Return to Falcon Ridge

The McLendon Family Saga

Book Six

By
D.L. Roan

Description

Torn between his first love…and a forbidden attraction he can no longer deny.

Jonah McLendon is no stranger to polyandrous love. Having grown up in a poly family, he didn't think twice when his high school sweetheart, Chloe, revealed her secret desire for a ménage with his best friend. There was only one problem. He didn't expect to fall for Pryce, too.

Beaten within an inch of his life after Chloe exposes their secret, and Pryce having been shipped off to a religious boarding school a half state away, Jonah tells the biggest lie of his life and leaves Falcon Ridge with his heart in pieces. When he returns a year and a half later, the last thing he expects to find is his best friend engaged to the girl who betrayed them both.

No longer the scared, confused kid he once was, Jonah is determined to get to the bottom of Pryce's sham of an engagement, but the truth behind Chloe's betrayal could change all their lives forever.

www.dlroan.com

ISBN-13: 978-1542499576
ISBN-10: 1542499577

Cover Design by JAB Designs
Copy Editing by Kathryn Lynn Davis
Proof Reading by Read by Rose

Interior eBook Design by D.L. Roan

Chapter One

Jonah McLendon stabbed a pitchfork into the dwindling mound of hay, his arms burning with fatigue as he tossed the load into the pen and moved to the next one. The dust and stench inside the stock paddock was stifling enough, but the humid air was so thick and hot that drawing a deep breath felt like drinking soup through a straw.

He paused a moment, leaning the pitchfork against the railing, and pulled off his sweat-soaked t-shirt, tying it like a bandana around his head to keep the sweat from dripping into his eyes. He was no stranger to pitching hay, had done it a million times in his family's barns, but the unusually hot summer and lack of ventilation in the rodeo arena was kicking his ass.

On any other Sunday he'd be down at the creek, swimming in the cool water and eating grilled burgers at his family's weekly summer picnic, but not today.

After breaking up with his girlfriend Chloe, and getting into a fight with his best friend—because he'd broken up with Chloe—Jonah needed time to think. With three dads, his mom, three brothers, and his twin sister Dani, there was never a moment's peace at his house. Add to that his four papas and Gran, his great uncle, Papa Joe's physical therapist, Breezy, and the damn paparazzi who followed his older brothers around like a pack of hungry wolves, and this Sunday's picnic would be one miniature pony and an emu short of a zoo.

Working alone in the empty arena to get it ready for the upcoming 4-H event was the perfect escape, but so far, he hadn't come up with a single plan to fix the mess he'd made with Chloe and Pryce. Nothing that would fill the hole in his chest, or dispel the incessant memories of the last time the three of them were together, half-naked and wrapped around each other like three strings of hot, sweet taffy.

"Hurry or we'll miss the fireworks." The frantic tone of Chloe's voice matched the pace of her hands as she worked his belt buckle loose and unzipped his jeans.

"I can't reach the snap," Jonah grumbled, his hand trapped between the back of Chloe's bra and his best friend Pryce's bare chest.

Good God, if they didn't get her naked soon, he was going to pass out. The damn reporters and their long lenses trying to get a snapshot of his famous country singer twin brothers made it impossible to find a moment's privacy anywhere except in his uncle Cade's workshop, and the sweltering air inside was suffocating. Add in the heat between the three of them, and they were about to have their own fireworks show.

"I've got it," Pryce said between his open-mouth kisses to the side of Chloe's neck. Her bra fell from her soft, plump breasts a moment later, revealing her pebbled, chocolaty nipples.

"Sweet Jesus, you're gorgeous." Jonah dipped down to taste one, laving the hardened tip with the flat of his tongue before he sucked it between his lips. Her Native American heritage had tinted her skin the color of mocha and cream, and he'd swear he could taste the sweetness.

"Ahh," she sighed, her head falling back against Pryce's chest, arching her back in a plea for more. He wanted more, too, but they were running out of time.

Only seventeen, he and Pryce couldn't buy alcohol for their Fourth of July bonfire, but a friend was lifting a case of beer from his brother's pantry and they had a very narrow window of time in which to pick it up without getting caught.

He pulled Chloe's panties aside and ran his fingers along her hot slit, finding her soaking wet and ready for them. She gasped when he slipped a finger inside. Pryce stifled her cry with a hot kiss, their tongues sliding against one another in a slow, hypnotic dance. Jonah's cock throbbed as he watched them, the sight so sensual and arousing he wanted to join them.

Chloe's fascination with his family's lifestyle had spurred her to wonder what it would be like to be with two guys at the same time. Maybe because of his family's unconventional dynamics—having three dads married to his mom—he'd had no reservations about sharing Chloe. Pryce had been reluctant at first, given his conservative, religious upbringing, and his concern it would somehow screw up their friendship, but one kiss with Chloe and he'd been hooked, too.

That one kiss had spiraled into something so erotic and powerful among the three of them, Jonah didn't know if he could stop it even if he'd wanted to. But lately he'd been having fantasies he had no business having, dreams of Pryce that were so hot he'd come in his sleep more times than he could count.

He closed his eyes, blocking out the disturbing, ludicrous images that had invaded his thoughts once again. "Come here." He grabbed Chloe's ass, hauling her up against him, crushing his mouth to hers, drowning himself in her taste in the hopes it would cleanse him of the insane desire to do the same with Pryce.

No such luck. Pryce's hard cock brushed against the back of his hand and his eyes flew open to find his best friend staring back at him. Jonah blinked, wondering if he hadn't imagined it, but when he opened his eyes again, Pryce was still looking at him with a lusty gaze, his erection now firmly pressed against the back of his hand.

Their gazes locked, Jonah watched with longing as Pryce leaned in and traced the shell of Chloe's ear with the tip of his tongue. Holy fuck!

They were so close. The desire to lean forward that one inch and lick his bottom lip—oh damn! Pryce shifted, pressing closer, with unmistakable intention, the zipper on his jeans cutting into the back of Jonah's hand.

Jonah's heartbeat thundered in his eardrums. He stared at Pryce over Chloe's shoulder. What was he doing? Could Pryce want this, too? If he didn't, and Jonah made a move, it could screw up everything. He was insane for even thinking it!

Pryce flexed his hips, pressing his cock harder against Jonah's hand, his eyes begging for both permission and forgiveness. Jonah's skin tingled with the sudden rush of adrenaline as he stared at his best friend.

Every cell in his body came alive with the exhilarating mixture of need and fear. Sweat dripped down his back, tickling his already sensitive skin. His heart pounding inside his chest, hyperaware that he could be making the biggest mistake of his life, Jonah turned his hand and cupped the iron-hard bulge in Pryce's jeans. When Pryce didn't flinch away, he tightened his grip and caressed the straining length of his cock.

Pryce's eyes glazed over with pure bliss, his lips parting on a guttural moan. The lustful sight stole the air from Jonah's lungs. He tore his mouth from Chloe's and gulped for every breath, pressing his cock against her belly, searching for the same exquisite pleasure he was giving Pryce.

Leaving a trail of kisses along Jonah's chest, Chloe slipped her hand into his jeans and wrapped her fingers around his cock, completely unaware of what was happening between him and his best friend. When she tilted her head back to look up at him, Jonah closed his eyes and kissed her, lost in the whirlwind of both new and familiar sensations.

Pryce thrust into his hand, sending a surge of blood rushing through his veins at lightning speed. Jonah broke away from Chloe's kiss, once again struggling to breathe. Chloe continued to stroke him, and Jonah closed his eyes, imagining that it was Pryce's hand on him instead of hers. Fuck! He was losing his damn mind! He could feel Pryce's hot breath against his lips, their mouths so close. All he had to do was lean in and take what he wanted. He held his breath instead, waiting, wanting, but too afraid to ask.

Pryce pressed his lips to his.

Jonah's world exploded. He devoured Pryce like a starving man, a growl ripping from his chest as their tongues met for the first time in a long, desperate duel.

Light from outside flooded the small workshop, and Jonah tore himself away from them. "Shit, it's Papa Daniel." He hurried to pull up his jeans, struggling against the tangle of arms and hands grasping for discarded clothes.

"Excuse me," Daniel said and turned to leave.

"Papa Daniel, wait!" Jonah zipped and buttoned his jeans and then chased his grandfather out the door, leaving Chloe and Pryce inside. "Papa Da—"

"Is that the Jessop girl?"

Jonah nodded, unsure of what to say.

"Are you and Pryce using protection?"

Jonah nodded again.

"Both of you? Even when it's only the two of you?"

Jonah's eyes widened and he shook his head. It wasn't like that!

"Remember who you're talking to, Jonah," Papa Daniel insisted, cutting off his explanation. "You're not the first guy in the world to kiss another guy and you won't be the last. Tell me you're being safe. That's all I care about."

"Yeah, we are." Jonah cleared his throat. Papa Daniel—who was not related by blood, but his grandfather all the same—and his great-uncle, Cade, had been a couple since before Jonah was born. He didn't have a problem with gay people, or any kind of people, but just because they *were gay didn't mean he was! He had to make him understand. "I know what that looked like, but—"*

"What you do and who you do it with is nobody's business," Daniel said, holding up a staying hand. "You've told me everything I need to know."

Jonah's cheeks grew hot and his palms felt clammy. He stared at his feet, feeling like he was about to pass out. Of all the times someone could have walked in on them. This was not happening!

"Do your mom and dads know?"

"God no!" Oh shit, please don't let him tell my parents! *"I mean—we're not—I haven't—"*

"I won't say a word," Daniel assured him. "Just..."

"Sorry we crashed your workshop," Jonah offered as Daniel glanced back at the door. "It's kind of crazy at our place with Con and Car being back, and all the reporters and stuff. It won't happen again."

Daniel chuckled. "If you don't tell Uncle Cade, I won't," he said. "And if her father or brothers catch either one of you, I'm denying everything."

The sound of a truck door slamming shut snapped Jonah from his erotic memories. He snatched his t-shirt from his head and was pulling it on to cover the bulge in his jeans when Pryce rounded the corner at the end of the stock chute.

Jonah picked up the pitchfork, stabbing it into the pile of hay as Pryce approached. "Aren't you grounded?" he asked, knowing Dirk Grunion had put him on lockdown for going to the bonfire.

"I snuck out."

"Go home," Jonah said with a sigh, not ready to have this conversation.

"We need to talk."

"Nothing to talk about." He tossed the hay over the gate with more force than he intended, half of it flying into the next stall.

"It's my fault," Pryce insisted. "I shouldn't have—"

Jonah pinned him with a glare. He was so sick of Pryce apologizing. He'd sent what must have been a hundred text messages saying he was sorry and begging to let things go back to the way they were. How in the hell did he think they could do that? Jonah mumbled a curse. He'd kissed his best fucking friend, and worse, he'd liked it! There was no going back from that.

"Then at least get back together with Chloe," Pryce said, turning his hat in his hands, his eyes—those damn sad eyes—pleading with him for something he couldn't give. "She's a complete mess, Jonah. She doesn't understand why you broke up with her, and I haven't said a word. I'll bow out and she'll never know."

"Do you think she's going to just let it go? Not ask a single question?" He tossed the pitchfork away and wiped the sweat from his face with the hem of his t-shirt.

"I'll tell her I found someone else," Pryce argued.

"And when she figures out it's a lie? What then?" He marched toward Pryce. "Let's go in the other direction. Say we tell her. Do you think she'll be okay with it? Do you think she'll understand?" he asked, knowing full well she wouldn't. "Hell, *I* don't even understand it!" He met Pryce's gaze, but quickly looked away when he saw his own confusion mirrored in his best friend's eyes. They'd screwed things up so royally. "I've thought about every possibility, believe me," he said with a sigh. "She doesn't deserve to be hurt like this, but if I don't break it off now, it's only going to get worse." He licked his lips, the desire to kiss Pryce still strong, even as pissed as he was at himself for feeling the way he did. "I still love her, man, but this…this isn't going away for me."

"It's not for me either," Pryce whispered.

Jonah placed his hand on Pryce's shoulder, cursing when he felt his friend's body trembling beneath his palm. He was a second away from pulling him into his arms and kissing the hell out of him again when another truck pulled up at the end of the covered paddock.

"Shit." He pushed Pryce back down the aisle in the direction from which he'd come. "Go home," he repeated as Chloe's three brothers filed out of the truck, the oldest brandishing a baseball bat.

They were bullies, all three of them. They'd given Pryce enough grief over the last year to last a lifetime, but Jonah had a feeling they weren't there for Pryce or even Chloe. They didn't know about their relationship with Chloe. No one did, except Papa Daniel. They'd been careful about that. Her brothers were there for him, revenge for punching Travis during a fight he'd had to break up at the Fourth of July bonfire. He'd had enough of their damn bullying.

"I'm not leaving unless you do," Pryce insisted, pushing back against him. "There's three of them. They'll kill you."

"Go, goddammit! I can handle them!" He shoved Pryce again and then turned to face the Jessop brothers.

Pryce was no lightweight. Working his family's ranch had made him lean and nice to look at, but he couldn't throw a punch to save his life. He wouldn't do anything but get in the way. This fight had been a long time coming and Jonah was glad to finally get the chance to make them eat their own bullshit for a change. There might be three of them, but he outweighed two of them put together. Thanks to his dads, and growing up with three brothers, he knew how to take care of himself.

"Go!" he shouted over his shoulder when Pryce didn't move.

"Look at the pussy run!" Travis Jessop snickered, slapping his brother, Finn, on the back.

Finn was the oldest, already out of high school and working as a mechanic over on the Reservation. He was also the biggest of the three. Six feet and some change tall, he was still shorter than Jonah, but he had a reputation as a dirty fighter.

Jonah clenched his fists at his sides, anger fueling his need for a good fight. "Go fuck yourself, Travis."

Travis's smile faded and his eyes turned dark and mean. "You and that—"

"Shut it, Trav!" Finn shoved the end of the baseball bat he was carrying into Travis' gut. The younger of the three, Wayne Jessop, laughed as Travis bent over and clutched his stomach.

Jonah smirked. At this point, they might beat the hell out of themselves and he wouldn't have to throw a single punch. That would be a damn shame. All this thinking had gotten him nowhere. What he needed was a good fight. Jonah eyed the pitchfork he'd tossed aside earlier; it was a few feet away, but he'd get to it if he needed it.

"Chloe's been telling some fucked up stories," Finn finally said, caressing the length of the baseball bat with his palm. "Seems you and that Grunion pussy popped her cherry then dumped her," he snarled, slapping the baseball bat into his palm.

Jonah's blood ran cold. Chloe knew Pryce's dad would kill him if anyone found out about the three of them screwing around. She'd promised not to tell anyone about them. He'd begged her not to when he broke up with her, and she'd goddammed promised! Now her brothers were there, threatening them because she'd lied? She'd screwed him and Pryce both, literally and figuratively.

"See? Here's the deal," Finn continued to taunt, taking a threatening step toward him. "If you tell me she's lying, I'll only have to kick *your* ass."

Jonah took a step back, ready to charge him if he came closer.

"But to be fair, just so you know all the rules." Finn gave the baseball bat a warmup swing. "If you tell me it's true, then I might have to kill you and that faggot friend of yours."

Jonah held his ground. "Do whatever you think you need to do," he said. It didn't matter what he told them. They'd never cared about Chloe. They were there for a fight and he was willing to give them one. He might get his ass kicked. He might not, but he wasn't going down without taking at least two of them with him.

Travis took the first swing.

Jonah dodged the punch and tackled Finn. Best to get the baseball bat out of the equation first. Finn hit the side of the stock pen hard, but Jonah didn't stop, landing several solid punches to his ribs.

"Fuck!" He pushed away from Finn, stars swirling in his head, a blow to the side of his knee making him wobble on his feet.

Wayne, the short, little shit he was, had taken his one cheap shot and bounced away, standing there laughing like he'd done something spectacular. Travis came at Jonah from behind, but he threw an elbow and charged at Wayne, taking him down to the ground. One punch to his face and the little bastard was choking on the blood from his broken nose.

Either Finn or Travis, he wasn't sure which, kicked him hard in the ribs and Jonah rolled off of Wayne, gasping for air. He grabbed the pitchfork laying an arms-length away in the dirt, but before he could swing it around, another boot came down hard on his chest.

Finn squatted and hovered above his face as Jonah struggled to breathe. "I'm disappointed," he teased, his lips pulled into a cocky grin. "Too bad your friend didn't stick around. Still would have kicked your ass, but at least it would have been interesting."

Jonah dug his fingers into the ground, fisted a handful of dirt, and flung it into Finn's face.

Curses flew. Finn fell back on his ass, his hands covering his eyes, and Jonah pushed to his feet, pitchfork in hand. Travis tackled him from behind and Wayne kicked him in the knee again, but before he went down, he shoved the pitchfork into the ground beside Finn, two of the prongs skewering Finn's hand.

Finn's scream was the last thing he remembered before the baseball bat connected with the back of his head. The lights went out, and the next time they came back on, he was laid up in the hospital, half his spleen missing, four broken ribs, his eyes so swollen he could barely open them.

His room was stacked three-deep with people: his brothers, mom and dads, the cops, his twin sister screaming at him to tell them what happened, and all of them asking questions he couldn't answer.

Thankfully, the sheriff ordered everyone but his dad, Grey, out of the room. Jonah's respite was short lived. Panic rushed through his veins when they told him they'd found Pryce's truck alongside his at the arena. For a brief moment, his heart stopped altogether, thinking Chloe's brothers had gotten to him, too.

"Dirk Grunion says he saw Pryce sneaking out of the house and followed him to the arena," the sheriff said. "Says they didn't hear or see anything when they picked Pryce up. Is that what happened?"

Jonah swallowed, the small effort causing more pain thanks to the breathing tube they'd shoved down his throat during surgery. "Is Pryce okay?" he choked out.

"Other than being beaten black and blue by his dad?" Grey mumbled with a huff. "It's a wonder he's not in here with you."

The sheriff shook his head with a curse. "I have half a mind to arrest that son of a bitch for child abuse." He tucked his pen and pad back into his shirt pocket and considered Jonah with a critical eye. "Does that kind of thing go on often?" he asked Jonah, "Dirk beating on his kid? Or was Pryce a part of what happened to you and you're covering for him?"

Jonah held his tongue, confirming Dirk's story but nothing more. Pryce's parents were religious nut-jobs, but that never stopped Dirk from beating the hell out of Pryce every chance he got. There was no doubt Dirk had gotten his hands on Pryce after finding him at the arena. Because of the decades-old feud between their two families, Pryce had been strictly forbidden to associate with Jonah. If they ever found out what they'd done with Chloe, or God forbid that Pryce had kissed him, Dirk would kill him.

Anything he said would out them both, so he kept his mouth shut, and hoped Pryce did the same. He never got the chance to find out. Before he'd even gotten out of the hospital, the Grunions had shipped Pryce off to some Podunk private, religious school three hours away.

In the weeks that followed, his older twin brothers, Connor and Carson, hounded Jonah to spill the beans about what had happened but there was no point. It was hard enough living up to their rock star status. He'd never be able to look them in the eyes again if they found out about him and Pryce, even if they did share a girlfriend. They weren't fucking each other so it wasn't the same.

By the time he started his senior year, the level of suckage in his life had only gotten deeper. Travis and Wayne had run their mouths, posted all kinds of garbage and lies on the internet, and turned most of his friends against him. Out of shape from sitting on his ass recovering all summer, he didn't make the cut for the football team. And Pryce was gone. Jonah had tried to call him, but the school he'd been transferred to refused to even let him leave a message, and Pryce didn't call him.

The only upside was that Chloe had moved to Colorado with her mom the day after Pryce left, which meant he wouldn't have to see her any time soon. Forever wouldn't be long enough as far as he was concerned.

Depressed and pretty much screwed, he wished every day that he could just disappear. The town he'd called home his whole life was now his own personal hell. The entire state of Montana wasn't big enough to hide in, but he didn't know where else to go.

On a trip to Billings with his dads one weekend, he stumbled across a military recruiting booth and took a few flyers, talked to one of the recruiters who'd told him about all the traveling he'd done since he'd enlisted, all the cool places he would get to see on the government's dime if he joined.

The chance to put a continent or two between him and home sounded exactly like what he was looking for, but joining the military required him to finish high school first. After poking around on the internet for ideas, he told his parents he wanted to start college early. Probably because they felt sorry for him, they let him double up on his classes online and he finished all of his required credits in a matter of a few weeks.

On his eighteenth birthday, he drove straight out to Butte to enlist in the Marines. What a wasted trip that was. The enlisting officer scared the living hell out of him with tales of his tours in the last war. Jonah decided real quick that the military wasn't for him. He'd already almost died once. As screwed up as his life was, he wasn't suicidal.

He didn't know why he told his parents he'd signed up for the military; maybe because it sounded honorable and brave when he was anything but. Either way, it was too late to tell the truth. When it came time to leave, he said goodbye, leaving his mom crying and his entire family believing he was headed to California to begin his military career. He got in his truck and headed north, not stopping until he got a flat in the middle of a snowstorm somewhere near Anchorage, Alaska.

Chapter Two

Eighteen Months Later

Jonah clicked the button on the gate opener clipped to the sun visor, somewhat surprised when the heavy wooden panels, scorched with the Falcon Ridge brand, swung open. At least his parents hadn't changed the code. Foot to the gas pedal, he steered his truck effortlessly over the snow-covered cattle guard, the gate closing securely behind him.

A year and a half. It seemed longer since he'd told his family the biggest lie of his life and ran away for parts unknown, his tail tucked firmly between his legs. Judging by the number of trucks parked in front of the house, things hadn't changed much. Filled with both relief and apprehension, he drove along the gravel driveway and parked beside one of his dads' trucks and cut the engine. There truly was no place like home, but did home still have a place for him?

A month ago, tucked away in the Alaskan hole-in-the-wall town he'd been hiding in, he'd dared to check his email and found a message from Papa Daniel. He'd ignored it for a few days, knowing that if Papa Daniel was writing it couldn't be good. A few more emails followed, one after another, until he'd finally caved and opened them. Sure enough, Papa Daniel and Uncle Cade had discovered his lie and threatened to tell his parents if he didn't come home and straighten it out himself. And to make things worse, he'd forgotten his mother's birthday.

He'd been such a coward. Still was in many senses of the word, but he couldn't let his great uncle and grandfather take the heat for his lie. He may not be ready to face down the rest of the demons that haunted him, but he had to face this one. He loved his family. He just wasn't so sure they'd still love him when the truth came out. *If it came out.*

He hadn't known what to expect when he arrived at Falcon Ridge, but finding an empty house certainly wasn't on the short list of possibilities. Wasn't even on the long list.

"Mom? Dads?" When no one greeted him in the kitchen, he rushed up the stairs to check the bedrooms, but all was quiet. Even Cory's room was empty, the basement, too. He stood alone in the middle of the living room, the lack of a fire burning in the hearth making the house feel cold and lonely.

Not once in his entire life could he remember having the house all to himself, and now that he did, it didn't sit right. He felt empty inside, just like the house, and all the demons he'd been running from threatened to close what little bit of distance he'd managed to put between them.

"To hell with this." He rushed back outside to his truck, retreating from the eerie silence to call his mom.

"Jonah?" his mom, Gabby, squealed when she answered. "Where are you? How are you?"

"I'm at home. Where is everyone?"

"You're home? Right now? Are you okay?"

He closed his eyes and took a deep breath. "Yeah, everything's fine. Where are you?"

"We're at the hospital—or the outpatient center—with Papa Daniel."

Jonah bolted upright in the front seat of his truck. "What happened?" He'd just spoken to Daniel not ten days ago and he'd seemed fine. He didn't tell his mom that, of course. They'd be in the dog house for sure if his parents knew they'd lied for him.

"No, honey, he's fine. It's..."

Jonah held his breath as he waited for her to finish. *Please let him be okay.* He didn't think he could take another emotional shitstorm worse than the one already wreaking havoc on his life.

"It's Uncle Cade," she finally said.

"Uncle Cade?" *What the hell?* Papa Daniel had said he'd been sick but that it was nothing to worry about. Now Cade was in the hospital?

"He had another gallstone," his mom said.

Jonah sighed in relief. Uncle Cade had had a similar procedure before he'd left for Alaska and it hadn't seemed all that serious.

"Honey." The tone of his mom's voice changed and he could feel her question burning in his gut before she asked it. "We've tried calling you for months. Why haven't you returned our calls?"

"I know, Mom. I'm sorry." He was sorry for a lot of things, but most of all, for not calling her on her birthday. *Dammit!* He punched the steering wheel, biting back a curse when his cold knuckles popped. He'd meant to pick her up some flowers on his way through town but completely forgot. Again. "I'll explain everything when you get home," he said, shaking out the pain in his hand.

"Okay. I—"

"Will you be home soon?" he asked, wondering how much longer he had to come up with a plausible story. Telling them where he'd been wasn't such a big deal, and with their tendency to overreact, he could easily lie about his reason for lying, but as to *why* he left? So far he had nothing but the truth, and he sure as hell wasn't about to tell them that.

"No. We're not sure how much longer we'll be."

"Let me talk to him," he heard one of his dads say in the background.

"Your dad wants to talk to you," Gabby repeated.

"Dad Grey?" *Please not Grey.*

"Yes, Grey," Gabby said, snapping his last thread of hope. "Matt and Mason took a ride up to the ridge to look for a few strays."

Jonah banged his forehead against the steering wheel until it hurt as bad as his hand. He loved his dads. All three of them were larger than life, but Grey was the one he knew he'd disappointed the most. He would never understand what was going on inside his head. Coupled with Grey's tendency to overreact, he was facing a ticking time bomb.

Jonah rubbed the sting from his forehead with a sigh. He'd have to tell them eventually. Grey wouldn't let him off the hook that easily. He just wished he had more time, like maybe a decade. *At least a chance to talk to Matt and Mason first.*

He slouched in the seat and propped his boot on the dash, a bad habit he'd learned from Uncle Cade—another thing his dads would ream him out for if they ever caught him doing it. "Put him on," Jonah said and braced for the worst. "And take your time coming home, Mom. I'm not going anywhere."

"Okay, honey. I'll be home soon. I love you! I can't wait to see you!"

"Love you, too."

"Jonah?" Grey barked into the phone before he'd even finished saying goodbye to his mom.

"Hi, Dad." He cringed, expecting a barrage of grueling questions.

Grey didn't disappoint.

"Are you okay? Did you get an unexpected leave or something? You should have called. And why haven't you—"

"I'm okay, Dad," he tried to interrupt, but the questions kept coming. *Where have you been? Why didn't you call your mother on her birthday? Why haven't you returned any of our calls or texts?*

He'd have to answer every single question eventually, and he would, but not yet. Not over the phone. He let Grey talk, not bothering to respond until there was a long pause and he knew Grey was done.

"Jonah?"

"I'm here, Dad. I'll talk to you when you get home. Do you know which direction Matt and Mason went to look for the strays? I'd like to ride out and let them know I'm back." He couldn't sit in the empty house to wait for them. He'd hoped to talk to Mason before Grey got home. The McLendon overreaction gene seemed to have skipped Mason altogether, and he was hoping to get some advice on how to spill the beans to Grey and his mom and still keep his head intact.

"They're out in the north tract up by the ridge," Grey answered, but said nothing more, no doubt waiting on Jonah to say enough to hang himself.

Jonah pinched the bridge of his nose, wishing he hadn't called. "I'm sorry, Dad. I'm…" *Just sorry.* "I'll explain everything when you get here. I have a lot to talk to you about. Just…not now. Okay?"

"It better be a damn good explanation," Grey grumbled.

Jonah didn't respond. What could he say? *I'm screwed up. I'm not the son you think I am.*

"Damn, I gotta go," Grey said and the line went dead.

Jonah stared at his phone a minute before he shoved it into his pocket and trekked out to the barn. Familiar childhood scents of horsehide and hay tickled his nose and some of his anxiety drained away. He walked down the wide aisle, smiling when he saw a familiar nose peeking out over the last stall door at the end.

"Hey there, boy." Jonah slid his palm over his horse's velvety nose, letting him get reacquainted with his scent before he opened the stall. Paladin's hot breaths billowed from his nostrils like steam in the frigid winter air, warming his cold hand. Montana in February could be brutal, but compared to the Alaskan tundra he'd just left, it felt more like spring.

"You remember me?" he asked, looking Paladin over. A year and a half may have passed since he'd last ridden the gentle giant, but judging by the way Paladin shook his head and stomped his hooves, he hadn't been completely forgotten. "Yeah you do." He smiled as he nuzzled the star on Paladin's forehead. "I've got your treat right here, buddy."

He pulled a carrot he'd swiped from the fridge from his coat pocket and fed it to the horse before opening the stall door and walking him down to the tack stall. He'd thought about taking one of the four-wheelers out to find his dads, but he didn't feel like moving a dozen vehicles out of the equipment shed to get one.

"We need some time together anyway, don't we," he said in a soothing tone as he ran the curry comb over Paladin's sorrel winter coat.

When Paladin was saddled and ready, Jonah gave him a pat on the shoulder before placing his foot in the stirrup and pulling himself up with remembered ease. "You ready, old boy?" It had been a while since he'd ridden, but he and Paladin fit together like a hand and well-worn glove. "Let's ride."

A biting north wind hit him in the chest as he rounded the barn and spurred Paladin into a trot toward the north tract. To guard against the chill, he pulled the brim of his Stetson down and flipped up the collar of his sheepskin coat. Snow blanketed the ground and covered the trail, but after twenty years of riding the ranch, he could get to where he was going with his eyes closed.

As he led Paladin toward the ridge, he looked out over the snow-covered hills, sparkling like diamonds in the midafternoon sun. Alaska had its beauty and northern charm, but nothing looked as pristine and magical as Falcon Ridge in winter.

Something in the distance caught his eye and he eased Paladin into a walk, stopping altogether when he saw the tip of a large boulder jutting out from the snow beside the creek. Pictures of his ex-best friend flooded his memories, seizing him in the saddle.

The first time he'd met Pryce, Jonah had been sitting atop that boulder, sulking because his dads had refused to let him ride in that year's spring rodeo. *You may be six-foot-tall, but you're not old or tough enough to ride those bulls* his dad, Mason, had insisted. At fourteen, he'd been all arms and legs, standing almost as tall as Grey, and like all kids, thought he was invincible.

He laughed at the memory now because his dads had been right, but that particular day he'd been mad as hell and looking for a fight. When he'd caught the kid from next door wading along the edge of their creek with a camera in his hand, he knew he'd found one.

The Grunions owned the ranch on the other side of the creek, and were the sworn enemies of the McLendons. He hadn't known why then, but his brothers had told him more times than he could count not to play on their land or Old Man Grunion would skin him alive. He'd seen them from time to time around town, knew they had a kid his age, but he'd never spoken to them or seen Pryce in school.

When Pryce had gotten closer to where he sat that day, Jonah picked up a rock, testing the weight of it in his palm before he decided it would serve his purpose. He'd waited patiently, barely breathing, and as still as a mountain lion about to pounce on its prey, until Pryce waded into range. *One more step.* Jonah cocked his arm back, took aim, and flung the rock across the creek. It landed a good three feet in front of Pryce, doing nothing but splashing a bit of water on his shorts.

Pryce froze mid-step and looked up at Jonah, his brows furrowed in confusion. "That was rude," he'd said, and reached down into the water to retrieve the rock, but instead of throwing it back like Jonah had expected, he studied it for a minute, then looked back up at Jonah. "Imagine if you were a rock," he'd said, "and you'd laid there your whole life, for hundreds of years, and then someone came along and picked you up and threw *you* into the water."

Jonah had stared at the awkward kid for God knew how long before he'd burst out laughing. It was the most absurd thing he'd ever heard. Rocks didn't know shit. Who cared what happened to them? He'd watched in silence as Pryce walked to the edge of the bank and set the rock down, positioning it just so before he gave it a nod, climbed to the top of the steep bank on the other side, and disappeared without even a wave goodbye.

Jonah had thought him more than a little odd, maybe even a little *gifted*, but before he'd left that day, he'd waded across the creek and retrieved the rock, setting it back in the place he'd found it, cursing himself when it was all said and done for caring about some stupid rock.

His curiosity piqued by the memory, Jonah tugged on Paladin's reins and guided him over to the boulder, cursing himself again as he dismounted and stomped through the snow to where he'd sat so many years ago. He cleaned the snow off the top of the boulder, digging until he'd cleared as much of it away as he could. He found one rock, but it was too small. Another was the wrong shape. Tossing them aside, he searched for the rock Pryce had *saved*. He hadn't thought of it since that day. It could have washed into the creek during one of the spring thaws years ago for all he knew, but for some strange reason, he needed to find *that* rock. He kept searching, moving more snow and picking up more rocks, none of them the one he was searching for.

"Dammit!" he shouted into the wind and plopped down onto the boulder. What was left of the wet snow leached into his jeans. He was too pissed to care as he stared at the thick layer of ice covering the creek bed, at the place where Pryce had stood that day. Only this time, instead of the awkward kid next door, he remembered the guy who'd become his best friend, the guy who'd tried to save him the day he'd almost died, the guy he'd fallen in love with.

Chapter Three

"Jonah?"

Jonah turned at the sound of his dad's voice to find Matt sitting high on his horse beside Paladin, while his other dad, Mason, trotted across the field toward them. He pushed to his feet, his chest aching at the very sight of them.

"Good Lord, Son, it *is* you!" Matt slid from his saddle into the snow and tackled him in a hug so strong he thought he'd break. "God, I've missed you," Matt said, his eyes glassy with tears when he finally let him go. Matt hurriedly swiped them away with his forearm and stuttered his way through a torrent of questions. "What the heck are you doing here? Is everything all right? Does your mom know you're back?"

"Yeah, she knows." Jonah nodded. "I called her a little while ago."

Mason pulled his horse up short and dismounted. Jonah's eyes stung with his own tears as Mason approached him in a rush. He fisted his hands into the front of Jonah's jacket and yanked him into his arms without a single spoken word, crushing Jonah with his familiar silent strength.

He didn't know why, but Mason's hug slayed him. The tight ball of shame and regret that had set like a bucket of concrete in his chest for the last year-and-a-half, unexpectedly broke free and he choked back a sob. Mason tightened his grip. Jonah fought against the emotions he'd denied for so long, the knot in his throat only getting larger and harder to swallow.

Mason gave his back a few hard slaps before he loosened his grip but he didn't let go. "It's good to have you home, Son," he said, holding him at arm's length, looking up at him with so much pride and love it hurt to look back.

"I need to talk to you," Jonah said as he hurriedly wiped the tears from his eyes. He was ready to confess everything, right then and there.

"I figured as much." Mason gave his shoulder a reassuring squeeze. "We have something we need to talk to you about, too, but let's get the horses to the barn and get out of the cold. My balls are almost frozen solid."

Jonah laughed, the sound getting stuck behind the lump in his throat and coming out as a choked cough. "Did you find the strays you were looking for?" he managed when the knot eased.

Mason shook his head, letting out a disappointed sigh. "We found their frozen carcasses up in the north pasture, before the climb to the ridge."

"You think it's a bear?"

"Mountain lion," Mason said. "Probably driven down from the ridge by the deep freezes we've had." He shook his head and glanced up at Matt. "I hate it, but it looks like we're going to have to go hunting soon. We can't have it sneaking into the valley picking off the calves once the season starts."

"Maybe I can go with you," Jonah suggested. He'd been thinking about staying up at the cabin anyway. And it had been a long time since he'd been hunting with his dads.

"Good idea," Mason said.

"Come on! We'll race you home!" Matt hooked his arm around Jonah's neck and pulled him toward his horse.

"Uh, what part of frozen balls did you not hear?" Mason asked, swinging himself back up onto his horse, his face scrunched up as he readjusted himself in the saddle. "No racing for me."

Matt and Jonah mounted up at the same time and they all turned their horses toward the barn. "He's been whining about his balls for the last hour-and-a-half," Matt said and gave Jonah a nod. "Ten bucks says I beat you to the gate."

"Make it fifty." Jonah turned his heels into Paladin's sides, giving him a few quick clicks of his tongue and they were off.

"That's cheating!" Matt yelled, but when Jonah glanced over his shoulder, his dad was only a few lengths behind him.

They were neck-and-neck when the pasture gate came into view. He glanced over at his dad, noticing his knees tucked in tight, his chest low, the brim of his hat riding low on his brow as he pushed his horse to the finish line. Matt rode with all the skill of an old-time cowboy and the grace of a jockey, just like he'd taught Jonah and his sister so many years ago. Christ, he'd missed him.

"I win!" Matt shouted as they pulled their horses to a stop at the gate, Matt ahead by a full length. Jonah shook his head, reaching into his pocket to pull out the cash but Matt waved him off. "I'll give ya that one," he said with a wink. "Paladin hasn't been ridden that hard in a while, but don't think I'm not holding you to a rematch once you get him back into shape."

"Deal." Jonah gave his horse a pat on the neck, catching Matt's gaze when he realized what he'd agreed to. He hadn't decided how long he was staying, or *if* he was staying. He might be back on the road before nightfall once Grey and his mom got home and he told them the truth about where he'd been.

"Come on." Matt jerked his head toward the house. "We'll leave the gate open for my slow-poke brother and get some of your gran's lamb stew on the stove. That ought to warm him up quick enough."

After the horses were stalled and watered, Jonah sat in the living room, stoking the fresh fire in the fireplace as his dads alternated between the kitchen and the shower. The house felt like home now that it was no longer empty. Matt had helped him carry his things up to his old room, which was exactly the same as he'd left it, all the way down to the dark blue sheets on the bed. He'd spent a moment looking over his old football and baseball trophies from what seemed like a lifetime ago. When he saw the picture of him and Pryce, mingled with a few others of him and his family, he'd shoved them into his drawer and fled his room like it was haunted.

Mason brought in a tray loaded with bowls of soup and cups of coffee. Jonah rose and took it from his hands, setting it on the coffee table before he squatted down on the floor and dug in. Matt joined them a minute later.

"Man, this is good." He hadn't had a home cooked meal since he'd left, and his Gran's lamb stew was his all-time favorite. He shoveled spoonful after spoonful into his mouth like a starving man.

"So, what have you been up to, Son? Or should I call you Private now? What do they call the new guys in the Marines?" Matt was the first to break the ice with a string of questions.

Mason elbowed Matt in the side, earning him a searing glare. Jonah swallowed the last bite of soup, looking longingly into his bowl, wishing there was more so he'd have an excuse not to answer.

With no distractions left, he set his spoon down into the bowl and cleared his throat. He glanced up at his dads sitting on the sofa across from him and pushed to his feet. There was no way he could say what he had to sitting down.

"I…" *Damn, this is hard.* Why the hell had he lied in the first place?

"Look, we know somethin's up, so just spill it and we'll sort it all out as we go," Matt said. "Did you get court-martialed? Injured? Stationed somewhere your mother is going to have a breakdown trying to cope with? What? Oh! Did you meet a girl?"

"Let him tell it in his own time," Mason argued.

"At this rate, he'll never tell us," Matt grumbled back. "We need to get this out of the way so we can tell him—"

"Not yet," Mason warned through clenched teeth.

"Tell me what?" Jonah saw Matt and Mason exchange another heated look. "What's happened?"

"Dammit." Mason whispered the curse and stood, his hands on his hips as he, too, began to pace. "Have a seat," he instructed Jonah, motioning for him to sit on the sofa beside Matt.

Jonah's pulse skyrocketed as he crouched down onto the edge of the sofa, his knee bouncing uncontrollably as he glanced between his dads. "What in the hell is going on? Is something wrong with Mom?"

"Well, we'd hoped to—I mean…"

"Spill it, Dad."

"Uncle Cade has cancer," Matt said.

"What?" He almost gave himself whiplash glancing back and forth between Matt and Mason, looking for a sign that this was some kind of cruel joke. But…his dads would never joke about such a thing. Shock flooded his system, his skin tingling with it as he tried to process the news. "Cancer? Uncle Cade has cancer?"

Mason nodded, his silence speaking volumes.

"But I just talked to him a few weeks ago and he said he was fine." The words slipped from Jonah's lips before he realized what he'd said.

"You've talked to Uncle Cade?" Matt asked. "And you didn't bother calling us?"

Jonah swallowed, nodding reluctantly. "Dads, I'm so sorry," he said through the tears that continued to clog his throat. "I never joined the Marines. Uncle Cade found out somehow and he was going to tell you," he rushed to explain. The last thing he wanted to do was throw his uncle under the bus, especially when he had fucking cancer. "I asked him not to tell you because I wanted to make it right. I lied to you and Mom. To everyone."

The room fell silent, no one speaking or moving for what felt like forever before Mason cleared his throat and came to sit beside Jonah, his elbows resting on his knees as he stared into the fire. "If you didn't join the Marines, then what…where the hell have you been all this time?"

Jonah slid to the edge of the cushion and scrubbed his hands over his face, mirroring Mason's position. "Alaska, mostly."

"Alaska?" Matt pulled back and stared at him.

"Uncle Cade has cancer?" Jonah asked again. That was impossible. Uncle Cade was like…Superman. He couldn't get cancer.

"We'll get back to Uncle Cade in a minute," Matt said. "What in the hell were you doing in Alaska? And the last time I checked, they do have phones there. Where were you that you couldn't have called us? Camped out in a damn bear cave?"

"I didn't have a plan when I left, okay? I just started driving and didn't stop until I got to Anchorage." When his dads didn't say anything, he kept talking. The more he talked, the easier it got. "I met a guy at a gas station who hauled equipment for one of the big gold mining companies. He said he thought one of them was looking for an equipment operator, so I rode up there with him on his next haul to check it out.

"I didn't get the job, but word travels fast up there, faster than here believe it or not, and one of the smaller operations gave me a job running paydirt. The front end loader I drove was a monster rig, but it wasn't much different than running the tractors here at the ranch once I got the hang of it."

He didn't tell them they'd hit one hell of a pay streak and his cut for the season had been ten times the average yearly salary at the ranch, or that he'd almost fucked his boss to keep the job. Kyle had honed in on him from the start. Jonah had tried to ignore him, managed to brush him off through the first season, but by the end of the second, Kyle had refused to take no for an answer. He'd thought he could do it. He'd wanted to fuck Pryce, and did in his dreams almost every night, but when Kyle touched him, he'd felt nothing but revulsion.

"Jonah?"

His mom's voice echoed through the house, followed shortly by Grey's. He looked over at Mason, his eyes pleading for them to help him out, but neither one of his other dads offered a single ounce of support.

"Don't look at me," Mason said with his hands held up in surrender. "You dug yourself into this hole. You'll have to dig yourself out."

"And don't think for a second this conversation is finished," Matt rumbled under his breath as they rose from the sofa.

"Jonah!" Gabby rushed across the living room and jumped into his arms, her tiny frame trembling in his grasp as he hugged her back. "Oh my God!" She kissed his temple, then hugged him again, her arms so tight around his neck he nearly choked. "You're here!" She pulled back and cupped his cheeks, her gaze searching every inch of his face. "You're really here!" She hugged him again, even harder this time.

"Easy," he chuckled, but she didn't let go. Over her shoulder, he caught Grey's stoic glare and some of the joy of seeing his mom again was consumed by trepidation and regret. This was going to be harder than he'd imagined.

Gabby let him go and he lowered her to the ground, setting her carefully on her feet. "I'm sorry I didn't call on your birthday," he said, but the apology fell flat and didn't lessen his guilt. "I was going to stop in town and get you some flowers, but I was so tired by the time—"

"Don't worry about it." His mom grabbed his hands, pulling him into another hug. "You're here now. That's all that matters."

"Son." Grey nodded with a grin that conflicted with the sadness in his eyes. Gabby moved to the side, but didn't release her hold on him as Grey pulled him in for a hug, giving his back a welcoming slap. "Damn good to have you home. Looks like you've grown another two inches since you've been gone."

At six feet six, he was two inches taller than Grey, but Grey would always be the bigger man, bigger than life itself.

"It's the boots," he said, and stuck his leg out to show off the only thing he'd splurged on since he'd gotten paid last fall. They weren't much to look at, but the thick soles were better insulation against the cold than the ones he'd worn on the ranch.

Grey shared a glance with Matt and Mason behind him, and then looked down at Gabby before he removed his hat. "I'm guessing these two have already told you about Uncle Cade."

Jonah nodded, the lump in his throat returning.

"Oh, honey, I'm so sorry I didn't tell you when you called," his mom said, "but Papa Daniel thought it best not to tell you over the phone."

"How is he?" Jonah asked as Gabby walked him toward the kitchen, all three of his dads in tow.

Matt and Mason each gave her a kiss on the cheek before they all took a seat at the long picnic-style table, his mom sliding in beside him.

"He's pretty well, all things considered," she said with a sigh, a sadness in her eyes he'd never seen before as she addressed not only him, but Matt and Mason as well. "They removed his gallstones and put in stents to keep them from coming back. The tumor in his pancreas is a little smaller than they thought, but it's still not good." She took his hand and gave it a squeeze. "The doctors say he has about eight months, maybe a year."

"Shit." The curse came out as a whisper. *Eight months.* Uncle Cade had been like a grandfather to him, the coolest one out of five for sure. He didn't even seem old enough to have cancer. How had this happened? "Is he still at the hospital? I'd like to go see him."

"We just dropped him and Daniel off at their house," Gabby said, "but the doctors warned he'd be out of it for a while. Breezy is going to stop by after she closes the clinic, but it might be best to wait until morning."

Jonah nodded silently. A lot had changed since he'd left. Breezy Youngblood had married his older brothers, Con and Car, a few weeks before he'd left town, and they'd since built a huge log cabin on the other side of the ranch. He'd also seen the rehabilitation center she'd opened in town as he'd driven through, right beneath Con and Car's new recording studio. Still not sure he'd have the nerve to go through with his unannounced return, he'd shielded his face beneath the brim of his hat as he'd pulled through town, in case they recognized his truck as he drove by. He loved his brothers, and Breezy, too, but he wasn't looking forward to the ass kicking Con and Car were sure to lay on him when they got wind of his deception.

"So, tell me where you've been," his mom said as she rose from the table. "I see your dads put some soup on, are you hungry? Did the Marines feed you well? You look healthy, but I know you must have missed—"

"I'm not hungry." Jonah cut her off. The single bowl of soup he'd scarfed down earlier curdled in his stomach. "Mom, I…" He glanced up at Mason and Matt in one last plea for help, but knew by the looks on their faces they'd give none.

"What?" she asked, the sudden silence in the room drawing her attention to their standoff. "What's happened?"

Jonah pushed from the table and stood in front of her, humbled and ashamed by the fretful look in her eyes. She'd aged since he'd been gone. She was still beautiful as ever, her long brown hair pulled up into a sloppy bun, tendrils of her curls caressing her rosy cheeks. But he could see the tiny, new worry lines at the corners of her eyes and mouth. He couldn't lie to her another moment.

"Mom, I didn't join the Marines."

She stared up at him, the crease between her eyes deepening as her brows pinched closer together. "What do you mean? I thought—"

"I lied," Jonah said, steeling himself against the disappointment he expected would overtake her confusion any second.

The sound of her open palm connecting with his cheek echoed through the kitchen, the sting stunning him to his core. She covered her gasp with her hand, her eyes wide with shock and tears before she flung herself at him and wrapped her arms around his waist. "Oh my God! I'm so sorry!" she cried against his chest.

Jonah stood paralyzed, his arms out to his sides, his jaw still stinging as she clung to him. She'd slapped him. His mom, who'd never hurt fly, had slapped him. He looked over to his dads, all three of them wide-eyed, their mouths gaping in shock.

“Do you have any idea how much I’ve worried about you?” Gabby pushed against his chest, but then hugged him again. “I’m so sorry I did that,” she sobbed, then pushed him away again. “Every time I turn on the news there’s a new war, horrific stories,” she railed, poking her finger into his chest. She stared up at him, covering her mouth with her trembling hand as more tears filled her eyes. “I can’t believe I hit you.” She hugged him again. “I don’t know what came over me. I’m so sorry.”

“It’s okay, Mom. I deserved it.” He did, and more. Jonah caressed the sting from his cheek, the physical impact having far less affect than the idea that he’d hurt her so deeply.

“I’m sorry I lied to you,” he said, addressing first his mom, then his dads, who still sat in silent disbelief. “I’m sorry for everything.”

Chapter Four

The next morning, the unmistakable scent of fried bacon enticed Jonah from his dreams. He opened his eyes and rolled from the sofa where he'd crashed in the basement the night before, making a pit stop at the bathroom before he pulled on his shirt and trudged like a zombie up the stairs to the kitchen. His stomach rumbled as the familiar scents of home grew stronger. It felt like a lifetime since he'd had more than a bowl of half-frozen cereal for breakfast.

"Mornin'." Matt was the first to greet him, his voice gruff with sleep.

Jonah gave him a lethargic wave as he made a beeline for the half-full carafe of coffee. He didn't bother with a mug, pouring cream straight into the carafe until it looked the right color, sloshing it around to mix it up a little before he guzzled the strong brew he'd come to depend on.

Behind him, Matt cleared his throat. Sucking down the last sip, Jonah glanced over to see him staring, his brow arched with obvious disapproval.

"Sorry," Jonah offered, flipping on the water and soaping up the carafe to make a new pot. "Bad habit I picked up. No place to wash dishes at the dig site except in the creek, so I learned to improvise."

Matt scoffed and retrieved a new filter and some fresh grounds from the cupboard. "While I'm disappointed that I'd never thought of doin' that myself, it's a habit I'd be breakin' pretty damn fast if I were you. Your mom sees you doin' that and you'll be sleepin' in the barn."

"If I see him doing what?" Gabby asked as she walked in, pushing up onto her tiptoes to give Matt a good morning kiss.

"Morning, Mom." Jonah hugged her back when she pulled him into her arms.

"Why'd you sleep in the basement?" she asked, her gaze roaming the contours of his face in that way all mothers do when they think something is wrong with their child. "Are you not feeling well?"

"I'm fine." Jonah pulled away from her and grabbed the stack of plates from the end of the counter, braving an attempt to set the table in his now semi-zombie state, the caffeine beginning to seep into his sluggish bloodstream.

His room held too many ghosts, and after the night he'd had dancing around his parents' questions about why he'd left, he'd been exhausted and crashed in the basement instead.

"Just fell asleep on the sofa. Didn't feel like getting up to go to bed." The last thing he needed was for his mom to revert back to treating him like the baby of the family. She had his younger brother, Cory, for that. *Speaking of which...*

"Where's Cory?" Jonah asked, snagging a slice of bacon from the pile on the plate Matt carried to the table. *Mmm, Bacon.* "I thought you said he'd be home last night."

"He had a last minute call come in and decided to stay the night at the fire station," Gabby said with a worried scowl. She wrapped her arms around him again and squeezed. "Why do all my babies have to grow up and leave?"

"I'm sure he's fine," Matt assured her, though Jonah wondered if his kid brother wasn't avoiding him.

Of all his siblings, he'd missed Cory the most. His older brothers, Connor and Carson, hadn't been around much when they were growing up, always on tour with their band until they'd moved home a few weeks before he'd left. Sharing a womb was about the only thing he had in common with his twin sister Dani. He and Cory had grown up together, been buds as well as brothers, but it wasn't enough to make him stay.

Cory'd been mad as hell at him the day he'd left, locking himself in his room. When he'd gone up to say goodbye, Cory had ignored him, refusing to even open his door. He'd tried to call him the next day, but that and the rest of his calls went straight to voicemail until he'd finally given up. Cory would never understand anyway.

Mason and Grey ambled down the stairs as Matt was bringing the last of the scrambled eggs to the table, each of them kissing Gabby before they said good morning to him and began piling food onto their plates.

"Shoot! I forgot the juice!" Gabby rose from the table to retrieve it from the fridge. "I swear I'd forget my head if it wasn't attached."

His dads shared a glance Jonah had long ago learned meant they were worried about her. He didn't ask why, but made a mental note to talk to Connor and Carson about it later when he went over to receive what he suspected would be one of many ass-chewings coming his way.

"So." Grey cleared his throat, diverting their attention back to the table. "What are your plans now that you're home?" he asked, leveling a discerning stare at him.

Jonah looked away. No longer hungry, he concentrated on dividing his scrambled eggs into three separate sections on his plate, trying to think of a convincing answer.

He hadn't really thought about it. That he was still here surprised him. He'd figured his dads would demand more answers than he was willing to give, and then he would leave and go back to moving paydirt in Alaska.

When his mom had called an abrupt end to their questioning the night before, and they'd let it drop without an argument before they'd all gone to bed, he'd been more than a bit shell-shocked.

"I guess I'll help you through calving season, if that's okay," he said with a shrug. "I haven't really thought about it beyond that."

"We can use all the help we can get, Son," Mason said, pointing for Jonah to pass him the butter. Jonah cut a slice for his own biscuit before he handed it over. "It's been a hell of a winter so far and, if Murphy's Law has anything to do with it, I'd guess it isn't over yet."

Grey eyed him over the rim of his coffee cup as he took a long sip. Jonah glanced away again, his stomach tightening at the banked questions in his father's gaze. Gabby may have bought him some time last night, but Grey wasn't through with him yet.

The kitchen door swung open, a cold breeze blowing in with his twin sister, Dani. Her hands full of grocery bags, she froze in the doorway when their gazes met.

"What the…?" Her eyes wide with surprise, the bags dropped to the floor.

"Dani!" Gabby exclaimed, her silverware clanging against her plate when she bolted to her feet in surprise. "I completely forgot you were coming today."

"Jonah!" He'd barely made it to his feet before Dani tackled him, wrapping her arms and legs around him like a monkey climbing a tree. "Oh my God! I hate you so hard right now!"

He hugged her back, sitting her on her feet when she finally let him go. "I've missed you, too," he said with a sleepy chuckle.

"You're such a jerk!" She gave him a hardy shove. "I've texted you like a million times! Why haven't you called me?" She turned to their parents, her hands on her hips as she glared in disbelief. "And why didn't anyone tell me he was home?"

"It's my fault, honey," Gabby said and rushed to hug her. "Everything has been such a jumbled mess with Uncle Cade. And then when I saw Jonah I was so shocked. I completely forgot."

"Speaking of forgetting." A stranger's voice filtered through the family chaos, followed by an uneasy, throat-clearing cough. The room fell silent. Every head turned, their attention focused on the kitchen doorway. "Hi," the guy said with a nervous wave, his gaze bouncing from one dad to the next, finally settling on Dani.

A feral growl rumbled in Grey's chest as Dani ran over to her guest. "Crap, I'm sorry. Dads, Mom, this is Ashley," she said, hooking her hand over the guy's shoulder and pulling him farther into the room.

"Ashley?" All three of their dads asked in unison as they rose from the table, their expressions ranging from skeptical to murderous.

Jonah studied the tech geek, with his dark-rimmed glasses and thrasher haircut. Dwarfed by everyone in the room but Dani and Mom, and a little on the thin side, Jonah had to hand it to the guy for not tucking tail and running for his life.

"Ash," he said and extended his hand to Mason first, the only one not trying to castrate him with a glare.

"My dads, Mason, Matt, and Grey," Dani said as Ash shook each of their hands.

"And I'm Gabby," their mom said, stepping between Ash and Grey to introduce herself, and effectively cutting off Grey's route of attack. Jonah snickered at the slick move.

"Nice to meet you," Ash said politely before extending his hand to Jonah.

"That's my jerkwad twin, Jonah." Dani introduced him with an arched brow and a smirk.

Jonah shook Ash's hand with relief. He wanted to freaking kiss his sister. He'd been praying for a distraction, something to take the focus off of him for a while, and Dani had just provided it. Their dads, Grey especially, had always been overprotective of his twin. Dani's arrival from college with a guy in tow would keep them off his back for at least a day.

Thank you, he mouthed to Dani, earning him another scowl.

Grey crossed his arms over his chest, awaiting further explanation from Dani.

Dani rolled her eyes. "Chill out, Dad." She picked up the bags she'd dropped and began loading the contents into the fridge. "Ash is just a friend. He's here to help me set up the control room for the drone surveillance. Calving will start any day, and this is the only weekend he's free."

"Oh, don't let them scare you," Gabby said to Ash, eying Grey in particular as she ushered him to the table. "You're the first guy Dani's brought home and they're a little surprised."

"Lucky me," Ash mumbled under his breath with a forced smile and a nervous nod, taking a seat next to Jonah.

Jonah couldn't help but laugh. He immediately liked the guy, but *just friends* or not, Ash was in for one hell of a shock if he thought coming home with Dani was going to be a typical meet-the-parents initiation.

"What, exactly, will you be working on while you're here, Ash?" Mason was the first to speak, offering Ash the bowl of eggs after scooping another helping onto his own plate.

And they're off. The subject of his defection officially deflected, Jonah's appetite came back with a vengeance and he dug into the lukewarm eggs on his plate, listening as Ash and Dani explained their plan.

"I've already cleaned out the old office in the calving barn," Dani said, shoveling her food into her mouth like a starving orphan. "That part I could handle, but I don't have a clue how to connect all the equipment. Ash is my tech genius. Once we have the monitors set up and the digital recorders installed, he'll get the drones connected to the controls and we should be good to go."

"So, you're going to monitor the herd and the heavies with drones?" Jonah asked.

"Oh my gosh! That's right!" Dani said with a feigned gasp. "You wouldn't know about our plan because, wait for it…you haven't freaking called me!" She took a sip of the juice Gabby set in front of her, giving him a saccharin smile. "Maybe if you'd returned even one of my text messages you wouldn't have to ask."

"Dani arranged for a tech firm to test out the new cattle monitoring technology they're trying to market," Ash interrupted their stare-off, giving Dani a shrug when she kicked him in protest under the table. "The Federal Aviation Administration needs to see performance reports before they'll approve the program for mass implementation, so your parents agreed to let them try it out during calving season."

"Cool," Jonah said, genuinely impressed with his twin's ingenuity. Of all his siblings, Dani was the most focused on the family ranching business and he fully expected her to take over when Grey decided to retire.

"I'm not completely sold on the idea," Matt grumbled. "We still don't know who's gonna be flyin' the darn things, and the last thing we need is a bunch of spooked, pregnant mammas breakin' through the fences tryin' to outrun an out-of-control drone. Cows aren't the smartest creatures on the planet, you know. And the stress isn't good for them."

"The tech company has a drone pilot on standby waiting for our call as soon as the first calf drops," Dani added. "And they didn't spook at the media drones flying all over the ranch when Connor and Carson came home last year. *And*, if this works out, and the F.A.A. gives their blessing, we might even be able to use the bigger drones to help rotate the pastures this summer."

"Sounds like we're going to be out of a job soon." Mason chuckled, giving Matt a playful shove. "Though, it'll be nice not to freeze our asses off trenching through three feet of snow for around-the-clock checks this year."

"Or our balls," Matt joked.

Gabby choked on her orange juice and Jonah covered his mouth, trying not to laugh. "Could you please refrain from talking about your testicles in front of our guest?" she asked after a few pats on the back from Mason. "I'm sorry," she addressed Ash. "Since Dani and her brothers moved out, they've had no use for manners."

"That's okay, Ma'am," Ash assured her with a chuckle. "I'm used to much worse at the frat house."

Grey dropped his fork onto his plate. "How long will he be staying?" He addressed the question to Dani, but his searing gaze never budged from Ash, who visibly wilted beneath Grey's scrutiny.

"I have to be back in Billings for class by Monday afternoon, Sir," Ash replied, his voice a little shaky.

Oh yeah, Jonah thought. He wouldn't miss this weekend for the world.

"I'll fix up Con and Car's old room for you," his mother offered.

"He can sleep in the basement," Grey insisted, breaking his stare long enough to glance at Jonah, daring him to argue.

"No problem," Jonah said, willing to sleep in the barn before he argued with Grey. Though judging by the tremble vibrating through the bench seat from Ash's bouncing leg beneath the table, the guy would be sleeping with one eye open no matter what part of the house he stayed in.

"He can't sleep in the basement," Gabby argued. "There's only a sofa down there. We can't make our guest sleep on a sofa when there's a perfectly good bed upstairs."

Grey stared up at Gabby like she'd just branded his balls. "I'm going to be repainting the upstairs this weekend. Start the remodeling for the grandkids nursery like you've been asking."

"This weekend? During calving season?" Gabby argued. "Stop being ridiculous. Breezy's not even pregnant yet."

"I'm not being ridiculous," Grey insisted, turning back to his eggs. "I'll call Papa Joe, then. He can stay there. I'm sure Mom would love the company."

"The basement's fine, Mrs. McLendon," Ash offered. "Really. I sleep on the sofa all the time when my roommate and his girlfriend are—"

Dani kicked Ash under the table again and he jumped in his seat.

"Anyway," Ash cleared his throat. "I'm used to it."

Matt rose from the table, his empty plate in hand, and gave Dani a kiss on the top of her head. "Until this old cowboy is replaced by one of your drones, the sun is up, which means we've got work to do. Nice to meet you," he said to Ash with a friendly nod. "See you at dinner."

"I'm going to run over to see Uncle Cade and Papa Daniel," Jonah said. Taking advantage of the opportunity to escape, he followed Matt to the sink with his plate.

"Oh my gosh. I completely forgot." Dani gasped. "Did you tell him about Uncle Cade?" she whispered to their mom.

"They told me," Jonah said with a sigh. "I still can't believe it."

Dani rose from her seat, her hurt feelings obviously forgotten, and wrapped her arms around his waist. "I can't either." She sniffled. "I cry every time I think about him not being here."

Jonah held her, choking back his own tears, until she finally let go. "I'm sorry I didn't call you," he said as she wiped at the wet tracks she'd left on his shirt. They may have fought like cats and dogs growing up, but seeing her cry had always been his weakness. "I really have missed you, Boo."

"I hate it when you call me that," Dani grumbled.

"But Con and Car call you that all the time."

"Yeah, well, they're my older brothers, and learning impaired." She pinched the front of his t-shirt, catching a few chest hairs between her fingers, and gave it a mean little twist.

"Ouch!"

"I've missed you, too." She released him, poking him in the collarbone for good measure. "But you're not off the hook. I want details, as soon as we get done setting everything up."

"Deal."

"And tell Uncle Cade and Papa Daniel that I'll be over to see them after dinner."

"Want a ride over?" Grey offered.

Jonah shook his head. The last thing he needed was to get cornered inside Grey's truck. He knew Grey would never hurt him physically, but the disappointment and hurt he saw in his eyes every damn time he looked at him, felt like a punch to the gut all the same.

"I'll walk," he said. "I need to stretch my legs after being cooped up in the truck for two days."

"I'll walk with you, then." Grey pushed from the table, depositing his empty plate into the sink before he leaned down and gave Gabby a kiss on the cheek. "Don't worry about the dishes. We'll do them when we get back."

"I'll get them," Gabby insisted, her worried gaze darting between her husband and Jonah. "Grey, wait."

Her whispered plea went ignored and Grey turned back to Jonah. "Go get dressed. I'll meet you at the end of the driveway."

Minutes later, dressed and anything but ready to face Grey, Jonah trudged down the front porch steps, his hot breath wafting behind him in the cold air. The small figure looming in the distance grew larger with each step he took. Dread built in the pit of his stomach until he stood side-by-side with Grey.

They walked in silence for a while, the gravel and snow crunching beneath their boots the only sound until they reached the end of the driveway and stepped onto the blacktop road. The walk would have been shorter if they'd cut through the open fields, but he knew why Grey had chosen the long way around and there was no use in putting it off any longer.

"I know you're disappointed in me," Jonah said, his gaze fixed on his boots scuffing along in a slow, hypnotic rhythm, his hands still cold despite the warming packets his mom had slipped into the pockets of his sheepskin jacket before he'd left. "I'm disappointed in myself," he continued when Grey didn't respond. "I'm not ready to tell you what happened, or why I had to leave—I may never be ready—but I am sorry I lied."

Grey remained silent as they walked. Jonah glanced over at him to see his stubble-covered jaw ticking in time with their steps, his dark brows pinched together in a heavy scowl. Out of the three, Grey had been the stern dad, always fair, but quick-tempered and never restrained in expressing his anger or disappointment when he screwed up. Jonah didn't know what to expect when Grey'd insisted on joining him for this walk, but silence certainly was not among the choices.

"Do you want me to leave?" Jonah finally asked, the idea of leaving home again so soon not as easy or appealing as he'd thought it would be.

"What?" Grey stopped in his tracks and looked up at him. "God, no. Your mother would kill me. I mean, I don't want you to leave either. I just…" He kicked a clump of snow, sending a spray of smaller white clumps skittering along the pavement ahead of them. "Dammit, this parenting thing is hard!"

"I'm not a kid anymore, Dad. You don't have to—"

"Have to what? Worry?" Grey shook his head, his lips curling into a sardonic smile as he glanced past Jonah into the field across the road. "You know, I had a shit-ton of things I wanted to say to you, but honestly, I'm speechless. The level of selfishness in what you did is astounding."

"Would you have let me go if I'd told you the truth?" Jonah argued. "That I didn't have a clue where I was going, except out of my damn mind if I'd stayed here?"

"It's been a year-and-a-half!" Grey shouted, balling his fists into Jonah's coat. "Six months without one single phone call! Your mother deserved better!" Grey released him and took a step back. "Sorry," he said and paced to the other side of the empty, two-lane road, his hands laced behind his head, staring up into the sky. "The funny thing is," he continued with a huff and turned back to face Jonah. "I'm angrier with myself than I am with you."

"Dad, I never meant to hurt you, or Mom, or anyone. I just couldn't see any other way out."

Grey stopped in front of him. As hard as it was, Jonah held his gaze, hoping his dad would see how sorry he was. Grey nodded and pulled him into a hug. "I know, Son. I believe you, and I'm sorry."

"You shouldn't be sorry," Jonah insisted, his words laced with surprise. "This had nothing to do with you or any of the family."

"Oh, but it does," Grey insisted. "I've somehow managed to make you feel like you couldn't trust me—"

"Dad, it's not that!"

Grey released him, but held him by the shoulders. "If there's anything I know I've done right, it's that I didn't raise a coward. Whatever's got you twisted up inside, stop running from it. Face it like the man we've taught you to be. And if you can't do it alone, then let us help you. If not me, then *one* of us."

"Dad, I…" Jonah looked away, unable to look his dad in the eyes when he knew the truth would be an even bigger disappointment than the lie.

"No. Look at me," Grey insisted, giving his shoulders a firm shake. "I don't care what it is. Nothing could ever disappoint me more than to see you tuck tail and run from it. Do you understand? Nothing."

The sincerity in Grey's eyes made Jonah feel more like a coward than ever. He was right. For the second time since he'd returned home, his resolve to keep what happened between him and Pryce a secret began to crumble. He knew his dads would still love him even if they didn't understand but would they look at him differently? Would the pride and love he saw in Grey's eyes dim to resignation and tolerance? His confession was on the tip of his tongue, but then Grey pulled away and began walking again.

"Dad, wait." Jonah jogged to catch up with him.

"Whatever you need to say, just spit it out."

"What…what's wrong with Mom?" Jonah asked, the cowardly move shoving him right back into the closet and nailing the door shut. He just couldn't chance it. Not yet.

"What do you mean?" Grey asked.

"I saw the way you, Matt, and Mason looked at each other this morning. Is she okay?"

Grey sucked in a deep breath and let it out with a long sigh. "When Con and Car left, she was sad, but she had you, Dani, and Cory to distract her. You left, Dani's living on campus in Billings, and Cory's gone four nights a week since he started at the fire station in Clarkston. I imagine he'll be moving out completely soon."

"Guess the house is kind of quiet, huh?" If his mom felt the same weirdness he'd felt when he'd come home to an empty house, there was no wonder. Five minutes of that and he'd been ready to break.

"Yeah." Grey sighed again. "And *the change* has hit her pretty hard," he said, emphasizing the words with air quotes. "She hasn't been herself lately."

"Yeah, I got that." Jonah rubbed his cheek, remembering the shocking sting of her palm. "But isn't she too young to be going through that?"

Grey shrugged. “Doc says everyone’s different. All we can do is open the windows at night and hide the knives. And don’t you dare tell her I said that.”

“I won’t.” Jonah laughed, leaning into the arm his dad draped over his shoulders. “So, we’re good?” he asked when Grey offered no further chastisement. Dare he hope that was the end of it?

“Not by a long shot,” Grey said with a wicked grin as he turned them toward Uncle Cade and Papa Daniel’s house. “While I think your mother’s reaction was punishment enough for now, you’ve still got a lot of ground to cover to make things right.” He squeezed Jonah’s shoulder before letting him go. “You can start by figuring out a way to get that yahoo your sister brought home the hell off my ranch.”

Chapter Five

"I have to go," Pryce said, but made no move to leave the warmth of Chloe's naked body. Snuggled beneath the covers in her room above her aunt's bakery, the morning's baking having already begun, the scents of cinnamon and vanilla wafted up through the vents. Combined with the sated, languid feeling that had settled in his bones from their predawn lovemaking, he had no desire to go home.

"I should be downstairs helping Aunt Bev." Chloe stretched out beside him and the sheet shifted across her body, her bare breasts playing peek-a-boo with the cold morning air. Normally he'd be hard pressed not to touch her. He was getting hard again just thinking about it, but this time he was satisfied with just looking.

More days than not, he was still shocked someone so beautiful would give him a second glance, but she had. For months, he'd been the awkward third wheel in her and Jonah's relationship, the awkward kid period. Somehow, when the dust had settled and he'd come home from boarding school—a place he would forever remember as *The Hole*—she'd fallen in love with him, too. There wasn't a single day since she'd come back that he hadn't felt like the luckiest guy on the planet, except when it came to his parents.

"I'm going to tell them today." His stomach rolled as the words left his lips. He'd gone over what he was going to say to his parents a million times in his head, but saying it out loud…

Chloe rolled onto her stomach and propped up onto her elbows, her messy morning hair flowing over her shoulder and tickling his side as she studied him. "Want me to come with you?"

He shook his head. This was something he had to do on his own. If his parents had the scorched-earth reaction he anticipated, he didn't want her anywhere near them. "I'll be fine," he said and flipped her onto her back.

She yelped in surprise and he kissed her neck, tickling her with his stubble as he settled himself between her thighs. He reached over and snatched the marriage license they'd filed for the day before off her nightstand and held it up between them. "One…more…month," he said between kisses. "We'll have the rent for the apartment in Billings. You won't have to work two jobs—even though I know you'll miss working at the rehab center with Breezy—but, we'll finally be free."

Chloe smiled but there was something in her eyes that he didn't understand, a sadness that didn't match his excited mood. "What's wrong?" He swiveled his hips, teasing her with his cock. "I have time for one more if you want."

Chloe shook her head, pressing her front teeth into her bottom lip. "Pryce…I…"

The knot in his stomach pulled tighter and he rolled to his side. He knew that look. Something was wrong. "What is it?"

She scrubbed her hands over her face and took a deep breath, her gaze fixed on the ceiling. "I wanted to tell you this last night, but I didn't know how."

Pryce's heart stopped beating. A full three seconds passed before he remembered how to breathe again. Whatever she was about to say wasn't going to be good.

"Jonah's back," she blurted out and sat up beside him.

He watched her grab hold of his hands, stared down at them as she threaded her fingers with his, but for some reason, he couldn't feel them. "When?"

"I overheard Breezy on the phone yesterday before we left the rehab center."

"No." He blinked a few times to clear the haze from his eyes but it didn't work. "When did he come back?"

Chloe bit her lip again, her gaze searching his. He tried to hide his utter shock but it was useless.

"Day before yesterday," she finally said in a whisper. "This changes nothing between us," she insisted, holding his palm to her cheek. "I love you, Pryce. You know that, right?"

Unable to speak, he stared at Chloe, seeing the truth in her eyes—a truth even she couldn't deny. She did love him, but it wouldn't be enough. It would never be enough because she still loved Jonah, too. So did he. How did this not ruin *everything*?

"I have to go." He swung his legs over the side of the bed and scooped up his jeans.

"Pryce, listen to me."

Dodging her reaching hands, he marched into the bathroom, ignoring her pleas to open the door. He'd never told her about what had happened between him and Jonah, and never would. She wouldn't understand. Hell, he didn't even understand it. He wasn't attracted to any other guy on the planet, which worked out great because there was no problem as long as that *one* guy had left town. But now Jonah was back, and he freaking *loved* him! And Chloe was still in love with him, too, and everything was just…fucked!

God, please let me wake up and this all be a nightmare.

"We need to talk about this." Chloe followed him around the room as he gathered his boots and socks.

"There's nothing to talk about," he said and sat down on the edge of the bed. "Jonah's back. You still love him and—"

"I do still love him," Chloe admitted. She sank down onto the floor at his feet, taking his sock from his hand as she stared up at him, her big brown eyes full of sorrow and the same fear he felt. "He was my first, Pryce. I'll always love him in some way, but he left me. He left us."

She laid her cheek against his thigh and he couldn't stop the urge to run his fingers through her hair.

"What my brothers did to him was terrible," she continued. "I never meant for any of that to happen, and no one deserves what they did, but he broke up with me, and I fell in love with you. Jonah coming back doesn't change that."

He left you because of me.

He couldn't say the words. Even if it weren't true, he wanted to believe her, wanted it more than he'd ever wanted anything, but he could feel the threads begin to unravel, threatening the life he'd already planned out in his head. The only part Jonah played in that life was in his memories and fantasies.

"Go tell your parents about our plans," Chloe said as she reached for his boot. He shoved his foot inside and she pulled his pant leg down before she pushed to her feet and slid into his lap, wrapping her arms around him. "We'll be fine," she whispered and kissed his cheek. "You'll get your college fund, start your new job at the equine clinic in Billings, and we'll get married, just like we planned. You'll get your degree and be the best large animal vet in Montana. In a month, Jonah, Grassland, your parents, and my brothers will all be behind us. None of it will matter."

~*~

"I don't understand." Pryce sat at his parents' kitchen table an hour later, his dog Timber at his feet, trying to process what his mother was saying. "I thought the second mortgage was going to be enough to get us through calving season."

His mother set a bowl down in front of him and he crinkled his nose. "Oatmeal is good for you," she said after he pushed it away and took a careful sip of coffee instead. He'd eaten enough oats to choke a horse over the last six months, and after the bomb Chloe'd dropped on him earlier, he wasn't hungry anyway.

"The second mortgage was used to make up for the crop we lost last fall," she continued as she sat in the seat across from him, steam rising from her own bowl of goopy cereal. "Your father's medical bills wiped out our savings and every day we get more bills in the mail, doctors, specialists, tests and more tests."

"But what about the insurance? Don't they pay the bills?"

His mother shook her head. "They only pay a portion. Your father's heart condition is getting worse, not better." Always prim and proper, her back ramrod straight in the chair, she brought her spoon to her mouth and took a ridiculously slow bite of her oatmeal, returning her spoon to the bowl before she blotted her lips with her napkin. "You're going to have to quit your classes," she said without preamble, the words so unexpected he'd thought he'd heard her wrong.

"What?"

"We need you here," she continued, taking another measured bite of her breakfast as if she hadn't just landed a sucker punch to his gut.

"I'm not quitting college." It was his only hope of getting the hell out of there, the cornerstone to his entire plan. "I can do what needs to be done at night and on the weekends. Most of my classes are online right now anyway, and—"

"You were late this morning because you stayed in Billings last night," she argued, and he didn't feel a single ounce of guilt for having lied to her. "You've already told me you'll have more classes on campus next semester," his mother continued. "The drive from Billings is too much."

"I told you I'll handle it." He downed the last bit of coffee and rose to get more, using the time to regather his control. This conversation was not going as he'd planned.

After leaving Chloe's, he'd decided she was right. At least he hoped she was. Just because Jonah was back, didn't mean anything had to change for them. All he had to do was make it through the month and everything would be fine, but taking the first step toward that freedom was telling his parents he was leaving.

He knew his dad didn't give a damn about anything but the ranch, but he'd expected more support and understanding from his mom. He was still bitter at her for shipping him off to boarding school instead of kicking his dad out when he'd beaten the life out of him, but he understood. She would never leave his dad, especially when he was so sick.

"We simply can't afford it now," she continued when he returned to the table. "And sit down. It's rude to stand over someone when they're eating."

Pryce ground his teeth together, sinking down into his seat again. He saw the red blush creep up her neck as she swallowed the bitter aftertaste of her admission, and couldn't help but feel sorry for her. She'd come from money. A lot of money. Their ranch, their home, everything they owned had been passed down from her great grandfather. They'd never been as well off as the McLendons, but they'd always had more than enough to make ends meet, until his dad's heart gave out. He hadn't thought Dirk Grunion even had a heart until it had stopped beating one day.

Regardless of their financial slump, thanks to the college fund his grandfather had set up for him, he'd never had to worry about money for school. And in one month, when he turned twenty, the bank would sign over control of it to him and he'd be free.

"Grandfather left me plenty of money for school," he said and brought his mug to his mouth, testing the temperature before he took a sip.

"Your college fund is gone, too."

Coffee spewed from Pryce's lips, the cup slipping from his grasp, spilling the hot brew down his chest and into his lap. "Fuck!" he shouted and jumped from his seat, ripping his shirt over his head and unzipping his pants.

"Watch your language! And stop shouting. Your father's still sleeping," his mother admonished, sitting calmly at the table, showing not one ounce of remorse or guilt, or giving a damn that he was burning alive.

He picked up a dish towel from the counter and ran it under some cold water before he applied it to his scalded chest. "What the hell do you mean it's gone?"

"At least one good thing will come of this," his mother said with an annoyed sigh as she rose and brought her half-empty bowl to the sink, ignoring his question. She took the towel from his hands and wiped the spewed coffee from the front of her dress. "Ever since you started going to that campus your language has been horrible, and I will *not* tolerate it in this house!"

"Oh, but you'll tolerate *him*!" Pryce pointed at his father's upstairs bedroom. "You'll tolerate him abusing your own son, stealing *my* college fund, ruining my *entire* life, but you can't handle the word *fuck*?"

His mother flinched when he shouted the word, so he shouted it again. "Fuck! Fuck-fuck-*fuck*!"

"Pryce, please! Those are the devil's words and I can't allow them. I won't!"

He stood frozen in the middle of their kitchen, staring down at her as if he was seeing her for the first time. Not as his mother, but as the cold, rigid woman who'd stood by all those years and said nothing. *Did* nothing.

"God will provide, Pryce. He always does. We just have to pray."

"I'm leaving." The words spilled from his numb lips without regret. "I don't know how, or when, but I'm marrying Chloe Jessop and we're moving to Billings."

"You will not marry that girl!"

"I'll get my degree, and when I do, I will never set foot on this ranch again." He bent and snatched his shirt from the floor. "Tolerate that." He pulled his shirt back over his head and tucked it into his jeans.

"I forbid it, Pryce! Do you hear me?"

"*Pray* about it, Mother," he said with a snarl before he grabbed his hat from the back of his chair, stuffed it onto his head, and walked out the front door.

Chapter Six

"Chloe?"

"Huh?" Chloe glanced up from her desk to see her boss, Breezy McLendon, standing in front of her. Lost in her thoughts of Jonah, she'd been unable to concentrate all day, and now that Pryce wasn't answering her calls, focusing on her job was impossible. "Sorry, what did you say?"

"Can you start Mrs. Hasting on her upper body exercises? I need to check on Mr. Rawlings to make sure he's not cheating on his repetitions again."

"Yeah, sure." She sprang from her chair and hurried over to Mrs. Hasting, forcing the distractions from her mind before greeting her with a smile. The last thing she wanted was for a patient to injure themselves because she wasn't as focused as she should be, but damn it was hard. She knew this day would come. Jonah was bound to come home eventually.

"Are we using the purple band today, or the yellow one again?" Mrs. Hasting asked, drawing Chloe's attention once again from her distracting thoughts.

"The yellow one." She helped the older woman position the resistance band around her waist. "Breezy said you're not ready for the purple one yet."

"I sure wish I was." Mrs. Hasting sighed. "I'm tired of not being able to reach into my cupboards for my good china."

Chloe smiled. "Give it a little more time and you'll be serving Sunday dinner on your best china soon enough. You don't want to overdo it, or you'll be starting from square one."

"Good Lord, no! I don't want that."

Chloe helped the older woman through her rehab exercises, taking special care to make sure she didn't over stretch her injured shoulder, but Jonah and Pryce were never far from her thoughts.

Despite her attempts to dismiss the agitating flutter, her heart raced at the thought of seeing Jonah again. He'd broken up with her, shattered her heart with excuses that more than a year later still didn't make sense. 'He didn't want to date anyone' didn't cut it, not after what they'd done with Pryce earlier that very day.

Maybe she'd gone too far. She hadn't outright asked Pryce to kiss her in the beginning, but watching how loving Jonah's fathers were with his mother had made her curious, and Jonah had been all too eager to convince Pryce to join them. One kiss turned into another, until the three of them were making out on a blanket, the gentle sound of the water trickling over the river rocks muffling their collective moans and gasps. Her first time with Jonah—her first time with anyone—had been sweet, and beautiful and her heart had been forever after his, but there was something magical and raw about making love with him and Pryce together. She'd never forget their first time, the feel of lying between them, their heavy, masculine bodies bracketing her, loving her.

Side by side, she pressed her forehead against Jonah's bare chest as he thrust inside her, his skin hot from the summer sun and wet from swimming in the creek. Behind her, Pryce kissed her neck, her shoulder, his fingers dancing tenderly over her flesh as he rolled his hips against her bare backside.

As Jonah pulled out slowly and pressed back in, she turned her head and searched out Pryce's mouth. His kiss was different than Jonah's, different than any other, ever. Pryce always kissed her as if the world was ending and it would be their last. Compared to Jonah's confident, tender strokes against her tongue, Pryce consumed her with passionate urgency that made the ache between her thighs unbearable without his touch.

She reached behind her and threaded her fingers through Pryce's dark, damp hair, pulling him closer, kissing him deeper, giving herself over to him, as Jonah loved her body and soul.

Jonah's grip tightened on her thigh and he guided her leg to rest atop his hip. The new position opened her wider and Jonah thrust deeper, touching a place inside her that sent her head spinning and heartbeat soaring.

"Oh my—ahh!" Breaking her kiss with Pryce, she clutched at Jonah's sinewy forearm.

Jonah stilled inside her. "Too much?"

Chloe shook her head, biting her lip as she adjusted to the feel of him seated so fully inside her.

"Can Pryce come inside you, too?" Jonah asked, pulling out with a slow tender stroke.

Pryce gasped behind her and she turned to see him staring at Jonah, a lost, uncertain look in his eyes that made her heart ache. His entire life he'd been made to feel unworthy and ashamed of physical affection. He'd never been kissed until he'd kissed her at Jonah's urging a few weeks ago. In that moment of uncertainty she fell in love with Pryce, too.

"Yes." She kissed Pryce again, reaching behind her to pull him against her, inviting him into her body, wanting him there.

"I...I don't know. I've never..." Pryce looked down at her, desire and shame battling for dominance in his mossy green eyes before he glanced up at Jonah again.

"It's okay," she said in a whisper against his lips and turned back to Jonah. "Tell him it's okay."

Jonah's eyes softened. He leaned down and kissed her, his gaze never leaving Pryce's as he pulled completely out of her. He reached over her and found Pryce's hand, guiding it between her thighs. Fingers pressed inside her. Jonah's or Pryce's? She didn't know, and her insides ached at the new erotic feeling.

Pryce's needy groan vibrated against the shell of her ear, sending excited chills racing over her flesh. She rolled her hips, searching out Pryce's touch as Jonah ground his cock against her pelvis, pushing her into Pryce's hardness.

Jonah slowly drew his hand back, but Pryce lingered, fingering her as his hips flexed with more urgency until she could feel the tip of his cock prodding against her entrance.

"Come inside me," she begged, pleading, hoping beyond hope that Pryce wouldn't stop.

The three of them lay perfectly still in the summer sun, trembling and silent, their world teetering on the edge of some precipice she could have never imagined when she'd spoken her curious thoughts a few weeks past.

Pryce sank deep inside her with a single thrust, a throaty groan escaping him before he jerked back out, his entire body tensing against her when he plunged in again. Jonah reached down between them, the tip of his finger sliding over her clit, circling and pressing harder as Pryce filled her over and over, until he pulled out and Jonah took his place.

"Fuck," Jonah cursed as he filled her. "You feel so good, Lo." He covered her mouth with his own, kissing her deep and long, his tongue sliding against hers in tandem with his thrusts: one, another, harder, deeper, until he pulled out and Pryce entered her once again.

One after the other, they loved her together in a rhythm that felt so natural and good, all consuming, fulfilling her in a way that making love with Jonah alone never had. She tensed in their arms, the throbbing ache in her core spreading through her limbs, sending a fire racing along her skin to the tips of her toes and back up again. Her nipples pebbled against Jonah's chest, her scalp tingling with the same pleasure. She trembled as she thrust against Jonah's hand—reaching, searching, needing more, until the throbbing ache consumed her and her entire body quivered between them.

"Chloe."

Chloe snapped her head up to see Breezy standing in the doorway. Mrs. Hasting was already done with her exercises and walking the resistance band over to the shelf where they were kept.

"I'll get that for you." Chloe rushed over and took the band from her.

"Thank you, dear."

"I'll walk you out to your car." Breezy offered her arm to the elderly woman. "Chloe, can you note her repetition counts in her file and meet me in my office before you go?"

"Yeah," Chloe said with a disappointed sigh. She'd screwed up and let her distracting memories get the best of her again. "I'm on it," she muttered as Breezy turned to leave with Mrs. Hasting.

She pulled the file from the stack on her desk and walked it into Breezy's office, not bothering to notate the file before she sank into one of the two chairs in front of the desk.

Breezy walked in a few minutes later, closing the office door before she took a seat at her desk.

"Whew! What a day." Breezy brushed her hair from her face and moved a sloppy pile of forms from one corner of her desk to another. "Did you note the file like I asked?"

Chloe shook her head, her gaze focused on the file in her hand. "I didn't keep track." Letting Breezy down was more than embarrassing. With little experience and no training, Breezy had taken a huge chance giving her this job. She'd spent the last six months teaching her how to manage the billing and scheduling, and was only just beginning to trust her with some of her patients' rehabilitation activities, and she'd blown it. "I'm really sorry. It won't happen again. I promise."

Breezy studied her for a moment before she nodded and reached for the file. "Chloe, are you okay? It's not like you to be so distracted."

Chloe sucked in a breath and shook her head. "Sorry, I'm…"

What could she say? She couldn't tell her about her past with Jonah. He'd never told his family about them, and she'd promised Jonah she wouldn't tell anyone. And she hadn't told anyone but Aunt Bev about her and Pryce for fear that Pryce's parents would find out about them.

But Breezy knew the Grunions. Pryce had told her about Breezy and her husbands trying to help him before his parents sent him away to that dreadful school. Maybe she'd understand and not fire her if she tried to explain that part of her distracting morning. If she lost this job before Pryce's trust fund was released, she'd probably have to drop out of school. Breezy had been kind enough to schedule her hours around her classes when no one else would.

"Chloe, you can talk to me." Breezy walked around the desk and sat in the chair beside her. "Whatever it is, if I can help you, I will."

Chloe shook her head. "It's nothing like that. I mean, I don't need money or anything. I just… You know Pryce Grunion, right?"

Breezy nodded, her expression a mixture of confusion and concern. "Is he in trouble?"

"No. Maybe." Chloe debated what to say. If Pryce had done what he'd set out to do that morning, then his parents already knew, and something could be wrong. If he hadn't, then all she could do was hope Breezy would keep their secret. Chloe took a breath and released the truth.

"Pryce and I are getting married," she said in a rush, finding a sense of relief in saying the words aloud. "He was supposed to tell his parents this morning, but he's not returning my calls. I'm worried about him."

~*~

Breezy McLendon sat back in her chair, Chloe's confession knocking her for a loop. Pryce Grunion? It wasn't that Pryce was a bad kid, though he wasn't much of a kid anymore. To the contrary, she loved Pryce. She'd never told anyone but her husbands of her suspicions that Pryce could be her half-brother. Not even Pryce knew, unless Dirk Grunion had decided to tell the truth about his affair with her mother, something she doubted the self-righteous bastard would ever do.

Chloe was a nice girl. She'd had some troubles after her parents' divorce, but she was smart and had pulled herself together well enough. She was a good person with a good head on her shoulders, working two jobs and taking online classes in business management to hopefully one day take over her aunt's bakery.

Considering the path Chloe's brothers had chosen—the eldest in prison before the age of twenty-one, and the other two known as the town's trouble makers—Chloe was well on her way to making a good life for herself despite the odds being stacked against her. Something Breezy could appreciate considering her own past.

There was, however, one problem with Chloe's confessed plans to marry Pryce. A big problem. A secret of which she was certain Chloe was naively unaware.

Pryce was in love with Jonah. Or he had been at one time.

Except for a few tense moments in passing, she hadn't spoken to Pryce since the day after Jonah's attack. Pryce's father had beaten him that day, for what she still didn't know. Neither he nor Jonah had ever spoken of what had happened, but the day after Jonah was beaten, they'd found Pryce sitting on their porch steps, his face swollen, fresh angry bruises marring his skin, fear in his eyes.

Carson and Connor had drilled Pryce about his involvement in the attack, all of which he'd vehemently denied. It was then that she saw it: the love in Pryce's eyes, his fear of losing Jonah. He'd never have hurt Jonah. He'd even braved another round of his father's wrath to sneak out of his house to talk to her, worried Jonah hadn't survived.

She'd tried to help him, talk him into filing charges against his dad, or calling child protective services for him, but Pryce had refused. His parents shipped him off to a religious boarding school the very next day. To this day Carson and Connor suspected Pryce at least knew something he hadn't told the police, but they hadn't seen the look in his eyes that day. She knew in her heart he loved Jonah, and that Jonah had loved him, even if neither had been ready to admit it.

"I'm sorry. I know it's sudden, or at least seems that way," Chloe continued, pulling Breezy from her memories of that day. "We've been together since I moved back home, but we had to keep it a secret. I mean, you know his parents. I'm sure they're not going to throw us an engagement party."

"No." Breezy withdrew the pen she kept tucked behind her ear, tapping it on her knee in an urgent rhythm. "I don't expect they will." Dirk Grunion had been sick for months, but she wouldn't put it past the man to hurt Pryce if he could. The fact that Pryce wasn't answering Chloe's calls wasn't a good sign.

"I'll never understand those people." Chloe pulled her phone from her pocket and glanced down at it, her brows furrowing before she stuffed it back into her pocket with a huff.

"Still no word?" Breezy asked.

"No."

Breezy pushed aside her concerns and tossed the pen onto the desk. Pryce was an adult and his father likely far too ill to hurt him. It was Jonah that worried her the most now. What would he think about Pryce getting married?

"I'm sure Pryce is fine," she said and pulled Chloe into a hug. "Congratulations on your engagement, though. Pryce is a good man, and nothing like his father, thank goodness."

Chloe nodded. "He is a good man." She picked at her fingernails, not meeting Breezy's gaze. "I'm lucky to have him."

Breezy smiled despite her worry. "I think you're both lucky to have found each other." When Chloe didn't respond, Breezy shifted in her seat and asked, "Are you sure that's all that's bothering you? Is there something else you want to talk about?"

Chloe shook her head, but then shrugged. "Is... I...We'll be moving to Billings," she finally blurted out. "Not for another month or two, when Pryce gets his grandfather's inheritance and starts his job at the equine clinic there, but I'll give you notice as soon as we have things figured out."

Breezy took a deep breath, partly in attempt to hide her surprise, and partly in disappointment. "I'll miss you." She clasped Chloe's hand with a reassuring smile. "You've been a godsend around here, keeping me organized and out there with my patients instead of in here pulling my hair out."

"Yeah right," Chloe said with a snort. "I haven't done such a great job of *that* today."

"Agreed," Breezy said with a laugh. "But," she glanced down at her desk, "you can make it up to me by separating that stack of files. Carson called me earlier, all bent out of shape about Jonah. I got distracted and mixed the approved files with the ones waiting on my signature for submission to the insurance companies. I can't make heads or tails of them."

"Deal." Chloe pushed from her chair to inspect the pile.

Breezy watched her for a moment, her thoughts racing. She wanted to be excited for them both, but any joy she felt was tempered with the truth. If Pryce had once loved Jonah, would he be happy with Chloe? Maybe she'd been too quick to assume he was gay. Maybe he was bisexual, like Papa Daniel. But, even if he was, did Chloe know? Had he been honest with her?

"Breezy?"

Breezy looked up to find that Chloe had paused, half the stack already separated. Yes, she was going to miss her.

"Is Jonah okay?" Chloe asked with an awkward hesitation. "Is he home for good, or just visiting?"

A funny feeling stirred in Breezy's gut. "Do you know Jonah?" she asked. "Were you friends in school?"

Chloe nodded, but then shook her head. "We...we hung out sometimes." She shrugged and went back to flipping through the files. "I'm sorry. It's none of my business. I was just curious."

Call it women's intuition, suspicion, or just plain hope, but she could have sworn there was more than friendly curiosity behind her question.

Breezy raced through her memories, trying to find one with Chloe and Jonah together. She had seen them a few times when she'd first come back to Falcon Ridge to help Papa Joe after his stroke. Jonah had never mentioned her specifically, but then again she'd been so entangled in her own troubles with Connor and Carson back then that she hadn't paid much attention.

Could they have been…together? *No. Maybe. Probably not.* A threesome seemed more than unlikely considering Pryce's stringent upbringing, but then again, she knew she was right about Pryce and Jonah. Call her crazy, but there was something in Chloe's tone that made Breezy believe there was more to the story. A lot more. Maybe she did know about Pryce and Jonah.

Her mind racing with a flood of frustrating possibilities, Breezy stood. "He's home for now." She took one of the files from the stack and opened it, staring at the pages inside. Chloe wasn't the only one with focus issues today. After her conversation with Con and Car earlier that morning, her attention to her job had been tenuous at best.

"We're having a welcome home dinner for Jonah this evening," she said, a stroke of genius hitting her like a bolt of lightning. She set the folder back on top of the stack, considering the idea, debating the possibilities and consequences.

Whatever had happened between the three of them, Chloe deserved the truth. And if Jonah was staying at Falcon Ridge for good, then he and Pryce needed to settle whatever had happened. The last thing the family needed was another generation trapped in the useless Grunion and McLendon feud. She refused to let that happen. Pryce and Jonah deserved better.

"Why don't you and Pryce come over tonight?" She clasped Chloe's hands, excitement overrunning caution. "I'm sure Jonah would love to see him again."

Chloe shook her head, panic exploding across her face. "No! No, I don't think—"

"It would be great! They can catch up and we could talk about wedding stuff. Gabby *loves* weddings! Oh! We could throw you an engagement party!"

"Oh, no! That's not necessary. And I can't come to dinner." Chloe turned back to the pile of files. "I…I have to help Aunt Bev at the bakery."

"Tonight?"

"Yeah, she has three birthday cake orders, and Mr. and Mrs. Nutter's fiftieth anniversary cake to make before noon tomorrow."

"Wow, that's a lot of cake."

"Tell me about it," Chloe said with a huff. "Thank you, though. I appreciate the offer."

"Well, okay, but please consider the engagement party. Gabby and I would be honored."

Chloe gave her a nervous nod. "I will, but we're not really planning anything special. Just an appointment at the courthouse."

Breezy laughed. "Don't let Gabby hear you say that. She's a sucker for big weddings."

"I know," Chloe said with a tight chuckle. "I remember your wedding cake."

"Oh my gosh! That's right! I'd completely forgotten your aunt made it!" Breezy smiled bigger as another idea hit her. "We can call your aunt and bring her in on the engagement party planning!"

"Oh, I—She's been really busy lately. I can't ask her to—"

"Nonsense!" Breezy insisted. "I'm sure she'd love it! Oh, she does know, right? About you and Pryce?"

"Yes, but—"

"Perfect! I'll stop in and see her, *if* you decide you'll let us do this for you of course."

Breezy knew she was being inappropriately pushy, but she couldn't help it. She didn't want to do something to break her and Pryce apart. On the contrary. If Pryce was in love with Jonah, and Chloe was in love with Pryce… She didn't quite know how or where Jonah fit into the equation with Chloe yet, but there was something there. She could feel it. She just needed time to fit all the pieces together: time and a plan, which was coming together quite nicely if she did say so herself. Gabby would be proud!

"You did what?"

Standing in her husbands' recording studio an hour later, Breezy closed her eyes and took a calming breath. Sometimes having two husbands was impossible.

"Carson, you weren't there. I know what I saw. There's something going on between them."

"Like you know what you saw with Pryce?" he argued, setting his guitar down into the stand beside him.

"Don't start," Breezy warned. "You're wrong about Pryce. He was in love with Jonah."

"Even if that's true—and I believe you that he might have been," Connor said with a staying hand when she attempted to argue, "things have obviously changed. Jonah's been gone a long time and we still don't know what happened to him. This whole thing could have nothing to do with Chloe."

Breezy wanted to argue, but Connor had a point. She turned and walked to the large picture window. On the second floor above her rehab center, Con and Car's recording studio overlooked the full length of Grassland's Main Street and the snow-capped mountains in the distance, a view she'd always found soothing.

Now that she'd had time to think about it, pushing the three of them together didn't seem like the smartest of ideas. But what if she was right? "They could be making a huge mistake."

"A mistake that's not yours to correct," Connor said, stepping up behind her. He folded his arms around her and drew her back against him, kissing the side of her neck before he rested his chin atop her head. "Baby, sometimes we have to learn lessons the hard way. Car can attest to that."

"Aw, man. Fuck you," Carson said with a smirk as he appeared beside her. He leaned down and kissed her cheek, reaching up to caress the spot he'd kissed. "But Con's right. We can't go stirring things up between Pryce and Chloe because of some *feeling* you have."

"Even if your brother could be irrevocably hurt by this?"

Carson grumbled beside her. "Let's not talk about Jonah. He's not my favorite person right now."

"But if they get married—"

"It's not our place," Connor insisted.

She tried to argue. The words were on the tip of her tongue, but the feel of Connor's mouth on her neck as he kissed his way up to the shell of her ear, stole her resolve and she melted against him.

"We have our own mission today, remember?" Con traced seductive circles over her belly, reminding her of their planned rendezvous. He trailed his fingers up between her breasts, cupping one with his big hand. "We're not going to make a baby any sooner by worrying about Jonah."

She glanced up at Carson, the heat in his eyes warming her from the inside out. "Are you sure you want this, too?" she asked one final time. Connor had been ecstatic when she first mentioned her desire to begin trying for a baby, but Carson had been understandably hesitant. They'd only just begun to rebuild their music career after the fallout from their label cancelling their contract. But now that their studio was finished and their fans were hungrier than ever for their next album, the timing seemed perfect to try.

"I told you last week that I'm on board for all the baby making you want to do, darlin'," Car said. He teased her lips with a flirty, seductive flick of his tongue and she opened to his deep, longing kiss. "In fact," he hummed against her lips, pushing his hand inside her blouse to tease her, "if I remember correctly, I showed you in the shower this morning how committed I am."

Fiery need zinged through her limbs and she pulled him closer. "Show me again."

Chapter Seven

The sun was setting when Jonah parked his truck in front of Con and Car's house. Having spent the morning visiting with Uncle Cade and Papa Daniel, the afternoon prepping the calving barn for the first wave of chaos that would begin at any moment, the day had been mentally and physically exhausting. The last thing he felt like doing was sitting at the dinner table dodging his family's inquisition. But Grey had been right. He was done running. From his family at least.

He shoved the truck door open and slid out into the snow. The sooner he got started, the sooner this would be over and he'd be one step closer to putting it all behind him. The next step in that process was talking to Con and Car.

He'd arrived early, hoping he'd have time to clean up before dinner after they'd beat the hell out of him for lying to Mom. He'd get in a few good punches, but he wasn't kidding himself. Con and Car would get the better of him. He steeled himself for a brawl and reached up to knock on the door, but Breezy pulled it open and tackled him before he could.

"Jonah!"

He stumbled back a step, Breezy's arms and legs locked around him in a crushing grip. "I see you've been taking climbing lessons from Dani." He chuckled, a little dazed by her enthusiastic welcome. He liked Breezy, and was happy his brothers had found someone like her to spend the rest of their lives with, but other than helping them plan their wedding, he hadn't spent much time with her before he'd left. The only thing he knew for sure was that she was just like his sister, which didn't bode well for him.

"You've grown a darn foot since you left," she said and squeezed his biceps. "Both tall and wide! Look at you!" She released him and he set her on her feet. "You may not have joined the Marines, but you sure look like you did. Except for that haircut." He dodged her hand when she ruffled his moppy hair. *Yep. Exactly like Dani.*

"Yeah, I know. Mom's already threatened to get her shears out if I don't go into town next week and take care of it."

"Come in! It's getting cold pretty quick out there." Breezy pulled him inside and closed the door. "You're early, and I haven't set the table yet, but would you like something to drink?"

"Sure." He waved off her offer to take his coat. He'd need it when his brothers dragged him back outside. He glanced up the stairs as she led him toward the kitchen, expecting an ambush. "Where's Con and Car?" he asked when none came.

"They had a conference call with one of the producers of the benefit concert they're doing in California next month. They'll be a little late."

Great. That meant the entire family would witness the impending fireworks show. He should have come before he went to visit with Uncle Cade and gotten it over with.

"The new house turned out great," he said, taking in the lofty rooms and modern design. "Car always wanted to live in a log cabin, just never expected something this big."

"They did go a bit overboard," Breezy said as she opened the fridge and pulled out a bottle of lime soda. "It's still your favorite, right?" Jonah took it and gave her a nod. "Good, because I have a whole case of it in the basement you can have. Sodas are off limits for a while."

Jonah snorted and unscrewed the cap, taking a swig of the syrupy caffeine-laced goodness. "Do Con and Car know that?" Soda was his brothers' form of crack.

"Well, they do as of a few weeks ago, when we officially decided to start trying for a baby."

Jonah choked on the last bit of soda trickling down his throat. "Wow!"

A baby? That was quick.

He walked over and put his arm around Breezy's shoulders. "I'd say congratulations, but I'm afraid you're going to need condolences when you get a look at my brothers' parenting skills, or lack thereof."

Breezy laughed. "We're not there yet, but I'm sure they'll be great fathers when the time comes, *Uncle* Jonah."

"Whatever you say," Jonah threw his hands up, "but I can personally attest to them being shitty babysitters." He hooked his hat on the back of the barstool and took a seat, while Breezy hopped up onto the one beside him. "The stuff me and Dani got away with?" He let out a long whistle. "And make sure they keep their porn better hidden."

Breezy gasped. "They don't have porn!"

He dodged her playful slap, laughing at her shocked expression. "You keep telling yourself that, sister. I know my brothers. They have a stash somewhere."

"Oh, stop. They do not."

"You're probably right." Jonah nudged her elbow with his. "I could get used to the whole *Uncle* thing, though."

"Oh yeah?" She took a sip from her glass of water. "I think you'll make an awesome uncle, too."

"Yeah," Jonah sighed. "I can take him on camping trips like Uncle Cade took us."

"Ugh, you're as bad as Car. What if it's a girl?"

"Whichever." He shrugged and stared at the soda bottle in his hand, the knot that had been stuck in his throat the whole time he was visiting Uncle Cade threatening a repeat appearance. "We'll camp out in the back of my pick-up truck and count the stars. Did you know that's how I learned to count?"

"I didn't."

"Yep. Uncle Cade taught me." He swiveled around and leaned back against the bar, picking at the bottle label. "I was a bit slower than Dani in school. Mom tried everything she could think of to teach me, but for whatever reason numbers were never my thing. Uncle Cade came by the house one night and picked me up. It was just me and him, and we rode out to the middle of the north pasture where there wasn't a tree or a cloud for miles. The moon was dark and the sky was lit up like a Christmas tree with so many stars." His memory of that night was so vivid, as if it were only yesterday. "I'll never forget it, being out with Uncle Cade, doing grown up stuff, you know?"

"Yeah." Breezy sighed. "I know what you mean."

"He'd told me that God had lost a star and needed our help to find it, but the only way we could keep track of the ones we could see was by counting them." Jonah laughed at how silly it all seemed now. "We counted all the way to a hundred, star by star, and something finally clicked. I started to see the patterns in the numbers." His voice cracked on the last few words and he swallowed against the lump in his throat.

Breezy draped her arm around his shoulders. "I'm so sorry about Uncle Cade," she said. "I know it hurts. We're all torn up about it."

He unscrewed the cap on his soda bottle and took a long swig, then swiveled back around to face her. "Can I ask you something?"

"Anything," Breezy said with a hopeful look in her eyes he didn't quite understand.

Jonah hesitated, screwing and unscrewing the bottle cap, still unsure he wanted to know. "How bad is it?" he finally asked. "I mean, they told me the basics today, but I know they aren't telling me everything. How bad is he going to get?"

Breezy let him go and stared into her glass of water. Her shoulders rose and fell on a long sigh before she answered. "Everyone's different, so it's hard to say. Pancreatic cancer is one of the worst kinds. It's probably going to get really bad before the end."

"Damn."

"Exactly," Breezy said, staring back into her glass, "but try to act normal at dinner tonight, okay? Cade's a proud, stubborn man, and he's especially sensitive about being pitied right now. He wants everything to stay normal for as long as possible."

"Yeah, I get it."

They sat in silence for a moment. The refrigerator kicked on, then off. The fire in the living room crackled and popped. Breezy's warm welcome and their conversation had lulled his anxiety of seeing his brothers again, but the quiet stirred his nerves back to life. He was about to get up and walk it off when Breezy placed a hand on his forearm.

"Can I ask *you* something?"

Jonah closed his eyes and propped his elbows on the bar. *Let the inquisition begin.* He'd hoped to talk to her and his brothers at the same time, if there was anything his parents hadn't already told them, but he should have known she wouldn't let him off so easily. He'd rather duke it out with Con and Car. Hell, a trial by combat would have been easier than facing Breezy alone. She knew too much, even if he hadn't told her everything.

"No, I didn't join the Marines," he began, his speech already prepared and practiced. "I lied because I didn't know what else to say. It was wrong, and I'm sorry. I was in Alaska, but now I'm home, and I don't plan on leaving again any time soon."

"I'm glad," Breezy said, pausing with a nervous swallow, "but that's not what I was going to ask."

Jonah glanced over and caught her gaze, her intentions clear in her eyes. "No." He reached for his hat, but Breezy snatched it from the back of the chair before he could get his hands on it. "I'm not talking about that," he insisted.

"Have you spoken to him?"

Jonah ground his teeth together, fighting the urge to leave, with or without his hat. He couldn't. Where else would he go but back to Alaska? He was trapped, and that same feeling that made him want to leave in the first place returned with a vengeance.

"No, I haven't seen him," he finally said when it became apparent she wasn't going to let it go.

"Are you going to call him?"

He stared at his hat in her hands, Grey's words echoing back at him.

"Jonah."

"I don't know, okay?" He snatched his hat back and headed for the door.

"Do you know Chloe Jessop?"

The mere mention of her name stopped him dead in his tracks, chilling the blood racing through his veins. He'd spent the last year and a half trying to forget that name.

"How do you know her?"

"She works for me."

That couldn't be. "I thought she moved to Colorado with her mom after her parents split."

Breezy grabbed up the half empty soda bottle and handed it to him. "She got into some trouble and moved back to Grassland to live with her aunt. She asked about you today and I was curious." Jonah watched in shock as she walked back around the bar, checking something in the oven as if she hadn't just stabbed him in the heart. "I got the impression the two of you were close."

Jonah ground his teeth together to keep from cursing. He slammed the bottle back onto the bar and slapped his hat onto his head. "We're not, and I'd be more careful in choosing your employees if I were you."

He opened the front door and four hands fisted into his coat, yanking him from the house. Con and Car pushed him down the steps, and shoved him face down in the snow. "Get the hell off me!" His mouth and nose filled with snow as he shoved against the two-hundred pounds of McLendon muscle sitting on top of him.

"Suck it up, buttercup." Carson pushed his head back down as Connor untucked his shirt and shoved a fistful of snow down his pants. "This is just the beginning."

"Whoa! What do we have here?"

Connor backed away and Carson let him go. Jonah shoved himself to his feet and pulled his shirt back down.

"Let me see it!" Carson pulled at the back of his shirt and he twisted away.

"No!"

"Fuck off! Let me see it," Carson insisted and turned him back around. He tried to pull away, but Connor blocked him and Carson shoved the back of his coat and shirt up.

"Damn!" Carson let out a long, low whistle. "That's some serious ink."

Jonah's cheeks heated as both his brothers studied his tattoo, the bitter cold biting into his skin, not to mention the snow that was melting down the crack of his ass.

"Is that…?" Carson traced the stream that ran beneath the falcon's outstretched wings, across his spine and faded beneath his shoulder blade. The tattoo artist had taken his crude sketch of the creek and their ranch and made a masterpiece from it, adding the falcon flying above.

"It's home." Connor glanced up at him, then back around at the ink. "And Papa Jake's family tree carving."

Jonah twisted free from his brothers and yanked his shirt and coat back down.

"It's fucking awesome, man." Carson plucked his hat from the snow where it had fallen when they'd tackled him. "I'm jealous."

"Me too," Connor added and Jonah dodged his playful shove. "Who did it?"

Jonah dragged in a sharp, cold breath and shook his head. They didn't give two spits about getting a tattoo. They were going to do everything they could to drag this out and he wasn't playing. "Can we just get this over with and get through dinner? I'm wiped and hungry."

"Get what over with?" Connor asked innocently and hooked his arm around Jonah's neck, guiding him back to the front door. "You tired of us already, bro?"

"Aww, poor wittle Jonah," Carson teased with a baby voice. "Working a whole day on the ranch and you're all tuckered out. You need a nap?"

"No." Jonah stopped and pulled away from Connor's grip, his fists balled at his sides and ready to go at it.

"Are you sure?" With a sarcastic frown, Connor reached up to pat the top of his head. "You look tired."

Jonah jerked his head away. "I'm not spending the whole night looking over my shoulder for the two of you to get it out of your systems."

"Get what out of our system?" Carson asked innocently.

"I know you're pissed at me for leaving and lying to Mom. So throw a punch already and let's get it over with." He raised his fists and widened his stance.

Connor burst out laughing. He stepped to Jonah's side and Jonah flinched, expecting a punch to the gut when Connor put his arm around his shoulders again instead.

"Oh dear brother," he teased with a mocking smile. "Let me break this down for you. If we lay a single finger on you, Breezy will cut us off for a month, which doesn't bode well for the baby making situation I'm sure she's already told you all about." He slapped Jonah's back and herded him up the steps. "Nope. We're just going to have to find some other creative and unusual punishments."

Jonah cringed. Living on a working ranch during calving season, he knew the kinds of things his brothers could rope him into.

"I still think if he swings first we could get away with it," Carson said, his arms crossed over his chest as he blocked the doorway.

"No one's fighting today," Connor said. "Besides, I heard Mom's right hook packs one hell of a punch."

An hour and a half later Jonah sat inside his brothers' home at the head of their long dining table, Papa Joe at the other end, flanked by the rest of his family, plus one. Dani's friend, Ash, had apparently drawn the short straw and got himself seated next to Grey, not that he believed for one second that luck—good or bad—had anything to do with it. He'd tried to intervene for the poor guy and take Grey's seat, which only earned him a growl from Grey who'd hip-checked him down to the head of the table before he scrambled in beside Ash. He didn't know what the big deal was. Anyone with eyes could see Dani wasn't the least bit interested in the guy.

Whatever. All in all, the evening had gone smoother than he'd anticipated. Uncle Cade had been winded when he and Papa Daniel arrived—his first trip out of the house since his surgery—but he'd dug into his dinner like a starving man. Judging by the weight he'd lost since he'd been gone, Jonah figured it was a good sign he was doing better, for now.

Cory had finally made it home. His kid brother had filled out and bulked up since he'd left. A lot. Jonah thought about asking him if he wanted to work out together sometime, but other than a cursory greeting to keep Gabby happy, Cory had avoided him at every turn.

He shoveled in another mouthful of his Gran's homemade mashed potatoes and shrugged it off. Cory would come around eventually.

After receiving an earful of grief from his grandfathers, and a proper scolding from Gran, he'd survived relatively unscathed so far, and was enjoying another home-cooked meal. God what he wouldn't have given for food like this in Alaska.

"I'd like to make a toast," his mother said, clinking her fork against her wine glass as she stood. "To Jonah, and to having all my children home safe and sound."

"The prodigal son returns," Cory mumbled with a smirk as he raised his glass of tea, meeting Jonah's gaze for the first time since he'd arrived.

"What the hell is that supposed to mean?" Jonah asked, fed up with Cory's cold shoulder.

"Ouch!" Cory flinched in his seat and rubbed his leg, glaring at Matt.

"Don't ruin this for your mother," Matt warned through gritted teeth.

"You know, you really shouldn't use words you can't spell," Dani added.

"Shut up, Dani," Cory shot back.

"She's right," Papa Joe chimed in, pointing his fork at Cory. "Big words don't suit you anyway."

"Just because I chose not to go to college right out of the gate like Miss Einstein over there, doesn't mean I can't spell!"

Grey turned and looked at Cory and his baby brother shrank back down into his seat, but he apparently wasn't done. "At least I didn't leave home. In fact, I'm the only one who stayed," he grumbled, nodding at Connor and Carson.

"What the hell, dude?" Carson responded with shocked agitation.

"This isn't about you, Car." Jonah tossed his napkin onto the table. Enough was enough. If Cory wanted a fight, he'd give him one. "Why don't me and you step outside and settle this. There's no sense in ruining dinner for everyone."

"I'm ruining dinner?" Cory shot up and tossed his own napkin onto his plate. "Screw this. I'm out of here." He shoved his chair under the table, throwing off Mason's grip on his arm as he made for the door.

"Cory!" Gabby shouted after him.

"Get your ass back in that seat." Matt ordered.

"The hell I will!" Cory turned and pointed at Jonah. "You can all sit around and pretend he's the patron saint of this family, but I won't!"

"What are you talking about? What's wrong with the two of you?" Gabby asked, glancing between him and Cory.

Cory glared at him, seething. "No brother of mine would have gotten a girl pregnant and then run off and left her."

Gabby and Gran gasped. Papa Daniel choked on his last bite and grabbed for his glass of water. Jonah's blood ran cold. "What are you talking about? I didn't—"

"Chloe may be marrying a Grunion, but Pryce is more of a man than you'll ever be!" Cory spat before Jonah could finish his adamant denial, and then marched from the room, the front door slamming behind him a few seconds later.

Chapter Eight

"I didn't…" Stunned, Jonah looked around the room, every shocked gaze searing him with either accusation or disbelief.

"Didn't what?" Papa Joe asked.

"I didn't get Chloe or *anyone* pregnant," Jonah promised. "I have no idea what Cory's talking about"

"Who's Chloe?" Clearly as dumbfounded as the rest of them, Gabby sank back down into her seat.

"Chloe Jessop," Breezy said and looked up at Jonah. "She works for me, managing my office, and I assure you she's neither pregnant nor a mother."

"But she *is* marrying Pryce." Jonah stared down at Breezy, his words coated with the familiar, bitter taste of betrayal. "That's why you asked me about her earlier, isn't it? You knew and you didn't tell me."

"I didn't know how to tell you," Breezy insisted.

"Tell him what?" Mason asked from the far end of the table.

"That Chloe and Pryce are getting married," Breezy finally said the words aloud, her gaze falling to her plate.

"So what's the big deal?" Matt asked with a shrug. "What does this have to do with Jonah?"

"And why would Cory think you'd gotten her pregnant?" Grey asked with a shrewd glare. "Were you and her…? Was that why you left? Because of a girl?"

"Not exactly," Carson mumbled. "Ow!" he yelled when Connor elbowed him in the ribs. "*Ow!*" he shouted again and jolted in his seat when Papa Daniel kicked him under the table.

Jonah glanced between his brothers and Papa Daniel.

They know!

"Should have guessed a girl was involved somehow," Matt mumbled, shaking his head.

The room exploded with warring voices, then began to shrink and spin around him.

Pryce is getting married? To Chloe?

Heat bloomed in his gut and spread up his spine, making the tips of his ears burn like the sun and his skin blister with a fine coat of sweat.

Con and Car know about me and Pryce. Did Papa Daniel tell them what he saw that day?

His dads began shouting, arguing.

Pryce is getting married to the girl who betrayed us both.

The voices in the room grew louder. His mom was saying something, but he couldn't quite make it out through the ringing in his ears.

Memories of the attack mingled with the noise in the room and visions of Chloe. Over the last year and a half, memories of her twisted with the ones of her brothers mocking faces as they'd beaten the life out of him.

At first he hadn't been able to believe her capable of such betrayal. She'd hated her brothers. But the more he thought about it, the more sense it made. Nobody knew about them except the three of them and Papa Daniel, but he wouldn't have told *her* brothers.

After he'd broken up with her, she'd probably run home crying and told her brothers everything. He'd thought she'd gotten her revenge, but now she was marrying Pryce, twisting the knife even deeper. How could Pryce do this? Unless…*he doesn't know*.

He could only imagine how easy it was for her to sink her seductive claws into him again. Pryce's trust fund was the perfect incentive, too, not to mention her brothers' lethal brand of intimidation. Good God! Had her brothers bullied him into marrying her?

"Enough!" Papa Daniel's loud voice boomed through the room and the chaotic shouts quieted. "I will not have my grandson's personal life debated at the family dinner table!"

Jonah bolted for the door.

"Where are you going?" Gabby yelled after him.

"Out!"

He shoved one arm through the sleeve of his coat, grabbed his hat from the bar and rushed out to his truck. He didn't bother to turn on the heater as he navigated down the long driveway in the darkness, flakes of snow and fine sleet pelting his windshield.

The engine was barely warm by the time he reached the Grunion Ranch. He steered his truck down the long, paved driveway, noticing the front gate busted from its hinges on his way in. The lights from the old colonial-style home, with its vast pillars and wraparound porch, glowed in the distance. The driveway forked, the left leading to the main house, the right fork leading to the stables and barns. He saw a light shining through the stable windows and cut the wheel.

Dirk Grunion's truck sat outside the barn and Jonah tensed. He slowed his truck to a stop and cut the engine and lights, second guessing his plan. Third guessing it. *Damn.* The last thing he wanted to do was dust things up with Pryce's old man.

The barn door slid open and the light poured out into the snow-covered yard. A tall, lean man walked out, his dark Stetson shielding the snow from the hard angles of his face, but it didn't take more than a second to know it wasn't Dirk. The tension in Jonah's gut slid lower to his groin and he sucked in a breath.

Pryce.

The image of his friend had long been seared into his memories. He knew every plane and line, every freckle and scar, every dip and taut cord of lean muscle, but there was something different about the shadow that moved through the darkness with purpose.

Jonah watched breathlessly as Pryce opened the truck door, leaned inside to retrieve something then slammed the door with enough force that he could hear it over the yards of distance between them.

Pryce dropped whatever he'd retrieved and bent over to pick it up, kicking at the snow when he couldn't find it. In spite of himself, Jonah grinned. He sat and watched his old friend curse and stomp through the snow until he'd found whatever it was he'd dropped, then trudge back into the barn, sliding the door closed hard enough it bounced back open a foot or two.

Jonah yanked his keys from the ignition and slid out of his truck, zipping up his leather jacket on his way to the barn. Hopefully Pryce was alone, but even if he wasn't, he couldn't wait another second to get to the bottom of this bullshit marriage business once and for all.

He was almost at the door when something flew through the gap and pinged off the truck's front bumper, followed by a string of curses. Jonah peeked around the door and jumped back again as another piece of greasy metal was hurled into the snow.

"Stupid piece of...!" The sound of metal against metal echoed inside as Pryce pounded the hell out of whatever he was working on.

Jonah waited a beat, and then curled around the edge of the door, protecting all his important parts from flying debris. Pryce was bent over, panting, his arms outstretched and braced against the fender of a horse trailer, cursing a blue streak.

"You never were good with a wrench," Jonah said as he slid the barn door closed behind him.

Pryce looked up and Jonah's gut tightened again. The air left his lungs and he forced himself to draw in his next breath as Pryce stood to his full height, taller than he remembered. His green eyes pierced Jonah with a stirring mixture of frustration and surprise, his lips pressing into a hard line, his nostrils flaring with each labored breath he took. Damn he looked good. Too good.

"I get by well enough," Pryce said, then bent down, picked up another wrench and went back to work on the trailer's axle, biting back another curse when the wrench slipped and he busted his knuckles.

Jonah marched over and reached for the wrench, but Pryce jerked it away and took a step back. Jonah held out his hand, watching a storm of different emotions swirl across Pryce's face until he finally gave in and handed it over.

"What are you doing out here so late fixing a trailer?" Jonah asked as he squatted onto his haunches and went to work to loosen the stubborn bolt.

Pryce didn't respond. Jonah glanced over his shoulder to see him busying himself with the other parts strewn across a makeshift workbench. His gaze lingered on his back, and then trailed predictably lower. A warm wave of lust flowed through his veins and rushed to his dick. The way those Wranglers hung low on Pryce's hips and cupped his ass and thick thighs… Had he been working out with Cory?

The wrench slipped. "Dammit!" Jonah cursed and shook his hand, the cold making his busted knuckles sting that much more.

"Here." Pryce grabbed a shop rag from his pocket and rushed to his side. The second their hands touched Pryce jerked away with a muted gasp.

Jonah pretended not to notice. He wiped the blood from his knuckles and turned back to the disabled trailer. "The wrench broke," he said, holding up what was left of it.

"Yeah." Pryce sighed and ran a greasy hand through his hair, leaving a smudge on his forehead. "Just like everything else around here." He balled his fists and kicked an empty feed bucket across the aisle.

Pryce paced back to the workbench and Jonah watched him, feeling like a fish out of water gulping for air. He wanted to pull him into his arms and take away whatever was eating at him, but Pryce wasn't his to hold. Never had been. Never would be.

"Grrrrraaahh!" Pryce shoved the workbench, sending it and all the trailer parts tumbling to the dirt floor.

"Hey!" Jonah rushed up behind him and locked his arms around his shoulders. "It's only a busted wrench."

"Don't touch me." Pryce twisted out of his grip and shoved him away, his hands trembling with anger. "Don't!" he warned when Jonah took a step closer. "And it's not just a broken wrench!" He ripped the ruined tool from Jonah's hand, hurling it to the other end of the barn with another frustrated growl.

"What the hell's happened to you?" Pryce had never had a temper, not once since they'd become friends had he seen him act like this.

"What do you care?" Pryce shot back.

"What do you mean, *'what do I care'*?" The last time I saw you we were still friends!"

"Just leave," Pryce ordered and marched back over to the upturned workbench. "It's what you do best," he grumbled, bending down to scoop up a handful of parts.

"What *I* do—you left first!"

"I had no choice!" Pryce snapped. "My parents sent me off to that hellhole! I didn't have a choice and you know it!"

"And you think I did?" Jonah argued. "You have no idea what it was like for me after you left." He bit back a curse, remembering

Chloe's brothers' vicious taunts and threats. Football, school, all his friends, the Jessop brothers had screwed up everything he'd loved, and even threatened to post pictures of him and Pryce online, pictures he still didn't know if they did or didn't have. "Travis and Wayne made my life a living hell for months, and I couldn't say a goddamn word to anyone without risking your parents finding out about us!"

Pryce didn't move, not a single breath.

"I tried to call you," Jonah continued. "You wouldn't even see Breezy when she drove over to try to talk to you. For all I knew you blamed me for being sent away and were never coming back!"

Pryce spun around. "I never blamed you." He dropped his gaze to his hands, fumbling with the trailer part he'd picked up from the dirt. "Breezy came to see me?" he asked.

"Yes." Jonah took a hesitant step toward him.

"So, she knows, then."

Jonah shook his head. "I've never told anyone, but I think she figured it out somehow."

Pryce crossed his arms over his chest. "That's probably my fault."

Jonah took another step, inching his way closer like he would an injured wild animal. "She told me you came over to the house to check on me the day after the fight." He gripped Pryce's shoulder. "She said your dad beat you up pretty bad." He raised his hand, hesitated, but couldn't stop himself. Pryce sucked in a breath when the back of Jonah's finger skimmed his cheekbone. Jonah turned his hand and cupped Pryce's jaw, taking in all the changes now that he was close enough to see them. Cory wasn't the only one who'd grown up since he'd left.

"He, uh…" Pryce cleared his throat, still focused on the part in his hands. "My father was waiting by my truck when I left to go get help," he finally choked out. "I tried to get him to come help you, but he refused. When I tried to go back, Craig, his old foreman, forced me into my father's truck, and uh…" He shook his head, his Adam's apple bobbing with his anxious swallow.

"He's a bastard," Jonah said, gripping Pryce's nape, drawing him close enough to smell the sweat on his skin.

"Well, I don't have to worry about that anymore." Pryce turned back around to the overturned workbench. "He can hardly get out of bed lately."

Jonah hadn't realized how close he'd come to kissing him until he found himself lips to felt with the back of Pryce's Stetson.

"He's dying," Pryce said.

"What?"

"Yep. Heart failure." Pryce skirted away from him, around the table, and began picking up the remaining trailer parts. "The doctors say they might be able to help him, but he's getting worse."

"Holy shit," Jonah whispered into the cold air.

Pryce chuckled. "Yeah, and now if you don't mind, I have to get this trailer fixed and get a load of hay stacked up in the pasture before sunrise."

"What? Why tonight?"

"Half our stock is going to freeze to death if I don't make some sort of windbreak before this storm blows in tomorrow night. I won't have time to fix the broken water tank heater and get the extra feed out if I don't get this done tonight."

"Where's your foreman, or the other ranch hands for that matter?" Jonah asked as he bent down and picked up a handful of bolts beside his boot and tossed them onto the workbench. "Why aren't they out here helping you?"

Pryce furrowed his brows as he doubled his efforts, moving with deliberate purpose, cleaning the dirt from the trailer parts and reorganizing them on the table. "They're gone," he said. "Most of them anyway. We can't pay them, and no one's going to work for my father for free, except me apparently."

"What about when the calving starts? You got any help coming?" Pryce couldn't possibly think he could do everything on his own.

"Our calves aren't due for another two months, but I've got a skeleton crew lined up if I need them."

"If you need them?" Jonah jerked the part out of Pryce's hand and took him by the shoulders. "You can't do this by yourself. Forget the storm. You could lose more than your stock." One accident and he could lose his life!

"I've already lost more than you could possibly imagine," Pryce said through gritted teeth.

Jonah fisted his hands into the front of Pryce's coat and backed him against the side of the horse trailer. All the months he'd spent telling himself he was wrong, that he didn't want Pryce, that he *couldn't* want him, were nothing but wasted time. This need inside him hadn't gone away just because he did. Every ridiculous excuse he'd meticulously crafted evaporated in a single breath. There was no other truth but the one in front of him, and he was done running from it.

"You didn't lose me," Jonah breathed, their faces so close his hat tipped back and fell to the ground behind him.

Pryce's hot breath coated Jonah's lips with a teasing taste of him. "But you lost me," he said and met Jonah's gaze.

"So it's true." Jonah's angry words sliced through the cold air between them. "You're marrying Chloe." Familiar resentment rose to the surface and he didn't bother to fight it. He pressed his hips against Pryce's, feeling the hard lie Pryce was about to tell for what it was. Even if he was in love with the traitorous bitch, Pryce couldn't deny the truth any more than he could. "Did you tell her about us?"

Pryce licked his lips, his body tensing in response to the seductive contact he still so obviously craved, his gaze dropping to Jonah's mouth. "There is no *us*," he breathed. "It was only one kiss."

"Wrong." Jonah descended on his mouth, prodding with his tongue until he pushed past Pryce's lips to claim the boy-turned-man the way he'd craved since the last time their lips touched.

Pryce pushed against his chest with a protesting grunt, but his token resistance subsided when their tongues clashed in a frantic duel. Jonah pressed his weight against him, trapping him against the trailer, countering each of Pryce's desperate strokes with his own. The long denied need for his best friend's taste drove him to reach deeper. He gripped Pryce's face and tipped his head back, their teeth clicking together in their haste for more. Welcomed heat flooded Jonah's veins as he thrust his tongue alongside Pryce's as deep as he could reach before retreating and moving in for another drugging taste. Damn, he'd needed this.

Pryce threaded his fingers through his hair and pulled him closer. The vibrant sting to his scalp raced to Jonah's groin and a growl rumbled through his chest. He ground his cock against the ample bulge in Pryce's jeans, extracting a mirroring desperate groan from him before Pryce twisted away, gasping for air.

Reluctantly, Jonah backed off, but didn't release him. He braced his forearm against the trailer beside Pryce's head, their feverish breaths billowing around them in a cloud of desire and lust.

With a firm grip on Pryce's chin, he gazed down at him, nowhere near satisfied. "Now there's two kisses," Jonah panted. "And you can bet your ass there will be more." He punctuated his point by trailing his lips along Pryce's jawline, the seductive feel of his five-o'clock stubble making them both release a shuddering breath.

Pryce shoved him away and Jonah let him go. He hadn't taken more than a step when Pryce cursed. "Chloe?"

Jonah glanced back at him, then over to the open barn door where Chloe stood frozen, her eyes wide with shock.

"Chloe, it's not what—dammit wait!" She bolted like a spooked colt and Pryce shot out of the barn after her. "Chloe!"

Chapter Nine

Pryce's last thread of hope slipped from his grasp as his fingers slid from Chloe's locked car door. He dropped to his knees in the snow and watched her taillights weave and swerve until they disappeared around the bend in the driveway. It was over.

Chloe hadn't said as much, hadn't said a single word, but she didn't have to. The hurt and betrayal in her eyes was enough. He'd lost her. He'd lost everything in a single day.

He didn't know how long he'd sat there in the dark, but his knees were numb and didn't want to cooperate when he finally pushed to his feet and stumbled his way back into the barn.

Jonah sat on an overturned bucket, up to his elbows in grease. When he noticed Pryce standing in the doorway, he stood, wiping his hands on the shop towel.

"All done," he said, nodding at the trailer axle. "Water seeped into the hub and froze up the ball bearings. A little heat was all it needed."

"Get out," Pryce said with a growl and shoved the barn door the rest of the way open.

"You can't marry her."

"I said get out!"

When Jonah refused, Pryce marched across the distance between them and punched him. Jonah flailed back, his hand covering his jaw, shock in his eyes. Good. Pryce took another swing, but Jonah dodged it and tackled him around the waist, forcing him to the ground.

"Get off me you son of a bitch!" Pryce shoved at the larger man straddling his hips, but Jonah didn't budge.

"Not until you hear me out!" Jonah captured his wrists and pinned them to the ground beside his head.

Face to face, Pryce looked up at the man he'd loved, the man who'd just cost him the only thing he had left to live for. Fiery anger burned its way through his chest and he thrashed against Jonah's hold, bashing his forehead into Jonah's smirking face.

"Sonofa*bitch*!" Jonah jerked back, and then rolled to his feet. "You broke my nose!"

Pryce scrambled to his feet and shoved him toward the door, ignoring the blood dripping from between Jonah's fingers. "I'm going to break more than that if you don't get out of my damn barn."

"She sent her brothers to beat the hell out of me!" Jonah jerked free from his hold before they reached the door.

Pryce stilled, sucking in breath after icy breath. What the hell kind of nonsense was he spouting now?

"Yeah, I bet she didn't tell you *that*, did she?" Jonah wiped the blood from his mouth with his coat sleeve.

"She didn't have anything to do with that!" Pryce argued.

"Then how did her brothers know about us?" Jonah snapped, collapsing back down onto another overturned bucket.

"What?" Icy fear pierced through the haze of anger and froze Pryce in place. The edges of his vision blurred as his heart beat against his chest. *They couldn't know.*

Jonah saw the panic in his eyes and shook his head. "I don't think they know for sure about me and you," he said with a grimace, massaging his jaw, "but they sure as hell knew about us and Chloe." Jonah pushed from the bucket and paced to the other side of the aisle. "She used them to get revenge for me breaking up with her."

Pryce furrowed his brows then released a sigh of relief as the pieces fell into place.

"That's not what happened," he said, leaning against the doorframe.

"No?" Jonah asked. "Then how did Finn know? Why did he threaten you right before he beat the piss out of me?"

Pryce shook his head in denial.

"I'm not making this shit up, Pryce! Finn said as much, for crying out loud! Right before him and his brothers damn near killed me!"

Pryce closed his eyes, squeezing them tight, as if he could shut out the memory of that day. "She didn't tell them anything," he sighed and turned away. He walked over to the bucket Jonah had used as a work stool and sank down onto it, propping his elbows on his knees. "She thought she was pregnant."

Jonah's head jerked back. "What?"

Pryce picked up the wrench Jonah had been using and twirled it between his fingers. "She was going to tell you the night you broke up with her."

"She was pregnant?"

"No." Pryce bit back a curse. None of this would have happened if he hadn't touched Jonah. "Her period was late, and she got scared," he continued. "When you broke up with her she didn't know what to do. Her parents had gotten into a huge fight that day and her mother was gone when she got home. She couldn't tell her dad, so she called Aunt Bev."

"Her aunt told them?"

"No you jackass." Pryce shook his head. "How many of your phone conversations have your brothers and sister eavesdropped on?" He glanced up at Jonah and saw the second he got it. "She didn't even know they'd heard her talking until the day after the fight, when word got around that you were in the hospital. She'd seen the bruises on her brothers' faces and the hole in Finn's hand from the pitchfork you skewered him with, and put two and two together. Chloe told her mom, but she didn't want anything to do with it. Her mother had been beaten up pretty bad in the fight with her dad and was more worried about getting out of town. She made Chloe pack her clothes and they moved to her other aunt's house in Colorado the day after I left."

"While I was still in the hospital." Jonah released a long sigh and sank down onto his haunches. "That explains why Cory thought I'd gotten her pregnant."

"What?"

Jonah shook his head and stood. "It doesn't matter." He walked over and offered Pryce his hand.

Pryce stared at it, and then looked up at Jonah. "You think this fixes anything?" He stood and walked back to the barn door, flinging it open. "You just cost me the one person I had left in this world who loved me for me."

"Pryce, I'm—"

"Go home, Jonah."

"She doesn't—"

"I said get out!"

He waited by the door. Jonah held his gaze, then dropped his chin and started walking. When Pryce reached to pull the door closed behind him, Jonah stopped and looked down at him. "She can't love you if she doesn't know this part of you."

Pryce stood motionless, unable to breathe as Jonah dipped his head and gave him a soft, disarming kiss. He remained rooted to that spot in the cold darkness, his eyes closed until Jonah started his truck and rolled away. When the air was still and silent, he glanced up at the night sky, wondering if his mother was right. Was God punishing him?

Physically and emotionally zapped, he wandered back into the barn, going through the motions of working, but not getting anything done. He wound up sitting on the overturned bucket, staring at his phone, debating whether or not to call Chloe. He'd already typed out and erased a dozen text messages.

What could he say? Sorry seemed spectacularly inadequate, though he *was* sorrier than he could possibly express. He couldn't take back what she'd seen. She wasn't stupid, and any denial he offered would only salt the wounds he'd inflicted by lying to her in the first place.

He dropped his head into his hands and released a frustrated growl. God, why had he let Jonah kiss him? When he'd looked up and saw him standing in the doorway, tall as a cottonwood and broad as a mountain, his arms crossed over his muscled chest, he'd wanted to fall to his knees in front of him, do all the forbidden things he'd dreamed of doing night after night—only this was real. Jonah was home, and any belief he'd gotten him out of his system was blown to hell and back.

The friction and heat, the need, the cold air that stung his lungs as he'd tried to breathe Jonah in, the anger, the guilt, the passion that stirred in his groin when he'd looked Jonah in the eyes and saw the truth—they'd all spun in his head and everything went sideways.

He glanced back down at his phone, thumbing through all the text messages and calls from Chloe he'd ignored throughout the day. All he could think about every time the damn thing rang was the hope he'd seen in her eyes that morning when she reminded him of their plans—plans that were now nothing more than a pile of steaming cow manure, like his college fund and their engagement.

Maybe it was for the best. Even if she hadn't seen him kissing Jonah, he'd never be the man she deserved. He'd never be able to buy her a house, or the new car she desperately needed. They couldn't move to Billings if he had to pay full tuition and he sure as hell wasn't moving her into his parents' house, even if they didn't disown him.

He could drag out his classes, take one here and there when he could afford it, but at that rate he would be thirty by the time he got his diploma and a job that paid enough to make ends meet. Chloe deserved so much better than that. She deserved better than him, someone who'd done nothing but lie.

He shoved a hand through his hair and stood, kicking the trailer tire on his way to the tack stall. None of it mattered now. He reached into the cabinet and shifted through the bottles of ointment and sprays to the back where he kept his stash, not that a single bottle of whisky was a stash by any standard. Jonah had lifted it from Keven Parker's big brother's graduation party two years ago. It was still three-quarters full, so he wouldn't exactly say he was the sinning drunkard he'd imagine his father calling him, but all bets were off tonight. Hell couldn't get much worse than this, so as far as he was concerned, he had nothing left to lose.

~*~

Parked behind her aunt's bakery, Chloe sat in her car and stared at the clock on the dashboard, the late-night numbers blurring in and out of focus through her tears. The heater cycled between lukewarm and inferno, depending on how close her car came to overheating. She should have taken it in for a tune up last month, but her brothers worked at the only mechanic's shop in town and she wasn't about to give them a dime. Between her classes, her hours at the rehab center and helping her aunt at the bakery, she hadn't had time to drive all the way to Clarkston.

As if the fates could hear her thoughts, a light on the dashboard flashed red and the engine sputtered and died. "No!" She slapped the dashboard. "No-no-no!" Numbed body and soul, her fingers trembled as she turned the key, but got nothing in response.

Another wave of tears streamed unchecked down her cheeks. The last straw broken, she laid her forehead against the steering wheel and released a sob, jolting upright in her seat when the horn blared. She glanced up at the loft above the store in time to see Aunt Bev's bedroom light switch on. "Dammit." She hurriedly wiped away her tears before she grabbed her purse and got out.

"Chloe, honey, what are you doing out here so late?" her aunt asked when she greeted her at the bakery's back door.

"I had to work late at the clinic." She ducked past her aunt, shielding her eyes behind her long hair as she headed for the stairs. "Sorry I woke you."

"Chloe."

The stern tone of Aunt Bev's voice pulled her to a stop.

"Chloe, look at me."

She turned around, glancing up through the tears that continued to flow despite her efforts to hold them back.

"Oh, honey. You never cry. What happened?" Aunt Bev rushed to her side and pulled her into her arms.

She'd thought she'd cried all she could on her way home, nearly running off the road twice before she'd reached town. Now, inside her aunt's safe embrace, the crack across her heart split in two. The pain was so intense she didn't think it would ever stop.

When she'd stepped inside the barn and saw the man she loved in the arms of the man who'd broken her heart, kissing him like he would die if he didn't, her entire world crumbled. Helpless to move a muscle, she'd watched them with morbid fascination. Jonah's large, hard body, old muscles and new, crushed against Pryce's lean form with desperate demand. Pryce had wrapped himself around Jonah with an urgency he'd never once had for her. The vision was an inspiring picture of erotic abandon so beautiful it took her breath away. But then Pryce broke away and she'd heard Jonah's possessive declaration. This was not their first kiss, and it wouldn't be their last.

The ugly truth invaded the scene in front of her, turning and twisting the picture, distorting and reframing it until it came into focus, appearing undeniably different than the beautiful passionate kiss she'd just witnessed. Jonah hadn't broken up with her because he didn't want her. He'd broken up with her because he wanted Pryce. And Pryce wanted him.

"Oh, Aunt Bev. It's terrible." Chloe sobbed into her aunt's shoulder as they stumbled to the small table in the back of the bakery's kitchen. She slid into the chair and hugged her aunt's hips, afraid if she let go she'd fall apart completely.

"It's okay honey. Let it out."

Aunt Bev's permission was just the incentive she needed. The flood gates opened and all the hurt poured out. Through her sobs, she told her aunt everything: Jonah coming home, Pryce ignoring her calls, the kiss, the passion she'd witnessed between them, the way she'd felt when she first saw them together, then the sting of rejection and betrayal that had sent her running.

"They don't want me," she cried, another surge of tears falling when there should be none left to cry.

"Do you want them?" Aunt Bev asked, handing her another tissue.

"Yes. No! I mean, I love Pryce," she said and dabbed at her swollen eyes. "I always have, but he lied to me, Aunt Bev. He doesn't want me, not the way he wants Jonah."

"That's not what you said, though." Her aunt stood and retrieved a glass from the cupboard, filling it with water and sitting it in front of her before she sat back down.

"I don't understand," Chloe choked out and reached for the glass.

"I can't believe I'm about to say this—and I'm in no way advocating it if you're not one-hundred percent sure about what you want—but, honey, you need to be honest with yourself. You said *'they'* don't want you," Aunt Bev clarified. "Do you love them both?"

Chloe blushed and shook her head. "That's not what I meant."

"Isn't it?" Her aunt took the glass from her hand and set it on the table. "It's me you're talking to, remember? I know all about the thing you had going with those two boys before your brothers did what they did, and who can blame you? Pryce is a good-hearted kid. His parents are a little bonkers, but he loves you like there's no tomorrow, and we both know he'd never hurt you on purpose. And Jonah is a McLendon. Every woman in Grassland has had a fantasy or two about those men, even me."

"What?" Chloe choked out.

Aunt Bev dipped her chin and raised an incredulous brow. "I'm a middle-aged woman, Chloe. I'm not dead yet. And yes, in my youth I spent my fair share of hours dreaming of being the jelly in Jonah's dads' creamy peanut butter sandwich."

"Aunt Bev!" Heat rushed to Chloe's cheeks and she turned away, unable to look her aunt in the eye imaging her with…doing…*that*!

"My point is," her aunt continued, taking Chloe's chin in her grip and turning her head to meet her gaze, "if you still love Jonah, then you've been lying to Pryce, too."

Of course she still loved Jonah. She'd told Pryce as much just that morning, but…maybe Aunt Bev was right. She hadn't been completely honest. Seeing Jonah again had been like throwing gasoline onto a dying fire. Jonah was and always would be her first true love. She'd ached for so long after he'd broken up with her, making herself sick trying to figure out why. Nothing she'd come up with had been even close to the truth. She'd never once imagined Jonah with another guy, much less Pryce. But the vision of the two of them together dispelled any hope her aunt's words may have inspired.

"It doesn't really matter now, does it," she said with a sober sigh.

Aunt Bev sat back in her chair and crossed her arms over her chest. "I can't tell you what is or isn't going on between those two, but I know Pryce loves you. If you can love two people, why can't he?"

That was the crux of it, wasn't it? "He's gay, Aunt Bev. Even if he does love me, I can't…I obviously don't have what he needs."

"Oh, honey." Aunt Bev laughed and pushed from her seat. "I sleep in the room next to yours. Trust me. Pryce has no problem taking everything you've got to offer."

"Oh my God." Chloe cupped her hands over her face with a mortified groan.

"So you've screamed," Aunt Bev said with a teasing grin. "Over and over and ov—"

"Stop! I did not scream!"

"Okay, so, maybe 'moan' is a better word."

Chloe turned her back on her aunt, unable to look at her, but also unable to hold back her laugh.

"Sleep on it tonight," Aunt Bev urged and turned Chloe to face her. "Then go talk to Pryce in the morning. He at least owes you an explanation, and you both owe each other the truth." Chloe nodded reluctantly. "And then the two of you, whatever you decide to do, should go talk to Jonah."

Chloe shrank away from her aunt's embrace. "I don't know if I can do that." She still felt ashamed about what her brothers had done to Jonah.

"Yesterday you were ready to get married, to tackle the world with Pryce," her aunt argued. "Well, honey, that world out there can throw a lot worse than this at you. Believe me."

Chloe turned and looked at Aunt Bev, her heart aching at the loss in her eyes, loss that had dulled over time, but was still clearly present. Having been only three when her uncle drowned in a rafting accident, she didn't remember him, but her aunt had loved him deeply. She'd often wondered why her aunt had never remarried, but she understood now. If her pain had been even half of what she'd felt tonight…

"Not everything in this world is black and white, Chloe," Aunt Bev said as she walked to the table and picked up the mountain of crumpled tissues, tossing them into the trash. "It's time to pull your big girl pants on and face the truth. You might surprise yourself."

Chapter Ten

"Ouch!" Jonah jerked his head from Matt's hands and cupped his nose.

"It doesn't look broken," Matt said and pushed Jonah's hand away, dabbing at the cut with a cotton ball, "but I'm not a doctor. You should go see one later to make sure."

Jonah dodged his ministrations and hopped off the tailgate. "We don't have time if we're going to get this done."

Matt grumbled a curse and tossed the bloody cotton balls into the trash. "Tell me again why I'm trailerin' two loads of hay and feed over to the Grunion's pasture before the sun's even up."

"Because, Dad, it's the right thing to do." Jonah marched to the cab of his truck and pulled a pair of work gloves from his glove box.

"The last time I checked, Dirk Grunion wouldn't piss on any one of us if we were on fire," Matt argued. "In fact I'm pretty sure he'd be the one to strike the match."

That was truer than Matt could ever know. The idea that Dirk knew the Jessop brothers had him cornered, and didn't do a damn thing to stop them, made him momentarily rethink his plan, but Pryce wasn't at fault. If he didn't help, it would be Pryce who lost their family's ranch.

"This isn't about Dirk." Jonah hefted a bag of feed from the pallet in a nearby stall and tossed it into the bed of his truck. "Pryce is my friend. I screwed up, and I owe him."

Matt shook his head. “Grey’s not gonna like this.”

“Then don’t help.” He shrugged and loaded another bag. “But I’m still doing it. Tally up whatever I take and I’ll get the cash the next time I’m in town.”

“It’s not about the money, and you know it.”

Jonah shrugged. “If you’re not going to help, I’ll load up the rest of it when I get back from herding their cattle down to the barn.”

“I’ll help,” Matt scoffed, and grabbed him by the arm to stop him, “but you’re not goin’ anywhere until you tell me what this is about.”

Jonah hung his head. “Dad, I can’t.”

“You can and you will,” Matt insisted. “Dammit, kid, this has gone on long enough. Does this have to do with what happened at dinner last night?”

Jonah looked away, anywhere but directly at his dad. “You wouldn’t understand.”

“You’re damn right I don’t understand! Son, if you didn’t get Chloe Jessop pregnant, then why does Cory think you did? And what the hell does Pryce Grunion have to do with it?”

Jonah sucked in a breath, holding it as the truth scrambled to the tip of his tongue. He looked at his dad and couldn’t do it. He couldn’t say the words! “I don’t have time to talk about this right now. The storm that’s coming is bad and it will be here—”

“Fuck the damn storm!” Matt jerked him back when he tried to turn away.

“I love him!” Jonah snapped, and then nearly passed out from the tandem rush of relief and fear flooding his bloodstream. He braced his hand on Paladin’s stall to keep from stumbling. “I love him, okay?” He tried to meet his dad’s gaze, but couldn’t. His lungs pumped hard to drag in each breath and push it out, but he didn’t think it was working.

“Hey.” Matt grabbed his arm and steadied him on his feet. He shook him, hard, and Jonah glanced up, expecting to see nothing but disappointment in his eyes. “That’s all you had to say, Son.” Jonah stood toe to toe with his dad, staring down at him in disbelief.

“That’s it?” he blinked. “You’re not going to ask me why, or how your son could possibly be in love with another guy? A Grunion?”

“Whoa!” Matt held up his hands, shaking his head as he backed away. “I don’t need to know the when, who, how and what’s-it’s of *anything* when it comes to *that*.”

"Me either," Mason said from behind him.

Great. Just...*great*. Jonah's stomach rolled and dropped to his feet. He glanced over his shoulder to see Mason walking toward them, but he couldn't make himself turn to face him. He didn't have to wonder how much he'd heard. He could only imagine the worst.

Matt caught his gaze again and narrowed his eyes. "Wait a minute. You thought I wouldn't—that *we* wouldn't love you? Because you're gay?"

"I'm not gay!" Jesus, he knew they wouldn't understand. "It's only Pryce," he said, trying to find the words to explain, but after a year and a half of searching, he still had none that made sense. "It's only…him."

"And Chloe," Mason added.

Jonah turned and leaned against the stall, still unable to look at him. "At one time, yes," he reluctantly admitted. He really didn't want to be having this conversation now, if at all, but his dads obviously weren't going to let it go. "We were…something."

He flipped off his hat and shoved his hand into his hair. Despite growing up in a poly family, he didn't even know what to call what they'd had, but it had been perfect while it lasted, until he'd screwed up and given in to his twisted attraction to his best friend. And then he'd blamed Chloe. He still didn't know if everything Pryce had said was true, but if it was… Damn, he'd really screwed up.

"So, this is why you left," Matt sighed and shoved his hands into his front pockets. "I swear, kid. We've all scratched our heads around here for a damn year tryin' to figure you out. It's a wonder we're not all bald."

"Look at me, Son." Mason placed a hand on Jonah's shoulder, his grip and tone commanding Jonah's full attention. "I'm only going to ask you this once, and I want an answer. An honest one."

Jonah closed his eyes and nodded, already knowing what Mason was going to ask.

"Did Dirk Grunion have anything to do with beating the hell out of you?"

Jonah shook his head. "No, sir. He didn't." He pushed off the stall and paced to his truck, bracing his forearms against the fender as he decided where to begin. "He was there, but he didn't lift a finger."

He told them everything, from beginning to end, not sparing a single detail. He told them about the first time the three of them fooled around, the first time he'd realized he wanted Pryce too, about breaking up with Chloe because he'd thought she wouldn't understand.

Then he told them about her brothers and how they'd bullied him and Pryce in school, all their threats, and then how they cornered him at the rodeo corral and took turns beating him until he passed out, how they ruined his entire existence after Pryce left, and how he'd blamed Chloe.

When neither of his dads spoke, or asked a question, he continued, telling them what happened the night before, about the kiss and what Pryce had told him about Chloe, and then her walking in on them. He explained that the Grunion ranch was in trouble, about Dirk Grunion being so sick. He spilled it all, and when he was done, he felt like puking.

Mason grabbed a hold of him and yanked him into his arms. "Christ, kid, why didn't you come to us?"

When Mason let him go, Jonah finally met his gaze. "I couldn't." He turned his hat in his hands, his nerves raw and edgy. "You know how crazy Pryce's parents are, especially when it comes to us. If I'd have said anything, you all would have ripped the whole town apart to get your hands on everyone involved."

"Damn right, we would have!" Matt said.

"And then everyone would have known about us, including Dirk Grunion," Jonah insisted. "And he would have killed Pryce."

"You think we wouldn't have protected him?" Mason asked, his brows pinched into a hard line of disbelief. "We've never lumped Pryce into our feud with the Grunions and you know it."

"But you don't know Dirk, Dad, or what he's done to Pryce. Nobody could protect him from that man. Nobody's ever protected him."

"Except you," Mason said, gripping his shoulder with a sad but proud grin.

"Son of a bitch!" Matt cursed. "And you want us to save his cattle? When he did *nothin'* to help you?"

"Dirk's dying," Jonah reminded them. "Pretty soon it sounds like, and if I don't do something, Pryce will have nothing. He'll lose the ranch, his home…" He closed his eyes and remembered the look on Chloe's face before she ran off. "I've screwed things up between him and Chloe, too, and I have to do something to try to fix it."

"You can't take all this onto your own shoulders, Jonah," Mason said. "The Grunions have made their bed."

"I have to try!"

"I agree." Mason held up a staying hand. "We'll help, but we can't pull our trucks and trailers onto their ranch and go herding up their cattle without permission."

"Yeah," Matt scoffed. "One dead heifer and Dirk will sue our pants off, if he doesn't call the sheriff on us the second we set foot over his property line."

"But Pryce will agree," he assured them. He had to. "He's the one in charge now, the only one as far as I can tell. He said most of their crew took off when they couldn't pay them."

"Go get Pryce. We'll talk to him," Mason suggested, halting him when he moved for the driver's door of his truck. "But, Son, don't get your hopes up. Dirk Grunion isn't the only one with a prejudice against us. His momma is just as likely to spit in our faces as Dirk is."

"Yes, sir." Jonah slapped his hat on his head and sprinted around his truck.

"Jonah," Mason called out to him before he could jump inside. "I'm proud of you," he said from the other side of the truck bed. "You may not have made all the right choices, but your heart was in the right place. I know you'll make things right."

Jonah wanted to run back around and hug his dads, but they were running out of time. The weather reports predicted the winter vortex to move through just after sundown. If they were going to save Pryce's cattle, then he needed to get his ass in gear and get to Pryce.

The barn door was open when he pulled up alongside Dirk's old truck; the one that had been parked in the same spot the night before. The dawning rays of sunlight gleamed off his rearview mirror and he squinted to see if Pryce was inside. When he didn't see him, he cut the engine and headed into the barn.

"Pryce?"

The horse trailer sat unmoved, the tire propped on the axle but missing the lug nuts, so he obviously hadn't been able to get the hay out to the field for the windbreak he needed.

"Pryce?" An answering groan came from the back of the barn. "Pryce? Is that you?" He sprinted to the last stall and peered over the door. "What the hell?"

He flung open the stall door and rushed over to the lump huddled in the dark corner, picking up the near-empty whisky bottle and tossing it aside. “Pryce!” He tapped him on the cheek and shook him by the shoulders. “Come on, cowboy. Wake up.”

“Jonah?” Pryce mumbled, his eyelids cracking open for a split second before his face scrunched up. “What er you doin’ here?” His slurred words were no more than a whisper with his whisky-roughened voice. “I toll you-da-leaf.”

“Get up!” Jonah draped Pryce’s arm over his shoulder and hoisted him to his feet, but Pryce stumbled and twisted until Jonah lost his grip and Pryce fell back to the ground.

“Go. Away.” Pryce crawled back into the corner, searching through the hay until he found the whiskey bottle. “Let me die in peace. It’s better this way.”

“Give me that!” Jonah swiped the bottle from his hand before he could take another swig and tossed it over into the next stall. “You have to get up! My dads are going to help you, but they need to talk to you first.”

“Your dads?” Pryce glared up at him. “Why would they ever help me?”

“Because I asked them to, asshole. Now get up! We have to get you on a horse and get those heads rounded up before noon or you’ll lose them all.”

“Pryce?”

Jonah whipped his head around to see Chloe standing at the stall door and he froze. The mere sight of her took his breath away. He hadn’t had time to see much of her before she bolted last night, but looking at her now, even with her red-tipped nose and puffy eyes, she was a sight to behold.

She’d grown up, too, all the curves she’d had in all the right places had filled out to perfection, his favorite ones accentuated by her skin-tight jeans. Her chestnut hair hung long over her slender shoulder, longer than it had ever been, and curled at the ends by her belt. He remembered exactly what those silky strands felt like between his fingers and he balled his fists to keep from reaching out to touch her.

“What’s wrong with him?” she asked and rushed to Pryce’s side.

"As far as I can tell, he's ass over ears deep into his first drunk." Jonah stooped down and grabbed him by the back of his Wranglers. "Help me get him up."

"You got him drunk?"

"No," Jonah grunted and hefted his friend up onto his feet again. "He did that all by himself."

"Chloe?" Pryce's head bobbled as he looked up at her, stumbling over his own feet as they dragged him out of the stall. "I'm sooo ssssorry," he slurred against her neck as they sank down onto the back edge of the trailer floor together. "God, you smell good."

"I wish I could say the same for you," Chloe said, wrinkling her nose.

"I need to get him sobered up and on a horse ASAP." Jonah peeled Pryce's coat off his back and down his arms.

"What are you doing?" Chloe pushed him away. "It's freezing out here!"

"I don't have time to explain everything," Jonah argued and went for the buttons on Pryce's shirt.

"Well, you're going to have to anyway." Chloe pushed her way between him and Pryce. "Less than eight hours ago I walked in here to find you kissing *my* fiancé, and now you're trying to undress him. Was he drunk last night, too? Is that what happened?"

"What? No!" Jonah choked back the frustrated curse on the tip of his tongue and took a step back. "Lo, I'm sorry. I shouldn't have kissed him, but if you saw us, then you know he was kissing me back." *Shit.* He hadn't meant to say that. The hurt that flashed in her eyes reached out and stabbed him in the heart. This was not going the way he needed it to.

"Listen," he said and gripped her by her wrists, pulling her to him when she tried to twist away. "I'm sorry," he gritted out. "I'm sorry about a lot of things. Most of all I'm sorry for walking away like I did. I know we need to talk, all of us, but if I don't get him at least sober enough to mount a horse, and over to see my dads soon, he's going to lose the ranch."

Chloe's brows furrowed and she drew her head back to look up at him. "What do you mean, lose the ranch?"

"It's true," Pryce said and hopped down from the trailer, stumbling like the room was spinning until he found his way into the nearest stall.

"You should go. I'm no good for you." The sound of his zipper being lowered was followed by his euphoric sigh. "Gives a whole new meaning to pissing like a race horse," he said as he glanced around the stall. "Not that we ever had a race horse. Ha!" He belched out a sarcastic chuckle. "We won't even have a cow come tomorrow."

Jonah sighed and turned back to Chloe. "The ranch is in trouble," he whispered.

"I know," she mumbled and glanced back at Pryce as he tried unsuccessfully to button his jeans. "I didn't know it was that bad, though."

"My dads are willing to help get the windbreak up and the cattle fed before the storm, but they need his permission to get the equipment onto the property. His dad won't give it, and who knows what his mother will do."

Chloe rolled her eyes. "Probably call the sheriff."

"Exactly," Jonah said. "We're running out of time. The storm rolls in tonight and it's supposed to be a bad one."

Chloe closed her eyes and took a deep breath, then opened them again and looked back at Pryce leaning against the stall door and looking like he was about to puke. "So you didn't stay last night?" she asked, then turned her accusing gaze up at him.

Jonah shook his head and shoved his cold hands into his pockets. "We got into a fight after you left and he kicked me out."

Her focus shifted to the cut on his nose. "He do that?"

"Yep." Jonah gingerly touched his nose. "Shocked the hell out of me, too. Didn't know he had it in him."

"Good." Chloe bit out.

"He loves you, Lo."

Chloe nodded, but looked away. "Yeah, well, apparently he loves you, too."

Jonah took her hand, but she snatched it away, turning her back to him, staring at Pryce. "I'll get him up to the house and in the shower."

Chapter Eleven

"Whoa!" Pryce stumbled alongside Chloe and she tightened her arm around his waist, eyeing the front steps and wondering how in hell's blazes she was going to get him to the door.

"Wait a minute." Pryce stopped and hunched over, bracing his hands on his knees as he finally lost the battle against the copious amount of whiskey sloshing around in his stomach.

Chloe turned her head, holding her own stomach at the sound of his retching heaves.

"Ugh," Pryce grunted again. "I think I'll just sit down for a minute."

"No-no-no!" She lunged for him and pulled him back up before he hit the ground. "We have to get you into the shower."

She glanced up at the grand, intimidating house again. The whole time she and Pryce had dated, she'd never stepped foot inside. She'd had no desire after she'd had the pleasure of meeting Pryce's mom.

Shortly after they'd begun dating, his mother had followed Pryce into the bakery one day when he'd snuck inside to see her on their weekly trip into town. They're relationship was still new and had been kept under tight wraps until that day, but she'd gotten it in her love-struck head that the woman couldn't possibly be as rigid as Pryce had led her to believe. Was she ever wrong.

She'd walked right up to the woman and introduced herself as Pryce's friend, shook her hand, offered her and Pryce a cup of coffee and one of her aunt's delicious cherry scones, all with a friendly smile that slowly faded to panic as the harsh woman stared at her like a three-headed calf. No *hello.* No *nice to meet you.* Not even a smile back. She'd looked Chloe up and down with a critical eye, nodded and ushered Pryce out of the store, leaving her rooted in place with disbelief.

"I'm not going to make it." Pryce doubled over again.

The front door swung open. Chloe glanced up to see Mrs. Grunion standing in the doorway, wrapped in a canary yellow robe.

"What in the world?" She rushed down the steps into the snow and hip-checked Chloe out of the way. "Pryce, what's wrong with you?"

Pryce stood upright, wobbling back a step and jerking his arm free from his mother's hold. "Nothing," was his one-word answer.

"You're drunk!" Mrs. Grunion sneered with disbelief.

"You think?" Pryce sneered back, his lips curled into a snarl.

"You got him drunk!" she fumed at Chloe with fire in her eyes.

"I didn't." Chloe shook her head, not sure if she felt more offended or annoyed.

"I knew this would happen!" Mrs. Grunion turned back to Pryce before Chloe could argue further and wrapped her arm around his waist to assist him.

Chloe hurried to his other side to help, but Mrs. Grunion reached across and tried to push her away. "I'm trying to help!" Chloe insisted.

"I think you've helped enough," his mother snapped, and then Pryce snapped.

"Let go of me!" He tore himself from his mother's grasp, taking her by the wrists when she ignored his order. "Let. Go."

Chloe sucked in a breath when she saw the anger in Pryce's eyes as he stared down at his mother. She knew he'd grown tired of her constant criticisms and religious hammering, but this was entirely different. Pryce had always been overly tolerant and placating when it came to his mom—so much so she'd urged him on more than one occasion to stand up for himself, but something had changed. What she saw was more than assertiveness; it was white-hot hatred and rage.

Pryce released his mother and made his way to the steps. Halfway up he stopped and looked back at Chloe. "Can you make me some coffee while I'm in the shower?"

"Sure." Chloe nodded.

"I'll make it," his mother insisted and turned her glare on Chloe. "You can go now."

"She's not going anywhere," Pryce said, continuing up the steps.

Mrs. Grunion rushed up to the door, her flimsy house slippers flipping up snow in her wake, and angrily whispered something to Pryce. Chloe made out the words '*inappropriate*' and '*rebellion*' before Pryce stopped again and slowly turned to look at her.

"She will come inside, and you will serve her a cup of coffee in your best china, or I will leave here today and you will lose everything," he said, his voice eerily void of emotion and resoundingly sober. "Am I clear?"

"We'll see what your father has to say—"

Pryce turned slowly, robotically, and took a step back toward Chloe.

"Wait!" His mother grabbed his coat sleeve, her gaze darting to Chloe. Her lips pressed into a grim line of determination but Chloe tipped her chin up. She still didn't have the answers to the questions she'd come to ask Pryce. She didn't know where they stood, on anything, but she was not going to let this woman intimidate her. "Fine," his mother said and marched through the open front door.

Pryce held Chloe's gaze until she stood on the step below him. "Are you okay?" she whispered.

Pryce closed his eyes and nodded. "I will be, once I get this awful taste out of my mouth and my head stops hurting."

Chloe wanted to push up onto her tiptoes and kiss him, but didn't, his vomit-scented breath only one of the things that held her back.

"I owe you an apology," he said, cupping her neck with his cold hands. "And an explanation. I'm sorry. Thank you for at least giving me the chance to say it to you in person."

Chloe bit her lip. An ocean of questions swelled inside her chest, but she held her tongue and took his hand. Now wasn't the time. "Come on. Jonah's waiting."

Pryce escorted her into the kitchen, his snow-covered boots scuffing along the pristinely polished wood floors, leaving a sloppy wet trail in their wake. He pulled out a seat at the cozy kitchen table and she lowered herself into it with a quick glance at his mother.

"I'll be back down in a minute," he said and gave his mother a warning glance before he turned and left. A warning she quickly learned meant nothing the second Pryce disappeared at the top of the stairs.

"You will stop seeing my son," his mother said as she fed the coffee grinds into an antique-looking percolator.

Chloe studied the woman. She was petite and slender, with salt and pepper hair as long as her own, that hung in a sleep-tousled braid down the middle of her back. She couldn't see more than an angled profile of her face, but her hands were delicate and frail, and trembled as she worked. Chloe contemplated her age, thinking she had to be younger than she looked.

"Did you hear me?" his mother asked when she didn't respond.

Chloe steeled her spine and spoke with largely feigned confidence. "With all due respect, Mrs. Grunion, that's not your decision to make."

His mother mockingly chuckled and shook her head. "Respect. People like you know nothing about respect."

"People like me?" How dare she? The woman knew nothing about her. Was this some sort of narrow-minded prejudice against her native heritage?

"I will not have you corrupting my son any further with your vile sinfulness!"

Vile what? "Mrs. Grunion, Pryce is a good man. I love him and he loves me. There's nothing sinful about that."

"You call this love?" She pointed at the ceiling, no doubt referring to Pryce's inebriated state. "I've worked too hard to raise my son, my *only* son, to be a good, decent, God-fearing man, and I will *not* stand by and watch you drag him to the gates of hell."

Chloe bolted from her seat, the words *he's already in hell because of you,* perched on the tip of her tongue when a loud thud sounded from the floor above them, followed by a garbled choking sound.

They both looked up at the ceiling, fright zinging through Chloe's system. "Pryce!" Had he lost his balance and slipped in the shower?

"Dirk!" his mother shouted at the same time and they both raced for the stairs.

Unsure of where she was going or what she'd find when she got there, Chloe followed closely behind Mrs. Grunion until they reached the upstairs hallway, past one closed door, then another.

The third door opened and Pryce stepped out, a white towel wrapped around his hips, and nearly collided with his mother as she passed by in a frantic rush. "What the…"

"Dirk!"

Chloe clung to Pryce as his mother rushed into the bedroom at the end of the hall, her mournful sob followed by a call for help. "Call an ambulance!"

Pryce rushed to his mother's side. Chloe followed to see his father sprawled out on the bedroom floor beside the bed.

"Father?"

"God, please save him!" his mother cried out, kneeling over Dirk, trying to arouse him.

Chloe pulled her cellphone from her pocket and dialed nine-one-one, rattling off the Grunion ranch address before she pushed Pryce and his mother out of the way. Her hands trembling, she felt for a pulse and began CPR when she found none.

"One-two-three-four," she counted off.

"Please save him!" Mrs. Grunion repeated in a chanting rhythm from the foot of the bed.

Pryce knelt beside her and began breathing for him. Over and over she felt for a pulse, and kept pumping his chest until she found one. "His heart's beating."

"Oh thank the Lord!" his mother shouted and fell to her knees beside Dirk's head. "Dirk, honey, can you hear me?" She kissed his face in a frenzy.

"He's breathing," Pryce said and took his mother into his arms. "Give him some room."

The ambulance sounded its sirens when it pulled up to the front door minutes later and Pryce ran down to greet them. Chloe watched as they loaded Dirk onto a gurney. She followed them down the stairs and out onto the front porch.

"What happened?" Jonah asked breathlessly as he came running up to the house.

"I think my father had a heart attack," Pryce said in a daze, watching them load his father into the back of the ambulance, his mother climbing in beside him.

Chloe took Pryce's hand and found it cold and trembling. It was only then she realized he was standing outside in only a bath towel.

"Pryce, you're going to catch pneumonia," she said and pulled him back into the house.

"Go get dressed," Jonah ordered as he rushed in behind them and closed the door. "We'll take you to the hospital."

"What about the storm, and all the cattle?" Pryce asked, shivering as he held the towel around his hips.

"I'll take him," Chloe insisted. "Do you think your dads will still help you?"

Jonah nodded and pulled out his keys. "I'll take care of it. Here, take my truck." He handed the keys to Chloe. "I saw that you drove your aunt's car over, and you'll need something bigger if you don't make it back before the storm."

Chloe took the keys as Pryce scrambled up the stairs. Jonah turned to leave and she reached into her own pocket for her aunt's keys. "Jonah, here, take my aunt's car back to your house."

Jonah caught the keys and gave her an appreciative nod.

"Jonah, wait."

Jonah stopped in the doorway, one foot inside, one out, and peered back around the opened door.

"Thank you," she said, feeling the sudden desire to run into his arms. He'd always been her gentle giant, giving the best hugs just when she needed them most.

Jonah only nodded and then ducked outside, the door closing behind him.

By the time she and Pryce gathered a change of clothes for his mother and arrived at the hospital, they'd already admitted his dad. His mother refused to leave his side long enough to come out and brief Pryce on his condition. The nurses said they'd find some information and get back to them, advising them to wait in the emergency waiting area, but no one had come to tell them anything yet.

"Why did you come back?"

Pryce's unexpected question broke through the hour of silence they'd spent waiting.

Chloe lifted her head and met his somber gaze. "We should talk about this later," she said, pushing from her seat. She walked to the window overlooking the parking lot and propped her hip on the sill, crossing her arms over her chest to ward off the chill seeping through the glass.

Pryce followed her. "I need to talk about it now." He tugged her arms free and took her hand in his. "You're the only one who matters to me, Chloe. I need to know if I've lost you."

She bit her lip and turned away, blinking back her tears. "That's not true."

"That I haven't lost you?"

She shook her head and glanced up at Pryce, looking him in the eyes to see if he would deny the truth. "I'm not the only one who matters to you." Pryce lowered his gaze, but it was too late. She'd gotten the answer she was looking for.

"I don't know what to say." He let go of her hand and paced to the corner. She wanted to reach out to him, to comfort him, to tell him she understood, but she didn't. Following her aunt's advice, she needed to let him explain what had happened.

"Jonah was my best friend," Pryce began, "my only friend." He turned and stared out the window, looking lost in the past as he spoke. "It's funny," he said with an unwitting grin. "He was way out of my friend league when we first met, or at least I thought he was. I was the new geek in school, scared to death." He turned to Chloe, but didn't look directly at her. "I was homeschooled until then, so public school was…intimidating, but Jonah most of all. He was good looking, a big name on the football team. I assumed he was one of the untouchable popular kids, you know? A *McLendon*."

Chloe nodded and Pryce turned back to stare out the window. "I guess it was six months, maybe longer, before I realized that I was his best friend, too." Pryce shrugged. "I just assumed he had a ton of other friends he never talked about, but eventually I figured out that there was only me. I'd never had a best friend before, and I can't describe what he meant to me. I mean, maybe I was in love with him then, too.

"And then when you and Jonah started dating, I just knew I'd lost him. I figured it was only a matter of time before he'd start ignoring me like the rest of the world did. When that didn't happen, I was so grateful. I would have done anything for either of you. And then *things* happened."

A rosy blush crept up his neck. He was so different than Jonah in that way, shy and insecure about physical affections. When he began to fidget and pick at something on the window, it took everything she had not to reach out to comfort him. "I'd never kissed a girl before you," he said with a sheepish grin. "I've told you that."

"You did," she nodded, grinning as she remembered their first kiss, Jonah sitting on the riverbank beside them.

"And then we uh…you know." He glanced up at her, but quickly looked away, back out into the parking lot, watching the storm clouds roll in. "I fell in love with you," he said with a shrug. "I remember thinking how stupid I was to fall for my best friend's girl."

"Did you ever tell Jonah how you felt about me?"

"God no!" Pryce said. "I was too scared to lose you both. I grabbed ahold of anything I could get and held on for dear life, but then it didn't seem to matter after a while. I stopped feeling like an outsider and more like I was a part of something special, a part of both of you."

"You were," she said. No longer able to resist, she wrapped her arms around his waist and laid her head against his chest. "You were a part of us."

"I know, but things got so mixed up," he said with a regretful sigh. "Our times together, sometimes it was like we melted into this one singular being. I couldn't tell him from you, or you from him and all I wanted was to crawl up inside you both somehow and live there forever."

Chloe closed her eyes, remembering feeling the exact same way and she missed it. She'd mourned the loss of that feeling the most when Jonah had walked away from her.

"It was my fault, Chloe. I made the first move on him, and if I hadn't, none of this would have happened. He wouldn't have broken up with you. Your brothers wouldn't have known anything, and Jonah would've never left."

Confused, she drew her head back and looked up at him. "Why would Jonah break up with me because you made a move on him?"

Pryce closed his eyes, his head falling in shame. "I kissed him," he said on a regretful sigh. "And he kissed me back."

"When?" she asked, wondering how long she'd been oblivious to their attraction.

"It was the day in his uncle's workshop, right before his grandfather walked in on us. You were between us, we were both kissing you and then…I don't know why I did it. It wasn't something I'd planned on doing. I touched him, and when he didn't pull away, I pressed harder against him. My entire world exploded. More than I could ever dream of wanting was right in front of me, and I honestly don't remember, but the next second we were kissing each other with you between us…and then his grandfather walked in."

Chloe thought back to that day, remembering it with pristine clarity. Had she been so enraptured by what they were doing to her, she'd never noticed them kissing each other?

Pryce pulled away from her embrace and paced back to the corner. "He broke up with you because of me. When I went to the arena that day, I went to tell him to get back together with you. I told him I would back out, that I wouldn't come between the two of you, but he said it wouldn't change anything. He still wanted you, but he wanted me too, and he didn't think you'd understand. *I* didn't think you'd understand, and I didn't want to hurt either of you."

"And then my brothers showed up," Chloe said, her heart racing at the thought of what they'd done to Jonah.

Pryce nodded. "He says Finn told him that he was there because we took your virginity and then he broke up with you. Jonah told me last night that he'd thought you'd sent them to get back at him, for breaking up with you."

Chloe groaned and dropped her head into her hands. "How could he think I'd ever do something like that?" She hated her brothers to the very core of her being, even more now, if that were possible. For Jonah to believe she'd sent them to hurt him was unthinkable.

"Jonah was in the hospital," Pryce reminded her. "I was sent away, and then you moved to Colorado with your mom. He didn't know about them listening in on your phone call to your aunt. By the time he'd recovered and got home, there was no one left to ask for the truth. And he was afraid to tell his parents what happened because of my father finding out."

"No one left but my brothers." Chloe stared at the floor, imagining all the awful things they'd done to him. She of all people knew how cruel they could be. After Finn was arrested for beating his last girlfriend while in a drunken rage, she'd hoped Travis and Wayne would see the light, but so far they'd only gotten worse. Since graduating they'd headed down the exact same path as Finn, without looking back.

"He said they made life hell for him."

"I don't doubt it. No wonder he left." She sank back down onto the window sill and stared out the window. The leafless trees had already begun to sway in the gusts of wind that had suddenly blown in, the wintery sight making her shiver.

"Here." Pryce shrugged off his jacket and draped it over her shoulders.

"Thank you," she said, drawing in Pryce's familiar clean scent as his residual heat warmed her.

"I thought I could forget Jonah," he said after a moment of silence between them.

"Are you attracted to other men? Besides Jonah, I mean?" she asked, one of a dozen questions that had plagued her through the night. As embarrassing as it was knowing Aunt Bev had heard them making love, she'd been right in reminding her of Pryce's obvious physical attraction to her, but what if she wasn't enough. What if he preferred men more than women?

"Absolutely not," Pryce insisted. "It's only ever been Jonah, and you."

Their nerves on edge, they both jumped when an ambulance pulled up to the emergency entrance and sounded the siren. They watched as another patient was unloaded, the emergency nurses and paramedics swarming the small space until they all disappeared behind a set of double doors.

"I thought I could forget about Jonah too," she admitted when the chaos ended and the room fell silent again.

Aunt Bev had been right about that too. She had wanted them both, and her heart still did. Seeing Jonah again had proven that much. Watching Jonah and Pryce together had awakened those old feelings. Her body remembered and craved to be between them again. And if the dreams she'd had the night before were any indication, the two of them making love to each other while they both made love to her, most certainly wouldn't be a deal breaker.

"I have a confession to make," she said, swallowing against the dryness in her mouth. Would Pryce forgive her for lying to him, too?

"I know you still love him," Pryce said, cutting her off before she could confess what she'd only admitted to herself no more than a few hours ago. "I've known from the beginning your heart was never fully mine."

"Then why haven't you said anything?" Her agitation diluted her guilt. "Why would you want to marry me if you thought I didn't love you?"

"I've never believed you didn't love me," Pryce argued. "I just…understood, because I loved him, too."

"You still do."

Pryce nodded. "God help me, I do." The sound that escaped his chest was an odd combination of a sigh and a tortured cry.

"Pryce, look at me."

"Do you know how screwed up this is? I mean, I can't be gay. I can't…"

"Look at me." She took him by the chin and made him look at her. "We can't help who we love."

"But *this* isn't…" He bit his lips and shook his head in denial. "I don't know if I can do this, even if I want to. All my life I've been taught that it's unforgiveable. The church would crucify me. My mother, God. I can't even think about what she—"

"Pryce, I've never stepped foot inside a church, but doesn't it say somewhere that God doesn't make mistakes?"

His cheek dimpled with his sarcastic smirk. "My mother would say I was possessed by a demon." He ran his fingers through his hair. "I can see it now, the deacons lining up in my living room for the exorcism."

Chloe laughed. She couldn't help it. If anyone was possessed, she'd say it *was* his mom. "Please don't tell me you believe that. Have you ever levitated or spouted obscure obscenities in some language you've never heard before?" she asked when he didn't respond. "Because now would be a good time to tell me if you had."

"No," he chuckled.

"You're not possessed. You're just different," she assured him. "I learned a long time ago that people don't like different. Being Native American comes with its own set of prejudices and judgements, you know."

"I've never cared, or even thought about that," Pryce said.

"And I don't care about you loving Jonah," she retorted. "As long as you love me, too."

"I do love you," he said. "More than you'll ever know."

"I love you, too." She cupped his face, pulling him down to her until their lips met in the sweetest of kisses. "I will always love you, Pryce."

"There's something else," he said against her lips and pulled away.

"What?"

Pryce mumbled a curse and balled his hands into fists, sending alarm rushing through her veins, chasing away the chill.

"What happened?" she insisted. "It can't possibly be worse than me walking in on you and Jonah doing the tongue mambo."

"My college fund," he finally said. "It's gone."

Chloe furrowed her brows in confusion. "What do you mean, *gone*?"

Pryce sank down onto the window sill beside her. With a frustrated growl, he bent over and fisted his hands into his hair. "My father," he said. "I'm guessing they took it to pay the bills at the ranch. I didn't stick around long enough to ask after my mother told me."

"Oh my God." She draped herself over Pryce's back. "Oh, Pryce, I'm so sorry." That money was the key to his dreams, the key to everything. "What are we going to do?"

Chapter Twelve

Jonah collapsed onto the chair beside Dani's friend, Ash, to catch his breath. His arms and legs burned with fatigue from using muscles he hadn't had need of driving a front loader over paydirt for the last year and a half.

"Nice shiner," Ash said, his gaze trained on Jonah's black eye.

"Thanks," Jonah said with a smirk. "It feels a lot worse than it looks."

The sun had set. The storm had blown in hard just as he and Mason stacked the last of the Grunion's hay bales on the windbreak wall they built in the stock pin. Their herd had been surprisingly cooperative. They'd managed to separate out the pregnant heifers and packed as many of them as they could into the barns, then filled the feed troughs with an extra rich ration for the ones left outside. Keeping their bellies full and packing them together behind the wall of hay should help them stay warm enough, but he'd go over and check on them once it was safe enough to go back out.

"Damn, it's really whipping out there." Ash ducked as a heavy gust hit the barn and the rafters creaked above them. "I was hoping to beat the storm out, but it looks like I'm stuck here until it's over."

"We're good in here," Jonah assured him and took a long swig of water. "This barn is as close to a concrete bunker as you can get."

"If you say so." Ash turned back to watch Dani stomp and pace at the other end of the barn.

Jonah hoped whoever she was talking to on the phone had a set of steel balls on him. "Boy, she's chewing somebody a new one."

"Yeah," Ash sighed. "Sounds like the drone pilot is going to be a few days late."

Jonah shook his head at his sister's hair-brained scheme. "How the hell they planned to fly one of those in this mess is beyond me anyways."

When Ash didn't offer a response, Jonah looked back over at him, taking note of the lost and sappy look in his eyes. Poor guy had it bad. "She's friend-zoned you, huh?"

Ash glanced over at him and then released a disappointed sigh. "Is it that obvious?"

Jonah laughed. "To everyone but her and Grey," he said, "but Grey's been bent out of shape since the day she started wearing nail polish, so I wouldn't take it too personal."

"I don't understand her," Ash said and went back to watching Dani.

Jonah nearly spewed his mouthful of water to keep from choking when he laughed out loud. He clapped Ash on the back. "Welcome to the club."

A barrage of curses echoed above the sound of mooing heifers about to give birth, and the wind whipping against the roof. He studied his sister as she ranted on. He may have been gone for a while, but she hadn't changed a bit. Like Ash, he didn't get her most of the time, but the one thing he did get was her love of this place and everything it stood for. Falcon Ridge would always be a part of her, and she'd always be a part of it.

"Listen, man, can I give you some advice?" Jonah asked.

Ash looked up over his dark-rimmed glasses as if to say *do I have a choice?*

"You can take it or leave it, but the right guy for Dani wouldn't feel like they're stuck here."

"That's not what I meant," Ash said with an agitated sigh.

"I know." Jonah held up his hands in surrender. "I'm just trying to save you some heartache. She's one-hundred percent devoted to this ranch, and any guy who wants to be with her is going to have to understand that. That kind of passion isn't something you can learn. It's something you're born with."

"Dammit!" Dani shouted as she tucked her phone back into her pocket, kicking one of the stall doors on her way into the office she was using, slamming the door behind her.

"I'd better go see if I can help," Ash said with a groan, but Jonah stopped him.

"Give her a bit," he warned. "Trust me. You do not want to go in there right now."

The single door at the opposite end of the aisle opened and Grey blew in with the snow. Jonah's gut tightened. Ash tensed beside him. Jonah jostled him with his elbow. "Don't worry, man," he said under his breath. "He's here for me, not you."

"Heard anything about Dirk?" Grey asked, ambling toward them.

"No." Jonah took out his phone to see if he had a signal in the storm, but it wouldn't matter even if he did. None of the three of them thought to exchange numbers. The best hope he had of hearing anything was if Pryce called the ranch line, which would go straight to voicemail this time of night. He thought about calling the hospital and having him paged, but decided against it. Pryce had enough to worry about.

"Matt tells me the Grunion herd is tucked in, mommas are in the barn. They should be fine."

"Yes sir," Jonah nodded. "And the calves aren't due for another couple of months so it shouldn't be too much trouble once the storm blows through."

"Does he have a crew lined up for when that happens?" Grey asked.

"Pryce said he's got a few hands on call." Jonah took off his hat and ran his hand through his sweat-soaked hair, wondering when the real interrogation was coming.

"Ash, can you give us a minute?" Grey asked.

Right on cue.

"Sure." Ash bolted for the barn door like a spooked colt with its tail on fire.

"I'm guessing they told you," Jonah said and sank back down onto his chair.

Grey hitched his pant leg up and propped his boot on the chair Ash had abandoned, resting his elbow on his knee. "Pryce Grunion, huh?" he asked with a twisted grin.

Jonah's instinct was to go on the defensive, always had been when it came to Pryce, but he bit his tongue, giving Grey a single nod. No sense in denying it now.

"I'm not here to bust your balls, Son. I'm here to try to help you figure things out, or just to listen if you need me to."

Jonah blinked, squinting up at his dad. "What?" *Did Mom slip something into his supper?*

Grey dropped his foot and sank down onto the chair beside him with a huff. "Look, I had my suspicions about you and Pryce. We all did."

Jonah stared at his dad. "What?" he repeated, the statement too weird to believe.

"It's not like we placed bets or anything, but yeah. I figured the two of you were up to more than just fishing every chance you got. Look," he paused and shifted in his seat, "I'm not ignorant to the fact that you grew up in an unconventional family. It isn't a far stretch to think you would do your own share of experimenting. Hell, your dads and I drew straws on who would have to have *the poly talk* with you when the time came. We just didn't get around to it until it was too late I guess."

Jonah rolled his eyes. Now he got it. "You think I have some screwed up idea about how this is supposed to work? Because you guys didn't 'teach' me the right way?" He shoved to his feet and paced to the other side of the aisle. "Let me guess. I'm not supposed to fuck the guy, only the girl. Is that your big lesson for the night?"

"Don't go getting any stupider than you already are." Grey sat back in his seat and swung the other chair around to face his. "I don't care who you fuck. Now, sit down and shut up for a minute, will you?"

Jonah looked at the chair.

"Sit," Grey ordered. "I'm going to tell you something Papa Joe told me once, and I want you to listen to every damn word," he said after Jonah plopped unceremoniously into the seat in front of him. "Don't just hear me, but actually open up those ears God gave you and listen."

"Fine, I'm listening," Jonah grumbled. Whatever it took to get this over with. He knew Grey wouldn't understand. Mason and Matt had surprised him, sort of. He'd expected them to be shocked for a bit and then act like nothing was different. Grey, on the other hand.... He sucked in a breath, preparing for the storm. It wasn't like they could ship him off to military school. That ship had already sailed.

Grey shook his head. "You are your father's son, I'll give you that," he said with a chuckle. "We may never know for sure which one of us had the pleasure of siring you, unless you need a kidney transplant or something, God forbid, but my money's always been on Matt with that short-fused temper of yours."

When Jonah didn't take the bait, Grey chuckled again. "You're going to break a tooth if you grit your teeth any harder."

Jonah rubbed his jaw, unaware he'd had it clinched so tight. "Just get on with it."

"All right." Grey's smile faded and he squared his shoulders. "If that's the way you want to do this, what exactly do you intend to do about the mess you've gotten yourself into?"

"What do you mean?" Jonah asked.

"I mean, you say you're in love with Pryce. He's marrying this Chloe Jessop girl, if you haven't screwed that up beyond repair. What are you going to do about it, besides pilfer off half my ranch hands to save a herd of cattle that's only going to bring in half of what the Grunions need to save their ranch?"

"Dad, I'm sorry. I had to try."

"Trying isn't good enough," Grey argued, "not when it comes to someone you love."

Jonah stared at Grey, even more confused than before. What else did he expect him to do?

Grey leaned forward in his seat. "Up until now, you've handled things about as well as any idiot kid would. I can't fault you for that, but you're not a kid anymore. You're still young, damn young, but if you go down this path, especially with a guy like Pryce Grunion and his family, you'd better be prepared to take it all the way to the end. If you don't, Pryce will lose a hell of a lot more than a few head of cattle."

"I'm not running anymore, Dad, if that's what you're referring to."

Grey studied him a minute longer, his lips pressing into a grim line before he spoke again. "What part does Chloe play in this for you?" he asked. "Mason says the three of you were together before this happened."

"Yeah." Jonah sat up in his seat and mirrored Grey's posture with his elbows propped on his knees. "I don't really know," he admitted. "I loved her too before all of this. It started out with just me and her."

"Why didn't we ever meet her?" Grey asked, "if she was that important to you?"

Jonah shrugged. "We started going out right before Papa Joe's stroke. Then Con and Car came home and everybody was up their asses about all the stuff they were going through. I didn't think anyone cared, and to be honest, I was fine with that. I didn't want all the attention."

Grey nodded. "So, you loved them both, then."

"I did, once, yeah." Jonah shrugged. He could admit that, but he'd blamed Chloe for so long for what her brothers had done, it felt like a betrayal to allow himself to feel that way about her now. There wasn't a doubt he was still physically attracted to her, but he wasn't sure if he could let himself fall for her all over again when his body still ached from the damage done.

"And you're sure she didn't have anything to do with what those bastards did to you?"

Jonah shook his head. "I believe Pryce wouldn't lie to me, but I haven't spoken to Chloe yet. There wasn't time before the ambulance came and took Dirk to the hospital."

Grey dragged in a long breath and leaned back in his chair again. He looked down the aisle and then back at Jonah.

"Well, for what my advice has been worth lately, I'd say you need to talk to Chloe," he finally said. "Find out the truth one way or the other. Once the air is cleared, if the three of you want to make a go of it, as my son, I expect you to do whatever it takes to make it work."

Jonah nodded, sidelined by the entire conversation and unsure of what to say back.

"*Whatever* it takes," Grey repeated. Jonah looked down at Grey's hand as he cupped his shoulder, giving it a reassuring squeeze. "Jonah, whichever path you choose, one or both of them, or someone altogether different, it won't be an easy journey. Life never is. But you're a McLendon. We never do anything the easy way," he said with a grin. "I love you, Son. That will never change. If this is what you want, then we'll help you where and when we can, but there will be no more running, and no more lies. Understood?"

"Yes sir," Jonah choked out. He didn't know whether to laugh or cry.

Grey stood and offered Jonah his hand. Jonah took it and his dad pulled him to his feet. "But if I find out this girl did have an intentional hand in what happened that day, she will never be welcome in my home. Am I clear?"

Jonah looked him in the eyes for the first time since he came in. "Crystal clear."

"And I expect you to settle this thing with Cory when he gets home from the station after this storm."

"Yes sir," Jonah nodded respectfully, though he wasn't sure how the hell he was supposed to do that, or if he even wanted to. Cory knew him better than anyone. He didn't understand how his own brother would believe the Jessop brothers' gossip, especially a rumor as ridiculous and insulting as him leaving Chloe pregnant.

"Good." Grey's chest rose and fell with his heavy sigh. "Now all I have to do is convince Matt that we won't be sharing every Christmas and holiday with Pryce's parents, and then find a way to get that guy your sister brought home back to Billings in the middle of a blizzard. Got any ideas?"

Jonah did laugh this time. "You don't have to worry about Ash, Dad. Dani isn't the least bit interested."

"Interested in what?" Dani asked as she made her way down the aisle, the sounds of the storm having silenced her approach. Jonah wondered how much she'd heard, but shrugged it off. If she didn't already know everything by now, she would eventually.

"Hey, Boo." Jonah smiled awkwardly, then grunted when she punched him in the stomach.

"I told you not to call me that," she said as she wrapped her arms around Grey and gave him a quick hug. "Hi, Daddy."

"Hey, baby girl. What's the status on this drone experiment of yours?"

Dani blew out a frustrated breath. "Well, the pilot seems to have misplaced his balls and delayed his flight from Texas to avoid the storm, so he won't be here for another three days, and we've already got four calves on the way, so…yeah, I'd say we're screwed."

Grey grinned and placed a kiss on the top of her head. "I'm sure you'll figure out something. You two go on up to the house and grab some dinner. I'll take the night shift tonight."

"I've got it," Jonah insisted. "Probably not going to sleep much anyway."

"I'll stay too," Dani offered. "We've got some catching up to do." Jonah dodged another of her playful jabs.

"All right," Grey conceded. "But your mom's not going to let you skip dinner. I'll tell her to have a couple of plates sent out, for which I'm sure *Ash* will volunteer."

"Thanks, Daddy," Dani said, ignoring Grey's sarcasm.

"You bet." Grey gave Dani one last hug before he turned and started for the door, pulling the collar of his coat up around his neck.

"Dad, wait!" Jonah jogged to catch up to him. "Thank you," he said and wrapped his arms around Grey.

"No thanks necessary." Grey hugged him back. "I just wish you'd come to me sooner is all."

"I know." Jonah nodded sheepishly. "I will next time."

"Let's hope there isn't a next time," Grey chuckled and turned for the door, disappearing with another gust of snow.

Jonah followed Dani as she strolled slowly past the stalls, checking on the first few mommas already in the first stages of labor. They came to a stop at the end, the two of them standing side-by-side with their arms resting over the stall rails.

"Did you get the Grunion's herd squared away?" Dani asked and Jonah nodded. "Good," she replied. "I can't believe their crew split. I mean, I can, but that sucks."

"Yeah," Jonah said with regret. "Pryce is in a tight spot."

Dani snickered and caught his gaze, her grin devious. "You mean he *has* a tight—"

"Oh my God, shut the fuck up!" Jonah hip-checked her off the rail before she could finish the moronic innuendo.

"What are we going to do without Uncle Cade?" she said after a long silence between them, her voice small and worried.

Jonah rubbed the ache that bloomed in his chest each time he thought about Cade, unable to imagine their family without him. "I don't know, Boo." He draped his arm around her shoulders and squeezed. "I don't know."

Chapter Thirteen

Paladin's hooves crunched through the snow drifts as Jonah herded the next group of mommas toward the calving barn. After a long night explaining everything to Dani, which went better than he ever expected, and a few hours of sleep earlier that morning, he'd forced himself out of bed and back onto his horse, chugging a half pot of coffee along the way.

Calving season had officially arrived. They'd delivered dozens of calves throughout the night, another dozen that morning and more were on the way. The storm had blown out as quick as it had blown in, but the clouds still hung low in the sky and kept the temperatures well below *ball freezing* as Mason would say, even by Alaskan standards.

"Whoa there boy." Jonah eased his horse to a stop as the latest group of pregnant mommas reached the barn.

"Hold them here and I'll meet you on the other side," Matt yelled over to him from atop his horse on his way around to the other end of the long barn to get the pens open.

"Got it," he said, thankful for the easy task. Cutting the laboring mommas from the observation corral had been no small feat, but now that they were on the brink of a warm bed of ground corn stalks and fresh feed, they weren't in any hurry to go anywhere.

He tipped his hat at Jacob Duncan, Matt's assistant foreman, as he trotted out to start cutting the next group of mommas. Jacob had joined the crew the summer Jonah'd left, so he hadn't gotten to know much about him, but it seemed like the older man knew what he was doing well enough. It was too bad that he was only staying on through the end of the season. Good help was hard to find.

That thought reminded him that he still had to check on the Grunion herd, not that he needed reminding. For the tenth time that day Jonah turned in his saddle to look out over the fields. Through the leafless trees, he could see the Grunion barns, and the wisps of chimney smoke billowing above the treetops in the distance.

An hour had passed since he'd first noticed it, yet no one had come to return his truck, or to update him on Dirk's condition. He tried not to be selfish. It was probably for the best, especially if Pryce's mother was home with them, but the need to settle this thing between them pushed back with a vengeance and made it hard to ignore.

Grey had said to do whatever it took, but what was that? Where did he start? He'd already screwed up by pushing Pryce. Grey's warning had been sobering. What if he pursued this thing with Pryce and it didn't work out? What if he screwed up again? Grey was right. Pryce would lose everything. If his dad lived, or even if he didn't, Pryce wouldn't be able to go home, ever. His parents would disown him at best. He'd lose the ranch, his birthright, his family, Chloe. All of it.

Chloe was everything to Pryce. Jonah could see that now. If he backed out and just let them go, no one else would be hurt. It would be the right thing to do; he knew it in his heart, so why couldn't he make himself do it? Why couldn't he stop thinking about them? God knew he'd tried. He'd put so many miles and mountains between them they should be no more than a distant memory, but they weren't. They were everywhere, in his dreams and his every waking thought, impossible to escape.

Matt opened the gate and a few of the ranch hands began guiding the laboring cows into their pens. Jonah spurred Paladin around to head off a stray and walked her back to the gate.

"Come around and man the head catch for me while I get the first group tagged and vaccinated." Matt instructed.

Jonah complied, taking one last longing look across the fields as he rode around to the other end of the barn.

The rest of the afternoon passed in a chilling blur with few breaks in between. He was locked inside a pen, hunched over a newborn giving it its first vaccinations, when Grey walked in, a guy he'd never met before filing in behind him.

"Where's your sister?" Grey asked as they approached.

"Over here!" Dani yelled from a nearby stall.

"Clay Sterling." The visitor extended a hand over the top of the pen railing.

"Jonah McLendon." With a polite nod, Jonah pulled off his glove and shook the man's hand.

"Good looking calf," Clay said, studying the newborn at his feet before he followed Grey down the aisle.

"That's the last one for now," Dani said as she backed out of the next pen and closed the gate. "Oh!" She stopped short when she turned around and almost crashed into Clay. "Um, hi."

Already bent over the calf again, Jonah rose up and leaned against the railing, studying his sister, the bewildered look on her face simultaneously confusing and hysterical.

"Looks like your pilot found what he was looking for," Grey said with a wry grin, ruffling Dani's hair.

"What?" Dani jerked away from him and gave him a scolding look. Jonah furrowed his brows in confusion. She'd never rebuffed Grey's playful affection.

"Dani, this is Clayton Sterling. The pilot you were expecting? Clayton, this is my daughter Dani."

"Clay." He offered his hand and Dani stared down at it.

"Sterling?" Dani asked, her gaze darting between their visitor and Grey.

"We spoke on the phone last night? Drone pilot?" Clay reminded her. "Although, I'm not sure what I lost that I was supposed to be lookin' for."

Dani looked back down at his offered hand and then back up at Clay. "Balls," she said in a dazed murmur.

"Excuse me?" Clay asked with a chuckle.

"Balls—I mean…shit." She shook her head. "The calf." She brushed a wisp of hair from her sweaty, dirt-smudged face, turning back to the pen where the mother licked and cleaned her baby. "The calf has balls." She closed her eyes and swallowed. "It's a bull. The calf is a male. As in not female."

"Ah, the kind without balls," Clay said with a teasing grin.

Jonah choked back a chuckle and bent down to help the foundering calf stand on its wobbly legs, watching from the shadows and listening with amused curiosity as Dani stammered around the boot in her mouth. Good thing Clay was a fit guy. It looked like he could run fast enough. At least he hoped so, because he could hear the time bomb ticking down the seconds until Grey figured out why his sister was turning eighteen shades of red. That calf wouldn't be the only one losing its balls.

"You didn't tell me Clay owns Sterling Eagle Ranch," Grey said when Dani turned back around.

"Oh, no sir," Clay corrected him with a staying hand. "S.E.R. is my dad's passion. Mine is designin' ways to make it run more efficiently."

"Still," Grey nodded and slapped him on the back like they were old friends. "It's an impressive operation. Mason will be particularly interested in your genetics programs. What you've done with your Brahman stock is nothing short of genius."

Clay grinned sheepishly at the praise. "That would be my grandfather and brother Levi's mad scientist project, albeit a successful one. And I can pay the same compliment to this place," he said, swiveling around to take in the expanse of the calving barn. "You have one of the most well respected ranches in the territory."

"I thought you weren't coming until day after tomorrow," Dani said with a critical smirk, putting an end to their appreciation love fest.

"Well, Miss McLendon, as I tried to explain last night, I was at the mercy of the weather." Clay looked up at Grey with an apologetic grin. "I had to set down in Wyoming to wait out the storm, and the weather reports were callin' for the headwinds to last a lot longer than they did." Turning back to Dani, he offered his apologies for being late. "As long as we document the logs with the updated headcount before we start, we'll be fine."

"You fly your own plane?" Grey asked. "That's impressive. Maybe you could take me and Dani up on a ride sometime. Been a long time since I saw the ranch from above, and I don't think Dani ever has."

"Yeah, impressive," Dani grumbled. "You two go ahead. I'll stay right here, knee deep in cow shit and snow, both feet planted firmly on the ground."

"You don't like to fly?" Clay asked.

"Doesn't bother me a bit," Dani quipped, "but I have a commitment to the tech firm to get them as much data as we can, so I'll be in the office trying to figure out how to fly a drone."

Clay laughed and shook his head. "Relax," he said with a wink. "I'm in good with the owner. I'm sure he won't mind if we take an afternoon off."

"I wouldn't be too sure about that," Dani argued and stepped around him and Grey. "My friend Ash has everything set up in the office at the end." She hooked her thumb over her shoulder as she back-stepped toward the office. "Take your time. Settle in. Ash and I have plenty to keep us busy until you're ready."

The calf Jonah was helping struggled beneath his inattentive grip and he let him go, snickering at Dani's bullheadedness.

"You own the tech company, don't you?" Grey asked.

"Sure do," Clay said with a wry grin as he stared after Dani.

"She's been a little too excited about this project," Grey excused Dani's rudeness. "I'll talk to her."

"No, please. That's not necessary," Clay insisted. "I might actually try to hire her out from under you."

"Good luck with that," Jonah mumbled to himself as they walked past. If this guy didn't tone it down in front of Grey, he'd find himself shitting a drone instead of flying one.

"You can sure try," Grey said with a goodhearted chuckle of his own, "but she'd never take you up on it."

Jonah's mouth fell open. He didn't even bother to close it as the two of them stopped a few feet from the pen.

"Fair enough," Clay replied. "Well, I guess I'd better not keep her waitin'." He shook Grey's hand.

"It was nice meeting you," Grey said. "We'll chat more at dinner tonight, and I'll introduce you to my brothers."

"Sounds like a plan." Clay tipped his hat at Jonah on his way toward the office.

"Huh," Jonah harrumphed confoundedly as he watched the man leave. *What the hell just happened?* Maybe his mom *had* started spiking Grey's food.

Grey stuck his head back inside the barn and his loud whistle split the air. "You've got company."

Jonah wiped his hands on the towel hanging over the railing and left the new calf with its momma. “Who is it?” The cold air outside burned his lungs as he followed Grey out into the snow, stopping short when he saw his truck rolling slowly down the driveway toward the barn.

“Whatever it takes, Son,” Grey reminded him before heading up the hill toward the house.

The knot Jonah’d had in his chest when he woke up that morning returned as the truck stopped and Chloe cut the engine. He tried not to read too much into the fact that Pryce wasn’t with her.

“Hi,” she said as she hopped out and shut the door. She looked exhausted, but no less beautiful than she’d been the day before.

“Hey.” He shoved his hands into his coat pockets, not knowing what else to do with them. “How’s Dirk?”

Chloe’s smile faded. “Not good. It was a major heart attack. He’s in intensive care and they don’t know if he’ll make it through the night. Mrs. Grunion won’t leave his bedside.”

“How’s Pryce?”

Chloe took a deep breath and released it with a tired sigh. “Between his dad and the hangover, he’s exhausted. We got home a few hours ago, but after checking on the stock he crashed.”

Jonah nodded, unsure of what to say next. Was the Grunion’s place home for her now? Had they reconciled and decided his fate without him? His earlier doubts all but forgotten, jealousy raced through his veins as he stared at Chloe, imagining Pryce naked in her arms. He knew from experience how good she felt, how intoxicating she could be, but he also knew Pryce needed more. If she thought this was over, she was sorely mistaken.

“Will you come to dinner tonight?” she asked with an uneasy smile before he could voice his challenge. “It won’t be anything fancy. Mrs. Grunion doesn’t have much in the pantry and we didn’t think to stop on the way home.”

“Dinner?”

Jonah’s angry thoughts must have been evident in his expression because she took a step back from him. “Never mind,” she said with disappointment. “You’re probably exhausted too. It was a stupid idea.”

“Chloe wait,” he said when she turned to walk away. “I…” He what? Was he supposed to apologize again? Was he supposed to beg her to stop seeing Pryce? He didn't want that either. What the hell was he supposed to do? *Whatever it takes*, he heard Grey's voice in his head.

"Thanks for letting us borrow your truck," she said and turned again to leave.

"What about your aunt's car," he asked, still at a loss for words but unwilling to let her leave yet.

"Oh, um…" Chloe turned and looked over her shoulder. "The snow is still too deep to drive it anywhere, but I'm going to stay with Pryce for a few days so I won't need it. Is it okay if I leave it here until then?"

He released a resigned breath and shook his head. "Get in. I'll take you back to Pryce's."

Chloe was still standing in the same spot when he started the engine, but eventually made her way around to the passenger side and got in.

The tires spun in a few spots as he navigated the hills to get the truck turned around. The radio was off and before too long all he could hear was the sound of his heart beating in his eardrums. With her sitting so close beside him, all he could think about was how many times he'd made out with her sitting exactly where she was now, and all the times he'd pictured Pryce there with them.

How had things gotten so screwed up?

"I didn't tell my brothers to hurt you," she said, her voice slicing through one particular memory of him taking her virginity.

"Yeah, Pryce told me." He looked over to find her staring out the window, chewing her thumbnail as she always did when she was nervous.

"That's what I wanted to tell you at dinner tonight," she continued. "I thought you should hear it from me. I was scared. I didn't know my brothers were listening when I was talking to my aunt on the phone, and when I heard about what happened to you… I was heartbroken when you broke up with me, J, but I'd never have asked them to hurt you."

Jonah turned the steering wheel and pulled the truck to a stop at the head of Pryce's driveway. He stared through the windshield at the broken gate hanging from its hinges.

"What happened to you, Lo? Why did you move away and come back?" Pryce had told him about her mom leaving, and Breezy had said something about her getting into some trouble, but he wanted to hear it from her.

Chloe stared out the windshield, then back down at her hands as she continued to pick at her fingernails. "My mom and dad got into another fight, about my brothers, I think. She never told me." She closed her eyes and shook her head. "It doesn't really matter, I guess. I mean, they were always fighting about something." After a long pause, Chloe took a breath and let it out slowly. "My mom was a mess after their divorce, coming home night after night with one jerk or another from the local asshole of the month club." She visibly shivered at the memory and the hair on the back of Jonah's neck prickled against his skin.

"Did they hurt you?"

"No. Not really."

"Yes or no, Lo?"

"I handled it," she insisted. "I called Aunt Bev after graduation and she let me move in with her, gave me a job."

"Christ!" Jonah slammed his fist against the steering wheel.

"It's not your fault," she insisted.

"The hell it's not."

Chloe turned in her seat. "The world doesn't revolve around you, J. Even if none of this had happened, if you'd never broken up with me, my mom still would've left and made me go with her. You couldn't have stopped that."

"I should have been there."

"You were in the hospital, thanks to *my* brothers."

"Which wouldn't have happened if I hadn't broken up with you."

"Let it go," she said with a frustrated sigh and ran her fingers through her hair. "I don't blame you, Jonah, but you shouldn't blame me, either. You have to know I didn't do what you think I did."

"I should have known better," he finally admitted. "I did know better. I was just so screwed up when I got out of the hospital. Then when I found out you and Pryce were gone, I just... I'm sorry."

When she didn't respond, he wanted to reach over and take her delicate hand, make her understand, but thought better of it when he saw all the dirt from the day's work beneath his fingernails. He shoved his hands into his coat pockets instead and leaned his head against the headrest.

"Things are so screwed up," he said with a sigh. "I don't know where to begin to fix it, or if we even can, but I love him, Lo."

She looked down at her hands in her lap, her hair falling over her shoulder to hide her face. "He kind of makes it hard not to love him."

Jonah smiled, remembering the first time they met by the creek. "Yeah, he does."

"Did you ever really love me?" she asked, her tone more sorrowful than accusatory. "Or were you just using me as a way to be with Pryce?"

"What? God, no!" Jonah sat up in his seat and turned to her. "I didn't even know I felt this way about him until after the three of us started screwing around. That's why I broke up with you in the first place, because I *did* love you. I knew I couldn't change the way I felt about Pryce, and that you wouldn't understand. Hell, I still don't understand it."

The truck cab was quiet for more long minutes than he thought he could stand before she finally looked up at him. "I'm sorry for what my brothers did to you."

Jonah bit back a curse when he saw the unshed tears in her eyes. In all the time he'd known her, he'd never seen her cry, not even the night he'd broken up with her. "You don't have to apologize for them." Ignoring the dirt and grime on his hands, he reached out and took hers. "Your brothers are bastards. I don't blame you anymore, and I'm sorry I ever did."

Chloe nodded, blinking back her tears. "I'm still sorry," she said, her lips trembling. "You didn't deserve that."

As he watched the tears fall from her eyes, despite all her efforts to hold them back, the anger and doubt he'd held on to so tightly suddenly broke free from his grip and he pulled her into his arms. "Shh, don't cry. It's okay. I'm okay."

"They hurt you." She fisted her hands into the back of his coat and sobbed against his neck. "That's not okay."

He murmured reassuring words as he held her, but inside he was shaking like a leaf, as lost to her as he'd ever been. How could he ever have blamed her? How could he ever have walked away from her? How could he ever fix this when he knew she would never be enough for him, no matter how much he still wanted her? And, God help him, how was he ever going to let her go now that she was in his arms again?

"I've missed you," she said with a sniffle, hugging him even tighter.

"I've missed you too, Lo," he breathed against her hair, inhaling her familiar perfume. "I've missed both of you so bad it hurts."

Chloe inched closer to him and loosened her grip, nuzzling her face against his neck. The feel of her fingers tangling in the back of his hair sent all the blood in his veins rushing south, leaving him lightheaded and slow to respond when her lips parted and she pressed an open-mouthed kiss beneath his ear, then another.

"Uh." He cleared his throat and took her by the shoulders, but he couldn't make himself push her away. "Lo," he warned when she pushed up onto her knees and straddled him. "What- what are you doing?" *Oh, hell!* He gripped her hips as she lowered herself onto him, his cock reacting to the exquisite heat between her thighs, craving the friction she withheld.

"Come to dinner tonight," she said, kissing her way along his jaw. "Please. You have to eat."

Before he could respond, she pulled the door handle beside him and slipped out of the truck, leaving him gasping for air and painfully wishing he'd stopped her sooner.

"Chloe, I don't think—"

"Please," she repeated. "If not for me, then for Pryce."

Jonah closed his eyes, and when he opened them again and saw the pleading look in hers, he nodded.

"Seven," she said, closing his door, her lips turning up into a sad smile as she back-stepped away from the truck, not turning around until she reached the gate.

He sat wondering what in hell he'd just done, as he stared down the Grunion driveway until Chloe disappeared around the bend.

Chapter Fourteen

Jonah jerked his head back from the buzzing in his ear, and then slapped the annoying agitation away, only to wake up with an ear full of white foam.

"What the hell?" He sat up on his bed, opening his eyes in time to see Con and Car running from his room. "Grow the fuck up! Assholes," he mumbled, pulling the sheet up to wipe the shaving cream from his face.

"Dude, we couldn't resist." Carson chuckled as he stumbled back in. "Come on, get up. Mom's blowing her top. You're late for dinner, bro."

"What?" He glanced down at his watch, but it wasn't on his wrist.

"Here." Con appeared behind Car and tossed the watch onto the bed. "Didn't want to screw it up, so we took it off."

Jonah snatched it up and strapped it back onto his wrist. He must have been completely out of it if he hadn't felt them remove it. He glanced down at the time, and then tapped the watch face when he saw the late hour. "You broke it!" He held it up to his ear to see if it was ticking.

"We didn't break anything." Car marched to his bedside. He grabbed Jonah's wrist and looked at the time, then pushed the curtain back to show the last rays of the setting sun. "It's six-thirty. Like we said, you're late for dinner. Mom sent us up to get your ass in gear before we head out to take the night shift."

"Dinner!" He pushed Car out of his way and lunged for his duffle bag. "Shit! I'm going to be late!" After dropping Chloe off, he'd driven home and wandered up to his bedroom to think. He remembered dozing off, thinking he needed a quick nap, but damn! That was over two hours ago!

"Boys, let's go!" Gabby shouted up the stairs with way too much glee in her voice to be taken seriously.

"You know she's going to milk this for as long as she can, right?" Con asked. "Having us all home is her dream come true."

Jonah grabbed a clean pair of jeans and a shirt that at least smelled decent. "I'm going out for dinner," he said, fishing around in his bag. "Damn! I thought I had one pair of socks left!"

"Grab a pair of Cory's," Con suggested with a laugh.

"Gross!" Car said with a pinched smirk. "Have you smelled that kid's feet after he gets home from a shift?"

"Forget it. I'll go without socks." Jonah threw the duffle bag into the corner and rushed toward the bathroom.

"So, where ya goin'?" Car jammed his boot into the gap between the bathroom doorframe and the door before Jonah could close it.

"None of your business." Jonah pushed harder against the door. "Dammit! I'm going to Pryce's, okay?" he said when Car wouldn't budge. "Now get out!"

"Ooh-la-la!" Carson teased.

"Seriously?" Jonah released the doorknob and stared at his older brothers. "It's actually painful to know that you guys were ever on the most eligible bachelor list." He shook his head in disbelief. "I don't know what Breezy is thinking trying to have a kid with the two of you."

"We're just poking a little fun, bro," Connor said over Car's shoulder. "Don't get your britches in a wad."

"Yeah, man. Hey." Car stopped him when he tried again to close the door. "We really do hope it works out with you guys. We don't know this Chloe chick, but Pryce is…cool," he said with a shrug.

Jonah nodded, unsure of what to say. "Thanks," he finally offered, then motioned to Car's hand on the doorknob. "You mind?"

Once out of the clutches of his mutant older brothers, he rushed through a hot shower, scrubbing the day's grime from his sore body, thankful he didn't have enough time to daydream, or second guess what he was about to do.

"You're not staying for dinner?" his mom asked as he breezed into the dining room, dressed sans socks, to say a proper goodbye.

"I have plans." He bent down to give her a kiss on the cheek. "I'm sorry I didn't tell you. I wasn't sure if I was going, and then I fell asleep. I'll be here tomorrow. I promise."

"You'd better," she warned. "Papa Daniel and Uncle Cade are coming to dinner tomorrow and they have some big announcement to make."

Jonah froze. "Like what?" God, he hoped it wasn't more bad news. Uncle Cade was supposed to be getting better before he got worse.

"I don't know," Gabby said with a shrug, "but they've asked everyone to be here."

"I'll be here, I promise." He gave her one last quick hug before he sprinted toward the door.

"Cory just pulled up," Grey said as he passed him in the hallway.

Shit. "I'll talk to him," Jonah said on the way out the door. *Just not now.*

"Jonah!" He stopped short on the porch, his eyes adjusting to the darkness to see Breezy sitting on the porch swing.

"Hey," he said and turned to go, but she jumped up and ran over to him.

"I'm sorry about the other day," she offered. "I didn't want you to hear about Pryce and Chloe that way."

Jonah shrugged. "It's okay. I get it."

"Did you talk with them?"

Jonah sucked in a breath to sooth his agitation. It didn't work. He'd forgotten what it was like to have a dozen or more people poking around in his business every waking hour. He knew they only did it because they loved him, but it was still annoying as hell. "I'm headed over there now if I can ever make it to my truck."

Breezy smiled. "Good." She wrapped her arms around his middle and squeezed until he was forced to hug her back. "I knew you'd keep your promise."

"What promise?"

She pulled away and smiled up at him. "The one you made on my wedding day," she reminded him. "That you'd never give up on the ones you love."

Jonah tried to remember, but he'd been so screwed up on her wedding day, all he could remember was his brothers crying at the altar like two big babies and wanting to get the hell out of there. "I won't," he agreed anyway and extricated himself from her hold. "I need to go."

"Tell Chloe she can have the day off tomorrow if she needs it," Breezy said with a wink. "Or if she wants a ride into town, I can do that too!" she shouted after him as he descended the steps and jogged toward his truck.

He opened the door and slid inside the dark cab, jumping out of his skin when he caught his kid brother's silhouette in the passenger seat.

"Grey said you wanted to talk to me."

"Son of a bitch, Cor! You scared the hell out of me."

Cory didn't respond. Jonah used the moment to catch his breath. He looked at the clock on the dashboard and sighed. "Cor, I'm late. Can we do this tomorrow?"

"Whatever," Cory said with a sarcastic smirk and gripped the door handle. "I've said everything I needed to say anyway."

"Cory, wait." Jonah grabbed his shoulder. Cory jerked away from him, but didn't open the door. "Dammit, man, didn't they tell you?" Surely he'd heard the truth by now. Hell, even Dani knew.

"Tell me what? That you're an asshole?"

"Grow the hell up, Cor," Jonah sneered. "You know I'd never walk away from something like getting Chloe pregnant—and it never happened anyway! How could you believe something like that?"

"How could I not?" Cory railed back. "You fucking left! You lied to the whole family and were gone for over a year! Do you have any idea what it was like after you left?"

"Oh, poor Cory," Jonah mocked. "Had to do a few extra chores. What's the matter? You run out of fresh issues of Hillbilly Delights?"

"Fuck you, asshole." Cory shook his head. "You didn't hear Mom crying herself to sleep every night for a solid month after you left! You didn't see Mason staring out the windows at two in the morning, night after night, wondering why you hadn't called, thinking you were blown up in some terror attack halfway across the world! Or Matt nearly losing his arm fixing one of the tractors because he was trying to answer his damn phone—hoping it was you—instead of paying attention to what he was doing!"

"Cory—"

"Dani thought all of it was somehow her fault! Did you know that? She blamed herself every day for leaving for college, something she's been excited about for as long as I can remember."

"Cor—"

"And you have *no* idea what Grey was like, trying to hold it all together!"

"Cory I'm—"

"No!" Cory pointed at him. "Don't you dare say you're sorry!" Jonah sat in shock as his kid brother scorned him, his eyes alight with searing condemnation. "Save it for the rest of the family who believe your bullshit excuses."

"Cory! Dammit wait!" Jonah reached out to stop him when he shouldered open the door, but it was too late. His brother slipped out of the truck, slammed the door and disappeared into the darkness.

"Shit!" He pounded his fist against the steering wheel. He was reaching for the door handle to jump out and run after him when his phone rang. "Fuck!" What now? He fished it from his back pocket, the name on the screen barely registering before he answered. "Dani, it's not a good time."

"What's wrong?"

Jonah closed his eyes, the throbbing in his head pounding harder against his skull with every passing second. What wasn't wrong? "Nothing, what's up?"

"Have you seen Ash?"

"No. Why?"

Dani let out a frustrated grumble. "I haven't seen him since this afternoon when Clay was showing me how to launch the drone, and he's not answering his phone."

"Have you checked the bottom of the creek?" Jonah mumbled. Poor guy probably got one look at his competition and took a header off the ridge. Either that or Grey ran out of legal options.

"No, why? What would he—"

"Never mind," Jonah sighed at his twin's cluelessness. "I haven't seen him, but if I do I'll tell him you're looking for him."

"Okay, thanks. And Jonah?" Dani said when he was about to hang up.

"Yeah."

"Are you okay? You sound upset."

"I'm fine, Boo. It's…been a really long day."

"Mom said you weren't staying for dinner. Are you meeting Pryce?"

Jonah swallowed against the queasy feeling in his stomach that stirred to life at the reminder. "And Chloe," he added, glancing at the clock on the dashboard again. Already a half hour late, they'd probably started dinner without him by now. Not that he was hungry anymore.

"Good," Dani said, her deviant grin evident in her tone. "I won't wait up."

"Whatever."

"I'm just saying," she giggled.

"Go find Ash," Jonah insisted, rolling his eyes at his sister's insinuation. "Oh, and Dani?"

"Yeah," she said. "I'm still here."

"I really am sorry about all the shit I caused by leaving the way I did. None of this was your fault. You know that, right?"

"You've been talking to Cory, haven't you?"

Jonah sighed with regret—about so many things. "Yeah."

"Don't listen to everything he says, J. He's just acting all butt hurt because he's not the center of attention anymore."

"I don't think so," Jonah admitted. "He was wrong about me and Chloe, but he was right about a lot of other things. I screwed up."

"I'll talk to him," Dani said.

"No," Jonah insisted. "This is on me. I'll figure something out."

"Are you sure?"

"Yeah, I got it. Thanks, though."

"Any time."

Jonah said goodbye and pocketed his phone. He put his truck in gear, but kept his foot on the brake as he watched the flurries drift in and out of the headlamp beams. Maybe going to see Chloe and Pryce wasn't such a good idea.

~*~

He's not coming. Chloe stared at the clock on the wall, the small pile of spaghetti on her plate now an unappetizing lump of cold noodles. She'd second guessed her invitation, and everything that had happened leading up to it, a million times since she'd left Jonah sitting in his truck.

What have I done?

She hadn't been prepared to feel Jonah's arms around her, to hear his voice whispering so close to her ear. She hadn't realized how much she'd missed him, then to hear him say he'd missed her too? How many times had she wished to hear those words?

All of the feelings she'd thought she'd buried came rushing back. Her body responded to him as it always had. And he'd responded to her, too.

There was no mistaking it. He was at least still physically attracted to her. She didn't know why that had been so surprising, but any doubts she'd had about that part of the mess they were in had been laid to rest the second she felt his hard length against her inner thigh. The question now was, what did she do with it?

She knew what she wanted to do. It's what she'd always wanted from the moment the three of them kissed. Seeing the way Jonah's parents lived and loved each other, it was so different than anything she'd ever known. She wanted that with Jonah and Pryce more than she'd ever wanted anything, but how would it work if Jonah and Pryce wanted to be together, too? Or worse, what if they decided they couldn't?

Pryce was struggling to accept that part of himself. What if he never did? She could lose him, not only their dreams together, but all of him. He'd already taken a risk asking her to marry him. They both knew his parents would deny him their approval, but with his inheritance they'd had a way out, a way to survive if they disowned him. Now that the money was gone, he was trapped. He could lose everything he'd ever known if he did what she was hoping he would. Would he decide it wasn't worth it, that she and Jonah weren't worth it, and walk away?

"You're not eating." Pryce's tired words pierced the silence hanging between them.

She looked down at her plate and rested her head on the heel of her hand. "I'm not hungry anymore."

Pryce took the fork from her hand and laid it on her plate, then pulled her into his lap. "We'll figure something out," he said, though his voice held as much doubt as her own thoughts. "I don't know what will happen if my father dies, but that won't change us. It'll take a little longer, that's all. We'll be together just like we planned. I promise."

That's what she was afraid of, but before she could voice her biggest fear, there was a knock on the front door. Chloe jumped when Pryce's dog, Timber, barked.

"I'll get it." Pryce tossed his napkin on the table and helped her to her feet. "It's probably someone from the church bringing food."

Chloe followed Pryce to the front hallway, her heart pounding with both hope and trepidation. She hadn't told Pryce she'd invited Jonah to dinner. She'd tried, but couldn't find the words. She knew what she wanted, but didn't know how to ask them for it. As seven o'clock approached, then passed, she'd been glad she hadn't told him.

Pryce twisted the door handle and froze with the door half ajar. "Oh. It's you."

"Hey." Jonah's deep voice sent a welcomed chill down her spine.

Jonah didn't move and Pryce didn't invite him inside. Chloe moved closer to the door, but was too nervous to speak.

"How's your dad?" Jonah asked after an awkward silence.

"Not good." Pryce released the door handle, but still made no effort to invite Jonah in.

Jonah's gaze shifted around the large foyer until it landed on Chloe standing behind Pryce.

"Hey." Chloe offered a nervous smile. "You came."

Jonah nodded, then swallowed. "Sorry I'm late. I uh, fell asleep, and my family…they're crazy." He looked skeptically between her and Pryce when neither moved to let him in. "Did I get the night wrong?"

"What night?" Pryce asked.

"No." Chloe grabbed Jonah's hand, pulling him inside before she closed the door, locking it for good measure. She wasn't about to let him leave now that he was there. "It's tonight."

"What's tonight?" Pryce released Timber's collar and the big dog lunged for Jonah, yelping with joy.

"Hey boy!" Jonah stooped to his haunches to greet him. "I missed you too!" He laughed and scrubbed his big hands through Timber's thick fur. "You've gone grey in the muzzle."

"He's ten now," Pryce added then snapped his fingers when the dog tried to jump up on Jonah. "Timber, down!"

"Good boy," Jonah rewarded him when he was planted firmly on all fours, his tail still wagging.

"What are you doing here?" Pryce asked when Timber finally wandered off, addressing the question to Jonah but his gaze locked with Chloe's.

"I invited him for dinner," she sheepishly admitted. Her hand trembled as she took Pryce's hand, then Jonah's.

"Wait." Jonah stopped when she tried to lead them both to the kitchen. "You didn't tell him?"

"No, she didn't." Pryce snapped his hand free from hers and crossed his arms over his chest.

Chloe swallowed, the void in her stomach churning with uncertainty. She looked at them both standing before her, broad-shouldered and demanding.

"I thought dinner would be the least we could do for all the work he and his dads did yesterday," she offered shakily. Damn, this was harder than she thought it would be, but the memories of their past and how good they'd been together spurred her to grasp onto the small amount of hope her conversation with Jonah had given her. She sucked in another fortifying breath and stepped across the line that had been drawn in the sand eighteen months ago. "And we need to talk. All of us."

Jonah's eyes narrowed, and then darted to Pryce. "Do you want me to leave?"

Chloe held her breath as Pryce considered the question. He looked up at her through his lashes, his green eyes pleading for mercy, hers pleading for every dream she'd ever had. He rested his hands on his lean hips and took a deep breath, his tongue playing over his bottom lip, a nervous tell she'd always found distracting.

"No," Pryce finally said with a jerky shake of his head. "I don't want you to leave."

Chapter Fifteen

Pryce left them standing in the foyer and walked back into the kitchen, but couldn't sit at the food-laden table. He braced against the cold marble countertop instead, the air inside the room suddenly dense and hard to breathe.

Jonah's heavy footsteps echoed on the hardwood floor behind him. Pryce's grip on the counter's edge grew tighter the closer the sound got. A hand landed in the middle of his back and he flinched before he realized it was Chloe's.

"Thank you," she whispered, caressing what she thought was relaxing circles on his back, but each stroke only wound his tense muscles even tighter. Was he really doing this? Standing in the middle of his mother's kitchen with Jonah and Chloe was the last place on Earth he thought he'd find himself when he woke up that afternoon; another restless sleep filled with wet dreams of the three of them, mingled with white-knuckle nightmares of his entire life crashing in around him.

"Really, man, I'll leave if you want," Jonah offered again.

Pryce pushed off the counter and turned around to face him, but still couldn't look him in the eyes. "I don't know what I want," he said, the honesty in his words giving him a refreshing reprieve.

"I don't want him to leave," Chloe spoke up. "I don't know where to start or what to say first, but I know we can't go on like this."

Pryce looked at her, a diluted panic rushing through his veins. Deep down he'd known things between them had changed, but hearing her say the words aloud terrified him. What if he couldn't give her what she wanted? What if he lost her altogether?

"What *do* you want, Lo?" Jonah asked her, tucking his thumbs into his front pockets as he leaned against the kitchen doorframe.

Chloe sucked in a deep breath, held it for a second, her cheeks puffing when she blew it out in one steady rush. "I want you both. I want it all," she finally said. "I know it's selfish, but it's what I've always wanted."

Jonah didn't move. Pryce wasn't sure he took a single breath until he said, "I'm sorry I left you." He pushed from the doorframe and came closer. "I'm sorry I hurt you both. I screwed up everything, and no matter what does or doesn't happen here tonight, or in the future, I don't ever want to hurt either of you like that again."

Chloe's whimper caught Pryce's attention and he glanced over to see tears pooling in her eyes. The rare sight caused an ache to bloom in his chest. The whole time they'd been together he'd known she still loved Jonah. He knew she'd been hurt when Jonah broke up with her, but until that moment he hadn't a clue how deeply.

"The thing is," Jonah continued, "I want it all too, Lo. I don't have all the answers." Jonah's gaze drifted to meet his and Pryce forced himself not to look away. "You stand to lose a lot if we do this, Pryce, more than I ever realized before. I understand why you're scared, but you have to know that as much as I want to be with her, in every way possible, I want you too. I can't turn off that part of me, and neither can you. This won't work if we're not at least honest about that."

Pryce nodded, but could only swallow the knot in his throat in response.

"You're engaged to be married," Jonah reminded him. "Are you okay with me coming back, being with Chloe the way we used to be?"

Pryce nodded without reluctance. "She was yours before she was ever mine."

Chloe gave him a reprimanding nudge. "I loved you both," she insisted with a sniffle. "I still do."

"Believe me," Jonah said, "the last thing I ever wanted to do was come between the two of you. But, Chloe, I need you to understand what this means for me. What this means for us. Are you going to be okay with me kissing Pryce?"

Pryce's eyes snapped to Jonah's, the lust he saw making him instantly hard. Jonah noticed it too, raking his gaze down to the bulge in his jeans, then back up again.

"Are you going to be okay with us fucking each other?" Jonah continued, his tone making his intentions crystal clear. Pryce swallowed against the dryness in his throat. Fuck, was he really doing this?

He bit his lip to keep from moaning aloud at Chloe's jerky nod. "I wish you'd told me how you felt to begin with," she said. "Both of you." She pulled her hand from Pryce's and wiped away her tears. "I'd never imagined it before, but now that I've seen the two of you together, it's…um…kinda hot."

Pryce choked on a snort as a red hue tinged her cheeks. Jonah cupped her face, tracing her lower lip with his thumb. The tender gesture and the hunger in his eyes were so natural. It quelled the panic in Pryce's veins instead of making him jealous, cleansing his doubt with a rush of desire and the love that had once connected them all. She needed Jonah. Pryce needed him too, but could he find the courage to love him the way he wanted?

"I can't promise that I won't screw up again," Jonah continued, "but I can promise you one thing." Chloe looked up at him when he leaned closer. "I'm done running," he said, and then glanced back at Pryce. "I'll do everything in my power to make this work this time."

"Me too," Chloe said and lunged for Jonah, wrapping her arms around his middle. "I never stopped loving you." She reached behind her, fisting her hand in Pryce's shirt and pulling him to them. "I've never stopped loving either of you."

Pryce leaned in behind her, his eyes locked onto Jonah's as he nuzzled her ear. "We love you, too," he whispered. The words felt right. *They* felt right, even if he was scared out of his mind. He honestly didn't know if what they were about to do was right or wrong. He didn't know what to do or say next. He just knew he couldn't lose them again. Ever.

Jonah cupped the sides of Chloe's face and tilted her head back. He narrowed his eyes, a flash of regret flaring in them before he looked over her shoulder at Pryce. "I want to kiss her," he said, asking for permission he didn't need.

"Do it," she and Pryce said together.

Chloe gripped Jonah by the nape of the neck and pushed up on her tiptoes, offering herself to his best friend. Pryce ran his hands along her sides, letting her know he was okay, coaxing her to be true to herself, even when he couldn't. Her body trembled beneath his hands as Jonah lowered his head and placed a cautious kiss on her lips.

One touch, one spark, that's all it took. Jonah wrapped himself around her and crushed his mouth to hers, a gritty growl rumbling from his chest as he devoured her with a hungry urgency.

Pryce closed his eyes and listened to the sounds they made, feeling the weight of them press him against the kitchen counter. They each fell right into place, like precision-cut puzzle pieces, as if the last eighteen months had never happened. Nothing had changed between them. *Everything has changed,* he reminded himself, but this part, the two of them loving Chloe together, he could handle. He craved it with impunity.

Jonah hoisted her up to wrap her legs around his hips. He pressed her against Pryce, sandwiching her between them as he ground his cock between her thighs. Pryce reached around to unbutton her shirt. Every time the back of his fingers grazed Jonah's chest, he wanted to stop and feel the hard new muscles beneath his shirt he'd noticed the night in the barn, but he didn't. He'd grown comfortable and confident with Chloe, when it was just them. Now he felt like he was back to square one, an awkward fumbling virgin again waiting for instructions.

"Take it off," Jonah ordered between kisses. "Take it all off."

Pryce's hands shook as he worked her buttons free, struggling against her frantic movements to free her arms. When her bra was somewhere on the floor with her shirt, he removed his own shirt and jeans, kicking them to the side before he cupped Chloe's soft breasts, running his callused palms over her nipples the way he knew she liked, pinching them between his knuckles with just the right pressure.

"Yes." Chloe let go of Jonah and leaned back against him. "Kiss me," she ordered with a desperate sigh, turning her head so he could taste her kiss-swollen lips.

A hint of Jonah's cologne teased his nose as he slid his tongue deep alongside Chloe's, tangling them together in their familiar rhythm, only this kiss was different. Knowing Jonah had just kissed her, had just shared that same feeling, the lines began to blur again, making it difficult to tell where she ended and Jonah began.

The feel of Jonah's hot breath against his fingers sent a zing of fiery current down his spine. Chloe squirmed in his arms and he peered down to see what Jonah was doing and saw him bent over her, flicking her hard nipple with the tip of his tongue.

"Damn, Lo. You're even more gorgeous than I remember."

Pryce watched as Jonah trailed his tongue between one nipple and the other, until he stopped and glanced up at Pryce. With a wicked grin, Jonah opened his mouth and slid his lips over Pryce's index finger, taking it all the way to the back of his throat, and sucked hard.

"Holy—!" Pryce ripped his lips from Chloe's with a gasp. His throat tightened, trapping his answering moan as Jonah's teeth grazed along his skin, his hot tongue sliding along its length. When the heat of his mouth disappeared and the cold air kissed his wet skin, he whimpered at the loss of sensation, closing his eyes as he silently begged for more. His eyes flew open when he felt the prickly stubble on Jonah's cheek rake against his own.

"Let me in," Jonah demanded and then crushed their lips together.

Trapped against the counter, and paralyzed with uncertainty and desire, Pryce was helpless to deny him. His entire body tensed, his muscles tightening until he thought they would crush his bones into a broken heap, but then Jonah's taste exploded over his taste buds. Jonah pulled back and plunged in again, deep and fast, demanding. The tension snapped and Pryce melted, kissing him back, meeting him stroke for stroke, chasing the only high that had ever numbed his fear.

Fingers, Jonah's or Chloe's he didn't know, gripped the back of his hair, the sting to his scalp spurring his heartrate and sending spikes of stimulating current straight to his balls.

Chloe slid down their bodies between them, turning until her breasts were pressed against Pryce's bare chest. "That's so sexy," she hummed against the side of his neck before she pushed up and sucked his earlobe between her teeth, sending chills racing over his heated skin.

The kiss slowed, but the onslaught continued. Jonah's hot, frantic breaths puffed against his wet lips. "We need a bed," Jonah said, his hands roaming both Pryce and Chloe. "It's been so long, and if I don't get inside one of you soon, I'm going to lose it."

Pryce tensed again. "I…I'm not ready for that," he confessed with regret, his gaze locked onto Jonah's lips. Kissing was one thing, a big thing; he needed—*wanted*—to kiss him again, but no more. Not yet.

"I'm ready," Chloe said in an uncertain whisper. "We don't have to do anything different," she rushed to assure Pryce. "Not yet. Tonight can be like it always was." She dropped her gaze and sucked her bottom lip between her teeth. "That is…if you still want that," she added with a nervous shrug.

Jonah gripped her chin, making her look up at him. "I'll always want that," he said and kissed her forehead, then the tip of her nose. "I'll always want you."

Pryce watched with longing as their lips met in a slow, tender kiss. Drawn to them like a magnet, he leaned in and touched his lips to the corner of Chloe's mouth, accepting her invitation when she tilted her head to the side to make room for him.

Not as subtle, he flinched when Jonah gripped the back of his neck and pulled him into their kiss. Their mouths opened and their tongues tangled, their tastes mingling with their uncoordinated strokes and flicks until Jonah pulled away again.

"It's not enough," he mumbled and grabbed Chloe by the hips. He spun her around and lifted her onto the dinner table, tipping over glasses and sending her full plate of spaghetti crashing to the floor. "I can't wait any longer."

With two quick yanks, he had her jeans and panties pulled down to her ankles. Pryce watched in rapture as he parted her legs, buried his face between her thighs and devoured her unrestrained, his hum of approval echoing her pleas for more.

Chloe gripped Jonah's head with one hand and reached out for Pryce with the other. "Please," she begged, her voice snapping him back into the moment. He took her hand and she pulled him to her, the thought of what they were doing on his mother's table evaporating into nothingness as he bent over her outstretched body and kissed her.

Jonah's hand landed on his ass with a loud slap and Pryce jolted up. "Shit!" He cursed his nervous reaction, but Jonah gave him no time to wallow in it. He hooked his hand around Pryce's forearm and pulled him down onto his knees, glancing at him from the corner of his eye as he licked Chloe's slit. The scent of her sweet arousal tempted him closer and Jonah winked, scooting over to give him room between her legs.

"Yes," Chloe sighed, giving Pryce the confidence he needed to join in. Jonah angled his shoulders to allow him to slide in beside him. With one long lick, her sweet flavor exploded over his tongue like a bursting-ripe peach. He couldn't hold back his gratified groan. Jonah grinned and leaned in beside him for another taste, their tongues sliding together over her slick folds. "Oh my God." Chloe's back arched against the table when they reached her clit and swirled in opposite circles. "That feels *so* good."

Jonah shifted beside him, his presence disappearing as he pulled his shirt over his head. The heat of his bare skin brushed against Pryce's shoulder, then blanketed his back, his clean scent mingling with Chloe's arousal, a combination more intoxicating than any whisky he'd ever tasted.

As Jonah shifted back into place, the edge of a dark shadow along his side caught Pryce's attention, but he couldn't make out what it was before Jonah lowered his arm, hiding it from sight. He wanted a better look, but he had more demanding needs at the moment. He shoved his hand into his boxers and gripped his throbbing cock, stroking it in time with Chloe's mewling cries.

"Oh yeah," Jonah said in a gravelly grunt.

Pryce glanced over to find him mirroring his own rhythm, stroking himself, too, as he pleasured Chloe. Pryce licked his lips, unable to look away. Just like the man himself, the size of Jonah's cock had always been impressive. The sudden urge to reach over and wrap his hand around the long thick length hit him hard. Could he do it?

Caught in the grip of his fantasy, temptation coursed through his veins as Jonah's hand slid over and around the tip, his thumb spreading his pearly pre-cum in a compelling rhythm. The sight was so stimulating Pryce nearly came, but Jonah threw him off balance again, capturing his lips in another heated kiss, sliding his tongue deep and swiftly between his lips, demanding entrance.

Chloe's taste was strong on his tongue and Pryce grounded himself in it, reveling in the sensations bombarding him. The few times they'd kissed before, he'd been too shocked or ashamed to enjoy it, but this time was different.

Jonah's mouth moved over his, the assault slow and deliberate, forcing Pryce to feel him. He memorized every stroke of Jonah's hot wet tongue, the way he curled it up as he pulled out, and then plunged back in with an even greater hunger. The feel of prickly stubble scratching against his own and the clicking sound it made, the scent of Jonah's cologne, the texture of his silky hair between his fingers all rushed together, whipping his innermost desires into an uncontrollable storm that thundered through him with abandon.

"Wow."

The sound of Chloe's voice seeped through the riot of new sensations. Pryce turned and looked up to see her staring down at them, her legs spread, her fingers circling over her clit as she pleasured herself. Jonah chuckled and released him. It was only then he realized he'd practically crawled into Jonah's lap.

"Sorry, Lo," Jonah said with a wry grin, kissing her inner thigh. "We got a little carried away."

Chloe shook her head. "No apologies necessary," she assured them. "Please, continue."

Heat bloomed in Pryce's cheeks. He and Jonah exchanged a promising glance, but the moment was lost.

"Let's take care of our girl," Jonah suggested with a glance down at Pryce's engorged cock, "and then let her take care of us."

He could go with that plan.

"No, seriously, I'm good just watching the two of you," Chloe protested, but Jonah wasn't having it.

"I need inside you, Lo," he reminded her, leaning in to lick her pussy, prying her fingers away with his tongue. "It's been too long already."

"Oh damn," she said with a sigh when Pryce rejoined him. She collapsed back onto the table, propping her heels on the edge as they doubled their efforts.

Pryce kept a tight grip on his dick, helping Jonah bring her to the edge, surprisingly comfortable with the times their tongues touched, even shamelessly searching out the contact with each stroke.

"I'm close," Chloe panted, raising her hips off the table, pressing harder against their mouths. "So close!"

Pryce and Jonah's gazes met and they both grinned, just like old times, as they each slipped a finger inside her wet heat, curling them against the sensitive spot they'd found so long ago.

Pryce's balls drew up tight between his legs, his cock throbbing in his hand. He was done for. He couldn't hold back his release another second.

"Ahhh!" Chloe's channel tightened like a vice around their fingers and she cried out, her intimate muscles fluttering with her climax.

"Oh my—oh God!"

"Fuck, yeah," Pryce cried out as he came with Chloe, his seed spilling into his palm.

"I've always loved watching you come."

Pryce thought Jonah was talking to Chloe, but was surprised to find him staring at him instead, his lips slanted in a wicked crooked grin.

"Both of you," he added with a chuckle when Pryce blushed.

Unsettled by Jonah's admission, Pryce turned his attention back to Chloe. He kissed her inner thigh, trailing his tongue along the crease at the top of her leg before he rose and placed another tender kiss in the center of her chest, grinning when she jerked with a residual spasm. "You're so beautiful when you come apart."

"She's not done yet."

Pryce looked down to see Jonah rolling on a condom.

"We're going to make her come again." Jonah took Pryce's hand and drew it down to rest between Chloe's thighs. Chloe sucked in a breath, shuddering beneath his touch when Pryce slid his fingers through her wet folds and circled her sensitive clit.

Pryce watched as Jonah positioned the tip of his cock against her opening. Chloe's head fell back, her body arching off the table when he pushed inside, filling her fully with one steady thrust.

"Damn, Lo," Jonah ground out between clenched teeth. The sight of his hard cock disappearing inside her sent all the blood in Pryce's body rushing south again. How screwed up was he that watching his best friend fuck his fiancé made him so damn hard? He didn't know. He may never know, and in that moment he didn't care.

"I've missed you," Chloe said, reaching up to pull Jonah down atop her. She gripped Pryce's arm and drew him down beside her, too. "I've missed us so much."

"I've missed us, too, Lo." Jonah turned to him then, his gaze focused on Pryce's lips, but Chloe pulled him into another searing kiss before Pryce could act on the now familiar urge to kiss him. He watched them instead, feeling oddly complete as they reconnected, then joined them when Chloe pulled him into their kiss.

When their tongues swirled together, Jonah pulled away with a groan. "Gotta move, Lo." He pushed up to hover above them, his eyes squeezed closed as he began rocking inside her, filling her over and over, snapping his hips in a desperate rhythm. "It's been so long, this one is going to be quick, but I'll make it up to you."

Pryce captured her echoing moan, savoring the feel of her soft lips against his, but another shadow on Jonah's back caught his attention. Unable to ignore it, he sat up to take a look. What he saw took his breath away. The lines, the shadows, the way the falcon's wings appeared to move as Jonah moved, as if it had come to life and was flying right out of his skin.

Mesmerized, he traced the feathers across his shoulder blades, down to the creek that ran along his spine. Then he saw it: the familiar bend in the creek bank where they'd first made love to Chloe, together. Etched into the large boulder beside it were the letters 'JPC', but they were more like a brand. The vertical strokes of the 'J' and the 'P' overlapped each other like they were one letter, and the 'C' was bigger, surrounding the other two.

Too many emotions to count crashed into Pryce like a sea of tidal waves rolling in from every direction. To know what they'd shared that day beside the creek had meant as much to Jonah as it had him… It wasn't the first time Jonah and Chloe had been together, but it was *their* first time. To be a part of such a powerful memory, to know that he shared the same importance in Jonah's life as Jonah had in his… He couldn't fathom being loved in such a way, by Chloe, by Jonah, by anyone.

"I'm going to lose it if you keep looking at me like that."

Pryce's gaze darted to meet Jonah's. Dumbfounded, he swallowed, afraid he might choke on the lump in his throat. "I don't know what to say."

"What's wrong?" Chloe asked when Jonah paused.

Pryce looked down at her and smiled. "Nothing, baby." He leaned over and kissed the top of Jonah's shoulder, unable to contain his grin as he stared down at Chloe, knowing that she would forever be a part of them no matter what happened. "Absolutely nothing."

Jonah began moving again, his gaze fixed on Chloe. A new feeling of belonging overshadowed some of Pryce's doubt. Compelled to be a part of them, he lowered himself back beside Chloe and wedged his hand between were they joined together. His insides trembled as he slid through Chloe's slick folds and bracketed Jonah's cock in the 'V' between his fingers, the feel of his hard flesh sliding between them nearly sending him over the edge again.

Jonah sucked in a breath at the added sensation, his rhythm faltering. "Holy shit! Don't stop." The satisfaction that filled Pryce's heart sent his confidence skyrocketing. He increased the pressure, squeezing Jonah tighter, while moving his thumb over Chloe's clit to pleasure them both.

"Harder," Chloe demanded, reaching down to cup Jonah's bare ass, pulling him into her. "I'm almost there, J! I can't hold it back!"

Jonah complied. The table rocked back and forth with the force of his thrusts, the legs scraping against the hardwood floor. Pryce gripped his cock, running his thumb over his swollen head as he swirled his other thumb over Chloe, already so close to the edge. Another plate fell to the floor. A chair tipped over. Glass shattered somewhere in the distance, but their rhythm never waned.

"That's it," Jonah said. "I'm there, too, Lo." His hips pumped faster.

Chloe's body coiled tight. Pryce watched through hooded eyes as she chased her release. He marveled at her beauty, the way her skin glowed with sweat and anticipation. There had never been a time in their relationship without Jonah when he hadn't cherished making love to her, but he couldn't deny there was always something missing. Right or wrong, the three of them loving each other was the way they were meant to be together.

"Come with us," Jonah said and reached out to Pryce. As Pryce stroked his own cock, Jonah wrapped his hand around Pryce's, stroking it with him. Pryce held his gaze and did something he thought he'd never do in his life. He withdrew his hand and let Jonah take over.

His hips left the table at first contact, the feel of Jonah's hand sliding up and down his cock pushing him right over the edge. He came, hard, and fucking came some more. He didn't think it would ever end. His cum spilled over Jonah's hand in spurt after spurt until he thought his spine would snap, and then he collapsed onto the table beside Chloe in a boneless heap.

Chapter Sixteen

The bright light of a full moon reflected off the snow, casting long shadows through Pryce's bedroom window. Crowded into the bed, Chloe on one side of him and Pryce on the other, all of them naked beneath the quilts, Jonah stared at the ceiling, saying a silent prayer that he wasn't dreaming, or making the worst mistake of his life.

Opening himself up again to the idea of *them*, to the possibility that they could make this work felt like both the best and worst decision he'd ever made. He'd spent the last year and a half trying unsuccessfully to forget, but now that option wasn't just off the table, it was impossible.

Making love to Chloe again was like heaven on Earth, something he'd never thought possible. And now that Pryce was taking a chance too, it all seemed too easy, too good to be true. What if he couldn't go through with it? Coming out to his family had gone better than he'd expected, but he'd be kidding himself if he thought building a life together would be so easy.

Pryce may be willing now, but Grey had been right. Pryce would lose everything if this didn't work. What if he went all in and Pryce couldn't do the same when the time came? They'd be right back where they started, only Chloe wouldn't be the only casualty.

He listened to the sounds of them breathing beside him, wondering what it would be like to fall asleep and wake up with them both every day. He wanted that, more than he'd ever wanted anything.

No. He couldn't go back. No matter what happened, he had to see this through all the way to the end, but where was that end? He hadn't expected any of this to happen and had no plan beyond this point.

"What are you thinking about so hard?" Chloe asked, tracing the scar on his side from his fight with her brothers.

Jonah grinned despite his distracting thoughts. Even after more than a year apart, she still knew him better than anyone but Pryce ever had. They still had a lot to talk about, but not now. Not when she was naked and warm in his arms. He drew her thigh up and over his. "This," he said and tried to pull her astride him.

"Uh-uh. No way. We said thirty minutes," she reminded him with a playful shove. "It's only been twenty since we got out of the shower."

"You don't like after shower sex?" Jonah teased.

"I like after shower sex," Pryce said with a sated sigh. "Ow!"

Jonah chuckled when Chloe gave him a similar reprimand.

"We had sex *in* the shower," she reminded them.

As if he needed a reminder. Seeing Pryce pin her against the shower wall, watching his cock shuttle in and out of her tight pussy would give him wet dreams for a decade or more.

"No after shower sex," Chloe said as she settled back into bed, snuggling up to Jonah's side. Did she have any idea how difficult it was to keep his hands off her with her wiggling around like that?

"Tell us about Alaska," she insisted.

Jonah threaded their fingers together to keep her hand from wandering off and driving him crazy. "Where do I start?" he asked, with a nostalgic sigh. "It's beautiful. The mountains… I've never seen mountains so big, or so much snow." He took Pryce's hand in his free one and brought it to rest beside Chloe's on his chest. "You'd have a field day with your camera up there." He smiled at the thought of Pryce clicking away at the herds of moose that would migrate over the tundra near the dig site from time to time. "There's so many amazing things to see when you can get out and about. Most of the time, in the winter, it's too cold, though. Bone chilling cold." A shiver raced down his spine at the mere thought of it. "Nothing like we have here."

"What's it like in the summer?" Chloe asked.

Jonah shrugged. "Not much different than here, I guess. Just doesn't last as long. We pretty much lived on the dig site twenty-four-seven as soon as the ground thawed, so I didn't get a lot of chances to explore."

"Did you get to drive on the ice road?" Pryce asked.

Jonah chuckled, remembering how many times they'd hung out in his parents' basement watching the extreme trucking show.

"No." Not yet ready to let Pryce go, Jonah squeezed his hand when he tried to pull it from his grip. "I mostly worked in the south, but I did make a few trips over to Anchorage, and even got to ride up to Fairbanks once, but that was as far north as I got, or cared to go."

"Where did you get your tattoo?" Chloe asked, pushing up to sit beside him. "Roll over and let me look at it again. I still can't believe you put our initials in it, considering you hated me."

"Hey." He grabbed her wrist and she stopped to look at him. "I told you I never hated you." It wasn't exactly true. He'd hated not being able to let them go, but none of that mattered now. "I just didn't know the truth."

"I know. I'm sorry. I'm just surprised is all."

"The three of us together and the time we had before everything went sideways was the best time in my life, Lo. It always will be. I wanted it to be a part of me forever, no matter what happened."

Chloe's lips turned up in a weary smile. She twisted her hand free and pointed her finger at him. "You better stop or you're going to make me cry again. Now roll over and let me look."

Jonah feigned an irritated sigh and rolled toward Pryce, not that he minded. One. Single. Bit. Pryce scooted to the edge but Jonah drew him back, as close to beneath him as he dared try. Holy hell this was not good for the 'no after shower sex' rule. Then again...there was no rule that said he and Pryce couldn't fool around.

With Pryce tucked securely against him, he closed his eyes as Chloe traced his tattoo and tried not to think about how close his and Pryce's cocks were. Christ, he'd never been so horny. Every second he was around either one of them he wanted them naked and beneath him. But as comfortable as Pryce seemed downstairs, and even more so in the shower, he didn't want to scare him off by pushing him too fast.

"So, spill. Where'd you get the tattoo?" Chloe asked him again.

"In Anchorage," Jonah said, his lips grazing Pryce's shoulder as he spoke. He took advantage and kissed him there, settling his head on the pillow a little closer to Pryce's. "A guy I worked with had some amazing ink. He took me to see his tattoo artist there."

Pryce tensed and looked away, but Jonah could read the question in his eyes before he did. He grabbed his chin, turning him to look back. "There's been no one but the two of you," he said. "I won't lie. I fooled around a bit with one of the crewman's cousins a few times, and my boss tried to get me to fuck him, but I couldn't do it."

Pryce swallowed and looked away again, but eventually turned back. "So you've never…"

"No," Jonah answered him honestly. "Like I said, I've tried a few things, but we never fucked. You're the only guy I've ever wanted that way."

Pryce nodded his understanding. "Me too—I mean—it's the same for me."

He could feel the heat blooming in Pryce's skin beneath his fingertips and released him, letting the subject drop before Pryce retreated from the progress they'd made.

"Does it hurt?" Chloe asked a few minutes later, blessedly ending the awkwardness that had sprung up between them.

Jonah thought at first she was talking about his tattoo, but looked down to see her fingering the scar on his side from the chest tube they'd had to insert to re-inflate his lung. Luckily it was small enough that the tattoo artist was able to camouflage it under the tip of the falcon's wing.

"Not anymore," he told her, and it was mostly true. His knee gave him more problems than anything, but other than that he'd been lucky.

"My brothers are assholes," she said and placed a kiss on the raised scar.

"Where are they now?" There was never a time when he questioned whether or not he'd made the right decision to protect Pryce and not to report them, but he'd wondered if they'd picked up where they left off with him and started bullying Pryce again.

Chloe shrugged. "Finn's in jail for beating up his girlfriend pretty bad. Last I heard he had more time added to his sentence for assaulting a guard, but I don't know when he's supposed to get out. Never is fine with me. And Travis and Wayne moved back onto the reservation with our dad, but they still work in town at Gully's Garage."

Jonah snorted. "Note to self: do your own oil changes."

"Yeah. It's a good thing you're good with a wrench," Pryce added. "We've been running the small repair stuff from the ranch all the way to Clarkston. My father's truck needs a major transmission overhaul, but we can't afford dealer prices, so I've been limping it along until they get the new service station built near Carlton. I'm hoping they'll be a closer alternative."

"Have they bothered you?" Jonah asked. "I mean, since you've been back?"

Pryce shook his head. "We steer pretty well clear of them."

"My aunt talked to my dad when I came back to live with her," Chloe said. "I don't know what she said to him, but Wayne and Travis don't say much to either of us when we see them in town—just a few dirty looks here or there. And they never come into the bakery."

Dirty looks he could handle, but he couldn't help but wonder what would happen when they found out he was back. He wasn't scared of them, but he'd be dammed if he trusted either one of them not to jump him again the second they had the chance.

"Speaking of repairs, what am I going to do about my car?" Chloe whined and flopped back down onto the mattress. "I can't keep borrowing my aunt's. She has deliveries and supply runs to do next week."

"What happened to it?" Jonah asked, resettling himself between them.

Chloe shrugged. "I think it overheated. It's been cutting off lately but I haven't had time to run all the way out to Clarkston."

"I'll take a look at it tomorrow," Jonah said. "I can take a look at your dad's truck, too, if you want," he offered Pryce. "As long as you can limp it over to the ranch so I can use our tools. Your tools suck." Jonah playfully nudged his thigh, leaving his leg lying atop Pryce's. He was surprised when Pryce didn't try to move away.

Pryce chuckled and then let out a long, frustrated breath. "Everything around here sucks."

Unable to resist the opening, Jonah rolled toward him and pressed his hard cock against his thigh. "Do you suck?" he asked with a coy grin, flexing his hips.

Pryce tensed, frozen like a statue beside him, barely breathing. "Um..."

Jonah looked down at the tent in the sheet. He certainly wasn't turned off by the idea. "Will you let me?" he asked, letting him off the hook. One day, and hopefully soon, he would get to feel his mouth on his cock, but right now he had to tread lightly. He rolled over on top of Pryce instead and straddled his thighs, their straining cocks mere millimeters apart.

"Can I help?" Chloe asked, her lips turned up into a seductive grin.

Pryce sucked in a hissing breath when she wrapped her fingers around the base of his hard shaft. "Ah!" He flinched when Jonah cupped his balls, thrusting up into Chloe's grasp. "What happened to no after shower sex?"

"Thirty minutes are up," she teased with a flick of her wrist.

Jonah chuckled, but he didn't want Pryce to do something he truly didn't want to do. "I'll stop if you want," he offered, and withdrew his hand. "Is that what you want?"

"Yes," Pryce choked out with a jerky nod.

Jonah attempted to hide his disappointment, but when he tried to move away Pryce stopped him. "No, I meant, *yes.* I want you to."

Not wanting to waste a single second, or give him a chance to change his mind, Jonah threw the blankets off and repositioned himself between his thighs. Chloe shimmied over and they met face to face, Pryce's fully erect cock positioned perfectly between them.

Jonah licked his lips, his gaze fixed on the drop of fluid leaking from the tip. He'd given exactly two blowjobs in his life, both while he was in Alaska, and neither of them the only cock he'd ever wanted. Still, he'd never shared a blowjob with another person, and knowing where to begin was a little more awkward than he'd imagined. Did he just dive in and suck him down, or wait for her?

Chloe took the decision out of his hands and ran the tip of her tongue along Pryce's length, root to tip, her eyes never leaving Jonah's. Hell on fire that was hot! His cock, already hard, pulsed at the thought of her mouth on him, too.

Pryce's garbled curse snapped his focus from the fantasy and back to the task at hand. He looked up at Pryce to see his face twisted, his mouth open in a rapturous silent cry. He held that sight, watching through his lashes as he leaned in and mimicked Chloe's move on the other side, taking his time to feel every velvety ridge and vein, grinning when Pryce thrashed his head to the side as he reached the tip, and then sucked him to the back of his throat.

"Oh damn!" Pryce curled up and grabbed Jonah by the hair, both pulling and pushing him as if he didn't know which way was up. "Stop! I'm going to come. You have to stop."

Jonah pulled off and gripped the base of Pryce's cock. "Can't have that. Not yet anyway," he said with a pleased chuckle.

Pryce released him and collapsed back onto the bed. "Holy shit."

Chloe giggled. "This is so much hotter than watching the two of you kiss."

"I'm glad you're entertained," Pryce joked.

Jonah slowly released his grip and motioned for Chloe to rejoin him. They went slow this time, tracing Pryce's shaft with alternating licks. When they met at the top, instead of taking him in his mouth again, Jonah pulled Chloe into a searing kiss, sharing Pryce's taste before lowering his mouth back over Pryce's erection.

"Fuck," Pryce hissed when Jonah's lips met Chloe's hand at the base. Unaccustomed to hearing him curse so often, Jonah laughed around his cock, which made him curse again.

Chloe stroked him as Jonah sucked him off. Up and down. Faster, and then slower until every muscle in Pryce's body was taut, his balls drawn up tight.

"That's it. I can't hold it back!" Pryce tried to twist away, but Jonah wouldn't let him. He'd waited a damn lifetime to taste him and he wasn't about to let him go now. "J, I'm coming. Get off!" Pryce shouted in a panic.

"Let him," Chloe coaxed and released her grip. She leaned over Pryce, kissing him, distracting him, giving Jonah free reign.

Jonah gripped his shaft and took him to the back of his throat again, then swallowed against his head, milking him until Pryce finally broke, coming with a string of guttural shouts.

Jonah swallowed every drop, sucking him dry as Pryce convulsed beneath him. When his cock finally softened, Jonah let him go and climbed up his body. He pulled Chloe to him and kissed her, long and hard, sharing Pryce's seed with her as he jacked himself off. Already throbbing, it didn't take long, only a stroke or two until his seed jettisoned onto Pryce's chest, a drop marking his dimpled chin.

With hooded eyes, Pryce met his gaze, then scooped up the drop and hesitantly sucked it from his finger before he collapsed back against the pillows with a defeated, but fully sated sigh.

The next time Jonah opened his eyes, the morning sun was shining brightly through the window. It took a second to understand the tangle of limbs and the instant boner the memories induced, but then he heard it, the sound that had woken him.

He sat up and listened, hearing the telltale swish of fabric and footsteps climbing the stairs.

"Pryce!" Jonah nudged him with a harsh whisper. "Pryce!" He shoved him again.

"Huh?"

"Someone's here!"

"What?" Chloe sat up and listened.

"Shit!" Jonah bounced to the foot of the bed, but before he could get more than one leg into his jeans the bedroom door opened.

Mrs. Grunion froze. He froze. Time stood still, and then the loudest ear-splitting screech filled the room.

"Heathens!"

Jonah dodged the picture frame she ripped from Pryce's dresser and hurled at him, managing to get his jeans pulled up and his junk tucked in before the next one hit him in the shoulder.

"Demons! Both of you!"

"Mother, stop!" Pryce jumped from the bed, tripping over the quilt on the floor.

"Get out!"

Wrapped in the sheet, Chloe searched for her clothes, spinning in a frantic circle until she remembered. "They're in the kitchen."

"You!" Mrs. Grunion charged at her, sinking her fingers deep into the bare flesh of her biceps with a punishing grip. "You worthless whore!" Chloe yelped. Her head bobbled back and forth as Mrs. Grunion shook her. "I told you to stay away from my son! You've ruined him!"

"Mother!" Pryce lunged for her, but Jonah managed to pry Chloe from his mom's grasp before he could round the bed. Pryce banded his arms around his mom and pulled her away. "Mother, stop it! She's not a whore! I love her, and she saved Father's life for God's sake!"

"Your father is dead!" his mom screamed, her entire body trembling.

"What?" Pryce's expression twisted in disbelief, releasing his mom.

"He's dead!" Mrs. Grunion repeated and twisted from his hold. Pryce stood motionless, shock riveting him in place. "And thank God for it! At least he never had to see this…this…abomination!" She sobbed, suddenly sinking to her knees with her hands folded in front of her face. "Oh, God please don't forsake my son," she prayed, mumbling memorized scripture verses between her cries.

"You'd better go," Pryce said, the defeated look in his eyes something Jonah was all too familiar with. He wanted to snatch him up and kiss him until that look vanished for good, but he didn't. Pryce's eyes were clouded with so many emotions Jonah couldn't count them all. It would only make things worse.

"Yeah, okay." Jonah took Chloe's hand and pulled Pryce into a hug. "Sorry about your dad," he whispered.

"Get out of my house!" his mother screamed again and reached for the lamp on the bedside table.

"Call us as soon as you can," Chloe whispered and kissed his cheek. "I love you," she managed before Jonah pulled her from the room, a split second before the lamp shattered against the bedroom wall.

They rushed down the hallway and stumbled down the stairs, skidding to a stop at the bottom where the pastor of Pryce's church stood with his wife. The pastor held Jonah's gaze, narrowing his eyes with malice and disdain as his wife whimpered and looked away, her grip tightening on her husband's arm.

"Get your clothes," Jonah instructed Chloe. She darted into the kitchen and he pulled on his shirt and boots while he waited for her return. A second later she rushed back in and handed him his coat, her clothes wadded into a ball she hugged to her chest.

"I believe that sheet belongs to Mrs. Grunion," the pastor said, stepping in front of the door when Jonah reached for the handle.

"David," his wife protested.

"No." The pastor raised his chin in defiance. "If she loves wallowing in sin so much, let her show her nakedness to the world."

"Go to hell," Jonah spat and pushed the pastor out of their way. A rush of frigid air spilled inside when he opened the door, but Chloe pulled him to a stop when he made to leave. "Chloe, let's go."

"If loving Pryce is a sin," she said in a sultry voice, "I'll wallow in it until my fingers are pruney, for *all* the world to see." She dropped the sheet to the floor and stood naked before them.

The pastor seethed, his face turning fiery red, but didn't avert his gaze. His wife whimpered and shielded her eyes.

Jonah scooped her up into his arms and darted out into the cold to his truck.

Chapter Seventeen

"You're still shaking." Chloe hadn't said a single word on their way back to the ranch to get her aunt's car. Unsure if the roads had cleared, Jonah had followed her back into town and up to her bedroom. He wasn't leaving until he knew she was okay.

"I'm fine."

"You're not fine." He took her coat and tossed it onto the bed. "Come here." He wrapped her tiny frame in a hug. He'd always loved the way she fit in his arms, but this felt different. He'd missed her a hell of a lot more than he'd allowed himself to believe.

"I'm shaking because I was just assaulted and called a whore by my future mother-in-law."

"You're not a whore, Lo." Jonah assured her. "You're beautiful, and kind, and trusting, and ours. Besides, I'm a hundred percent positive that guy and his wife are going to be saying Hail Marys for a year to get you out of their heads."

Chloe groaned against his chest. "I can't believe I did that."

Jonah chuckled. "It was perfect." He kissed the top of her head with a grin. "A little crazy, but perfect. You're perfect."

"I hated leaving him there."

"Me too." Jonah cursed the uncertainty and shame in Pryce's eyes when they'd left. He'd seen it more times than he could count after Dirk Grunion had beaten or humiliated him for one reason or another.

In the beginning it would take weeks for Pryce to shed the feelings of inadequacy and shame his parents heaped onto him. Things between he and Jonah and Chloe may have changed, but would it be any different this time? Would Pryce come back to them at all? Jonah had to believe he would. The horses were out of the barn and they couldn't go back.

"I'm calling him." Chloe pulled her cellphone out of her back pocket.

"No." Jonah took her phone. "Give him time, Lo."

She reached for her phone, and then sank down onto the edge of the bed with a frustrated growl when he wouldn't give it back.

"You know him, Jonah. His mother will fill his head full of bullhockey and he'll start second guessing everything again."

"I pushed him last night, farther than I meant to," Jonah admitted, "but he knows now. He knows what he wants, and if he wants it as badly as I do, he won't be able to deny it."

"That doesn't mean he won't try," Chloe insisted.

"And we won't let him." *Not this time.* Jonah handed her phone back and sat on the bed beside her. When she leaned into him, he wrapped his arms around her and pulled her onto his lap. "His dad just died. As screwed up as they were, I'm sure he's rattled. But he loves you, Lo. Don't worry."

"He loves you too." Jonah shrugged and Chloe turned in his lap until they were nose to nose, straddling him. "He's been in love with you from the beginning."

Jonah dropped his forehead to hers. "I know."

"You do?"

Jonah sighed. "Kind of. I mean, there was always a feeling between us, but I didn't understand it until I started dating you and we all started fooling around. It scared the hell out of me, Lo. I didn't know what to do. And then when we kissed, I just…freaked, and then ran. I never meant to hurt you."

Chloe stared at him. "What?" he asked when she grinned.

She placed a feather-light kiss on his lips. "I still can't believe you're here."

"I can't believe a lot of things," he whispered against her lips. How is any of this possible? "I don't know how to make all this work, Lo. I just know that we have to."

"I don't know either," she said with a resigned sigh, "but no matter what happens, you own a piece of me, Jonah McLendon. A big piece that I hope you'll never again try to give back."

"Never."

He held her gaze, hoping she knew just how much he meant it. Now that the air had been cleared and they were back together, he had no intentions of letting go of either one of them. He tunneled his fingers through her hair, biting back a groan when she shifted in his lap. Damn, would he ever get enough of her? He and Pryce had spent hours inside her, in one way or another, and it hadn't seemed to have even scratched the surface of his need.

"Good." She gave him a quick chaste kiss and peeled herself from his lap. "I need to shower or I'm going to be late for work, not that I'll be able to function when I get there."

Jonah jackknifed off the bed and shot across the room, capturing her before she could slip away. "I forgot to tell you." Her back to his chest, he slipped his hands beneath the front of her shirt, kneading her buttery soft flesh. "Breezy said you could have the day off if you needed it. After last night, and what happened this morning, maybe you should stay here, catch up on some sleep."

Chloe melted against him. "Breezy knows about us?"

"Mmhmm." Jonah nodded, or at least thought he did. He couldn't concentrate on anything with her in his arms. "We have a lot of catching up to do, Lo."

"That doesn't sound like sleep to me," she said, stopping his hands from traveling further under her shirt.

"I'm sure we'd get a few hours in before dinner."

"What about Pryce?"

"Pryce will be fine."

"No, I mean…" She turned in his arms and looked up at him. "I'm not sure we should do this. You know, without him."

Jonah tunneled his fingers beneath her waistband, pushing his hands deep into her jeans. He cupped her heart-shaped ass and drew her against his hardening cock. "He said he's okay with us, Lo. He has to be. It's the only way this will work."

"But still, it feels wrong, after we just left him there."

Jonah held his breath, and then released it in a disappointed rush as he let her go. "You're right."

As much as he wanted her, he couldn't. He trailed his fingers along her silken skin, tasted her lips one final time. Yes, he could. Oh, he could *so* easily let himself get lost in her, but they needed to set some ground rules before things got all twisted up again.

"Go to work," he said, giving her cheek a lingering kiss.

"Can you come over later? I'm sure Aunt Bev wouldn't mind making extra for dinner."

Jonah shook his head. "My mom called a family meeting for dinner tonight, something about Papa Daniel and Uncle Cade. I have to be there, but you should come."

"Is Cade okay?"

"I don't know. I hope so." He kissed the tip of her nose. "Come with me. It will be a good distraction and I want my family to meet you."

Jonah's eyes were drawn to her bottom lip as she twisted it between her teeth before she answered. "I don't want to intrude."

"You won't be intruding," he insisted and drew her back to him, unable to resist the urge to kiss her again. She felt so damn good in his arms after so long without her. "Come," he pleaded. "If I come back here tonight I won't be able to keep my hands off you."

"Okay." Chloe giggled and twisted out of his grip. "But I don't have a car."

"Give me your keys. I'll take a look at it on my way out. If it's something I can't fix today then I'll come pick you up."

Chloe retrieved her keys from a hook behind the door and handed them to him, then pushed up and kissed his chin. "Thank you."

"Call me if Pryce calls you."

"Oh, wait!" Chloe called after him as he paced to her bedroom door. "I need your number."

"Oh yeah." He pulled his phone from his pocket and entered her number as she read it off to him.

"I tried calling you," she said in a soft voice, "after I moved to Colorado, but it wouldn't go through."

Jonah entered his number into his cell, debating whether or not to tell her about her brothers taking his phone and screwing up his life. "I had my phone shut off for a while, and then got a new number," he said instead, not wanting her to feel guiltier than she already did for something that wasn't her fault. That part of his life was finished. He'd rather leave it in the past and start over.

He gave her phone back, along with one last kiss goodbye. "Try not to worry."

Eight hours later he pulled into Falcon Ridge for the third time that day, Chloe sitting rigid in the seat beside him. Her car was toast. He could fix it, but he'd need a lift and more tools than he possessed for the major overhaul it needed.

Curiosity had sparked an idea on his way home that morning when he'd driven by Gully's Garage. When he saw the closed bay doors and only one truck parked out front, he'd made a U-turn and pulled up to the dated building. Taking a chance that Chloe's brothers weren't there, he knocked on the door, relieved when Art Gully answered and invited him inside. One pot of hot sludge Art called coffee, and a very promising conversation later, he left with a nervous excitement about his future. Their future. He wasn't ready to share his thoughts with Chloe and Pryce yet, but if some of the missing pieces of his new plan fell into place, they might just be able to make this work.

"Don't be nervous." He laced his fingers with Chloe's, her vanilla scented lotion teasing his nose when he kissed the back of her hand. "My family will love you."

"Do they know it was my brothers who attacked you? I mean, do they think I asked them to?"

Jonah released her hand and pulled his truck to a stop in the usual spot behind Matt's. He cut the engine and unbuckled his seatbelt.

"Oh my God! They do!"

"No, they don't, Lo. I never told them what happened until a few days ago, after I talked to Pryce."

"But you did tell them about my brothers."

Jonah unbuckled her seatbelt, letting it slide away before he hooked his thumb under her chin and made her look at him, stealing a kiss before he continued. "They know you're important to me. Nothing else matters—to me or to them."

Chewing on her bottom lip, she closed her eyes and nodded. "You're important to me too, and I don't want to screw this up."

Jonah chuckled. "Lo, our family dinners are usually such a circus you could stand on your head naked in the middle of the table and no one would notice."

"I doubt that," she said with a snort.

"Come on. It's getting cold out here." Jonah opened the door and lowered her to the ground, taking her hand as he led her across the snow-dotted yard, up the steps and through the front door. "Just remember. If you're ever in doubt about something to say, give it a second or two and Con or Car will say something stupid and divert everyone's attention."

"Jonah! Is that you?"

Chloe's grip tightened around his hand as he pulled her down the hallway toward the scent of his Gran's apple cinnamon pie.

"Hi Gran!" He returned his grandmother's enthusiastic hug.

"Jonah McLendon, you're late! And good Lord! No one told me you were bringing company!"

"Shoot, I forgot to tell you!" Gabby grumbled from her perch at the bar where she sat slicing lemons for the lemon water she always drank with dinner.

"Sorry," Chloe offered with a nervous smile, glancing between him, Gran and his mom. "I don't have to eat if there's not enough. I'm not hungry anyway."

"Nonsense, girl." Gran pulled her into a welcoming hug. "I always make extra. I'm Hazel, Jonah's grandmother, and it's so nice to finally meet you, Chloe."

"Don't smother her," his mom insisted and then did just that when Gran finally let Chloe go. "Sorry," Gabby offered. "I'm just so excited to meet you, too."

"And you must be Chloe." Papa Joe's booming voice reverberated from the kitchen doorway.

"Yes, sir." Chloe turned and offered her hand. "Nice to meet you."

Jonah grinned when Papa Joe raised his brow in question. *Here it comes.* "Nice to meet you, too, Miss Chloe," he said and took her hand, bending over it to bestow a flirty kiss. "You keep calling me Sir, though, and it might go to my head."

"Oh, stop your flirting." Gran snapped him with the dishtowel in her hand. "But he's right," she whispered to Chloe with a wink. "You don't want to feed that ego of his. Trust me."

Papa Joe chuckled and released her hand. "Call me Joe."

"Thank you, Joe," Chloe said with an anxious smile.

"Mom, do you have those lemons—oh Chloe! You're here!" Breezy stormed in and tackled Chloe in another hug. "I'm so glad you came! I wasn't sure you wouldn't change your mind."

"I did, a thousand times," she admitted, casting Jonah an apologetic glance over Breezy's shoulder.

"Well, I'm glad you didn't," Gabby said, handing Breezy the bowl of sliced lemons. "We can always use the extra hormonal support around here."

"Gabby, hon, have you seen my phone?" Matt stopped short when he rounded the corner. "Well, hello there." His hands resting on his narrow hips, he glanced between Jonah and Chloe. "Is this her?" he asked, and Jonah nodded. "Well, damn, Son, you didn't say how pretty she was." Matt draped his arm over Chloe's shoulder and turned her toward the hallway. "It's nice to meet you, Chloe. I'm Matt, Jonah's good lookin' dad. The smart one, too, but don't tell anyone. They'll expect me to behave."

"I heard that!" Gabby shouted after them. "You'd better catch up to them. There's no guessing what he might tell her," she warned Jonah and handed him a steaming bowl of fresh greens. "Take these to the table on your way."

"Thanks, Mom. I knew you'd love her."

With a gentle squeeze, Gabby stayed his retreat to the dining room. "Have you heard from Pryce since this morning?"

Jonah shook his head, heat creeping into his cheeks. He hadn't told her about him and Pryce, not directly. He figured his dads had told her, but still, the idea that his mom knew he and Pryce were…whatever they were, was more than a little awkward. "Chloe and I are trying to give him some time. We'll probably call him after dinner tonight."

The corners of her mouth turned down into a worried frown. "I hope he's okay. It must be so hard for him without you and Chloe there."

With that one expression, the awkwardness vanished and the knot in Jonah's stomach relaxed. He stared at her in awe, his chest aching with so much love and appreciation he could barely contain it. "I love you, Mom." He gave her the biggest hug he could manage without hurting her or dropping the bowl of vegetables.

"I love you, too." She hugged him back before she took his cheeks between her palms and kissed his forehead. "A mother is only as content as her unhappiest child. If Pryce and Chloe make you happy, honey, then of course I'm delighted for you."

"Finally," Grey huffed behind them. "Somebody around here finally made you happy." He ambled over and pulled Gabby into his arms.

"Oh stop," she said with a playful shove. "You know you make me happy."

Before he was trapped in the kitchen and forced to witness his parents making out, Jonah snuck around them and headed for the dining room with the bowl of greens.

"Not so fast." Grey snagged the back of his shirt before he could make his escape. "We need to chat."

Chapter Eighteen

"Don't keep him long," Gabby warned and took the bowl from Jonah's hands. "Dinner's getting cold and we can't leave Chloe in there all by herself with your brothers and the Papas."

"Oh, she's not alone." Grey snickered and cut Jonah a sly grin. "Breeze and Gran are keeping her plenty busy talking about wedding stuff."

"What?" Jonah bolted toward the hallway, but Grey still had a commanding grip on his shirt.

"I was joking!" Grey let him go, pulled out two beers from the fridge and handed one to him. Jonah gave him a questioning glance. It wasn't his first beer, but he was still a few weeks shy of legal drinking age, and it was his first drink with one of his dads.

"You're close enough," Grey said and clinked their bottles together. "Besides, it looks like you could use one."

That's an understatement. "I talked to Chloe." Jonah twisted off the cap and tossed it into the trash can. "She didn't know about her brothers."

"Oh, yeah." Grey waved him off and took a long pull from his beer. "I figured you had all that worked out if you were bringing her home."

"Then, what did you want to talk to me about?"

"A couple things, but first," Grey leaned in to speak in a hushed whisper, "what happened with Ash?" He took another long sip, leaning back to look around the corner to make sure no one heard him. "What did you say to make him leave?"

"He's gone?" Dani had called looking for him, but never said he'd left.

"He called a ride and high-tailed it back to Billings last night before dinner."

Jonah shook his head and leaned against the counter. "You honestly don't know, do you?"

Grey cocked his head. "Know what?"

Jonah laughed. He couldn't help it.

"What?" Grey insisted. "What did you say to him?"

"Nothing." Jonah held his hands up in surrender, his beer dangling between his fingers. If Grey couldn't see what was happening between Clay and Dani, right before his very eyes, hell if he'd be the one to break it to him. "I didn't say a word to the guy."

"Really?" Grey stared at him a moment, a cocky grin on his face. "Huh, that was easier than I thought it was going to be."

Jonah hung his head in an attempt to hide his incredulous grin. "What else is going on?" While he loved sharing a beer with Grey, a far cry from where he thought he'd be a week ago, he needed to move this conversation along so he could get back to Chloe before his other dads did or said something crazy he'd never be able to live down.

Grey checked around the corner once more, and then pulled him deeper into the kitchen. "I've spoken to our lawyers about Chloe's brothers."

"What?" Jonah's blood ran cold.

"You were a minor when they attacked you. Finn Jessop was damn near twenty. I might not be able to do anything about her younger brother, but Finn and Travis need to answer for what they did to you."

"No."

"Jonah, as a parent I can't just let this go."

Jonah downed the rest of his beer and tossed the bottle into the trash. "You have to, Dad."

"I want you to talk to the lawyers, listen to what they have to say."

Son of a bitch. What part of 'let it go' did he not get? "Dad, I appreciate what you're saying, but the answer is still no. I'm handling it my way."

"How exactly?" Grey asked.

"Grey! Jonah! Get your boots in gear!" Mason called from the dining room. "I'm starving!"

"You're not the only one." Uncle Cade's voice boomed from the front foyer.

"We'll talk about this later," Grey said and led the way toward the roar of voices that always filled their house at dinner time. "And we still need to talk about Cory."

"Where is he?" Jonah asked, having not seen Cory's truck when they'd pulled up to the house.

"He couldn't get his shift covered."

"Sorry we're late," Papa Daniel said as he and Uncle Cade shucked their coats and met them in the hallway.

With more strength than Jonah expected, Uncle Cade pulled him into a back slapping hug. "It's good to see you home, kid."

"You, too," Jonah offered, at a loss for words at how much better Cade looked.

The four of them filed into the crowded dining room together and Jonah rushed to the empty seat beside Chloe.

"Hats off," Gabby reminded him with a pointed glare.

"Sorry." He flipped off his hat, hanging it on the back of his chair.

Chloe turned to him with a mischievous smile. "Your dad was just telling me about the time you tried to make your own cowboy boots by wrapping your legs and feet in duct tape."

"Dad!"

Matt slapped the table and threw his head back, almost tipping over in his chair with laughter.

"Car told me to do it," Jonah grumbled, unfolding his napkin and laying it across his lap. "That shit hurt!"

"Can we at least not curse at the dinner table?" Gabby insisted.

Jonah cringed. "Sorry, Mom."

"We had to rip it off piece by piece," Matt squealed through his laughter, his eyes watering with tears.

"Yeah, real funny." Jonah squinted across the table at Car. "Took me six months to regrow the hair on my legs."

"You were six," Car protested. "How much hair could you have had?"

"None, thanks to you."

With a clap of her hands, Gran called the room to order. The family bowed their heads, while Papa Joe stood and began a prayer to bless the food and thank God for bringing their family together. Jonah took Chloe's hand, giving her a wink when she glanced over at him. When she closed her eyes again, he looked around the table and took in the sight of his family.

His mom sat between Grey and Matt, Mason on Grey's right. He hoped to God that Grey got this thing with Chloe's brothers out of his system. He didn't know if Chloe would freak or not, but her reaction wasn't his biggest concern. All he wanted was to put the past behind him and start over. If he could get Pryce on board and everything worked out with Art Gully, he could do just that. He took a deep breath and said a silent prayer that Grey would back off and let him handle it.

Papa Joe cleared his throat. Jonah looked and found him staring at him, his eyes narrowed in warning. Jonah quickly closed his eyes, but opened them again when Papa Joe continued.

His grandparents sat across from his parents, Gran between Papa Nate and Papa Jake as Papa Joe prayed at the head of table beside them, Dani at the right of them. Breezy sat between Con and Car, her head bowed, her lips pressed into a determined line before they curled up into a smile and she squirmed in her seat. He darted his gaze back to Con and caught the naughty grin on his lips as he fiddled with something beneath the table. Jonah rolled his eyes. If she wasn't pregnant before Easter he'd eat his hat.

Beside him, Uncle Cade sat shoulder to shoulder with Papa Daniel, their heads also bowed, their hands clasped together and resting on the table. Jonah stared at their hands, watching Papa Daniel's thumb caress small circles over the back of Cade's weathered knuckles. They'd never been ones to display their affection for each other around the family, but that had apparently changed since he'd left and Cade was diagnosed with cancer. The sight did funny things to his insides. Would he ever be able to share that sort of open affection with Pryce?

Chloe squeezed his hand when Papa Joe expressed special thanks for bringing him back home to Falcon Ridge, for the opportunity to meet Chloe, and then another plea to give Pryce peace in his time of mourning for his dad.

"Amen," Jonah repeated when Papa Joe ended his prayer, unable to resist the urge to pull Chloe's hand to his own lips. "Thank you," he said and kissed her palm.

"For what?"

For still loving me. "For not running for your life when you had the chance."

Chloe shrugged, the corner of her lips curling into a grin. "I still could."

"It's too late now," he teased. "You're stuck with me forever."

"Can the two of you stop sucking face long enough to pass the rolls?" Papa Joe asked with a grunt, pointing to the bread basket in front of them.

"Joe McLendon!" Gran reached across Papa Jake and poked Papa Joe's arm. "Can we get through one dinner in my lifetime without me having to scold you?"

"I don't know. Can we?" Joe shot Gran a sideways glance, waiting for the basket of hot yeast rolls to make its way down to his end of the table.

The sounds of clanging forks and hums of appreciation dominated conversation as they all dug into Gran's cooking. Jonah hummed his own blissful appreciation when the taste of her buttery mashed potatoes exploded over his tongue, making every second of subjecting Chloe to his family's antics worth it.

"Where's Clay?" Connor asked after clearing a few bites from his plate.

"Who's that?" Breezy asked.

"The drone pilot," Dani said with a sour smirk.

"He's a lot more than a drone pilot," Grey added with the enthusiasm of one of Con and Car's fans. "His family owns one of the biggest ranches in the country."

"And their breeding program is the gold standard in the industry," Mason added. "I might take him up on his offer to fly down and check out their operation."

"You'd think he shits gold bricks," Dani muttered under her breath.

"What was that, Dani?" Car asked.

"Nothing," she quickly covered. "Apparently *Golden Boy* had to fly off to check on his other pet project somewhere in Idaho."

"Golden Boy?" Breezy asked.

"*Clay,*" Grey said pointedly to Dani, "has his hands in a lot of technologically advanced projects around the country. One of the wind farms he's setting up in Twin Falls had a problem after the storm, but he should be back tomorrow."

"Dani, I thought you'd be more interested in what he does." Breezy said, reaching for her glass of water. "You don't like him?"

Dani shrugged and picked at her salad.

"Oh my God!" Car snorted. "You do like him! Like…*like*-like him."

"That was mature," Con mumbled.

"What? No!" Dani protested, her face scrunching up like someone had stuffed her mouth with cow manure. "He's…I don't *like* him!"

Jonah held his tongue as he watched his sister's cheeks turn bright pink, but he couldn't hold back his laugh when Breezy elbowed Car in the side hard enough to make him spit and choke on his food.

"Stop trying to embarrass your sister." Grey pointed his fork at Car.

"What?" Car asked with feigned innocence. "She's totally into him!"

"I am not!"

"He's twenty years older than her," Grey said dismissively.

"He's the same age as Con and Car!" Dani argued.

"Exactly," Grey agreed. "She wouldn't be the least bit interested—"

"Speaking of storms," Gabby interrupted their astronomically dysfunctional conversation. "The news is calling for some kind of super vortex system to move in next week. It's supposed to be worse than the last one."

A melody of collective moans circled the table and the subject was officially changed.

Round one goes to Mom!

"I'm moving to Florida," Papa Nate grumbled.

"I second that motion," Papa Joe and Papa Jake said in unison.

"None of you are going anywhere without me," Gran warned. "And I'm never leaving Falcon Ridge."

"I don't know about Florida, but..." Uncle Cade pushed his chair back from the table and rose to his feet. "Your Papa Daniel and I are going on a little road trip."

The room fell silent for all of five seconds.

"What? When?" Dani, Papa Joe and Breezy asked in unison.

Uncle Cade raised his hands, urging them all to quiet down.

"We're leaving next week," Papa Daniel said.

"So soon?" Gabby asked, her worried gaze darted between Uncle Cade and Papa Daniel. "Cade just had surgery."

Uncle Cade nodded. "I'm already feeling better than I have in months," he said. "I have my last follow-up on Wednesday, and if all goes well we'll head out right after."

"Are you sure that's wise?" Gran asked. "To be so far away from your doctors? What if you have complications, or another infection?"

"We all know I only have so much time left," Cade argued, visibly shaken by their protests. He pulled at his shirt collar, fidgeting with the top button. "The doctors said I'd get better for a while before...before things get bad again, and I'm feeling fine now. We want to take some time for ourselves while we still can."

"Where are you goin'?" Matt asked, effectively ending the protests.

Uncle Cade looked down at Daniel, smiling when he nodded for Cade to continue. "Well, that's sort of what we wanted to talk to you all about," he said, then looked at Daniel again.

Papa Daniel stared at him for a moment before he, too, pushed back his chair and stood shoulder to shoulder with Cade, an anxious look in his eyes.

Jonah's mouth went dry. What was happening? *God, please don't let it be more bad news.* Uncle Cade had just said he was fine. How bad could it be if they were leaving Falcon Ridge?

Papa Daniel cleared his throat, and then took a sip of water, his hand trembling ever so slightly as he set the glass back on the table, his gaze focused on his and Cade's joined hands when he spoke.

"Cade asked me to marry him, and I said yes," he finally said. A fierce red hue colored Papa Daniel's neck and cheeks, rushing all the way to the tips of his ears. As fidgety as Uncle Cade, he picked up his napkin and wiped the sweat from his brow.

"We're going down to the courthouse after my doctor's appointment," Cade continued, "then take a few weeks on the road for our honeymoon, maybe run down to Colorado."

"And Utah," Daniel interjected nervously. "Thalia's going to meet us in Utah for a few days." Jonah's brows rose in surprise. It had been a while since Daniel's daughter had come to the States for a visit. "She…uh…she was going to come here for a visit next week, but with calving season, and us leaving and all…"

"You're getting married?" Gabby asked, her voice filled with cautious excitement.

Daniel nodded sheepishly.

The room exploded with excited shouts and whistles. The remnants of the meal forgotten, everyone sprang from their chairs and rushed around the table, tackling them both with congratulatory hugs. Gabby and Dani were crying. Breezy and Gran were crying. Hell, even Chloe was crying as she was pulled into Papa Daniel's arms.

"Come here," Papa Daniel said as he grabbed Jonah's forearm, drawing him into his embrace with Chloe. "I want you to be my best man," he said. "Will you stand with me?"

"Of course!" Jonah hugged his grandfather, unable to contain his smile.

"You will not be getting married at the courthouse." Gabby's decree floated above the congratulations and laughter. "I won't have it."

"You're in trouble now," Grey said with a chuckle.

"I think we're all in trouble," Mason grumbled. "You know how she gets with weddings."

"We'd better gas up the trucks," Matt added. "I feel an emergency run to Billings coming up. Maybe two if this storm gives us time."

"I'll call the photographer we used for our wedding," Breezy suggested. "He's fantastic and usually booked out for a year, but I might be able to call in a favor."

"Pryce can take the photos," Jonah insisted. "He's brilliant with a camera."

"Car and I can handle the music," Connor added.

A loud whistle split the air and everyone turned to look at Uncle Cade. "Simmer down," he commanded. "We don't want to make a big to-do out of it. In fact, the smaller the better." He turned to look at Papa

Daniel, a knowing twinkle in his aging eyes. "I'll be lucky to get him in a room with a judge as it is."

"A judge will do just fine." Daniel released Jonah and Chloe and turned to Gabby. "There's no time for frills and hoopla, honey. We're still in the middle of calving, and if there's a storm coming you'll need all hands on deck to prepare. All I want is to say 'I do' and get him on the road."

"How romantic," Uncle Cade said with a feigned smirk.

"Nonsense," Gabby argued. "Let us do this for you. It won't be anything extravagant, of course, not with only a few days to plan, but—"

"I'll help," Breezy said.

"Me too," Dani added, sliding into the family circle around the happy couple to wrap her arms around Daniel. "Papa, let us do this for you." She drew Uncle Cade closer. "We promise to keep it small."

"My aunt and I can make the cake," Chloe offered. The entire family turned to look at her and she wilted against Jonah's side. "I mean, if that's okay," she added.

"Of course that's okay, honey." Papa Daniel cupped her cheek, a tender gesture Jonah appreciated, knowing it meant that she'd already been accepted into his crazy family.

When Daniel let her go, Jonah wrapped his arm around her waist and drew her against his side, unable to resist the urge to kiss the top of her head and inhale her sweet scent. She was a part of him now, a forever part that made his heart both swell with pride and ache with emptiness. *One down, one to go.*

Solidifying Chloe's place in his life and his family's acceptance made Pryce's absence all the more noticeable. He'd told Pryce he'd give him time to decide, but he couldn't shake the feeling that doing so had been a mistake. An overwhelming urgency rushed through his body. He needed Pryce as much as he needed Chloe, and he needed to make sure Pryce knew that, before his mother planted the seed of doubt so deep he'd never be able to uproot it.

"What about the storm, and the calves?" Daniel's last protest pulled him from his worried thoughts.

"We've got it covered," Grey insisted.

"We'll have everything ready in plenty of time for you to leave before the storm," Gabby assured them with hope and determination in her eyes as the entire family waited with bated breath for Papa Daniel and Uncle Cade's consent.

"I guess we're having a wedding," Daniel finally said with a nervous chuckle.

"Yes!" Gabby popped onto her tiptoes and kissed Papa Daniel's cheeks, then Cade's. "Oh my gosh! I have to make a list!" Dinner forgotten altogether, she grabbed Chloe and Breezy's hands and dragged them off to begin their planning, Gran following in their wake.

"Jonah," Papa Daniel called him back when he attempted to follow them. "We wanted to ask you for another favor."

"Anything," he said with a nod, forcing himself to focus on their request instead of on grabbing Chloe, getting the heck out of there and calling Pryce.

"We'd appreciate it if you could stay at our house while we're away. You know, with another storm coming and all. Make sure the pipes don't freeze. Maybe keep a fire burning in the hearth?"

Jonah furrowed his brows. He'd be glad to keep an eye on the place, but stay there?

Uncle Cade elbowed Daniel and gave him a knowing wink. "Don't be dense, kid. We're well aware of what's going on. Pryce and Chloe are welcome to stay with you. I'm sure it can be a little crowded here, if you get my drift?"

Oh. Heat rose in his cheeks. "Um, thanks, but—"

"No buts," Uncle Cade insisted. "If it makes you feel better to think you're just helping us out, fine. Invite them or don't, but in case you do, I'll leave a case of condoms in the bathroom and some beer in the fridge."

Holy Christ. Jonah choked. *This is not happening.*

Jonah flinched when Cade thumped his chest. "Just stay out of our bed and the place is yours for a few weeks."

"No way." Jonah backed away, shaking his head. He knew better. "You've probably got the whole place wired with cameras."

"Only in our bedroom."

Jonah choked at Cade's suggestive wink.

"There's no cameras in our bedroom or anywhere else in the house," Daniel said with a sideways glance at Cade. "Is there?"

"Of course not." Uncle Cade rolled his eyes and then turned back to Jonah. "Daniel will get you the spare set of keys. Take them," he urged.

"Um…" He cupped the back of his neck, glancing between them. Weird or not, it would be nice to have some privacy for a few weeks to figure things out. "Fine. Yeah. Okay," he finally agreed before they offered up their stash of gay porn, too. "No frozen pipes on my watch."

"Good," Daniel nodded. "Now, the two of you go on. Get out of here and go check on Pryce. Be sure to convey our condolences."

"Yes, sirs." Jonah gave them a mock salute and started off for wherever his mother was holding Chloe hostage.

Chapter Nineteen

"Did you find them?" Chloe hurried down the crowded aisle at the craft store, the basket in her hands full of wedding supplies Breezy and Gabby had requested. It was their third and final stop, and if they didn't find what they were looking for, they'd have to come up with a plan B for the wedding cake.

"I have Captain America, but can't find The Shadow," Aunt Bev said, picking through the rows of miniature plastic superhero figures. She nodded at the section to her right. "I haven't checked those yet."

Chloe began at the top of the section and worked her way toward the end. She'd thought it was a joke when Jonah had sent her a picture he'd found online of a superhero wedding cake, showing two superheroes for the cake topper instead of the traditional bride and groom, but now that she knew what big comic book fans Daniel and Cade were, it was perfect! Now all they had to do was find The Shadow for Cade and they'd have everything they needed.

"Got it!" Aunt Bev snatched the figurine from the rack and danced an awkward happy dance, holding it up like a winning Bingo card. "It's going to be perfect!"

"Great!" Chloe took it and tossed it in the basket. "Let's get out of here."

"Chloe, stop worrying. Pryce will call you when he can."

On the way to the check out, she pulled her phone from her purse and checked for a message from Pryce, but there was only a text from

Breezy saying she'd closed the center early, asking if Chloe could meet her and Gabby at the coffee shop when they were finished. She texted back 'on my way' and dropped her phone into her purse.

Three days had passed since Mrs. Grunion had caught her and Jonah in bed with Pryce and thrown them out. He'd called twice, well, technically only once, to tell them the funeral was tomorrow, and a text to say he couldn't talk after her last phone call had gone unanswered. Jonah was getting the same cold shoulder.

"That will be sixty-seven dollars and three cents," the clerk said.

"I have the three pennies." Aunt Bev dug into her purse while Chloe retrieved the money Breezy had given her for the supplies.

"Drive over there and see him," her aunt suggested again as they walked to the car. "If Mrs. Grunion calls the Sheriff, you know I'll bail you out. But honestly, Chloe, I don't think she would. I hear she's taking Dirk's death pretty hard and won't even get out of bed."

Chloe bit her lip to keep from grimacing. Her aunt was getting more information through the town's gossip vine than she'd heard from Pryce. "He's asked me to stay away," she said, staring out the car window as they pulled out of the parking lot and headed back to Grassland. "I don't know what to do." She felt like she was losing him.

One night.

For a few wonderful hours everything had been perfect, and now it felt like it was all slipping through her fingers. After his family's dinner, Jonah had taken her back to the bakery. Alone in her small room, the air had grown heavy with lust and need. She'd wanted more than anything to make love with him, but couldn't. Not without Pryce.

Jonah hadn't pressured her, seemingly satisfied with just holding her in his arms for a while, but when he'd left, she felt like she'd disappointed him, too. He'd called her yesterday, but said he was taking the night shift in the calving barn and couldn't come over. Maybe he was telling the truth. She knew calving season to be a busy time for any ranch, but when he didn't answer her last text, she couldn't shake the feeling he was avoiding her now, too. She couldn't win. Losing either one of them would hurt the same as losing them both.

"Chloe?" Aunt Bev squeezed her knee. "Have you heard anything I've said?"

Chloe shook her head. "Sorry, I zoned out."

"Honey, it's only been a few days. If you've bared your heart to them and they know how you feel, that's all you can do."

"I know." Chloe nodded and looked back out the window.

"If they love you, they'll figure it out, but this is bigger than just you. You have to give them time to accept each other."

Chloe closed her eyes and concentrated on the rhythm of the shadows cast by the bright light of the setting sun as they drove along the country road. She appreciated her aunt's advice. She'd been astoundingly supportive considering their unorthodox choices, but she hadn't seen the look in Pryce's eyes when his mother told him his dad had died. She hadn't heard the regret in his voice when he'd finally called her. His mother was breaking him down again, manipulating him. Pryce had begun to stand up to her, but who knew what the desperate woman was capable of now?

She had to find a way to get to him before it was too late and he crawled back into the closet and slammed the door on them both.

By the time she helped Aunt Bev unload all the supplies at the bakery and walked down to the café, Breezy and Gabby were already waiting in a corner booth.

"Hi." Chloe greeted them as she pulled off her gloves. The second glove was tight and when she pulled harder, it popped off her hand and flipped over the table, landing in Gabby's coffee cup with a splash. Gabby flinched back in her seat, but the damage was done, her white blouse dotted with dark splotches.

"Oh my gosh! I'm so sorry!" Chloe snatched up the unused silverware packets on the empty table beside them, frantically unwrapping the napkins to mop up the mess, dropping one of the forks into Gabby's glass of water. Gabby caught the glass before it tipped over, but the water had sloshed out onto the notepad Gabby had been writing in, blurring the ink.

Chloe groaned, but Gabby took her hands, stilling her clumsy efforts to help. "It's okay," she said with a warm smile.

"I'll grab some extra napkins from the bar," Breezy said and jumped from her seat.

Gabby took the napkins from Chloe's hands and plucked her glove from her coffee cup, wringing out as much of the liquid as she could before wrapping it in a napkin. "Sit," she insisted with a lighthearted chuckle.

"I'm really sorry about your shirt." Chloe sank down into the chair, humiliated.

"My shirt will survive, but I'm not too sure about your glove." Gabby patted the coffee from the worn, cracked leather and handed it back to Chloe. "Maybe if you rinsed it out and held it under the dryer in the bathroom, but then the leather will probably shrink."

Chloe took the glove and stuffed it into her coat pocket. "I need a new pair anyway. I've already done that a time or two," she said with regret. "That's why it stuck on my hand."

"Sorry, they had to fetch a new pack of napkins from the back," Breezy said, handing the extra napkins to Gabby. Chloe flinched when Breezy gripped her shoulders in an awkward hug before retaking her seat beside Gabby.

"Let me get those." The waitress appeared and gathered up the sopping napkins and cold cups of coffee. "I'll bring a fresh pot and some extra cups. Be right back."

"Thank you, Lori. Take your time." Gabby told the waitress as she handed her one last napkin.

"Are you all right?" Breezy asked Chloe when the waitress was gone.

"I'm fine," she said with a sigh, glancing over at Gabby, who was dabbing the specks of coffee from her shirt. "A little nervous, I guess."

"Don't be nervous," Gabby insisted with a dismissive wave. "We're practically family."

Chloe choked on her nervous snort.

Breezy laughed and lifted her glass of water to her smiling lips, giving Chloe a wink over the brim. "It's overwhelming, isn't it?" she asked after a sip. "I felt the same way when I first came back to Falcon Ridge."

"Felt what way?" Gabby looked up from her shirt and caught Breezy's meaning, turning her surprised gaze to Chloe. "Oh, honey. I'm sorry. I didn't mean to be presumptuous, it's just that I see the way Jonah looks at you."

Chloe shrank back in her chair, her face aflame with embarrassment. If that was true, she was officially oh-for-two when it came to impressing her possible future mother-in-laws.

"And *I've* seen the way Pryce looks at you," Breezy said with a cat-like grin. "The McLendon men aren't the only ones with disarming charm.

"It's not the way they look at *me* that I'm worried about." Chloe slapped her hand over her mouth. *Dammit!*

"What do you mean?" Breezy asked, her brows furrowed in confusion.

"Never mind." Chloe shook her head. "I shouldn't have said that."

"But I thought you were okay with…" Breezy stopped, holding up her hand. "I'm sorry. It's none of my business."

"No! I'm fine with them," Chloe rushed to explain before they got the wrong idea. "I want them to be…together. God, sorry." She pressed her fingers to her forehead, embarrassed she would let such a thing slip out. "I shouldn't be talking about this with Jonah's mom and sister-in-law." She gathered her purse to leave, but Gabby reached across the table to stop her.

Gabby leaned in and whispered across the table. "We both understand the complexity of what you're going through, honey, more than most women could. We'll be glad to listen if you need to talk. We don't discuss details, mind you, but don't think for a second that anything you say would embarrass either of us, or that it would go any further than this table."

Chloe picked at the edge of the laminated table top, unable to look them in the eyes. They obviously knew more about being in love with two men than she did, but it was still awkward. "I'm afraid I'm losing them," she said, her fear outweighing her embarrassment.

"What do you mean?"

Chloe told them about what happened with Pryce's mom, including what she'd done to the preacher and his wife.

"You didn't!" Gabby gasped, slapping her hand over her gaping mouth, but a giggle slipped through.

"I did," Chloe groaned. "I don't know what came over me."

"I do." Breezy grinned. "Trust me, we women are capable of all kinds of crazy things when it comes to defending the men we love."

"And that includes Mrs. Grunion, I'm afraid," Gabby added with a regretful frown. "I know that she hurt you, Chloe, but however misguided it might have been, I'm sure Mrs. Grunion's overreaction was born of grief for her husband."

"I'm not so sure about that," Breezy said. "That woman is crazy."

"Pryce's mother is eccentric, yes, and staunchly religious, but I'm sure she's just grieving," Gabby argued. "Her husband was the one I worried about."

Chloe shook her head, still picking at the table edge. "You don't know her. The things she's done to Pryce…"

"Oh I've had my issues with her and Dirk," Breezy said. "You don't have to convince me that both can be equally cruel."

"But before all this happened Pryce was ready to leave. Now he won't even return my calls, or Jonah's, and I know it's because of his mom. And now Jonah's acting…different."

"How does Jonah feel about all of this?" Gabby asked. "You don't have to tell me, but have the two of you at least talked about it?"

Chloe glanced up at Gabby, but then looked away, the hopeless feeling inside her at odds with the hope she saw in Gabby's eyes. "Yes, we've talked. There don't seem to be any easy answers."

"Of course not." Gabby pushed from her chair and rounded the table, pulling Chloe into a hug. "Oh, honey. I know it all might seem a mess right now, but give it time."

"That's what my aunt said." Chloe swallowed her tears, refusing to give into them. She'd already cried more in the last week than she had her entire life.

"She's right, honey," Gabby said when she let her go and settled back into her seat. "Why don't you bring your Aunt to dinner tonight. It won't be as crazy as it was the last time you came over and we'll have a chance to get to know her better. And, maybe afterward, you and Jonah can take a walk over to see Pryce." She gave Chloe a knowing wink and Chloe blushed. "I know he asked you not to, but sometimes men need a little nudge to remember what's important."

"More like a shove off a cliff," Breezy said with a snort. "It's like they live in an alternate universe sometimes."

"Tell me about it," Gabby said with a sigh. "Grey is in such a state of denial about Dani. Sometimes I think he still sees her as a seven-year-old girl in pigtails. Did you know he keeps her old crayons in his desk drawer, like she's still going to come in and ask him to color with her one day?"

"I've got you beat," Breezy said with a shake of her head. She pulled out her cellphone and clicked on an app, then rolled her eyes as she held out the phone for Chloe and Gabby to see. "It's the baby cam they've already installed in the nursery. See the two-liter bottle in the corner of the room, over by the paint cans?" Gabby nodded. "That's the second soda today, and I guarantee I'll find both empty bottles buried in the bottom of the trash can when I get home."

"I thought soda was off limits," Gabby said.

"It is," Breezy grumbled.

"Ugh, I blame their dads." Gabby said with a chuckle. "But I can't wait to see the nursery! Grey's going to convert Con and Car's old room into one for her—or him," she added with a wink. "Oh I can't wait!"

"Don't get too excited yet. If they don't start following the diet the doctor suggested, I may never have a baby."

"Don't worry," Gabby insisted with a sly grin. "My boys come from good stock. You'll be shopping for furniture to fill that nursery soon enough."

"Yeah, well, I'm beginning to think it's never going to happen. You'd think with two husbands all I'd have to do was blink to be pregnant."

Gabby laughed and clasped both their hands. "Now I'm saying it to both of you. Give it time. Enjoy the journey. And after a while, if things are still in limbo, we'll bring in the big guns."

"The big guns?" Chloe asked.

"Jonah's grandmother, Hazel," Gabby said with a wink.

Breezy laughed out loud. "I'm not sure what she can do about me getting pregnant, but if anyone could whip the McLendon men in line, it's her."

"Chloe?"

At the sound of her name, Chloe turned around and found herself face to face with her brother, Travis. "Oh, God," she whispered. *Not now. Not in front of Breezy and Mrs. McLendon.* Although they worked in town, she hadn't spoken to either of her brothers since she moved in with her aunt, but by the look of Travis, and the stench of booze wafting in the air around him, he hadn't changed much.

"Hey, Sis," he said with a sinister lopsided grin. "Got a minute for your big brother?"

"No." The word was out of her mouth before she could stop it. "Leave me alone, Travis."

She shouldered her purse and tried to skirt around him, but Travis grabbed her arm. "I need to talk to you."

"Let go of her," Gabby ordered. "Or I'll call the Sherriff." Breezy grabbed Chloe's other hand and tried to pull her away from Travis, but his grip tightened and he jerked her closer.

"I'd heard a rumor that Jonah was back." He sneered at Breezy and Gabby. "Didn't take you long to go running from one shit packer to the other, though I guess it makes sense. Jonah's family does have more money."

"Shut up!" Chloe shoved at him, breaking free of his hold. "I know what you did to Jonah. You and Finn, and Wayne!"

"That fag had it coming."

"And an entire café just witnessed your confession." Gabby sneered.

Chloe looked around the small café, only then noticing the sudden silence, every gaze focused on the four of them.

Travis grabbed for her again, but Gabby gripped her shoulder and stepped in front of her, sending Chloe careening into Breezy, who helped her regain her balance. "How dare you attack my son!"

"Gabby, don't." Breezy tried to stop her, but Gabby twisted away.

"If you lay another hand on Jonah, Chloe, or any other member of my family," Gabby snarled at Travis, "my husbands and I will—"

"Get the hell out of here, Travis." Tom Delany, the café owner, shouted a curse as he rounded the counter and stomped toward them. Travis struggled against Tom's hold when Tom shoved him toward the front door. "I told you not to come in here again."

"I just need some money!" he shouted over Tom's shoulder, grabbing at the door frame to keep from being pushed outside. Chloe watched in horror as desperation overran the anger in Travis's eyes. "Twenty bucks! That's it! And I'll never bother you again!"

"You need help!" Tom shoved him through the doorway, then closed and locked the door. "Lori, call the Sherriff," he ordered. "Did he hurt you?" he asked Gabby, his gaze darting between the three of them. "I came in as soon as I saw him on the security monitor."

"No, we're fine," Gabby assured him, turning to gather her and Breezy beside her.

"Security monitor?" Breezy asked.

Tom pointed at the camera above the front door. "Had them installed after the break-in last month."

"Is he on drugs?" Chloe asked, watching her brother's agitated strides up and down the sidewalk in front of the cafe. He stopped when he caught her gaze through the window, and then took off running down the sidewalk.

"He's on something." Tom ran his fingers through his salt and pepper hair. "It's over folks," he said to the other patrons. "He won't be back."

"That's what you said last time," a woman grumbled as she rose and gathered her things.

"He's done this before?" Chloe knew her brothers were trouble, but in the months since she'd been back, she hadn't heard of them doing anything like this.

"Sherriff's on his way," the waitress called out from behind the counter.

"Thanks, Lori." Tom faced the three women, his fists propped on his hips. "Once, I think," he said. "I'm pretty sure he's the one who broke in, tried to steal the register and cleaned out the spare change from the tip jar."

"Broke in? Travis was always a bully, but never a thief."

"It's the drugs," Tom said with a regretful shake of his head. "I tried to help him a while back, but it didn't take."

"Looks like he's getting desperate," Breezy said.

"My God." Chloe braced against the back of a nearby chair. "Is he so addicted that he's spending his entire paycheck on drugs? Now he's robbing stores?"

"Art Gully let him go right before the break in," Tom said. "Held back his check to pay for a job he'd screwed up. That's when the break-ins started."

"There's been more than one?"

"At the new laundromat," Tom confirmed. "Two days after they hit the café. And someone tried to pry open a few newspaper stands last week, but last I heard no one knew who. The Sherriff's been working with the Reservation police, keeping an eye on Travis and his friends in the meantime."

"Obviously not a close enough eye," Gabby argued.

"I have to warn Aunt Bev."

"We'll go with you," Gabby insisted.

Chapter Twenty

Pryce stared at his reflection in the floor-length mirror, barely recognizing himself in the black wool suit. He'd grown a few inches since he'd worn it last. A year ago, maybe two? He didn't remember, only that it had been a while since he'd set foot inside his family's church—the only reason he owned a suit at all.

He turned in front of the mirror to check the length of the slacks in the back. His mother had let out the hems, but the coat was tight in the shoulders, and the tie was choking the life out of him.

"Dammit!" He clawed at the knot in the tie until it released its grip on his neck, yanked it over his head and flung it across the room. What did it matter if he wore a tie to his father's funeral? He was going to burst into flames the second he walked through the church doors anyway.

God help him, he was so confused. For days his mother had been a constant voice inside his head, reminding him of the eternal consequences of what he'd done with Jonah and Chloe. He thought he no longer cared about all the religious stuff he'd grown up believing. Mostly he didn't, he guessed, but the constant barrage of religious doctrine was sucking the life out of him.

She'd tortured him with tears and sermons of guilt-laden verses and prayers he no longer prayed. She'd confined herself to her bed, acting as though she no longer had the will to live, crying until she made herself sick. When that didn't work, she'd thrown temper tantrums and had breakdowns, throwing everything he owned out into the snow, then begged him to stay when he threatened to leave it, and her, behind. In the middle of it all, he could feel her pleas breaking down the wall he'd built between them, changing him, filling him with doubt and fear.

He was sick of it! He wasn't afraid of going to hell, probably already was, but the idea of walking into that church terrified him. He knew it shouldn't. He shouldn't give a damn about those people, but he couldn't shake the sticky shame he'd felt since the day his mother walked in on him with Chloe and Jonah.

The second he walked through the church doors they'd know what he'd done. Even if they didn't know, if he continued with Jonah and Chloe they would find out, and his mother would be cast out of the church. With his dad gone, she'd have nobody. Nobody but him.

What am I going to do?

He was screwed no matter what he did. He loved Chloe, he honestly did, with all his heart, but no matter how hard he tried, how deeply he buried his feelings for Jonah in his love for her, he could no longer deny he loved Jonah, too.

He couldn't choose between them. Even if he tried, if he forced Chloe's hand, she would choose Jonah a thousand times over him and he'd lose them both anyway. He wouldn't have to worry about hell, because living without them would *be* hell. It was selfish, but he'd rather die and burn for eternity than feel that kind of emptiness again.

But he couldn't just abandon his mother. Whether out of guilt or instinct, he loved her, difficult as it might be. He'd been ready to leave before his father died, but now…

It was so much easier to hate her.

The drama of it all had nearly driven him insane, until he woke earlier that morning to the smell of sausage and hotcakes. He'd thought he was dreaming when he'd reached the bottom of the stairs to see his mother in the kitchen, dressed in her usual prim style with her hair neatly braided and pinned in an elegant bun, smiling as she flipped a hotcake in the pan.

He'd finished half a plateful before he'd worked up the nerve to ask her what had brought on the sudden change. She'd said Pastor had called that morning and God had answered her prayers. He hadn't bothered to ask what was said to bring on the one-eighty turn of her mood, and said a silent prayer of his own that whatever it was lasted long enough to get through the funeral.

"Pryce, have you seen my onyx broach? Oh, don't you look handsome." His mother hurried across the bedroom, her long black skirt swishing against her ankles. She inspected the fit of his suit, smoothed out the wrinkles in the back and turned him around to face the mirror. "I do wish your father could see you," she said with a sad smile that curved into a frown when her gaze met his in the mirror. "Where's your tie?"

"I'm not wearing a tie," he said, jerking away from his mother's grasp.

"Not wearing a tie? But you must! It's church."

"It's father's funeral," Pryce insisted. "Not a regular service."

"It's the respectful thing to wear," his mother said with a warning glare. "Not to mention the rules of the church, or have you forgotten?"

"Mother, I love you, but I'm not—"

"Probably so, considering how long it's been since you've attended a service." She prattled on as if he hadn't spoken a word, walking over to the dresser to retrieve another tie. "Hopefully that will change today."

"Nothing will change," he insisted, taking the tie from her hands before she could string him up in another noose. "I'm not coming back to the church." He didn't know what he was going to do, but rejoining the church wasn't an option.

His mother stilled. He braced himself for her wrath, but it never came. Her narrowed eyes softened, her pursed lips turning up into a cunning grin. "I will not argue with you about this. Not today."

"Then don't," Pryce said with a tired sigh. His mother's strange mood kept him on edge, jumping from second to second wondering when she would start throwing things again, but he wasn't giving in. "I'm going to pay my last respects to my father. That's all." It was more than his father deserved, but his mother needed him. He refused to be a cruel bastard just because his father had been.

His mother looped the tie around his neck and Pryce yanked it off again.

"Enough of this rebellion!" she scolded him through a forced smile. "I will burn in hell before I let you continue down this path. Is that what you want? Your own mother condemned to a fiery grave for all eternity?"

His will to argue exhausted, Pryce closed his eyes and released his last hopeless breath. He draped the tie around his collar and stood like an inanimate statue as his mother tied the perfect knot. "There," she said and turned him back to face the mirror. "A proper young man at last."

Numb, Pryce looked back at his reflection, studied the solid grey tie. Was that all it took? A simple piece of silk tied around his neck to cover all his sins?

Memories from the night he'd spent with Jonah and Chloe flickered to life in his mind, so vivid they clouded his vision and sent his blood racing to all the inappropriate parts of his body.

He could feel the warmth of their hands on him, their silken tongues gliding along his skin, their mouths rising and lowering over his cock. The sound of Chloe's passionate hums filled his ears as he remembered her taking him inside her, but this time Jonah was there, too, staring up at him, his eyes filled with the same lust and wonder as Chloe's, and all of it was for him. The things they'd done to him felt so good it couldn't possibly be right, and no tie in the world could erase what he'd done, or the fact he hadn't given his dying father a single thought while he was doing them.

"Meet me down stairs and we'll pray with the pastor before he takes us to the church," his mother said, and kissed his cheek. Yanked from his memory, he suppressed the urge to slam the door behind her after she left, flinching when his phone buzzed in his pocket. Hesitant, he pulled it out and swiped to see the message.

Chloe: Thinking about you. Hope you're okay.

He smiled at the little heart she always sent, then pocketed his phone and sank down onto the edge of the bed. She and Jonah had called and texted him dozens of times since the day his father died. He'd avoided their calls at first simply because he couldn't deal with them and his mother's antics at the same time, not to mention risking her ire, but now…

He knew they would ask to see him again. When they'd knocked on the front door the night before it took everything he had not to walk out of the house and never look back, but before he could, his mother had slammed the door in their faces, cutting them off before he could explain.

Explain what, exactly? Why was he torturing himself? He loved them, but even if he was ready to be with Jonah—something he still wasn't sure he could do—he couldn't just walk away from his mother. She was being semi-tolerant this morning for some strange reason, but there would come a time when she would demand his capitulation or she'd disown him. If his father were still alive, he could almost live with that, but now she was alone.

His phone buzzed again.

Jonah: Chloe could come with you if you need someone.
Jonah: I could come too. Bring a bottle of whisky ;)
Jonah: Probably not a good idea, but... I'm here.

Jesus, would it ever end? Every text from them ripped him open, yet he couldn't bring himself to turn off his phone.

Jonah: At least respond to her, please.

He felt like such a douche. The last thing he wanted to do was hurt Chloe. He paced his room, typing out a quick reply to let her know he was okay and would call them after the funeral. When she didn't reply, he scrolled to her number to give her a quick call.

"Pryce! We're waiting!" Like a sharp dagger, his mother's voice cut through the closed door and lodged in his gut. He mumbled a frustrated curse and clicked off the phone, leaving it on his dresser. Something had to give, and right now he needed to focus on getting through the funeral.

After prayer, a solemn car ride into town, and more prayer, he ushered his mother into the church. Other than being a little warm due to the heated air inside, he felt okay. No flames erupted from his suit. No lightning bolts flashed. No choking sulfuric smoke swirled in the air. *So far so good.*

There was no casket, though his mother hadn't opted for cremation. Their religion didn't believe in viewing the deceased. Their soul had moved on, their body of no consequence.

A solitary picture was perched on a tripod in front of the pulpit, surrounded by lavish flower arrangements of varying vivid shades. The image was one he knew well, reflecting a younger version of his father, his eyes not as cold and judgmental as Pryce remembered them. Still, he looked away as he got closer. Even in death he couldn't look his father in the eye, partly out of shame, some guilt, but mostly out of deeply ingrained habit.

When they reached the front row, he was ushered to a solitary pew to sit alone instead of beside his mother, but he didn't protest. Nor did he care, to his surprise. All the time he'd spent worrying about their judgment of him had been a waste. Few, if any members looked at him with contempt or disdain. Some of the deacons even came over to shake his hand in polite greeting.

The true battle, as it turned out, was sitting in a room with those same people as they droned on about his father. The service began with yet another prayer, and then one member after another stood at the head of the church and retold their memories of a stranger named Dirk Grunion. More than once he'd wondered if they were at the right funeral.

His confusion turned to anger as the hour ticked by. He wanted to rush to the pulpit and shout out the truth. He understood the respectful custom, but the stories they told were outright lies! How could so many people be so blind? Dirk hadn't been a loving father! He hadn't been a just or honest businessman. Every ranch hand in the state had been burned in one way or another by his father's brand of 'honesty'. And a loyal husband? What a joke! He understood his mother's denial, but everyone in the room knew of his many affairs.

Blood filled his mouth. He unclenched his teeth, focusing on the pain in his cheek instead of the ache in his chest, waiting for the last word to be spoken so he could get the hell out of there.

"Pryce Grunion."

He jerked his gaze from the floor to the pastor standing at the pulpit.

"Your mother has informed us of your intention to re-declare your faith today," the pastor continued.

What? Shock pushed him to his feet. He looked at his mother sitting on the front pew, surrounded by the pastor's wife and deacons.

She smiled at him, her eyes filled with hope, tears streaming down her cheeks.

"Come," the pastor beckoned him to the podium. "Your decision will surely bring everlasting peace to your father."

His head spun. The room shrank. His skin prickled as sweat laced his back and neck. It all made sense now. His mother's sudden change, the deacons, everything.

His mother stood. "Pryce, the pastor is waiting."

"No."

"Pryce, please."

Pryce clawed at his tie, choking on his mother's betrayal.

"You have to, if not for me, then for your father!" She gripped his wrist and pulled him toward the altar.

"I said no!" He yanked his arm free from her hold, glancing up at the pastor, then back at the congregation who sat on their pews, their eyes now full of righteous condemnation. How could he ever have cared what these people thought of him? "I will never forgive you for this," he snarled before storming out of the church to the sound of his mother's sobs.

He walked.

As fast as his legs could carry him, he walked through the snow to the road and then followed it aimlessly. His feet and hands were numb, but he walked. The exposed skin on his face burned from the cold. Having left his coat behind, his body shivered and ached, but he kept walking. He didn't know where he was going, or how far he'd gotten when a truck slowed alongside him.

He turned and looked through the open passenger window and saw a familiar face. "Breezy?"

~*~

Content to let the sounds of the road fill the silence between them, Breezy focused on the drive home, sparing an occasional glance in Pryce's direction when she could.

Even before Chloe had finished sharing her fears for him yesterday at the cafe, she'd decided to have a talk with Pryce. It was time to tell him the truth, but now she was second guessing that decision. Having grown up beneath Dirk Grunion's ominous shadow, she understood the distant look in his eyes all too well. He was on the edge, and the last thing she wanted to do was push him too far. Her mind raced with thoughts of what could have happened to him to make him leave in such a way, though she'd suspected he wouldn't escape the funeral unscathed.

The Grunion house was empty when she parked in front. No tire marks scarred the fresh snow that had fallen on the circle driveway since she'd followed Pryce to the church. She didn't imagine it would be long before someone showed up looking for him.

"Thanks for the ride."

"Wait." She reached across the center console to stop him from leaving. "What happened?"

Slumped in the seat, Pryce stared out the windshield. "My mother happened."

"What did she do this time?"

"She did what she's always done," he said with a regretful sigh. "I don't know why I expected anything different today."

"Pryce, talk to me," she pleaded when he didn't elaborate. "I know you were probably too young to remember, and our families were never close, but I grew up here, too. Your mother is my aunt, and I know what she's capable of."

A shower of snow flurries melted against the heated windshield as she waited for him to speak. She was about to let him go when he finally opened up.

"I remember you and your brother helping in the barn during the summers," he said. "My father didn't like it. He and my mother used to argue about it a lot."

She imagined they did, knowing what she knew now. Dirk Grunion wouldn't want to be reminded of his sins.

"I know you're here to talk me into seeing Jonah and Chloe," he continued. "Between trying to keep what cattle we have left alive and dealing with her, I don't have time for anything else right now. Please tell them I'll call as soon as I can."

"Pryce, stop. I'm not here to talk about Jonah and Chloe," Breezy said in a rush before she lost the opportunity and her nerve. Pryce stilled, his hand on the door handle, waiting for her to continue. She swallowed against the butterflies working their way up her throat. Having thought about this moment for so long, rehearsing every word, and now that she had the chance to say them her mind was completely blank.

"What is it?" Pryce asked. "Is something wrong with Chloe or Jonah?"

"No." Breezy shook her head. "Other than Chloe's encounter with Travis yesterday, and worrying about you, they're fine."

"Travis? What the hell has he done?"

"She's fine," Breezy insisted. "Jonah's spitting mad, along with his dads, but that's not what I came to say."

"Then what? What is it?"

Breezy took a deep breath and tried to remember the words she'd practiced. Few came to her, so she decided to wing it the best she could. "You said you remembered your parents arguing about me and my brother helping on the ranch."

"Yes."

"The reason… Uh, this is so hard."

"Just say it."

"Fine." She took a deep breath and let it all out at once. "Your dad had an affair with my mother before she died, and I think he was my biological father, too."

"What?"

"It's true. I remember Dirk with my mom. I was only a few years old, but I remember. I think he was in love with her."

"But…she was my mother's sister."

"Exactly," Breezy confirmed. "I don't know for sure, but I suspect your mother knew about it. That's why she hated us being there. We were a constant reminder of his infidelity."

Pryce stared unseeing at the dashboard before he turned and looked at her with shock in his eyes. "You think… my father was also your father?"

"I know my brother was his," Breezy confirmed. "Dirk and my dad all but admitted it before my brother died. When I think back to what I remember of your dad, what he and my mom were like together… Pryce, my dad was a drunk. He and my mom, they weren't intimate. Not only was it probably physically impossible, but I know what I saw. Dirk loved my mom, for a long time. I can't help but believe he was my biological father, too."

"I can't believe it." All of the tension left Pryce's shoulders and he collapsed back against the seat. "I knew he had affairs. Everyone knew, but my mother's sister?"

"I'm not telling you this to upset you, or God knows put more of a burden on you than you already have," Breezy rushed to explain. "I'm telling you this because you deserve to know the truth. You're not alone, Pryce. Even if it's not true, I'll always be here and I want to help you."

Chapter Twenty-One

"Staring out the window won't change anything." Jonah sidled up behind Chloe and kissed the top of her head. She turned and burrowed into his embrace, her warmth seeping into his bones as he looked through the glass down his parents' driveway. He couldn't help but hope he was wrong.

"But Breezy said their talk helped him."

He hugged her closer, trying to ignore the sexual need that still coursed through him like wildfire. This waiting for Pryce thing was driving him crazy. "She also said he wouldn't promise anything."

Chloe turned in his arms again and they both watched for any sign of Pryce. "I hate that woman."

After what Breezy had told them, so did he. Christ, what a mess. When he'd made up his mind to do whatever it took to make Chloe and Pryce his, he'd never dreamed Pryce's mother would be his biggest challenge. How was he supposed to fight this?

"If he doesn't make it, we'll all take pictures of the wedding with our phones," he said. "I'm sure we'll get some good ones."

"You know I'm not worried about the pictures." She pulled free of his grasp, but he pulled her back.

"It will all work out. I promise. We'll think of something." How he would make it work was a mystery, but he had to, and soon.

"I miss him," she said with a wishful whisper, reaching around to pull him closer.

"I miss him too, Lo." The scent of her perfume trapped him and tested his resolve to keep his hands off her. He kissed her, this time just below her earlobe, extracting a whimpered sigh. "I'd barely gotten a chance to love either of you before all this happened."

"Chloe, have you seen the—oh. Sorry."

"It's okay, Aunt Bev. What do you need?"

Jonah suppressed his urge to protest the interruption. He'd gotten so little time alone with her since the wedding preparations began.

"I was looking for the extra icing you said you'd put in the refrigerator. I have a few touch-ups to do to the layers and I can't seem to find it."

Chloe popped up onto her tiptoes to give Jonah a quick peck, glancing out the window one last time before she followed her aunt into the kitchen. He watched her go, and then turned back to the window, not only hoping to see Pryce, but to also give his hard-on time to subside before his mom walked in and snapped the whip she'd been brandishing all morning.

Movement in the distance caught his attention. A spark of hope flickered through his veins a split second before disappointment doused the fire when Con and Car's truck rolled into view. He blew out a disappointed sigh. *Well, at least the extra table Mom requested made it in time.* He untucked his shirt, rolled up his sleeves and met his brothers on the front porch. Distraction was his best plan B, and there was an ample amount of it on the ranch today.

"That's the last one." An hour or so later Jonah handed off the last bolt of shimmery silver fabric to Mason. What in the world it had to do with Papa Daniel and Uncle Cade getting married he didn't know, but his mom had ordered a truckload of it.

Matt jumped into the truck and started it up. "I'm parking all the vehicles down by the barn to make room for that road hog they rented for their trip. Cory's driving it over so Grey and Mason can get it all decked out in time."

"Got it." Jonah fished out his keys to move his own truck when said road hog pulled up at the gate and honked, its loud air horns sounding more like a Mack truck than an RV.

"Practicing to be an engine driver for the station?" Jonah teased when Cory jumped out.

"Hell no," his brother snapped and tossed him the keys. "This beast is all yours."

"Hey, Cor," Jonah called after his brother. Cory stopped and turned back, a sour expression on his face. "You're right," Jonah said, shoving the RV keys into his pocket. "I've thought about all those things you said the other night. I have a lot to make up for, if I even can, but we were friends once. I hope we can be again one day, but can we call a truce in the meantime? At least for today?"

Cory's tense posture relaxed with his reluctant nod. He took a few steps back and offered Jonah his hand. "Truce."

Jonah shook his hand, and then nearly jumped out of his boots at the electrical shock that ran up his arm. "What the hell, bro?"

His brother doubled over laughing, holding out his hand to show the prank buzzer. "I found it in the cup holder in the RV. Must be one of Uncle Cade's remodeled inventions. Shocked the hell out of myself on the way over here."

"What in God's name would he need that for?" Jonah shouted with a muffled curse, shaking the sting from his hand.

Cory shrugged, still laughing as Jonah inspected the gadget. "Wanna go say a special *hello* to Con and Car?"

"Hell yeah!"

The rest of the afternoon passed in a blur. After tasering Con and Car, Gabby declared martial law and whipped everyone into her personal wedding army. The first floor of his parents' house had been cleared of all unnecessary furniture, most of which was stuffed into his room upstairs. The tables and chairs were set up, draped with linen and decorated with the silver fabric he'd helped unload. Gran and the Papas brought in a truckload of food which Dani, Chloe and Aunt Bev set up buffet style in the dining room, complete with a cheese fountain, whatever the hell *that* was. The altar was built. Con and Car set up the sound system and had their guitars tuned and ready.

Thirty minutes to go time and everyone was dressed and accounted for except Uncle Cade, Papa Daniel, the minister, and Pryce.

He's not coming. Having snuck away from the chaos, Jonah sat on the stoop outside the kitchen, his chin resting on his knees as he stared out across the barren fields. A small pillar of smoke billowed above the trees in the distance, above Pryce's house. Jonah closed his eyes and sucked in a breath, holding the cold air in his lungs until they burned.

What if I've lost him?

Breezy's news had given them hope, but now that it was clear Pryce wasn't coming, he was losing that hope. What would happen to him and Chloe without Pryce? Could they make it without him? At least now she knew the truth about him, but who would want to spend the rest of their life with someone knowing they would never be enough? Could he make her enough? Maybe. He was more than willing to try, but would it be enough for her?"

"There you are."

Jonah looked over his shoulder at Chloe and smiled. "Hey beautiful." Despite his sour mood, he'd never meant those words more. Her long hair was pinned up in a delicate halo on the top of her head, stray curly tendrils brushing her rosy cheeks. The deep purple in her dress made her skin glow like molten copper that made him want to see more of it.

She shivered against the cold and he thought to rush her back inside, but he wasn't ready to rejoin reality just then, and figured she needed a break too. Instead, he pulled off his leather coat. "Here, put this on."

"No, you'll freeze," she protested. "Let me go get mine."

"I'm fine," he insisted. "Come keep me warm." He lowered his feet to the next step and guided her down onto his lap with a wink. "Wouldn't want you to freeze that beautiful ass of yours on the cold concrete steps." Of course now that her ass was once again so close to his cock...

"What's wrong?"

Jonah gave her a sideways glance. As if she didn't't' know exactly what she was doing to him.

"Not that," she said with a playful swivel of her hips.

"Exactly that," Jonah growled, capturing her mouth in a long-overdue kiss. She parted her lips and their tongues met in what had become a familiar rhythm. She tasted like strawberries and vanilla icing, and his.

Chloe hummed her approval, but when they parted she threaded her fingers through his hair and made him look at her.

"I won't be distracted by your seductive kisses, J."

"No?" He grinned against her lips. "Let me try again." He kissed her again, not only in an attempt to distract her, but because he had to. He craved her like no other, not even Pryce.

"Still not working," she said with a grin when their lips parted next, although he counted the hitch in her breath a small victory. She ran her finger over the crease between his brows. "This isn't you. What's wrong? Why are you out here by yourself when your whole family is inside getting ready?"

"I told you my family was crazy."

"You're avoiding my question."

Jonah released his hold on her and snuggled her comfortably back in his arms. "Aside from Pryce, and wanting to murder your brother, you mean?"

"Travis is sick," she argued. "He needs help."

"I still want to hurt him for cornering you and my mom in the café like he did," he said with a sigh. "I think my dad might be right to try to prosecute him for the attack. Maybe if he's locked up he'll get the help he needs."

"Maybe," she nodded, "but that's not what's bothering you and you know it."

"Isn't that enough?" Jonah chuckled. When she didn't laugh with him, he knew the game was over. "Fine." He tipped his head back and released a defeated sigh. "I was thinking about what a mess I've made."

"I knew it!" Chloe squirmed in his arms, trying to stand, but he wouldn't let her.

"Don't worry," he rushed to assure her, refusing to let her go. "I'm not going anywhere, but I can't help but wonder if I made a mistake coming back."

Chloe shook her head in protest. "How could you say that? Don't ever say that."

Jonah looked out over the field again, wishing he had superhuman vision so he could see through the trees and know what Pryce was doing. "You were happy with him, Lo. If I hadn't come back, you'd still be engaged to Pryce and living out all the dreams the two of you had."

"It would have all been a lie," she said matter-of-factly. "And I'm still engaged to him. That hasn't changed."

"But what if it does?" he asked, forcing himself to share his primary fear. "Will I be enough for you? Will we be enough for each other?"

Chloe propped up in his lap and cupped his face in her hands. "Don't. Don't you dare go there, Jonah McLendon." She kissed his lips and then pulled back to look him in the eyes. "You said we'd figure something out and we will. Even if it takes a hundred years, we will not give up on him."

Jonah nodded and kissed her back one last time, but her obvious avoidance of his question dimmed the earlier spark between them.

"Aunt Bev and your mom are right," she continued, wrapping his coat tighter and snuggling back into his embrace. "If he needs time then we'll give it to him."

"They're here!" Breezy's shout carried through the closed door.

Chloe jumped from his lap and pulled him to his feet. He followed her inside and the ensuing chaos of Uncle Cade and Papa Daniel's arrival was enough to distract him from his depressing thoughts.

"What in God's name did you do to the RV?" Papa Daniel grumped, pulling off his overcoat. "Did you have to cover every window with hot pink shoe polish?"

"We left the windshield," Grey said with a devious grin and took his coat and gloves.

"I told them you'd be pissed." Papa Joe said. "Damn kids don't listen to nobody."

"If I'd listened to any of you, we'd all be crammed into a depressing office at the courthouse," Gabby argued as she breezed into the room and wrapped her arms around Daniel. "Relax. It's tradition."

"He's as cantankerous as a feral dog staring down a dog catcher," Uncle Cade warned. "You'd think he was doing a perp walk instead of getting married."

"You knew I would be," Papa Daniel argued. "How's my tie?" He asked Gabby. "My hands were shaking and I almost couldn't get it tied at all."

"It's fine," Gabby assured him and gave him a peck on the cheek.

"Are you set to stay at the house?" Papa Daniel asked and Jonah gave him an affirmative nod. "Good."

"Minister Farnes." Breezy hugged the middle-aged man in the white cloak who Jonah recognized from her and his older brothers' wedding. "I can't thank you enough for yesterday."

"Caleb, and it was my pleasure," the man insisted, hugging her back before he greeted Gabby and the dads. "Where should I set up?"

"Over here." Gabby directed him into the living room to the altar his dads had built.

"We'd better get started or you two won't make it out of here before the storm hits." Gran ushered Uncle Cade and Papa Daniel from the foyer.

"No one's leaving until I get some of that cake Chloe's aunt made," Papa Joe declared.

A shrieking sound like he'd never heard in his life sent alarm skittering down Jonah's spine.

"Good God!" Gran's hand flew to her heart. The entire family turned to see what had happened as Chloe flung open the front door and rushed outside.

"What set her dress on fire?" Papa Joe asked.

Jonah pushed through the foyer past his mom and papas, but pulled up short at the front door.

It couldn't be. Frozen as stiff as an ice statue, he stared out at the driveway, not ready to believe what he was seeing. Chloe hadn't finally come to her senses and run screaming for her life. She was running to Pryce, who was riding up the driveway, on a horse, in his black leather Stetson and sheepskin coat, looking sexier than Jonah remembered ever seeing him.

"Are you gonna stand there and suck wind like a dyin' goldfish?" Matt asked over his shoulder. "Or are you gonna go join your girl and welcome him home."

When all Jonah could do was swallow against the knot in his throat, Matt laughed and gave him a shove. Still stunned, he shuffled across the porch, down the steps and out into the snow.

"He's not wearing his coat," he heard his mom say behind him, but he didn't feel the least bit cold.

Pryce dismounted. Chloe squealed again as she jumped into his arms. Now that Jonah's feet were working, it seemed like he was stuck between gears, wanting to either run to Pryce, or stop completely and watch them together, but neither happened and he continued on one step at a time until he was standing in front of them.

"Am I too late?" Pryce asked.

Lost in his gaze, Jonah shook his head. "Nope." He fisted his hand in Pryce's shirt. In front of God, his mom and dads, his entire family, he yanked Pryce to him and claimed his mouth in a kiss he'd thought he would never feel again. He didn't care if he was going too fast, or if Pryce was ready or not. He was through with fighting forces he had no control over, done hiding, done sitting back and waiting for the stars to align. He was lucky enough to love two people, and he was staking his claim on them both, right here and now.

"Marry us," he said when their lips finally parted.

Chapter Twenty-Two

"What?" Pryce released Chloe and she slid to the ground between them, his heart hammering inside his chest.

"Let's get married," Jonah said again. "You, me, Chloe. Today. Right now."

"Today?" Chloe took a step back, glancing between the two of them.

"I…I can't—*we* can't get married. Not today!" Pryce swiped a hand over his forehead, almost knocking his hat off.

"Why not?" Jonah asked with so much excitement in his eyes Pryce could hardly stand to look at him. "The minister's here. We're here. You and Chloe have the marriage license, right?"

"Jonah, wait a minute," Chloe interrupted.

"Let's do it!" Jonah insisted. "You and Chloe will be legal. I'll be the stand in during the ceremony, but it will all be legit with the three of us. You can change your last names to mine or something. It's perfect."

Pryce tried to breathe, but very little air seemed to make its way into his lungs. Dammit, he knew this was a bad idea.

"Jonah, stop." Chloe pushed Jonah out of the way and cupped his face in her hands.

"Breathe," she coaxed.

"I'm fine." Pryce gripped her wrists and held her away.

"What's wrong?" Jonah grabbed his arm but he twisted away.

"You're what's wrong," Chloe said. "Geeze, J! I thought we were giving him time!"

"I said I'm fine!" Pryce grabbed his horse's reins. "I shouldn't have come."

"No!" Chloe took the reins from him and handed them to Jonah. "I'm glad you came. I've missed you. We've missed you," she said, glancing up at Jonah.

"Yeah." Jonah shrugged, stuffing his hands deep inside his front pockets. "I'm sorry, man. I guess I got a little carried away."

Pryce swallowed, his gaze wandering toward the house. "Breezy said your Uncle and Grandfather needed a photographer for their wedding."

"Yeah, they do." Jonah cupped the back of his neck and turned toward the house. "They're ready to start." He eyed the satchel Pryce had tied to his saddle. "That your camera gear? Want me to grab it?"

"I got it," Pryce insisted. They both reached for it and their hands collided. Jonah's was cold, and Pryce couldn't stop the urge to clasp his hand in his own. Jonah didn't flinch away from his touch and Pryce took advantage of the moment to try to make him understand. He brought their hands down between them, mesmerized by how oddly right they looked together. "Look, Jonah, I still want this," he said, unable to look him in the eyes.

Before he could finish what he was going to say, Jonah hooked his finger beneath his chin and tilted his head back to look at him. "I get it," he said with a crooked grin, his tall shadow blocking the early afternoon sun behind him. "I don't know what came over me. I'm just really glad to see you again."

Pryce stared up at him. Jonah looked so good, larger than life and more tempting than even a week ago. There was so much to say, but everything inside him wanted to climb Jonah like a tree and kiss him until the shame was gone, to feel his claiming touch until all his doubts and fears disappeared.

"Guys, we have to go," Chloe whispered. "They're waiting on us."

Pryce looked at her and his heartrate galloped in his chest. Literally galloped. The sun lit her hair like a halo and her glossy lips parted into the biggest smile. And how could he not have noticed that dress? "I've missed you so damn much." He grabbed her up again and twirled her around, soliciting a surprised squeal before she picked off his hat, holding it up to shield their faces while she kissed him, again and again and again.

"Keep that up and I'm going to get jealous."

Pryce walked her over to Jonah and she leaned over and kissed him too. Jonah cuffed his neck and pulled him into the kiss, like he had before, and Pryce nearly melted right there in the snow.

"Papa Daniel's gonna pass out in here waitin' on the three of you," one of Jonah's dads yelled from the front porch.

Pryce wrenched away and wiped the evidence of their kiss from his mouth.

Jonah plunged his hat back onto his head with a chuckle. "They already know," he said, walking Pryce's horse toward the porch.

Pryce stopped in his tracks. "They do?"

"Relax," Jonah said and hitched the horse's reins to the porch railing. "My great uncle and adopted grandfather are getting married today. Trust me, they're cool with us."

"Aunt Bev knows, too," Chloe said as they walked up the stairs.

"Oh thank God you're okay!" Jonah's mom rushed out the front door and tackled Pryce in a strangling hug.

"I'm fine, Mrs. McLendon," he choked out, glancing over at Jonah with a plea for help.

"Call me Gabby," she insisted when she finally let him go. He sucked in a much needed breath and fumbled to right his hat. "Or Mom," she added with an urgent smile. "Whichever you prefer is fine with me, but right now we need to get you guys inside before Daniel backs out and calls this whole thing off."

"I'm not calling anything off," someone, he guessed it was Daniel, said from inside. "Let the poor kid breathe."

If Pryce thought he was nervous before, his knees were knocking when he stepped inside. He walked from the foyer into the living room and the heat inside his coat jumped two hundred degrees. More than a dozen pairs of eyes stared back at him with curious amusement.

"Let me get your coat," one of Jonah's dads offered. He knew their names, but he'd not met them more than a few times in the past and didn't remember who was who. "Grey," he said, as if he'd read his thoughts. "And that one there is Matt," he nodded to the man standing beside Jonah's sister Dani and his younger brother Cory.

"And I'm Mason." Matt's identical twin waved from the front row of chairs by the altar. Pryce nodded to Jonah's brothers, Connor and Carson, as he handed off his coat and hat. Everyone who was anyone knew who they were, even if he hadn't already met them the day Jonah was attacked.

"Hi," he said to Jonah's grandmother, waving from her seat next to Mason. Her three husbands sitting beside her smiled and gave him a nod. He'd met them a few times too, but didn't remember their names.

"Good to see you again, kid." Cade's boisterous voice drew his attention to the altar. "You've met me and Daniel of course."

Pryce nodded politely.

"And this here is Minister Farnes."

"Please, call me Caleb." The minister nodded with a smile. "It's good to see you again, Pryce."

"You know him?" Chloe asked in a hushed whisper beside him.

Pryce nodded nervously. "Breezy introduced us yesterday."

"Did you bring your camera?"

Pryce flinched at the unexpected voice, not realizing Breezy was standing right behind him.

"Hey," he said when she gave him a sisterly hug. He still couldn't believe he had a sister. The feeling was strange, having been raised an only child the least of the reasons why. They'd talked about DNA tests, but he already felt the truth in what she'd told him. No matter what the tests showed, she'd already done more for him than any of his other kin had.

"Here." Jonah nudged Pryce's shoulder and held out his camera bag. "I need to get up there." He nodded to the altar. "I'm best man."

"Oh, okay." With sweaty palms Pryce took the bag and went to work.

The room was flooded with excited energy. Pryce adjusted the settings on his camera for the lighting and clicked a few test shots, making another adjustment before he moved to the other side of the room. The overwhelming nervousness he'd felt earlier disappeared as he lost himself in his lens.

Off to one side, Connor and Carson picked up their guitars and strummed a soft country melody as everyone took their places. *Click. Click.* He'd heard about the trouble they'd had with the paparazzi. A family wedding was a different kind of occasion, but taking any more than a few pictures of them still felt intrusive, so he quickly moved on and took another few of the family until the music ended.

"Dearly beloved, we are gathered here today, surrounded by those whose hearts are filled with His love for these two men."

Minister Farnes' smile was so kind and genuine as he spoke, the joy in his heart self-evident in the way he looked at Daniel and Cade. *Click.* Pryce had felt dead inside when Breezy had driven him over to the minister's house the day before. They'd stayed up until dawn talking. Well, he had. Minister Farnes mostly listened, but having someone to talk to who'd come from a similar religious upbringing, and now believed so differently, lifted a huge weight from his chest. He'd felt like he could tell him anything, and did, baring his soul until the wee hours of the morning.

Daniel said a few inaudible words, and then nervously cleared his throat, inciting an outburst of laughter from the family. *Click.* Cade drew Daniel's hand to his smiling lips and kissed his knuckles. *Click.* The minister continued and he zoomed out, taking a few pictures of the three of them standing together. With the sun filtering in through the shuttered windows behind them, the lighting on those would be fantastic.

Everyone bowed their heads in a prayer and he used the opportunity to quietly move to the back of the room. Chloe saw him and gave him a wink. He pointed the lens and zoomed in on her easy smile, his chest aching with love for her. *Click. Click.* He pulled out and framed one of her and her aunt sitting side-by-side. *Click.* She would love that one.

Daniel and Cade turned and faced each other, the movement drawing him back to the reason he was there. The minister joined their hands together, Cade moving quickly to lace his fingers with Daniel's. *Click.* They repeated words he'd heard before, but something in the way they said them gave him pause. He lowered his camera and gazed at the men in awe. They weren't an abomination, some freak of nature that deserved condemnation just for existing, or the evil McLendons his father had repeatedly warned him against. They were men who'd lived a lifetime by each other's sides, loving and supporting each other. Their love was real, a tangible force wrapping itself around them like a protective shield. If only he could capture it somehow in his lens, he could show the world how right their love was. *Click-Click-Click.*

A feminine sob caught his ear and he turned back to the family. Sitting between her husbands, Gabby dabbed at her eyes with a tissue, an uncontainable smile on her lips despite her tears. *Click.* Grey draped his arm around her shoulders and drew her to his side. *Click.*

Pryce scanned the room, capturing moment after moment, each one telling a story of love and a family like none other he'd ever experienced.

Another sniffle caught his attention and he pointed his lens back to the altar to see Dani wipe away a tear. *Click.* Standing beside Cade, her hands were clasped tightly in front of her as she fought not to cry. Their grandmother passed down a handful of tissues and Mason pushed up from his seat to hand them to her. *Click.*

Jonah glanced over at him, his lopsided grin drawing Pryce's attention to his dimples. *Click.* He zoomed in closer, focusing on Jonah's smiling eyes. The emotion in their depths changed suddenly from playful to a smoldering, primal awareness that made Pryce's gut tighten. Heat filled his face as more blood rushed south so fast it made his hands shake. *Click-click-click-click-click.*

"You may kiss your spouse," the minister said and Pryce whipped the camera over to the happy couple and clicked with the same excitement that erupted in the room as they kissed.

Cade pulled away from Daniel and faced the family, but Daniel turned him back and kissed him again. The family broke out into another round of laughter and cheers and whistles so loud they split the air. He tried to get it all, but the moment was too huge to capture with a single lens, so he stayed focused on the couple as the family surrounded them, exchanging heartfelt hugs and kisses and smiles of joy.

Pryce was flying by the time they cut the cake. He hadn't had so much fun in…well…forever. He'd captured countless random shots throughout the evening and couldn't wait to go through them all. Everyone drank and ate and he'd laughed so hard his sides hurt.

"Say cheese fountain!" Jonah shouted from across the room.

Pryce turned toward him and was blinded by his camera flash.

"Oh! Get one of us together!" Chloe jumped to his side and pulled him into a playful kiss as Jonah clicked away.

"Get in there with them." Dani took the camera from Jonah and gave him a shove. "Wait. What button do I push?" she asked, staring down at the camera in confusion. Jonah rushed back and showed her before he jumped in between Pryce and Chloe and wrapped his arms around their shoulders. "You're too tall. Lean down." She instructed, motioning with her free hand as she peered through the viewfinder.

They posed with their faces cheek to cheek for the camera.

"Kiss! Kiss! Kiss!" Daniel chanted.

"Oh, stop." Gran chastised him for teasing them.

"He's just trying to divert the attention away from us," Cade snickered as he hooked his arm around Daniel's neck and pulled him in for a kiss.

"Kiss! Kiss! Kiss! Kiss!" Carson repeated and the rest of the family joined him.

Chloe threw her head back and laughed. Pryce looked over at Jonah to see him smiling back, his eyes full of mischief and life and easy happiness. He didn't know if it was the champagne running through his veins, or the pure joy of the moment, but he grabbed Jonah by the shirt, squishing Chloe between them, and brought all three of them together in a playful kiss.

Jonah's family cheered and whistled as the flash captured the brazen moment. Instead of pulling away, they all lingered, their lips pressed together, their breaths mingling in the air between them. It wasn't a seductive kiss by any means, but more like a fusion of their lives, a shared closeness reserved only for true love. A love he felt for the first time he could honestly believe in.

When they finally withdrew, Chloe wrapped her arms around him and snuggled against his chest. Jonah stood behind her and wrapped his arms around them both, kissing the top of her head. "I love you, Lo," he whispered in her ear. "I love you, too," he said, kissing Pryce's cheek before he hugged them. The need to say it back clawed at Pryce's chest, the words perched on the tip of his tongue, but the flash of the camera distracted them and the moment was lost.

The sun was setting when everyone trickled out into the front yard to send Daniel and Cade off on their honeymoon road trip.

"Take good care of him," Jonah's grandmother, Hazel, said before she pulled Daniel into a hug. "He's the only brother I have."

"I always have," Daniel said.

"And if he shows even the slightest sign of complications, don't wait," she continued. "Get him back here immediately."

"You'd think she was my mother instead of my sister." Cade leaned down and gave Hazel a peck on the cheek. "I'll be fine. I feel fantastic."

"Oh, I almost forgot." Daniel caught Jonah by the arm and placed something in his hand. "Anywhere but our bed," he said with a grin.

Pryce didn't know what that meant, and judging by the blush coloring Jonah's cheeks he wasn't about to ask. Instead, he pointed his camera and clicked. Until he'd met Chloe, Jonah had always been his favorite subject, and today he'd had unlimited opportunities to indulge with them both.

"Say hello to Grant and Thalia for us," Gabby told Daniel as she handed him a basket full of leftover food and cake.

"I will." Daniel gave her one last hug, then he and Cade turned to the RV. Everyone scooped up handfuls of powdery snow and pelted the newlyweds until the door closed behind them, and were still laughing as they waved goodbye and the RV rocked down the driveway toward the road, the metal cans tied to the rear bumper clanging against the gravel.

With so many to help, the clean-up was a snap and in no time Pryce was sitting in front of a bonfire in the middle of the McLendon's back pasture, surrounded by Jonah's family.

"Well," Dani pushed to her feet. "I'm headed for the calving barn."

"I thought you got the night off since Clay isn't back yet," Jonah said, handing her his empty beer bottle when she offered to take it.

"I did. The rush is over and we only have a few more to watch," she said with a shrug as she collected the remaining empties, "but the storm moves in tomorrow, and I wanted to go over the data before he gets back."

"You push yourself too hard," Gabby said with a frown. "You need to slow down a little."

"I'm fine," Dani argued. "It's not like it's work." She bent down and gave her mom a peck on the cheek. "Love you for loving me."

"Love you for loving me," Gabby said back with a wink.

"She'll be passed out in her office chair within an hour," Grey said when Dani was out of earshot. "I'll carry her to bed on our way in."

"She's been a little off the last couple of days," Mason observed. "Maybe she's got a thing for that Ash kid."

"Shut the hell up," Grey tossed his bottle cap at him.

"What?" Mason shrugged and took a swig of his beer. "I'm just saying. You didn't have to run him off like that."

"All the men in my family are clueless," Jonah mumbled under his breath.

"Why would you say that?" Pryce asked.

"Because Dani isn't into Ash," Chloe clarified with a whisper. "Jonah thinks she likes that Clay guy who pilots the drones she's testing out."

"I know she does," Jonah argued.

"Well, we're going to head back to the house, too," Carson announced as he stood and stretched. "Got some work we need to finish up on the nursery."

"Yeah, like makin' the baby," Matt said with a sly grin.

"Matthew!" Gabby jostled him with her elbow.

"What? It's not like anyone here's buying that they're going back so early to compare paint swatches."

"Nope," Connor said and pulled Breezy to her feet. "The painting is all done." Pryce chuckled when he hoisted her over his shoulder. "Goodnight y'all. Nice to see you again, Pryce." He nodded as Connor and Carson marched by, Breezy giggling as they disappeared into the darkness.

"Only four more to go and we'll have this big ol' fire all to ourselves," Matt said, leaning in to nuzzle Gabby's neck.

"You don't have to tell me twice." Cory stood and tossed another log on the fire. "Pryce." He shook Pryce's hand, then bent down and gave Chloe a hug. "I'm going to be dreaming about that cake," he said with a wink.

"Careful, bro." Jonah stood and gave his brother a slap on his back. "I might think you're flirting with our girl."

"Not yet, but all bets are off if you break her heart."

Pryce watched the exchange with both fascination and trepidation. Living in the McLendons' world was like having an out of body experience he never wanted to end, but the end was coming and he'd have to go home soon. He glanced over his shoulder to where his house sat in the darkness, dread filling his chest like a bucket full of lead sinkers.

"Night, Mom."

Pryce stood with Chloe as Jonah said goodnight to his parents. He pulled her into his arms, soaking up every second he could before he had to return to whatever hell was waiting for him across the creek. Thanks to his chat with Minister Farnes, he felt better equipped to deal with it than he had the day before, but he was in no rush.

"Thanks for inviting me," Pryce said to Jonah's parents before he left. "I'll send over a drive with all the pictures as soon as I can get them copied."

"Bring it yourself," Grey said, and then stood to shake his hand. "You're welcome here anytime. Just take good care of my boy."

"Yes, sir. Goodnight, Mrs. McLendon. You did a wonderful job on the wedding."

"Thank you," Gabby said with a smile and a wave. "Hopefully I'll get to do it again soon?"

"Mom!" Jonah grabbed Pryce's hand, yanking him from the circle into the dark.

"Goodnight!" Pryce yelled again with a laugh.

Chloe screeched in the night and Pryce ran to catch up with them to see her perched on top of Jonah's shoulders, laughing as she tried to catch her balance.

"Can't we just stay out here forever?" he asked, picking his way along the frozen ground, the light from the flashlight in Jonah's hand swinging back and forth with his strides.

"Why? It's freezing!" Chloe plucked off his wool cap with a giggle, pulling it over her own head and rolling it down to cover her ears.

"I'm not ready for this day to end," he said, feeling so happy he couldn't muster a single protest of Chloe's brazen thievery, despite his cold ears. "I don't want to go home yet."

"Then don't." Jonah turned and held something up to him.

"What's that?"

He shined the light on the set of keys dangling from his fingers. "The keys to Uncle Cade's and Papa Daniel's house. They invited us to stay there while they're gone."

"Us?" He glanced between Jonah and Chloe, then back to Jonah.

"Us," Jonah said with his lopsided grin, right before he leaned in and kissed him senseless.

Chapter Twenty-Three

Chloe yelped when Pryce swept her off her feet and carried her over the threshold into Daniel and Cade's home.

"Are you sure this is okay?" she asked once inside and on her feet, glancing around the cozy room. "Eee!" she squealed again when Jonah grabbed her from behind and buried his stubble-covered face in the crook of her neck.

"It's perfectly fine, just like you," he growled. He pressed his rock-hard length against her backside. "I want this ass, Lo. You've been teasing me with it for days and now that Pryce's here, I'm not taking no for an answer."

She melted against his touch, tipping her head to the side to give his skilled tongue more room to roam. God help her, she wanted that too. She knew they needed to talk, but she craved this connection with them after the days spent apart from Pryce.

Missing his touch, she opened her eyes to look for Pryce and froze when she saw him leaning against the wall, his arms crossed over his chest, watching them with an unreadable look in his eyes.

"What's wrong?" Jonah asked him, kissing his way to the tip of her shoulder. "Get over here."

"You waited for me?" Pryce asked.

"What?" Jonah lowered the zipper on the back of her dress.

"You heard me." Pryce uncrossed his arms. His boots scuffed along the wood flooring as he crossed the hallway to stand in front of her, his gaze darting between her and Jonah. "Did you or did you not, have sex while I was gone?"

Jonah's grip tightened on her hips and he stiffened behind her.

"It felt weird without you," Chloe rushed to explain. "Since we didn't get the chance to talk about the rules, or what we were comfortable with."

Pryce's gaze roamed her face. His eyes softened, but she still couldn't tell if he was happy or upset.

"Did you want to?" Pryce finally asked, reaching up to finger one of her stray curls.

"Hell yes I wanted to." Jonah released her and stepped around to face Pryce. "And I won't apologize for it."

No-no-no! This isn't the way tonight was supposed to go!

"Then you should have," Pryce said.

What?

"What?" Jonah voiced her thought, his eyes narrowing in confusion.

"I'm not ignorant to the way this works," Pryce said. "I'm slow on some things, but I'm a fast learner." He pinched Jonah's coat zipper and pulled it down, then slowly pushed it off his shoulders. "If you want to make love to her, then make love to her."

Chloe sucked in a breath when Pryce ripped open Jonah's dress shirt, sending buttons pinging off the wall and bouncing along the floor. "If you want to make love to me, then make love to me."

The look they shared caused a chain reaction that started in her chest and ended with an ache in her core so strong she pressed her thighs together to ease it.

"Are you drunk?" Jonah asked him.

Pryce shrugged. "Not enough to fuck you, but enough to admit I want to." He glanced at Chloe, his lips curling up into a lazy smile. "I want both of you, so much."

No one moved. The air between them sizzled with banked lust and anticipation.

"Good enough," Jonah finally said, then tackled them both, pinning them against the wall with his broad body, devouring Pryce's mouth in a kiss so hot it scorched the air between them.

They collided in an explosion of moans and whimpers and frantic hands clawing at each other's clothes. Her dress fell to the floor, followed by her strapless bra. She yanked at Pryce's shirt, trying to find the skin-on-skin contact she craved.

"Ah!" Pryce flinched with a muffled laugh against Jonah's lips. "Cold hands!" he protested as he pushed Jonah's shirt off his shoulders and down his arms.

Jonah jerked away, thrashing his arms behind him until his shirt fell to the floor.

"Oh!" Chloe's muffled squeak blended with Jonah's growl when he crushed his lips against hers and demanded access. "Mmmph!" His hot, silky tongue tangled with hers in an urgent swirl. Her bottom lip stung from his playful nip before he tilted his head and plunged in again, deeper and slower, so hard her lips stung from the pressure.

Pryce freed her of her panties and she pulled herself up by Jonah's neck, wrapping her legs around his hips. She rode the ample bulge in his jeans, resenting the confining denim between them until she felt hands that couldn't anatomically be Jonah's working their way under her thighs and up between her legs.

"Lift her up," Pryce ordered and Jonah hoisted her higher.

A finger penetrated her entrance then slid up to the spot that throbbed with need.

"Oh, yeah," Pryce said with a hum. "She's ready."

Ready? She was going to implode if they didn't hurry.

"Damn," Jonah panted, reaching out to brace himself against the wall. "Oh fuck!" He sucked in a shuddering breath. "That feels good."

Jonah's hips bucked beneath her and she wished more than anything she could see what Pryce was doing to him.

"Going to feel even better when you're inside her," Pryce teased.

"Wait!" Jonah breathed against her shoulder. "Not yet. Stroke it a few more times before you put the condom on. Oh yeah. Just like that."

Chloe threaded her fingers through Jonah's hair and guided his mouth to her breast, the back of her head hitting the wall with a thud when he sucked her nipple into his mouth and flicked his tongue back and forth.

She bucked in his arms, pressing harder against his mouth. She was so close, right….there! She almost came when he raked his teeth over her nipple, but then he released her, throwing his head back with a shout.

"Gaw*dammit*, Pryce! Do you know how long I've waited to feel your mouth on my cock, and you do it now? When I can't see you!"

Pryce gurgled a laugh and Jonah jerked against her, biting his bottom lip until it turned as white as his teeth. Chloe grinned. She wished she could see him too, but figured it was best this way. Pryce was so insecure about his feelings for Jonah it was probably easier for him to get comfortable without everyone watching him.

The tendons in Jonah's neck pulled tight, his chest heaving with his erratic breaths. She leaned up and kissed his jaw, trailed her tongue along the taut tendons, and then sucked his earlobe into her mouth. "Does it feel good, J?"

"Oh-*fuck*-yeah!"

She gave a throaty chuckle and raked her teeth over the shell of his ear.

"I'm gonna come!" he shouted. "Seriously, Pryce. I can't hold—oh damn! Fuck-yeah! Uh! Ah!"

Jonah jerked against her as his orgasm ripped through his body. His arms and legs shook. His whole body trembled as he choked out curse after dirty curse.

His arms finally gave out and she slipped from his grip with a squeak, landing on top of Pryce, but Jonah caught her and steadied her on her feet. Her legs wobbled and she fell back against the wall, watching as Pryce took one final lick and looked up at Jonah with a saucy wink. "That was easier than I thought it was going to be."

"Fuck you!" Jonah said with a sated grin. He grabbed Pryce by his shirt and yanked him to his feet. "On second thought." He ripped Pryce's shirt over his head, spun him around and pushed him to Chloe. "Fuck *her* while I give you a taste of your own medicine."

Pryce grinned at her, his eyes blinking in a lazy rhythm. Jonah pulled and tugged at Pryce's belt buckle, then unzipped his pants and shoved them down to his boots. "I've missed you," Pryce hummed against her lips before he sucked his bottom lip between his teeth, his eyes rolling back with a pained moan.

"Are you okay?" She asked him, pressing her forehead against his, threading her fingers through his sweaty hair.

"Umhmm," Pryce hummed. "I really liked it."

Chloe giggled and kissed the tip of his nose. "I like it too."

"Son of a—"

"You're all suited up," Jonah said as he stood, leaning down to place an open-mouthed kiss to the top of Pryce's shoulder, "but you can't come until I'm inside her, too."

She and Pryce gazed at each other, his eyelids heavy with sensual promise. They'd never taken her together that way. They'd shared her pussy, alternating strokes, and Jonah had fingered her ass a few times when they were messing around, but she'd never taken them inside her at the same time. Tonight, she needed them both. Inside her, around her, loving her together.

Jonah lifted her right leg to rest on Pryce's hip. She understood his intent and lifted the other, wrapping her legs around Pryce the way she had Jonah.

Pryce held her against the wall and thrust his hips, filling her completely in one long, sweet stroke as he kissed her, his tongue sliding just as deep alongside hers. She tasted the sweetness of champagne and the saltiness of Jonah's seed, the idea that Jonah had come in his mouth sending her right back to the edge.

"Harder," she demanded against his lips. Pryce complied, thrusting up inside her over and over, pounding her against the wall.

"That's what I want to see," Jonah said behind them. "She's missed you, Pry. Give it to her hard."

"Christ!" Pryce's rhythm faltered and he almost dropped her. Chloe opened her eyes and looked over his shoulder to see Jonah pressed against Pryce's back, kissing his neck, grinding his hips against him.

Pryce thrust hard inside her and then suddenly froze, his entire body tensing against her.

"Relax, it's only my finger," Jonah whispered into his ear and Pryce groaned, the throaty sound deep and desperate.

Chloe throbbed around his girth and a whimper slipped past her lips. She knew exactly what Jonah was doing to him and she couldn't wait until he was doing it to her.

"Mmm—" Pryce pressed his lips into a tight thin line. The air in his lungs hissed out through his nose and he drew in another breath through gritted teeth.

"Don't come," Jonah rumbled in his ear.

"Sonofabitch!" Pryce panted, just before his knees buckled and they crashed to the floor.

Chloe yelped as she slid down the wall, landing in Pryce's lap with him still deep inside her. "Whoa!"

Pryce cried out with a laugh, falling back onto the floor, holding his side where she'd caught him with her elbow.

"Sorry!" She gasped and shifted to see if he was okay.

"No! Don't move!" Pryce gripped her hips and thrust up inside her. "Don't," *thrust,* "oh damn. So good," *thrust*, "move!"

"Yes." Jonah's deep voice hummed in her ear. He nudged her forward, pressing her down onto Pryce's chest, and then draped himself over her back. "Don't move a single inch."

"Oh-my-*gawd*." She pressed her forehead into Pryce's shoulder, her entire body tensing with anticipation as Jonah caressed one ass cheek, then the other, before gliding his hand down between them. The tips of his fingers grazed her rear entrance, but he didn't stop until his hand was between her and Pryce, Pryce's cock sliding between his fingers as he slid in and out of her.

Pryce uttered a string of unintelligible curses, thrashing his head to the side, his eyes squeezed shut.

She repeated Pryce's curse when the tip of his finger curled against her clit and circled through her wet arousal.

"Damn, Pry. You should feel how wet she is."

Pryce lifted his head and looked down at where they were joined. He positioned his thumb beside Jonah's finger, flicking and circling until she was ready to scream her release.

Jonah slid his hand free, drawing his fingers back up to her ass. She clenched her teeth and sucked in a breath when he circled the sensitive rim, pressing against it, but not pushing inside.

"Jonah, please," she begged, reaching back blindly to clasp his hand. "I can't take much more teasing."

"I can't either." Pryce gasped when she clenched around his cock in response to the feel of silky lube being drizzled between her ass cheeks.

Jonah chuckled. "I'm right there with you both," he said, positioning himself behind her. The hair on his thighs tickled the back of hers, and then she felt his rigid cock against the crack of her ass. "Has he taken you here?" Jonah asked her, finally pressing the tip of his finger inside her.

Chloe shook her head, gritting against the delicious sting. "We haven't."

"Mmm," he hummed, pulling his finger out and then sliding it back in a little deeper. "I'll go slow, Lo. Just breathe."

"No," Chloe insisted. "Now."

"Is that—holy—!" Pryce arched beneath her when Jonah added another finger. "I can feel that!"

"I can feel you too," Jonah said, crooking his finger inside her.

"I'm not going to last." Pryce's words were more of a plea than a warning. "It's not going to happen."

"Hold on," Jonah said, working his fingers faster and deeper, stretching her, filling her there as Pryce filled her from below.

Chloe heard the sound of a condom being opened and her heart leapt inside her chest. This was it. This was the moment she would finally hold them both inside her for the first time.

"Try to relax, Lo. Push out when I tell you. Let me guide you."

Too breathless to speak, she nodded and tried to focus on Pryce, but when the head of Jonah's cock pressed against her rim, she couldn't keep her eyes open.

"Now, Lo. Breathe!"

Pryce's body coiled up tight beneath her, his hands kneading her skin with bruising strength as Jonah rocked into her, stretched her, then finally penetrated her tight ring.

They all tensed, their bodies strung tight. She swallowed the scream building in the back of her throat, a chorus of desperate grunts and moans echoing around her.

"Holy shit." Pryce arched beneath her when Jonah pushed deeper.

"Beautiful." Jonah pulled out, and then pushed back in. "You need to see this, Pryce. See what it's like for us both to be inside her."

Pryce's only response was another moan and a jerk of his hips.

"Stop." Chloe couldn't move. Stretched and filled so full, she felt like she was on the razor's edge, literally.

"Is it too much?" Jonah pulled back a little and she reached behind her to stop him.

"Give me a second, please." The sting intensified, burning her from the inside out, but the pain quickly morphed into something else, a feeling she couldn't explain.

Pryce cupped her cheeks and commanded her to look at him. "We can stop, Chloe, if it's too much."

"No." They couldn't stop. She could do this. She had to. She wanted to.

"Lo?"

From her fingers to her toes, a tingling wave of heat rushed through her veins, chasing away the pain. Her skin prickled with chills and her head spun with a strange euphoric fog.

"So…full." She pushed back against them, testing the limits of her new high.

Jonah's grip tightened on her hips. Or was it Pryce's? She didn't know. Like Pryce had described, she couldn't tell where one man began and the other ended.

Jonah pulled out slowly, but instead of pain, the slow glide intensified the pleasure, making her insides throb and ache from the emptiness. "More," she demanded, sucking in a long breath when Jonah filled her again.

"Damn," Pryce cursed. "It's like you're fucking us both."

"Move with me," Jonah said, increasing his tempo.

"I…I'm not sure I can."

Jonah slid back in and held himself tight against her, filling her completely. "Pull out," he instructed and Pryce complied. "Oh yeah. That's it. Fuck yeah."

When Pryce drove back in, Jonah pulled out and the rhythm continued. Chloe rode the wave between them, feeling their bodies move as one, holding her lovers inside her body as she had for so long inside her heart, inside her soul.

Jonah draped himself over her back, his thick forearms shaking beside her. "I love you, Lo," he whispered in her ear. "I love you so damn much."

"I love you too." She turned and searched out Jonah, kissing him deep and hard as they rocked inside her.

Their lips parted. Pryce tipped her chin back toward him and their tongues mated in a similar frantic kiss. Jonah held himself above them and leaned down over her shoulder. Straining to reach them, he shared their kiss, their tongues tangling together in the open air. When she withdrew to catch her breath, Pryce and Jonah's mouths fused together with so much passion, watching them made her heart ache. How could she have ever been so blind as to not see their need for one another? The passion they shared, the feel of their hands, two mouths, two hard bodies enveloping hers, sent an instant tremble quaking through.

"Grrrah!" Jonah snapped his head back with a pained cry, thrusting his hips in a frantic rush. The friction ignited a throbbing in Chloe's core she couldn't fight. She threaded her fingers with Pryce's, pinning his hands beside his head, and braced herself against the rush of her orgasm as Jonah and Pryce emptied themselves inside her.

Chapter Twenty-Four

"Do you have to go?"

Pryce leaned his head back against Jonah's chest and stared out the window. The next storm had moved in and snow was falling, so heavily it blurred the meadow separating Daniel and Cade's house from the McLendons'. Chloe would be upset she'd missed it, but he and Jonah couldn't bring themselves to wake her after keeping her up so late.

"You know I do," Pryce said.

After spending the last two nights with Chloe and Jonah, the last thing he wanted to do was go back home and face his mother, not to mention the reading of the will that would no doubt leave him swimming in debt.

Jonah rested his chin on top of Pryce's head and blew out a resigned sigh.

Pryce turned in his arms, leaning into the kiss Jonah pressed to his forehead. "I'm working on it," he said, but the words sounded hollow even to him. After everything they'd done and confessed since the wedding, he still hadn't let Jonah fuck him. He hadn't lied when he said he wanted to. He did, but it felt like once he crossed that line he could never go back. Everything was changing so fast.

"It's not that," Jonah said, staring out the window.

"What is it, then?"

Jonah leaned his head against the wall beside him. "I guess I'm afraid if you go home you won't ever come back."

"I will," Pryce tried to assure him, but Jonah shook his head in rebuttal.

"She'll try to turn you against us again. You know she will," he added when Pryce tried to deny it, "and you've always been afraid to stand up to her."

"Yes." Pryce admitted, forcing himself back into Jonah's arms. "She will try, which is one of the reasons why I don't want to go back, but I'm not the scared, wimpy kid I was before you left, J."

Jonah chuckled, reaching up to caress the healing cut on the bridge of his nose. "No, you've definitely learned how to throw a right hook."

Pryce cringed, remembering their fight in the barn when Jonah first came back. "Sorry about that."

"Don't be," he said with a crooked grin. "I'm impressed."

"I can handle my mother," Pryce assured him, "but I need time."

"How much time?"

Pryce shrugged. "I think I've made good progress," he said with a saucy hum, trailing his fingers down to caress Jonah's cock through his boxer briefs. It twitched and hardened in his hand, but Jonah jerked away.

"How much time?" he insisted.

Frustrated, Pryce turned and stared out the window. "I don't know."

"A week? A month? A year?"

"I. Don't. Know." *Dammit!* How could he make him understand? "I don't have the luxury of the perfect family that accepts me for who I am." As much as he despised what his mother had done, Minister Farnes' advice kept playing on a constant loop in his head. "She's the only mother I have, Jonah, and you know what she's like. She'll kick me out despite needing me there, and even though I hate her right now, I can't abandon her."

"Marrying us isn't abandoning her," Jonah insisted.

Pryce held up a staying hand. "I can't talk about getting married right now."

"You're already engaged to Chloe!"

"That's different and you know it."

"Oh." Jonah smirked. "So it's being married to me that's the problem."

"You know it is, and you know why!"

"I thought we were past that," Jonah said, waving a hand between their mostly naked bodies.

"We are, but…" Pryce bit back a curse. The last thing he wanted to do before he left was fight with Jonah. "I want—I *need* time!"

"Time for what?"

"Time to deal with all of this," he argued. "Time to talk to my mother. Time to grieve my father. Time to get used to the idea that I have a sister, or-or that I want to fuck *you*, and that I'm not going to burst into flames the second I do."

Jonah chuckled and drew Pryce back into his arms, pressing his morning hard-on against his hip. "You will definitely burst into flames when I finally get inside you," he said with a cocky grin, "but it will be the farthest thing from hell you could possibly imagine."

Pryce's knees almost buckled at the tempting contact. "I hope you're right." A part of him wanted Jonah to bend him over a chair and do it already. He glanced around the room, taking notice of the back of the sofa. That would work.

"You know I'd never hurt you, right?" Jonah ran his hands down Pryce's back, under his boxer briefs to cup his ass.

Pryce gave him a reluctant nod. "Can you just give me some time to adjust to life outside the closet, before you nuke it with me still half inside?"

Jonah threw his head back and laughed. "I'd settle for a bulldozer, but yes, dammit. I get it." He kissed Pryce's jaw, then his chin, then sucked on his bottom lip before he plunged his tongue past it and kissed him slow and deep. Pryce melted at the newly familiar sensations, kissing him back until Jonah finally let him go.

"Just don't let her convince you that this is wrong," he said. "And answer Chloe's texts and calls if you're not coming back tonight," he added with another playful lick, dipping his knees to press their cocks together. "And don't get pissed if I can't wait for you to get back to make love to her again."

"I told you I didn't care about that," Pryce said in a breathy whisper, grinding his cock against Jonah's. "That feels…ah…really good."

Jonah pushed Pryce's boxers down and cupped his balls, rolling them in his hand as he stroked his cock in the other. "Let me suck you off one last time before you leave?"

Pryce closed his eyes when Jonah sank to his knees in front of him. As many times as Jonah's mouth had been on his cock in the last two days, he still couldn't hold back a gasp at the first contact of Jonah's silky tongue on his stiff flesh. He gritted out a groan as his hot cavernous mouth enveloped his cock head and he swallowed him to the back of his throat, hollowing his cheeks as he pulled off. Jonah descended on his shaft again, but stopped to flick the tip of his tongue under the head, mercilessly teasing his glans.

The fact that it was a guy sucking his dick was second to the knowledge that it was Jonah. For as long as he'd dreamed of such a possibility, the feeling was still so surreal. He looked out the window at the falling snow, then back down to Jonah, hoping he wouldn't wake up and find it all to be another one of those dreams.

Three hours later than he'd planned, thanks to Chloe's tempting shower invitation, Pryce climbed the front steps of his parents' house, camera bag in hand, and walked through the front door. The air inside was cold. Too cold.

"Mother?"

He dropped his camera bag onto the sofa on the way to the thermostat, only to notice the power was out.

"Mother? Are you here?"

When no answer came, he rushed up the stairs and into her room to find her huddled beneath the covers, dressed in her bathrobe. "Mother, what's wrong? It's freezing in here."

She rolled over and he saw the tracks of tears on her cheeks. "Where have you been?" She reached out her hand and he rushed to take it, finding it icy cold.

"When did the power go out?" he asked, ignoring her question and propping a hip on the side of her bed. "And why didn't you start a fire?"

"I did, but it burned out and there's no more wood in the bin," she said and rolled to sit up, wiping her tears from her eyes. He grabbed a tissue from the box on her nightstand and handed it to her, biting his tongue against the string of curses he wanted to shout. He didn't know if she was playing her usual games, trying to make him feel guilty for not coming home, or if she was still mourning his father. Either way, she knew crying was his weakness and she wouldn't hesitate to use it if she thought it would get her what she wanted. But she hadn't known he was coming home, and she'd obviously been crying a lot.

"Have you eaten anything?" he asked, pushing to his feet and crossing the room to open the curtains.

"I had some toast last night," she said with a sniffle.

Determined to get through the reading of the will and whatever came after that, he took a calming breath and marched to the bedroom door. "I'll put some soup on and get a fire started."

"I'll help." She swung her legs off the bed and made to get up, but Pryce stopped her.

"Stay here and keep warm until I get the fire going." He tucked her beneath the covers and handed her the box of tissues. "I'll come get you when the soup's done and we'll eat lunch in front of the fire."

Not giving her time to argue, he marched back downstairs and went to work. This was exactly why he couldn't leave her, or let her push him away. Whether she wanted to admit it or not, she needed him, but her tricks wouldn't work this time.

After bringing in several armloads of wood from the cord stacked in the barn, he built a roaring fire, and then dumped three cans of chicken noodle soup into a pot and set it to simmer on the gas stove. With heat and food taken care of, he pulled out his cellphone and texted Jonah.

Pryce: Is the power out there?
Jonah: Went out right after you left. You?

At least it wasn't cut off because of lack of payment.

Pryce: Yeah. Here too.
Jonah: Everything OK?
Pryce: For now.

Before his battery died, he called Donovan, one of the few hands he had left who'd been helping him with the herd, and made sure he was still available for when the temps dropped. Right now it looked like mainly a snow event, but the forecasters were saying there was the chance of another polar vortex coming down their way and he'd need help getting the stock packed back into the barn. The windbreak

Jonah's dads had built was still holding fast, so at least that was one thing he didn't have to worry about.

The soup hot, he poured it into two bowls, grabbed spoons and napkins and set everything up on the living room table, but before he called for his mother, he went to his father's office to look for the generator manual. He'd seen his father hook it up a few times, but never started it himself. It wouldn't run the house heater, but they'd need it for the other essentials if the power didn't come back on soon.

Manual in hand, he closed the file drawer and was about to leave when he paused, an open drawer in his father's desk catching his attention. Curious, he pulled the file drawer open further and peered inside. Touching his father's things had been a punishable offense for as long as he could remember. Dirk had never invited him to learn about the business end of the ranch, so reaching inside and plucking out a folder felt forbidden and risky, despite his father being dead and buried.

Inside the folder was a mound of feed receipts. Another folder contained what looked like stock bids, and several more were bulging with equipment repair logs. He thumbed through the folders, feeling both liberated and overwhelmed at the amount of paperwork. He'd thought he understood the amount of debt they were in, but if these bills were any indication of what they owed, they were in a lot of trouble.

The sound of footsteps moving down the stairs sent him scrambling. He shoved all the folders back into the drawer, careful to leave it ajar like he'd found it before he heel-toed it out of the room.

"Pryce?"

"Right here, Mother." He held up the manual as he met her at the bottom of the steps. "I needed a refresher in case we need the generator," he explained, guiding her into the living room. "Take a seat beside the fire. I'll hand you your soup."

"I can handle a bowl of soup," she argued, jerking her hand free of his and making her way to the chair. "Where have you been?"

"I told you. Out getting wood and making soup," he said, taking a seat on the sofa. The idea of eating anything turned his stomach, but he picked up the bowl and took a sip anyway, freezing with the spoon halfway to his lips when he caught his mother's piercing, stare.

"You were with *them*, weren't you?"

The way she said 'them' with a bitter, disgusted snarl was the last straw. Something snapped, literally. He could have sworn he'd heard it.

He placed his spoon back into the bowl and carefully lowered it to the table. His head spun as he stood, his ears ringing as his blood pressure rose. He bent down and took her bowl from her hands, and then pitched it like a fastball into the fireplace, shattering it into a dozen pieces, the soup sizzling against the burning logs.

"I was at Daniel and Cade's wedding—a *gay* wedding—with my *sister*!"

His mother furrowed her brows in confusion.

"Don't act like you didn't know Father had an affair with your sister. Breezy told me *all* about it."

"Lies!" She yelled and pushed to her feet. "All lies, spun by that wicked family to ruin our good name!" When Pryce didn't respond, she sank back into the chair, covering her mouth with trembling hands. "They've finally done it. They've corrupted you, turned you against me."

"*They* didn't turn me against you! You've done that all by yourself!" Pryce railed. "I stayed over there for the last two days because I couldn't stand the thought of spending another second in this house with you and your lies, and your screwed up head games!"

His mother closed her eyes, shook her head. "So you *were* with them."

Pryce's anger flared to an inferno. He leaned over and stared into his mother's cold eyes. "Jonah, Chloe, and I *fucked* each other's brains out for two solid days," he gritted out, his fists clenched at his sides.

His mother gasped, but he turned the knife even further.

"And in case you have *any* doubt, *yes*! I'm fucking Jonah, too! I'm bisexual, Mother. I like cock as much as I like pussy and Jonah's cock is—"

His mother slapped him across his face. "How *dare* you?"

Pryce jerked back, rubbed his jaw. He lowered his hand and found his palm streaked with blood, and then glanced down at his mother's hand to see her twisting the ring on her finger.

He chuckled. Maybe he'd finally lost it, but for whatever reason all he could think about was the look she'd have on her face when she figured out she was going to have to pawn her wedding rings.

"Get out of my house!" she demanded with another snarl, her hand trembling as she pointed at the front door.

Pryce chuckled again. "You love saying that, don't you? *'Your house'*," he repeated with a snort. "Have you seen the stack of bills on Father's desk? You don't own this house! The bank does, and before you even think about calling the Sheriff to throw me out, you think about this." He stepped closer and pressed his finger into the middle of his chest. "I'm all you've got left."

"God will take care of me!" she shouted. "And I have the church! Pastor—"

"Look around, Mother!" he shouted, his arms held wide. "Pastor didn't build you a fire. He wasn't here when the power went out. None of the church members are out buying groceries to fill your empty pantry, or chop more wood, or feed the cattle, or shovel snow! The only person God sent to help you was me, and lucky for you, I'm not a bastard like my father. *I'm* not leaving. I'll take care of things around here until we get this mess straightened out, but I swear-to-God, if you say one more word about Jonah or Chloe, or the McLendons, or utter a single one of your prayers in my presence, you'll freeze to death alone in this tomb you call a house."

He left her sitting by the fire, yanked his sweat pants out of the dryer, stayed in the shower until the hot water ran out, then went to bed early surrounded by a shoebox full of hand warming packets he'd found in his closet.

She was still sleeping in the chair when he woke up the next morning. He stopped in the foyer on his way out to get more wood, tempted to bring her a blanket, but decided it was best not to wake her. There was nothing left to say.

Jonah gave him a ride into town for some groceries, and Chloe went back to help her Aunt at the bakery. He didn't like the idea of her staying in town with Travis jacked up on meth, or whatever kind of drugs he was on, but she'd insisted she'd be fine. He had nothing else to offer her so he couldn't really argue.

Three days passed, the power flickering on and off for hours at a time. He spent most of that time out in the barn with Donovan, working to keep the herd fed and watered. His nights were spent in his room, going through pictures of the wedding or sexting with Jonah and Chloe.

Jonah had called him that morning to make sure he knew about the next big cold front moving in. After jerking off in the shower to the sounds of Jonah and Chloe going at it over the loud speaker on his phone, he'd met Donovan out in the barn and saddled up his horse. They'd spent most of the morning corralling the stock and packing the mommas back into the barn for the night.

"Supposed to be one for the record books," Donovan said as he closed the gate on his cattle trailer.

"Yeah." Pryce peeled his gloves off and tucked them into his back pocket. "I just hope the power stays on."

"You don't have to do this, you know," Donovan said, throwing his thumb over his shoulder at the trailer full of Grunion cattle they'd loaded up. "I know you're in a tough spot with your dad dying and all. I've been there myself."

"It's the only way I can pay you." Pryce shrugged. "Besides, you could be saving them from freezing to death if it's as bad as they say it's going to be."

"Still," Donovan huffed. "Even if you don't make auction, you can still use the beef."

Pryce laughed. "Even if I scrounge up enough cash to get every single calf to auction weight in time, I won't have enough to save the ranch."

"That bad, huh?"

"Yep."

"Well." Donovan slapped the side of the trailer. "Thanks for the beef. You need me to stick around and help you track that mountain lion?"

Pryce waved him on. "She's probably long gone. I'm just going to take a ride up to the ridge to see if there's any more tracks leading into the valley."

"Stay safe." Donovan tipped his hat. "Call me if you need anything."

"Will do."

When the truck and trailer disappeared around the bend of the driveway, Pryce mounted his horse and took off for the back pasture. It wasn't unusual to see mountain lion tracks after a big storm, but those they spotted along the creek were too damn close for comfort. He couldn't afford to lose any more heads of cattle or he wouldn't break even on the feed bills.

Once he reached the creek that ran between his ranch and the McLendons, he trotted along until he picked up the original tracks. They went on for what felt like miles before they finally crossed the creek onto McLendon land. Pryce pulled out his phone and tried to dial Jonah to warn him, but there was no signal. There was no use in going all the way back home to tell them. They'd only have to ride all the way back out again to kill it, if they could find it before the storm. Instead, he steered his horse down the bank and dismounted, leading him across the narrow crossing in the frozen creek, and up the steep bank on the other side.

The tracks continued along the creek bank for a few hundred feet, and then cut across the field. Pryce followed them for a while to a thick patch of brush jutting out from around an outcropping of rocks just outside the tree line. He stilled his horse and listened, pulling his rifle from the saddle holster when something rustled in the trees. His horse's ears twitched back and he danced nervously in the snow. Pryce turned in the saddle, his gun aimed, peering through the scope as he scanned the woods for any signs of movement.

By the time he heard the soft gallop of paws in the snow it was too late. His horse reared up in a panic, throwing him from the saddle as a mountain lion rounded the outcropping of rocks. His foot stuck in the stirrup, he was dragged a few dozen feet behind the spooked horse before he could twist free. When he slid to a stop, a second lion was barreling down on him from the tree line.

"Oh shit!"

Gun! Where was his rifle? Three inches of the barrel was sticking up out of the snow a few feet away and he lunged for it, rolling onto his back just in time to get off a shot. The big male hit the snow a few feet from him, leaving a bright crimson trail of blood in its wake.

He pushed to his feet and spun around, finding his horse in his scope. The female was on his tail, three yards and closing. He aimed, fired, missed, but the cat broke off the chase and cut down the ravine, across the creek and into the forest.

"Dammit!"

Pryce started to run after his horse, but the second his left foot hit the ground his ankle buckled, the pain so harsh it stole his breath. "Ow!"

He collapsed into the snow, rolled up his pant leg and pulled off his boot before the swelling got so bad he'd have to cut it off with his knife. He rolled down his sock and cringed at the deep blue knot already forming. He didn't know if anything was broken, but even if it was just a sprain, he was in deep trouble. He couldn't walk all the way back home in this condition, and with only one boot.

"Sonofabitch!" He pounded his fists into the snow.

He crawled over to the dead cat and pulled out his cellphone, holding it up in the air when he saw the no signal icon, as if that ever worked. He clicked over to his camera and took a picture of the dead cat, thumbed a text to Jonah and Chloe letting them know what happened and where he was in case it might go through, and then hobbled over to the outcropping of rocks, the pain in his foot growing worse with every step.

Hoping someone would see his rider-less horse and send help, he dug a hole in the snow at the base where two boulders met and crawled inside. With the rocks at his back and only one way in, he was safe as long as his ammo held out, and he didn't freeze to death before help came.

Chapter Twenty-Five

The door to Grey's office was ajar, but Jonah knocked anyway before he pushed it open and stuck his head inside. He'd learned long ago not to walk in unannounced. "Hey. Got a minute?"

"Sure. Come on in." Grey peeled his glasses off and closed the folder on his desk.

"Are you sure?" Jonah asked, running his sweaty palms down the front of his jeans. "I can come back later, if you're busy."

"Not at all," he insisted. "I was just watching Con and Car's latest video blog."

He turned his computer monitor around to show him, but Jonah held up a staying hand. "I've already seen it," he said with a nervous chuckle. "Douche on douche violence really isn't my thing."

Grey laughed. "You have to admit, the look on Car's face when the snowball hit him in the nuts was pretty damn funny."

Jonah could only nod, trying to steady his breathing. He didn't know why he was so nervous. He was only there to ask Grey for advice, and a small favor that would determine the outcome of the rest of his life.

"What's up?" Grey asked, leaning back in his chair, lacing his fingers behind his head.

"I want to buy Gully's Garage." *Dammit!* He hadn't intended to blurt it out like that.

"What?" Grey leaned forward in his seat, resting his elbows on his desk. His face twisted in confusion, his brows furrowing to a deep 'V'.

"I have the money," Jonah rushed to explain. "Well, most of it, but that's not the reason I wanted to talk to you."

Grey stood and walked around to the front of his desk, propping his hip on the corner. "I don't understand," he said as he crossed his arms over his broad chest.

Jonah shoved to his feet and began to pace, a nervous habit he shared with all his siblings. "That didn't come out right. Dammit! I practiced this whole speech."

"I don't need a speech," Grey said with a chuckle. "Just spit it out."

Jonah pulled out the rolled up folder he'd tucked into the back of his jeans and handed it to Grey. "I want to buy Gully's and start my own repair shop. My business plan is in there, with all my ideas. I've already talked to Mr. Gully. He's ready to sell, and I've even given him a deposit, but I don't know anything about land titles and insurance, or business licensing and all that stuff."

Grey unrolled the folder and flipped it open. He retrieved his glasses from his desk and slid them on to read Jonah's outline. It wasn't anything fancy. He'd copied the format from one he found online, and did a few conservative calculations on profit and losses and fixed expenses. He'd run the numbers every way he could think of and, with the agricultural equipment service part of his plan, he should be able to make his entire investment back in three years or less.

Grey glanced up over the rim of his glasses and Jonah's heart almost stopped. "How much of a deposit did you give him?" he asked.

"A grand." Jonah rattled off a string of silent curses. Great. He thought it was a crap plan and was already wondering how much he'd lost.

"I'm surprised he didn't ask for more."

"What? Why?" Had he missed something?

"Because that building, and the property it sits on, are worth a lot more than what you have listed here," Grey explained. "Have you had the property inspected and appraised? Are you sure there's nothing wrong with it?"

Jonah shook his head. "That's what I was hoping you could help me with. Well, that and all the other stuff I'm clueless about."

Grey closed the folder and laid it and his glasses back on his desk. "You said something about having the capital to buy it." Jonah nodded. "How, exactly? Did you already take out a loan from a bank?"

"No, I have the cash." Jonah shrugged when Grey arched a brow. "We got lucky last summer and hit a huge pay streak on the gold claim I was working on. My cut of it covers the sale price."

"And you're sure this is what you want to do with it?"

"It's what I'm good at, Dad, and Grassland needs this. And it's an income I can build a life on, with Pryce and Chloe."

He felt like he died a hundred times before Grey nodded and looked up at him. "And I'll get free equipment service?"

Jonah automatically responded with a *yes*, but choked it back. Falcon Ridge had a lot of equipment and he'd go broke in six months if he didn't charge him something.

"It was a joke," Grey said with a chuckle and hooked his arm around Jonah's shoulders. "But I can get priority scheduling, right?"

Jonah released a relieved breath. "So, does this mean you'll help me? That you think it's a good plan?"

"It's a fantastic plan, and of course I'll help you."

Jonah's internal celebration was cut short by a knock on the door. "Hey." Mason, stuck his head inside.

"Come in and listen to what Jonah has up his sleeve," Grey invited.

"Uh, yeah, I'd love to," Mason said as he lifted his hat and ran his fingers through his hair, "but Matt has one of the Jessop brothers hogtied out in the front yard, and I thought one of you might want to talk to him before he gets arrested for whatever he's about to do to him."

"What the hell, Mason?" Grey pushed past him and Jonah followed him down the hall. "Why didn't you stop him?"

"Hey, I did my part. See something, say something, right?" Mason argued when he caught up with them at the front door. "Besides, I'm not so sure I don't want to string him up myself."

"Dad! Stop!" Jonah bounded off the porch behind Grey.

"Fuckwad walked right up to the front door!" Matt grunted as he pulled on a rope he'd strung over a tree branch. The other end of the rope was tied around Wayne Jessop's waist, his hands and feet tied up behind him, and each time Matt yanked on it, Wayne was lifted higher above the ground like a hog-tied sack of potatoes.

"Help!" Wayne spit and sputtered, struggling against the rope.

"I'll help you, all right!" Matt said and gave Wayne a shove, sending him spinning in circles.

"Cut him down!" Grey ordered.

"I don't know," Mason said beside him. "I think I like our new tree ornament. Little late for Christmas, but he should be nice and ripe by next Halloween."

"Fuck! Jonah, dude, I fucked up, man. I know you hate me, but I'm not your problem!"

Jonah marched over with his pocket knife, ignoring the fear that flashed in Wayne's eyes, and sliced through the rope. Wayne landed in the snow with a muted thud.

"What the hell are you doing here, Wayne?" Jonah pressed his knee to the back of Wayne's neck. He would be lying if he said he wasn't tempted to give him more than a little payback while he was tied up.

"It's Travis, man! H-he-he's gone fucking nuts! I tried to warn Chloe, but she called the Sheriff on me before I could tell her to watch her back!"

Jonah flipped him over and yanked him up by his coat. "What has he done?"

"Nothing yet, I don't think, but he was crashing bad last night and talking all kinds of crazy shit about her and you." He looked over at Jonah's dads. "And your family," he added nervously. "He was gone this morning when I got up, and he stole my dad's car. I didn't come here to start shit. I promise!" he yelled when Grey stepped over to them. "I tried to find Pryce first, but that place is like a ghost town over there. Horses and cattle loose in the yard!"

"What?" Jonah released him and peered out across the fields, but he couldn't see anything through the trees. Pryce was supposed to have the stock in the barn by now!

Jonah didn't know which direction to run first. He pulled his phone from his pocket and called Chloe as he ran for his truck.

"Jonah, wait! I'll go with you!" Mason chased after him and jumped into the passenger seat.

"Hey—"

"Are you okay?" he asked Chloe the second she answered.

"I'm fine," she said with exasperation. "Wayne came by the bakery this morning acting all crazy, but I called the—"

"He said that Travis was coming after you. Have you seen him?"

"Wayne? When did you talk to him?"

"He's at the ranch!" Jonah put the truck in gear and spun out of the snow bank and onto the driveway, steering with one hand, and holding the phone with his shoulder as he shifted with the other.

"Wayne's at Falcon Ridge? Oh my God! Jonah, I'm so sorry," she said with a groan. "Why do my brothers have to be assholes?"

"He came to warn us about Travis," Jonah said, hitting the brakes to navigate around a fallen log on the edge of the drive. "He's talking all kinds of crazy shit and Wayne was worried he might try something stupid. Is your aunt there with you?"

"No, I'm at the clinic with Breezy."

"She's at the clinic," he repeated to Mason. His dad pulled out his cell phone and started dialing.

"We're fine, but… Jonah, I haven't heard back from Pryce all morning. You don't think he—"

"I'm on my way over there now," Jonah said. "I'll call you back when I know something."

"Jonah, you sound upset. What's going on?"

"I don't know, Lo. Wayne said he went by Pryce's before he came to the ranch and things didn't look right. I'll be there in five minutes and I'll let you know."

Mason pointed to a heifer standing in the middle of the road in front of Pryce's driveway as he hung up his phone.

"Got it," he said and slowed to a crawl to navigate around it. "You and Breezy call the Sheriff and lock your doors, and tell Aunt Bev to do the same," Jonah ordered. "I gotta go, but I'll call you right back."

"What the—?" Jonah hung up and floored the accelerator as he pulled past the gate. "How the hell did they get out past the cattle guard?"

"It doesn't look good," Mason said. "Isn't that Pryce's horse?" he asked, pointing out the passenger window toward the barn.

"What's it doing out here, and saddled up?"

"There's Mrs. Grunion." Mason pointed out the windshield when she came rushing out of the barn.

Jonah slammed the truck into park and jumped out, leaving the engine running. "What happened?" he yelled out to Pryce's mother, his heart racing faster with every frantic step he took.

"Get off my property!"

Jonah ignored her and ran into the barn, which was stuffed to the rafters with cattle. "Pryce!" He yelled out a few more times, but no one answered. "Where is he?" he demanded, taking Mrs. Grunion by the shoulders.

"I don't know," she cried. "Pastor is on his way out to look for him."

"Have you seen one of Chloe's brothers here?" Jonah asked, refusing to let her go.

"No! I haven't seen anybody but one of the hands, but he left hours ago!" she shouted, twisting away from him. While he felt a moment's relief that Travis hadn't been there, he still wasn't any closer to finding Pryce.

"Mrs. Grunion, listen to me!" Jonah took her by her shoulders. "His horse is saddled up, see?" He pointed to Pryce's horse as Mason walked it back over to the barn. "Now, think! I know he went out to herd the cattle back in. Did he come back? Is he still out there? He'll be dead in a few hours if I don't get to him before this storm blows in! It's already snowing! You need to tell me which way he went before I lose his trail!"

"What? There's another storm coming?"

"Jesus!" He let her go before he seriously hurt the woman. "Have you been living under a rock?"

"He-he-he was out here working all morning. When I came out to see why the stock was loose, his horse came galloping up to me!"

"Jonah, look at this."

Jonah raced to Mason's side and saw the jagged gashes on the horse's hind legs. "What did that?"

"Mountain lion," Mason said with a grimace. "We saw some tracks close to the fields the day you came home. We haven't had a chance to track it down yet." He flipped the leather flap beside the saddle. "The saddle holster's empty. That could be a good sign if he took his rifle."

"Pryce always takes his rifle," Mrs. Grunion confirmed, but then the seriousness of the situation finally registered. "Oh my God!"

"I gotta go find him!" Jonah gathered the horse's reins, but Mason stopped him before he could mount up. "Not this one," he said and took the reins from his hands. "He needs a vet."

"Shit! Yeah, you're right!"

"I'll take care of it." Mason jerked his head toward Jonah's truck as he pulled his phone from his pocket. "Go get Paladin. I'll call Matt and have him saddled up by the time you get back home."

"Please," Mrs. Grunion begged. "Please find him!"

Jonah sprinted for his truck, dialing Chloe as he ran.

"Is he okay?" she answered.

"He's not there, Lo. It looks like he had a run in with a mountain lion."

"A mountain lion?"

"Yeah, his horse is clawed up pretty bad. I'm on my way to go find him, but I have to go!"

"Oh my God, please, no!"

"He'll be fine," Jonah assured her, even as a thousand horrific scenarios ran through his mind. "I love you! Don't worry!"

"I love you too!" she cried. "Jonah, you have to bring him home! You hear me? You bring him home!"

"I will!" He hung up before he lost it, squeezing the phone in his hand until it cracked. The speedometer pegged sixty between Pryce's driveway and his, the tires kicking up snow and gravel as he barreled toward the barn. He would bring him home, in one piece and alive.

"Con and Car are on their way to the clinic to get Breezy and Chloe," Grey said through his open window when the truck skidded to a stop in front of the double doors at the end of the barn.

"Thanks." Singularly focused, he made a beeline to Paladin who was already saddled up and waiting for him beside two of his dads' horses.

"Take the ridge trail," Matt instructed as he mounted up.

"That's our land," Jonah argued. "What would Pryce be doing over on this side of the creek?"

"It's the last place we saw the tracks, and probably where the den is. It's the only thing I can think of that a mountain lion would defend viciously enough to attack a horse and rider."

Jonah nodded.

"Grey and I'll split the creek between the property lines. Cover more ground that way. We'll let you know if we find any tracks."

"Here!" Gabby shouted as she ran down the hill toward the barn. "I'll radio if we hear anything here," she said and tossed Jonah one of the two-way radios in her hands, then tossed Matt and Grey the others. "Please be careful, and let us know the second you find him."

"Thanks, Mom." Jonah tucked the radio into his saddlebag and kicked Paladin into gear.

Out of the barn, around the corral, and through the west gate, he rode hard toward the last place his dads had seen the mountain lion tracks, but he had to slow down when the wind picked up and the snow mixed with sleet, pelting him in the face.

He tucked his chin and pushed his horse through the snowdrifts. The landscape changed quickly from flat snow-covered fields to steep rocky hills and he had to go even slower. "Pryce!" He stopped and listened, but couldn't hear anything except the stinging sleet bouncing off his hat and coat. "Pryce!" He yelled out every ten feet or so as he approached the rocky edge of the ridgeline. There were no tracks leading anywhere. Pryce wasn't there.

"Jonah!" Grey's voice crackled over the radio. Jonah scrambled to untie his saddlebag and pull the radio out. *God, please let him say they found him.* "Go ahead," he said and released the button, holding his breath for Grey's reply.

"We found horse and lion tracks crossing the creek. Looks like he cut across the valley toward the ridge."

"I'm up here now, but I don't see anything!"

He turned Paladin around in a circle, searching for any signs of life, but the snow was blowing so thick and hard he couldn't see twenty feet in any direction.

"Check the outcrops over by the northern watering tank!" Grey instructed. "He might have taken shelter there!"

Jonah cursed. He was a half mile past it! "On my way!"

"Be careful." Matt's voice called over the radio.

Jonah pulled his rifle from the holster and kept it tucked under his arm, guiding Paladin back down the ridge toward where he hoped the watering tank was. He was navigating near white-out conditions when the dark tower appeared in the distance, the edge of the woods just behind it. If he could make it to the tree line he might catch a break in visibility long enough to pick up any remaining tracks.

"Pryce!"

Paladin's ears twitched to the right and Jonah stilled.

"Pryce!"

Something bellowed in the distance, but he couldn't tell if it was human, or just the trees creaking in the wind. He turned his horse to follow the sound, shouting Pryce's name every few steps, then stopped when he saw the outcropping of rocks in the distance.

"Pryce!"

"Over here!"

Jonah jumped from his horse and slogged through the knee-high powder until he saw a dark figure in the distance. "Pryce! Holy shit! I found you!" He latched onto his best friend and lover and tackled him into the snow.

"Ouch!" Pryce recoiled beneath him and drew his leg up to his chest.

"What's wrong? Are you hurt?"

"My ankle!" Pryce shouted through his chattering teeth. "F-f-foot got c-caught in stirrup when my horse reared."

Jonah struggled to his feet and helped Pryce to stand. "Is everything else all right? Did the mountain lion get you?"

Pryce shook his head. "J-j-just cold. Is my h-horse okay?"

"He's cut up pretty bad! Mason is looking after him. Wait here a second. I gotta radio my dads! They're out looking for you too!"

He ran back to Paladin and dug out his radio. "I found him!" he shouted into the speaker. "Up by the rocks, like you said!"

"Is he okay?" Grey's voice was barely audible over the sounds of the wind.

"He's got a twisted ankle, but he's alive!"

The radio crackled again, nothing but static coming from the speaker.

"Dad!"

He held the radio up to his ear, but still nothing.

"Dad!"

"Get up to the cabin!" Grey's voice crackled through.

What? Was he crazy? "The storm is too strong!" he shouted back. Holy hell! He couldn't make it all the way up to the cabin in these conditions.

"It's worse in the valley! You need to get above the storm, Son!"

Jonah cursed and looked over at Pryce. How was he supposed to get him and Paladin up the ridge to the cabin?

"Do you copy?"

A biting gust of wind cut across the treetops and loud crack filled the air. The top of a tall pine snapped off and crashed to the ground a few dozen feet behind him, spooking Paladin, but Jonah caught his reigns.

"We copy!" he shouted into the radio.

Chapter Twenty-Six

With Pryce mounted safely atop Paladin, Jonah picked his way up the rocky ridgeline toward the family hunting cabin. His dad had been right. The storm had blown in low and fast through the valley, but once they started climbing, the snow thinned and the winds calmed. It was still a hell of a storm, and the temperatures had dropped like a rock, but at least he could see where he was going. For now. They were running out of daylight and if they didn't reach the cabin soon, they'd never make it through the night. They had to be close. He knew the trail like the back of his hand, but covered in this much snow, everything looked different.

Paladin snorted and Jonah looked back to see Pryce hunched over the saddle horn, his gloved fists clenched in Paladin's mane. "Hey." Marching back, he could hear Pryce's teeth chattering over the sound of the snow crunching beneath his boots. He cupped his wind-burned cheeks between his hands. "Hang in there," he said, giving Pryce a soft shake. "We're almost there."

"I'm fine," Pryce insisted, the words stuttered and broken.

The hell he was. Jonah pulled off his coat, the cold air slicing through his shirt like a thousand knives, and unzipped the heavy wool lining. While every step hurt, walking kept him warm enough to keep going. Pryce didn't have that luxury. Unable to walk, he was going to freeze to death if Jonah didn't get him to the cabin soon.

He draped the wool lining over Pryce's back, tucking it in tight around him before he slipped his sheepskin coat back on and started walking double time, repeating Grey's words in his head with each step. *Whatever. It. Takes.*

The grey sky turned darker by the minute and leached into the landscape until everything blended together in the dusk. No longer able to feel his hands, he stopped to check on Pryce when he saw the outline of the cabin in the distance.

"Whoop!" He pumped his fist into the air. "We found it!"

Pryce stirred in the saddle and Jonah rushed to his side. "Hold on a few more minutes, man. We're here."

He tugged Paladin's reins and marched across the snow, gritting his teeth against the pins and needles stinging his feet with each step. If it weren't for his one splurge on the special boots he'd bought in Alaska, he would no doubt have lost a toe or two by now.

The small porch in the front was invisible beneath the snow, but it didn't take much to clear a path and pry open the door. He rushed back to Pryce and peeled him from the saddle, carrying him over his shoulder into the one-room cabin and set him down on the edge of the bed.

"Get undressed," he ordered, but Pryce didn't respond. "Hey," he tapped Pryce's cheek, and then shook his shoulders until Pryce opened his eyes and gazed drunkenly up at him. "Christ." Hypothermia was setting in quick.

He rushed to the shelves in the corner, pulled out every blanket in the stack and tossed them on the bed. Piece by piece, he stripped off Pryce's clothes, laid him out on the thin bare mattress and piled on the blankets, tucking them in as tight as he could. "I'll be right back," he said, but lingered, second guessing what he should do next: strip down and stay with him until he came around, or get the fire started. The temps were still dropping and they would both freeze if they didn't have some source of heat.

"Got to do it," he finally decided and left Pryce bundled up and shivering on the bed.

He gathered up the wood stacked beside the wood stove and piled it inside, tossed in some lighter knot and struck a match, blowing on the flame until it caught.

With the wood crackling, he rushed outside, cringing against the cold wind, and grabbed Paladin's reins. He hated the idea of leaving him out in the cold, but he had no choice. They were too far from home to unsaddle him and send him back on his own. Surrounded on three sides by jagged rocks and steep cliffs, he couldn't let the horse run free.

He walked him over to the side of the cabin, out of the wind, and tied him off to the porch railing, then grabbed his rifle and saddlebag and gave him a pat on the neck. "You've got a good winter coat, buddy. You'll be fine. I'll bring you some water as soon as I get Pryce warmed up and melt some snow," he said with a quick rub of Paladin's nose, and then rushed back inside.

Pryce was ice cold and shivering violently when he crawled beneath the covers and huddled against his naked body. Bare flesh to bare flesh, he wrapped himself around him and they shivered together. He rubbed Pryce's arms, his sides, his thighs, kissed every patch of bare skin within reach until he could no longer hold his eyes open and they drifted off into oblivion.

The crackling noise of his radio woke him sometime later. Though his hands and feet still felt like bricks of ice, the air inside the cabin was warm and toasty. Sitting up, he leaned over to check on Pryce. He still felt a little chilly to the touch, but he was no longer shivering and his breathing had leveled out.

Satisfied with the progress, he peeled himself from Pryce's side, his body sore and protesting every move. The radio crackled again, but no voices came through. He scrubbed his hands over his face and dropped his legs over the side of the bed. Now that they weren't going to freeze to death, they needed to rehydrate and find some food.

Each step less painful than the first, he walked over to his saddlebag and pulled out his radio, setting it on the table with the still-frozen bottles of water his dads must have tossed in, along with a handful of expired granola bars he'd found in the bottom of the bag. Taking a quick stock of the cupboards, he found a first aid kit, the pot he needed to melt some snow, along with a lockbox of beef jerky, a few pouches of just-add-water meals, and—thank-you-baby-Jesus—some coffee!

He lit the handful of candles he'd found and placed them around the room before the radio clicked again and this time, Chloe's voice came through loud and clear.

"Base to Jonah. Are you there?"

He rushed back to the table and snatched up the radio. "Jonah to base, we're here!" Pryce grumbled and shuffled beneath the covers. Jonah cringed and lowered his voice. "Hey, Lo. We're safe and sound at the cabin, over."

"Oh thank God!" she shouted and he scrambled to turn down the volume. "Is Pryce okay? Can I talk to him?"

"You have to let go of the button," he heard Cory say in the background, followed by the clicking sound that told him she had.

"He's sleeping, Lo." Jonah watched the covers move up and down with each of his breaths. "His ankle is twisted up pretty bad from getting stuck in the stirrup when his horse reared, but other than a little hypothermia he's fine. Don't worry."

"Are you going to be okay? The storm is still really bad outside!"

"We're fine, Lo. Promise. What about you? Did Travis cause you any trouble?"

"No. Nobody's seen him since last night, but I'm okay. Con and Car brought me to the ranch and I'm staying here until you get home."

Relieved, Jonah released a sigh. Hopefully Travis was gone for good. He'd have to remember to thank Wayne for the heads up when he got back, after he punched him in the throat.

"Are my dads there?" As much as he wanted to talk to her, he needed to get an idea of what was going on in the valley while they still had a signal.

"Right here, Son." The smile in Grey's voice made him feel proud he'd made it, that he hadn't given up. "The power and phones are out down here. No signal. Looks like the storm is going to sit tight through the night. You got everything you need up there?"

Jonah peeled back the curtain on the window beside the table and peered out at the darkness. "We're fine for a day or so, but we may need to be shoveled out of here."

Grey laughed. "As long as you're both okay and can keep a fire going, you'll be fine. I'm sure the two of you can think of plenty of ways to keep warm."

"Dad!" His face flushed hot despite the cold. He looked over at Pryce, then down at his cock and snorted, remembering the nickname Pryce had given him. Jonah and the whale weren't coming out to play anytime soon.

"Remember, there's a load of cut wood stacked beneath the porch," Grey continued. "You may need to dig down to it, but it should be dry, and enough to get you by until this blows through."

He'd forgotten about that. "Thanks." He was reluctant to ask the next question, but knew Pryce would want to know as soon as he woke up. "Is Pryce's mom okay?"

"She's staying in town with friends from the church," Mason answered. The whole family must be gathered around the radio. "I got the stock corralled back into the barn, and his horse bandaged up. All's good on the home front."

Relieved, he sank down into one of the four chairs skirting the table. A shiver raced down his spine when the cold, polished wood made contact with his bare skin. "I'm going to melt some snow and heat up some soup," he said. "Tell Mom and Chloe I love them."

"I love you too, honey," Gabby clicked back. "Oh! And there's some extra clothes and stuff packed under the bed if you need them."

"Thanks, Mom." He could hear the worry in her voice despite her attempts to hide it behind her smile.

"We'll listen for your call if you need anything," Cory said. "Don't worry about Chloe."

"Bastard," Jonah mumbled with a grin and clicked over. "No flirting with our girl."

"I love you," Chloe clicked back over one last time. "And tell Pryce I love him, too!"

"He knows, Lo."

"Tell him!"

Jonah laughed. "I will. Love you too."

What little bit of energy his short rest had earned him already spent, he forced himself out of the chair and back to work. With Pryce still fast asleep, he refueled the stove with the wood left inside, deciding to tackle getting more later if they needed it, then layered his clothes back on to fetch a bucket of snow.

He cursed when he opened the door, hurrying to shut it behind him. "Fuck my balls!" It hadn't been this cold in Alaska, for crying out loud!

He scooped out a bucket full of snow from the bank building at the edge of the porch and rushed back inside, his fingers already numb by the time he closed the door. He poured the snow into the pot he'd found and set it on the wood stove to melt.

After the boiled water cooled, he ran it out to Paladin, who seemed as snug as a bug, then repeated the process. He set the next pot on the stove for him and Pryce, and then went to work on making a bowl of soup. When everything was ready, he snuck back under the covers and snuggled against Pryce's back.

"Hey," he whispered in his ear. "You need to eat something."

"Huh?"

Jonah traced his fingers along Pryce's thigh and back up to his hip. He hadn't planned anything sexual when he crawled into bed with him, but the temptation to touch him was too strong to ignore. He reached down and wrapped his hand around Pryce's hard cock.

"Holy—" Pryce jackknifed from the mattress. "Cold hands! You and Chloe with your cold fucking hands!"

Jonah snatched his hand back with a laugh. "Sorry," he said, kissing Pryce's shoulder.

"Shit!" Pryce crashed back down to the mattress.

Jonah leaned down and traced his nipple with his tongue, drawing out a throaty growl. "Better?"

"Would be if I didn't have to piss so bad." He pushed back the covers and looked at his watch, than bolted back up. "We survived?"

Jonah laughed again as he rolled from the bed, tossing Pryce his jeans. "So far so good, except having to go outside to take a leak. Better get it over with now so you don't have to go out after your belly's full of hot soup. Sort of ruins it."

"You have soup?"

"Mmhmm." Jonah grinned. He couldn't help it. Pryce was alive, and so damn hot with his shaggy hair all ruffled like they'd spent the last six hours fucking rather than surviving a blizzard.

"I'm starving." Pryce rolled out of bed but then crashed right back down onto it with a groan. "Ow" he said, drawing a hissing breath through his teeth.

"Damn. I forgot about your ankle." Jonah rushed around to the other side of the bed and squatted down to take a look.

"I forgot, too."

Jonah cringed when he saw the swollen knot. "Man, that looks worse than mine did when I got sacked by Lenny Darringer that last game of my sophomore year. Remember that?"

"You deserved it for letting Skinny Lenny sack you."

"Hey!" Jonah gave him a playful shove back onto the mattress. "It wasn't my fault the entire offensive line was already half in the tank celebrating the *five* touchdowns I'd already scored." He straddled Pryce's thighs and kneeled on the mattress, one knee on each side of his hips. "What's the matter?" He inched up Pryce's chest until the tip of his cock was almost touching Pryce's chin. "Were you jealous?" he teased, sucking in a breath when Pryce glanced down at his cock and licked his lips. Was he going to do it this time?

Pryce tackled him, rolling him to his back. "I really gotta piss," he said with a grin and motioned to his stiff prick. "And this isn't going to help."

Jonah laid there a second, sucking wind while Pryce shimmied into his jeans. *So close!*

Pryce hissed when he tried to stand, his gaze darting around the cabin then down to his ankle. "Do you think there's something here to wrap it with?"

Jonah blinked away his hopeful visions. Pryce wasn't ready, and clearly in no condition to fool around. "I didn't see anything earlier, but I'll check again. We've got plenty of ice, though. Here, let me help you." He stood and tossed Pryce his shirt and coat. "Trust me, you're gonna need them."

"Screw going outside." Pryce dropped the clothes on the bed and hopped to the door, ignoring Jonah's offer to help. "I'm only cracking the door a couple of inches and lettin' her rip."

"Suit yourself." After rummaging through the first aid kit he'd found earlier, finding nothing that would help Pryce's ankle, Jonah grabbed two spoons and the pot of soup and headed to the table, laughing at the high-pitched yelp Pryce let out when he opened the door. "Told you."

"How the hell am I supposed to take a leak in this? My dick's never been this confused!"

"Really?" Jonah chuckled. "Could've fooled me."

"Not funny," Pryce tossed over his shoulder.

Something on the floor caught Jonah's eye. Pryce's wallet had fallen out of his jeans and Jonah bent down to pick it up, pausing when it flipped open to an old picture, the corners worn and creased. He instantly recognized himself in the image, sitting on the boulder by the creek, but he couldn't have been more than fourteen when it was taken.

"I'm never going to be able to watch Alaskan Ice Truckers again." Pryce tucked and zipped and hobbled over to the table, crashing into the chair beside him. "Oh! Hey-don't…" He tried to take his wallet back, but Jonah snatched it away.

"When did you take this?"

Pryce blushed from neck to ears, staring at the picture. He scratched an eyebrow, still not meeting Jonah's gaze. "The day we first met," he finally said, reaching for the wallet again, but Jonah was faster. "It was my first camera, okay? I was down by the creek, burning up film when I saw you sitting there, and I don't know. I just took a picture of you."

"And you've saved it? All this time?"

Pryce swallowed nervously, then nodded.

"Have you jacked off to this picture of me?" The idea did something funny to Jonah's insides and he couldn't help but fall a little farther in love with him at the thought.

"No!" Pryce snatched the wallet from his grasp and Jonah let him have it this time

"You have!" Pure, undiluted happiness bubbled up from somewhere deep inside when he saw the truth in Pryce's eyes.

"I have not!" Pryce insisted, but he couldn't contain his embarrassed grin. "Maybe," he finally admitted.

"You did and you know it!" Jonah cupped Pryce's neck, pulling him into a kiss, but neither of them could contain their laughter. "I'm flattered," he said when the laughing subsided.

"I'm starving." Pryce pushed Jonah back into his chair, still blushing.

Jonah handed him a spoon and they both dug into the pot of broth and rehydrated vegetables. "So what the heck happened out there?" he asked, his cheeks still aching from grinning so hard.

Pryce shook his head with a shrug. "Donovan and I were moving the last count of cattle into the corral and spotted some big cat tracks close to the interior gate, so I went to check them out after he left.

When I saw they crossed over the creek, I tried to call you but there was no signal out that far." Chills raced along Jonah's arms as Pryce told him about the eerie feeling he got seconds before the female charged him. "It was like my body knew something wasn't right before my brain put all the pieces together." He shrugged. "By then it was over, and the second cat was practically on top of me before I could pull the trigger."

"Damn." Jonah took another bite and laid down his spoon. "That means the momma is still out there."

"I listened for cub cries after I tucked into the rocks, but didn't hear anything."

"Yeah." Jonah got up and peered out the window again. "Matt said he thought they might be defending a den." He couldn't see anything but black darkness against the candlelight reflecting in the window. He'd have to keep a keen ear for any unsettled noises Paladin might make. The mountain lion probably wouldn't follow them this far up the ridge in the storm, but he couldn't take the chance of losing his horse.

"I hope my mother's okay in this storm," Pryce said. "She doesn't even know how to build a good fire."

Jonah looked over his shoulder to see him staring into the pot of soup. "Man, I forgot to tell you." He sat back down and retrieved the radio from his saddlebag. "She's staying with some friends in town. Wayne found half your stock roaming loose in your yard and we went over to see what had happened. That's when Mason saw your horse. She said her pastor was coming to help, so I assume he—"

"What? Wayne? Chloe's brother? What the hell was he doing there?"

Jonah told him about Wayne coming to warn them about Travis.

"Is Chloe okay?" Pryce yanked the radio from his hand. "Did Travis hurt her?"

"Relax," he said, laying a hand over the radio. "She's fine. Con and Car picked her and Breezy up, and she's staying at the ranch with my family. Nobody's seen Travis since last night."

"I still need to talk to her. Let her know I'm okay."

Jonah turned on the radio and they clicked over a few times, but heard nothing but static in return.

"We'll try again in a bit." Jonah took the radio from Pryce's hand and set it back on the table. "She knows you're okay." He laced his fingers with Pryce's, staring at the way they fit together, so differently than his and Chloe's, yet just as right. The seriousness of what had happened hit Jonah like a Mack truck. All the fear he'd beaten back since finding Pryce's horse cut up, and Pryce nowhere to be found, came rushing at him all at once.

"I lost you a thousand times today," he said, running his thumb over Pryce's knuckles.

Pryce's fingers tightened around his and Jonah met his tired gaze. Pryce's lips parted, his tongue peeking out and tracing his bottom lip in a nervous but hungry swipe. Jonah sat frozen, afraid to make the first move and get rejected again, but every cell in his body was primed and rioting for his touch.

Pryce swallowed, hard, his gaze dropping to their hands before he spoke. "I don't know what to do," he said, then pulled his hand free from Jonah's. He stood and Jonah blew out the breath he'd been holding, sure he was going to be left with another case of blue balls, until Pryce braced himself on the table and clumsily hobbled over to him. He shoved off his jeans then straddled Jonah's lap, their cocks pressed together between them, and spoke against his lips. "Show me."

Chapter Twenty-Seven

Pryce gripped Jonah's shoulders and held on for dear life, their mouths fused together in a desperate kiss as Jonah stumbled to the bed. Simultaneously terrified and turned on, every step Jonah took brought them that much closer to crossing the line he'd drawn between them, a line that blurred with every breath, every touch.

His back hit the mattress and Jonah tumbled down atop him. The weight of his body between his thighs, pressing him into the bed, felt strange but good, and freeing as he lost himself in Jonah's kiss.

When he'd seen that mountain lion barreling down on him, his life had flashed before his eyes. He'd heard the phrase before and thought it was just something people said to be dramatic, but it wasn't. It was as real as the pictures he took with his camera, but faster, clearer, even in the face of death. Hundreds of pictures of Jonah and Chloe had flashed before him with blinding speed. The church didn't matter. His mother didn't matter. There was no right or wrong, heaven or hell, only Jonah and Chloe and the regret that he'd not loved them the way they deserved.

Them.

They both owned his heart and soul. Now, with an ache so strong he could no longer deny it, he was finally ready to surrender his body to Jonah. He needed him as much as he'd ever needed Chloe.

He gripped Jonah's ass, kneading the firm flesh beneath his palms, pulling him harder against the demanding thrust of his hips. Jonah tore his mouth away, a deep groan rumbling in the depths of his throat as he ground himself against Pryce.

"Christ, I want to fuck you so bad right now," Jonah panted against his shoulder.

Pryce slid his fingers through Jonah's hair and lifted his head so he could look into his eyes. "I want you to."

Hovering above him, Jonah's eyes swirled with erotic hope. "Now?" he asked.

Pryce nodded.

"Are you sure? Because I don't think I could take it if you changed your mind again."

"I'm not changing my mind." He pulled Jonah down and kissed him again, seeking out every part of his mouth, taking it over and over again. Jonah devoured him with desperate urgency, but then he jerked away and scrambled to his feet.

"What-where are you going?" Jonah didn't answer as he rushed to the other side of the cabin, returning with a plastic box in his hand.

"Mmmph!" Jonah quashed his next question with another dizzying kiss, pinning his arms above his head as he settled back between his thighs.

Pryce wrapped his legs around Jonah's hips and bucked up beneath him, searching out the relieving contact. Jonah answered his demand with a snap of his hips, pushing him deep into the unforgiving mattress before he released one of his hands and reached for the box he'd retrieved.

Pryce chuckled when he looked down at the box and saw Jonah fumbling with a bottle of lube, a few condoms scattered on the mattress beside the box.

"What?" Jonah grinned with a shrug, twirling the bottle upside down and squeezing half of it into his palm. "I saw it earlier when I was looking for something to wrap your ankle."

Pryce arched a dubious brow.

Jonah laughed. "It's not like I was planning on getting trapped here with you. Lube is a survival staple in my family."

Pryce didn't have time to protest before Jonah grabbed their cocks and coated them with the gel. "Cold!"

"It'll warm up." Jonah gave them both a long, silky stroke.

He'd been right. It did warm, and quickly, but as good as it felt—oh God help him—a hand job wasn't what he wanted. "Wait." He pushed at Jonah's chest, but Jonah silenced him with another kiss. He tore himself away, gasping for his next breath as he tried to still Jonah's hand before it was too late, but Jonah released him just in time.

"Hold on," Jonah said, cupping his balls in his palm as he circled his virgin hole with his finger, pressing one inside, then another.

Pryce arched off the bed, the burn and stretch harsh but satisfying, making him want to both pull away and press down harder. "Oh fuck!" he shouted when Jonah curled his fingers and massaged his gland.

"Damn, Pry," Jonah said, circling his finger until Pryce cried out from the pleasure. "You're going to make me come just watching you."

In and out, Jonah worked his fingers, all the while setting his flesh ablaze, kissing his shoulder, his neck, his jaw, nipping and licking at his lips until he was ready to come apart at the seams.

"Now," Pryce demanded and grabbed Jonah's hand. He laced their fingers together, shimmying into place until the head of Jonah's cock kissed his hole. "Do it."

Jonah pressed into him, the tip of his cock stretching him until the stinging burn turned to a white-hot flame. "Sh—oh—damn!" He was too big! Through the blazing pain, Jonah's instructions to Chloe surfaced. He squeezed his eyes closed and tried to relax, bearing down on him despite the pain. If Chloe could take him, he sure as hell could.

"Uhhh…mmm…ummm…" Jonah grunted with each deliberate flex of his hips, throwing his head back, baring his teeth with a shout when he breached Pryce's rim and finally slid inside.

Pryce opened his mouth to scream, but not a single sound escaped.

"Oh-Christ. Oh-damn." Jonah panted in his ear. "So fucking good." He pushed up and hovered above him, his arms shaking. Pryce held his breath, afraid if he didn't that he'd scream like a girl, or worse, cry. "Are you okay?" Jonah asked.

Pryce nodded silently, blinking away the blackness bleeding into his vision of Jonah above.

"Hey, it's okay." Jonah relented, stilling inside him as he lowered himself down on top of him, the blanketing weight pushing him deeper, his length and girth filling him so full.

"Breathe," he coaxed, nibbling his way up his jawline. Pryce shook his head even as the burning in his chest intensified. "Breathe," Jonah whispered again, suckling his earlobe, snaking his hot wet tongue into his ear.

A shot of desire throbbed through Pryce's veins, straight from his heart to his cock. The air rushed from his lungs like a deflating balloon.

"That's it." Jonah continued his tender, soothing assault, nipping and stealing tastes of his skin and sweat. "I can't tell you how many times I've dreamed of this." With a feather-light touch, Jonah trailed his lips over his temple, across his forehead and down the other side of his face.

"Me too," Pryce managed when the razor-sharp edge of pain dulled to more of an overload of sensations.

Jonah grinned, and then pressed his mouth to Pryce's. Pryce tipped his head back and welcomed Jonah's kiss. Their tongues met in a slow wet glide, one after the other until the sharp ache inside rolled into a constant demanding throb.

"Can I move?" Jonah asked.

"Please."

Jonah pushed back up onto his shaky forearms, jostling the bed. Pryce bit his lip, expecting the searing pain to return, but when Jonah drew his hips back, the heat he felt was of a completely different kind. The good kind. The orgasm inducing kind.

"Nnuaahh!" He shuddered as the length of Jonah's cock glided through his sensitive opening, sucking in another ragged breath when he slid back in.

Jonah grinned. "I can't wait until it's my turn," he said, but Pryce couldn't think about that yet. Burning from the inside out, he couldn't think period. He fisted his hands in Jonah's hair, pulling him down until their mouths met in a clash of teeth and tangle of tongues. He loved him. He loved this man so damn much. If this was hell, he wanted to roll around in the flames for all eternity, coating himself in soot and ash, and everything Jonah.

The mattress springs creaked and popped as Jonah thrust inside him over and over again, slow, then faster, harder, the muted sound of their bodies colliding in a hypnotic rhythm giving him a high like none he'd ever felt. He hooked his legs around the back of Jonah's thighs, ignoring the pain in his ankle to pull him deeper inside with every inward thrust.

Jonah mumbled a string of curses and shifted above him, the new angle shuttling his cock over Pryce's gland and sending every nerve ending in his body into overdrive, triggering a blinding orgasm he had no hope of stopping.

"I'm coming!" He couldn't hold it back. His entire body convulsed beneath Jonah as spurt after spurt of cum jettisoned from his cock and splashed onto his chest.

"Uhm-uh-mmm-uaahhh!"

With one final deep thrust, Jonah held himself deep inside, coming with a shout that must have shaken the snow from the roof before he collapsed on top of Pryce in a heap.

Jonah sighed into the crook of his neck, in no hurry to move. Neither was he. As limp as an overcooked noodle, he closed his eyes and relived every moment they'd just shared, their bodies twitching in unison as if Jonah was reliving it too. He never wanted to forget this night, ever, not that he could.

"You saved me." The words sprang from Pryce's heart and spilled from his lips without thought.

Jonah chuckled. "Damn right, I did." He lifted his head and grinned. "You'd be a popsicle by now."

Pryce shook his head. "No. I mean…I'm…" His life had changed so much. He couldn't find the words to express what Jonah meant to him.

Jonah's grin faded, his gaze locked with Pryce's for a moment before he lowered his head and kissed his shoulder, his neck. "I love you," he whispered into his ear, the very words Pryce had been searching for.

Certainty flooded Pryce's veins like a soothing balm, the same certainty he'd felt when he first knew he wanted to spend the rest of his life with Chloe. For the first time since he'd realized he was falling in love with Jonah, he didn't feel the least bit ashamed or confused or sinful. He felt empowered, free, like he could do anything, be anyone, even a man in love with his best friend. He wrapped his arms around Jonah and let the truth flow from his heart for the first time, untainted by doubt and fear. "I love you, too."

A few hours later Pryce was awakened by a rustling sound outside. He peeled his eyes open to see sunlight flooding through the cabin window, followed by a rumble of muted voices. Before he could throw off the covers or wake Jonah, the cabin door flew open and Chloe rushed inside.

"Oh thank God you're okay!"

"Lo?" Jonah sat up, scrubbing the sleep from his eyes. "What are you doing here?"

Chloe rushed across the room and jumped into the middle of the bed, climbing between them and smothering them with excited kisses. "I thought I'd lost you both!"

Pryce winced when she jostled his swollen ankle, but he was so happy to see her. He pulled her into his arms, relieved to know she was okay, and returned her excited kiss.

"I stayed up all night listening for you on the radio. When I tried to reach you again this morning and nothing came through, I was so scared!" She straddled Jonah's hips and kissed him too, pulling Pryce into the kiss with them.

"Eh-hem." Pryce pulled away at the sound of another male voice. Heat rushed to his cheeks when he saw Grey standing in the open doorway, the sun's reflecting rays behind him casting an intimidating shadow across the room.

Pryce gave the elder McLendon a nod. "Thank you, sir. I'm sorry about crossing over onto your property, but I was worried—"

Grey held up a staying hand. "No thanks or apologies needed, Son." The corners of Grey's lips quirked up and he covered his mouth to hide his grin, coughing to clear his throat before he continued. "That's what family's for. I'm just glad to see both of you…alive. That was one hell of a blizzard."

Jonah and Chloe both shivered beside him and Pryce realized for the first time he was naked, nothing but a few layers of covers separating him from the frigid air filling the cabin.

"Are they okay?" Matt asked, striding up behind Grey. "Oh shit! Sorry!" He covered his eyes and spun around on his heels, reaching back to grab Grey and pull him back outside. "Y'all get dressed already! I'm freezin' my balls off out here!" he shouted and closed the door.

Pryce looked over at Jonah and laughed, seeing the reason for Grey's smirk and Matt's quick retreat. Plastered to Jonah's chest were several unopened condoms that had been strewn over the bed when they'd fallen asleep in each other's arms.

At Pryce's snicker, Jonah looked down and peeled one off with a chuckle. "Serves them right after all the times I've walked in on them and my mom."

"Oh my gosh!" Chloe gave them both a chastising shove. "You did it without me!"

A sense of panic tightened in Pryce's gut. "But, I thought you said you were okay with us...you know…"

"Oh! No, I am, but I wanted to watch!" She pursed her lips into a pouty pucker.

"Oh, there will be a repeat performance, trust me," Jonah said and tackled her onto the mattress, then pulled Pryce into a quick but thorough kiss before he rolled off the bed and pulled on his jeans.

Once cleaned up and dressed, Jonah called in his dads and they helped Pryce hobble to one of the snowmobiles they'd driven up the ridge. Relief rushed through Pryce the second he saw the sleek machines. Aside from his ankle throbbing like a sonofabitch, his ass was too sore to be perched on top of Jonah's horse for any length of time.

"I'll ride Paladin down," Matt offered. "Y'all get home and get Pryce to the hospital to have that ankle looked at."

Pryce thought to protest, but by the time they reached the McLendon's house the pain in his ankle was unbearable.

"Pryce!" His mother came rushing out the front door of the McLendon's house when the snowmobile rolled to a stop by the steps.

"Mother? What are you doing here?"

"Oh thank God!" She threw her arms around his neck and tackled him with so much force he and Grey nearly rolled off the seat. "Are you okay?" She ran her hands over him in a frenzied rush to check him over. Pryce twisted away and cast a questioning glance at Mrs. McLendon standing at the base of the steps, hoping his mother hadn't done something awful.

"I invited her to come wait for word that you were okay," Gabby explained, tightening her wool shawl around her shoulders. "Dani drove into town to pick her up."

"You let Dani drive into town?" Grey grumbled as he removed his helmet. "What were you thinking?"

"I'm thinking she's a grown woman and knows how to drive in the snow better than me."

A few seconds behind them, Jonah rolled up and jumped off his snowmobile.

"Jonah!" Gabby ran to him, checking to make sure he was okay. "Oh good! You found the clothes!" she said, noting the extra layers Jonah had thrown on under his coat.

Pryce's mother gasped when she saw his ankle. "We need to get you to the hospital!"

By the time he was admitted into the emergency room Pryce was beginning to think his ankle wasn't his only injury. Maybe they should take a look at his head while he was there.

His mother, Jonah, Chloe, and the rest of the McLendons all stood together as they waited for the doctor. No one spoke a spiteful word. As he glanced around the crowded room, it felt like he'd fallen to sleep in Jonah's arms and woken up in an alternate universe. Not once had his mother sneered at Chloe or given Jonah a sideways glance, or insulted Jonah's family. She'd even thanked them profusely for rescuing him.

"Mr. Grunion?"

Pryce caught himself looking for his father before he realized the doctor was asking for him. "Yeah, uh, that's me." Careful not to move his leg, he pushed himself up straighter in the bed.

"Looks like you have a hairline fracture to the tip of your fibula, but you lucked out and didn't tear any ligaments."

Pryce cringed. Lucky or not, the last thing he could afford with all the work he had to do was to be laid up with a bum ankle, not to mention the medical bills he couldn't pay.

"What about the hypothermia?" his mother asked.

"Well, thanks to his friend's efforts," he said nodding to Jonah, "as far as I can tell it wasn't serious. Make sure he drinks plenty of fluids and wears the boot we'll have fitted for him, and he should make a full recovery."

"Aww." Chloe leaned down and pressed her lips to his forehead. "Don't worry. We'll take good care of you."

Pryce looked at his mother, expecting to see her glaring at Chloe. There was some disappointment in her eyes, but mostly resignation as she smiled tiredly down at him. Something huge had shifted between them, and whatever it was, he wasn't about to question it.

Chapter Twenty-Eight

Pryce pulled at the straps on his ankle boot, wincing at the loud noise the Velcro made in the small, quiet office. Jonah arched a brow, reminding him for the tenth time that day that he wasn't supposed to take it off. Pryce didn't care. The damn thing itched worse than a plaster cast and he couldn't take it anymore.

"Sorry to keep you waiting," the senior Mr. Melrose, of the Law Offices of Melrose and Melrose, said in a rush as he walked in and closed the door behind him. "I had to find your file. My assistant still hasn't been able to dig out from the storm and I'm a complete idiot when it comes to how things are filed around here."

Pryce's gut tightened, the pressure lessening only marginally when Chloe laced her fingers with his. To her right, his mother unfastened her coat button, her back ramrod straight as she gave the family attorney a nervous nod. She'd been acting strange the last two days and Pryce was determined to figure out why.

Inviting Gabby over for coffee the day before had been beyond strange. Inviting Jonah and Chloe over for dinner had been the last straw. He'd cornered her in the kitchen after they'd politely refused, and demanded to know what she was up to. She'd insisted that she was only being polite and wanted to thank them for helping save his life, but Pryce wasn't buying it.

That morning she'd been especially nostalgic. She'd cooked his favorite breakfast and talked about all her favorite memories of him as a child. He might not have bought the new-leaf thing she was doing, but it beat the alternative, so he'd decided to let it go, hoping it wasn't just another of her ploys to manipulate him.

He tightened his hand around Chloe's and glanced over to Jonah. Nothing she could say or do would tear him away from the two people he loved.

"Well," the attorney began, peering through his fashionable bifocals at the documents in front of him. "Dirk's will is pretty straightforward," he said, still reading. "Mrs. Grunion, as his surviving spouse, he's left you with the ranch and the house, but as you may know, they come with a severe amount of debt: a second mortgage, a substantial line of credit, and a—"

"We're well aware of the debt," Pryce said.

Mr. Melrose paused and glanced impatiently over the rim of his glasses. Pryce shifted in his seat beneath the weight of his scrutinizing stare. He knew they were up to his eyeballs in debt. He didn't need anyone to itemize it for him.

"Yes, well," he continued, flipping to the next page. "There's the usual life insurance policies, which—"

"Policies?" Mrs. Grunion leaned forward in her seat. "There's more than one?"

The lawyer nodded and pointed his pen at her. "One policy for ten-thousand-dollars with you listed as the beneficiary, to cover his burial expenses, I presume," he said, and then nodded to Pryce. "And there is a term life policy for fifty-thousand-dollars to be paid to his oldest surviving heir. I'm assuming, as an only child, that would be you, Pryce?"

Pryce doubled over and rested his head in his hands, feeling his last hope slip through his fingers. As badly as he needed that money, he couldn't cheat Breezy.

"No, sir."

"Pryce!" his mother protested with a chastising whisper.

Pryce ignored her. "Breezy McLendon is his daughter—or at least we think she is."

"You don't know that!" his mother shouted.

Pryce confirmed the lawyer's questioning glance with a nod and a sigh.

"Okay," Mr. Melrose proceeded, jotting down a note in the file. "We'll have to do a DNA test to confirm this, of course, but it's not a problem we haven't dealt with before."

"He is Dirk's only child!" his mother insisted, pointing her finger at Pryce.

"Mother, please."

"I understand your surprise, Mrs. Grunion, but we have to follow the law in these cases." Mr. Melrose urged her to retake her seat and she reluctantly complied, her lips pursed in protest.

"Now let's see. Where were we?" Pryce was on the verge of walking out. He didn't need to hear any more. "There's the joint bank accounts, a nominal IRA, and then there's the matter of your college fund, Son."

Pryce nodded. "It's gone. I know."

"On the contrary. There's plenty here for you to attend the school of your choosing. Maybe even grad school if you're conservative and responsible."

Pryce's head shot up.

"What?" He met Jonah's confused gaze, then Chloe's before he stood and leaned over the lawyer's desk to see what the hell he was talking about.

"It's right here." Mr. Melrose handed him the latest bank statement and he scanned all the numbers to the total at the bottom, then back up to the date. It couldn't be. "This says there's over two hundred thousand dollars in the account."

Mr. Melrose nodded. "Of course, your mother is the executor until your twentieth birthday, an odd age if I must say. Most maturity dates are set at eighteen, or twenty-one. Sometimes twenty-five, but…"

Pryce stared at the numbers as the lawyer droned on. His gaze drifted off the page to his mother, who sat indifferent to the news that his college fund was not only completely intact, but had more than twice the amount his dad had told him was in it.

He looked back down at the numbers, his hand trembling as his mother's odd behavior and all the pieces of her diabolical plan fell into place, one by one.

"You lied to me."

"Pryce, please. Let me explain."

"There's nothing to fucking explain!"

"Hey." Jonah clamped his hand over Pryce's shoulder and he shrugged it off.

"You were going to rob me of my inheritance!"

"No!" she emphatically denied. "Your father didn't want you to know how much—"

"Oh I don't doubt he planned to get his hands on the half he didn't think I knew about, but you! *You* didn't want me to get *any* of it!" His mother shrank against the back of her chair, but he gave her no quarter. "You knew I would leave!"

"Pryce."

He threw off Chloe's cautioning hand and advanced on the conniving woman. "You knew I was planning on using this money! You *knew* I was going to marry Chloe and leave you, and you couldn't let that happen!"

"You're making a mistake!" She pushed up from her chair, but backed away when Pryce stepped closer. Her expression twisted with pleading pain, her eyes welling with tears. "I had to stop you, Pryce. Please understand. I was doing it to help you!"

"The only thing I understand, for the *first* time in my life, is what a manipulative bitch you really are!"

"Pryce, c'mon, man." Jonah pulled him back and this time Pryce acquiesced.

"Don't call me," he sneered, backing away from her at Jonah's insistence. "I never want to speak to you again, understand?"

"Pryce, please don't do this."

"And if you touch one penny in that account before my birthday, I'll burn it all to the ground!"

The world floated around him in a red haze as he followed Jonah and Chloe out into the parking lot to Jonah's truck. How could she do this? How could *anyone* do this to their own son?

"Where do you want to go?" Jonah asked and Pryce shook his head. He didn't have the faintest idea what to do next.

"Maybe we should go by the bank," Chloe suggested. "See if there's anything you can do to cash out the account early."

"They won't." His head fell back against the back seat. "I went to see the account manager the day before the storm to do just that, but she wouldn't tell me anything, not until the account is signed over to me."

Jonah put the truck in gear and backed out of the parking space.

"Where are we going?" Chloe asked.

"To talk to Grey," Jonah said as he pulled onto Main Street. "He'll know what to do."

~*~

Five days later, Pryce sat at the kitchen table in Daniel and Cade's house, staring at the student loan application on his laptop. Grey had called his attorney and they'd tried to find a way to keep his mother from withdrawing the money from his college fund account, but it was no use. All of the legal documents were in place and it was locked up tight. As executor, she could close the entire account if she wanted, and she'd done just that.

Officially twenty-years-old, Pryce had been waiting at the bank earlier that morning when the manager unlocked the doors. Ten minutes later he'd walked out without a cent. She'd closed the account and taken it all. Stolen it right out from under him.

"Why don't you take a break?" Standing behind him, Chloe squeezed his shoulders, and then ran her palms down over his chest, kissing the side of his neck. "I can finish the application for you."

Pryce gripped her hand with a tired sigh. "I need to do this." He wasn't giving up on his dream. Breezy had insisted he keep the money from his father's life insurance policy, but it would be a while before he saw any of it. With Jonah now a part of the equation to help with their living expenses, he might be able to make it work, but it wouldn't be easy. At least for the first few years. "The quicker I get this done, the quicker I can set up my classes for the next semester."

"Maybe I can distract him." Jonah had snuck up behind him and kissed the other side of his neck. "We were hoping to begin your birthday celebration early."

The mid-morning stubble on Jonah's cheek sent tempting chills racing along Pryce's skin, but he twisted away, determined to get this over with so he could get on with his life. "Let me finish this first, please. The classes fill up fast and if I don't get this loan, I'll have to find another way."

Someone knocked on the front door and Jonah released him with a chaste peck on the cheek. "I'll get it, but we're only giving you another hour before I'm hogtying you to the bed and having my way with you."

Pryce was tempted to slam his laptop shut and say to hell with it, but Jonah returned a few moments later with Gabby McLendon at his side.

"Gabby! Hi!" Chloe rushed over to give her a hug. "Can I get you something to drink?"

"No thanks. I won't be long," Gabby pulled an envelope from her purse. "I only came over to invite you all for dinner—Gran's making Pryce a special birthday pie—and to give you this." She laid the envelope on the table in front of Pryce.

He immediately recognized his mother's handwriting on the front and let out a frustrated sigh.

"I went to see her this morning. She wouldn't say much, but asked me to give this to you."

"I know you mean well, Gabby, but I don't want anything from her." He picked up the envelope and handed it back to her.

"Open it," Gabby insisted.

"Why should he?" Jonah snatched the envelope from Pryce's hands and handed it back to his mom. "He doesn't want anything to do with her."

Gabby took the envelope from Jonah and tossed it back on the table in front of Pryce. "I'm on your side," she insisted, "but I also understand the desperation a mother feels when she thinks her child is making a mistake that could affect the rest of their life." She pulled her shawl a little tighter around her shoulders and looked up at Jonah. "We're right sometimes, but sometimes we're wrong."

Jonah pulled her into his arms. "You weren't wrong, Mom. It was a mistake to leave."

"No," Gabby insisted as she pulled away. "I mean, I wish you'd told us the truth, but your dads are right. You've grown up, and I think going away on your own for a while was exactly what you needed."

"Are you saying my mother doesn't know stealing my inheritance is wrong?" Pryce asked unable to disguise his bitter sarcasm.

"Absolutely not," Gabby insisted. "Manipulating and lying to you the way she did, and her prejudices against your relationship with Jonah and Chloe are most definitely wrong." She walked around the table and grabbed up the envelope, placing it in Pryce's hand. "No mother is perfect, Pryce. We're human, even when our children think we're not, but this isn't about her."

She leaned down and gave Pryce an affectionate hug. "I'm not defending her, honey. You have every right to be angry with her, but a lifetime is a long time to live with that kind of rage festering inside you. Believe me, I know from personal experience that forgiveness isn't easy, but you need to let go. Don't do it for your mother. Do it for yourself, and Jonah, and Chloe. Do it to protect *your* heart and the ones you love."

Pryce was still staring at the envelope long after Gabby left. Every survival instinct he possessed was screaming at him to rip it up and toss the scraps into the fireplace. He held it up, pinched between the tips of his fingers. He could almost hear the hissing rip of paper, the thought of everything his mother had done pushing him to do it and never look back.

He slid his finger under the flap and ripped it open, plucking out the pages inside, rationalizing his decision as he unfolded the letter. He wasn't forgiving her. He just didn't want to live the rest of his life wondering what she'd had to say for herself now that he knew the truth.

My Dear Son,

Still bitter, Pryce rolled his eyes at the dramatic salutation.

I know you are angry with me, and you have every right to be. Your father wasn't a perfect man, Pryce. I know this, but he was your father, and my husband in the sight of God. I made a promise to honor and obey him in all things. I did my best, but ultimately failed you both.

Fearing it too large a sum for a young boy to respect and not squander, his reasoning for lying about the amount of your trust fund was sound at the time, but so much changed when he became ill. He'd demanded I use it to keep the ranch running, but in the end I couldn't. It is true that I panicked when I learned of your plans to marry Chloe, and the lie I told was unforgivable, but I ask you to forgive me all the same, as I forgive you.

A flash of anger burned in Pryce's stomach. *She* forgave *him*?

Pryce, I know you've made your decision, but I beg you to reconsider. I can't bear the thought of losing you to God's wrath. He's spared you once already, Pryce. I prayed harder than I'd ever prayed in my life the day you were attacked by that mountain lion, and I'm so thankful to Him for giving you another chance. Please don't throw that away.

He balled the letter up in his fist, unable to tolerate another word. Her self-righteous delusions bled through every line, her willful blindness to his father maddening. She'd always refused to see Dirk for who he really was: an abusive, hypocritical bastard.

They were perfect for each other.

He stood and walked over to the fireplace, knowing before he got there that he was doomed to read further. He mumbled a string of curses as he unfolded the crumpled paper, skipping over the bullshit to the last few paragraphs.

You were right about the house. It is a cold and lonely place now that you and your father are gone, as I knew it would be. I will be staying with Mrs. Florence in town for a while. I'm grateful for her hospitality and company until the winter passes and I can better manage on my own.

The McLendons have offered a fair price for the cattle and grazing land, and though your father would be angry, I intend to accept it. They are kind people, despite their sinful flaws, and I pray for them daily, as I pray for you. Pryce, I love you. I know you think otherwise, but I do, and I'm only doing what's best for you. The money in your trust fund is and always will be yours, as your grandfather intended, but I can't allow you to take advantage of his generosity. He would have never approved of the choices you've made, so I've deposited the money in a separate account and will keep it for you until you see the error of your ways. I hope you do so soon, before it is too late.

Please don't worry about me. I will be fine. The Lord has and always will provide. I hope you will come visit me soon.

I miss you. You deserve nothing but happiness and joy, Pryce. I will be praying for those things for you.

Love you always, and Happy Birthday,

Mother

Pryce stared into the flames as they consumed the pages, turning his mother's words into ashes.

"Are you okay?" Chloe asked as she slipped into the quiet room and put her arms around him.

"Yeah," he said and hugged her close, surprised at the relief he felt as the last piece of paper melted against the fire's flames. "I'm okay."

Chapter Twenty-Nine

Four months later.

Jonah turned the front door lock and walked out into the cool spring night air, turning around to look back at his dream. *My shop.* He jumped into his truck and sat for a second, staring out the windshield, taking everything in. With Grey's help, he'd closed the deal with Gully earlier that month, cleaned the place out, given it a fresh coat of paint and turned his first wrench three days ago. So far he was in the hole, but the agri-maintenance contracts were flowing in, just like they'd hoped, and Chloe'd said that by the end of the month they should make enough profit to pay the rent on the small house they'd leased in town. It wasn't much, but seeing the sign on top of the building with his name on it felt like a million bucks.

He gave his truck key a crank and the engine fired up, but before he shifted into drive, another truck pulled into the parking lot and skidded to a stop beside him. Jonah's gut tightened when Wayne Jessop got out and jogged around to his window.

Though they'd managed to forge an uneasy peace between them, Jonah still felt uncomfortable meeting him in an unlit parking lot in the middle of town. That reminded him. Now that Uncle Cade and Papa Daniel were back from their trip, he needed to talk to Uncle Cade about installing a security system.

"Hey," Wayne said nervously when he rolled down his window. "Sorry, I tried to get here before you locked up."

"Just about missed me." Jonah gave his hat a polite tip in greeting.

"Yeah, I'm glad I didn't. Saves me a stamp."

"What's this," Jonah asked, taking the white envelope Wayne handed him through the window.

"An invitation, for you and my sister, and Pryce too, of course."

"Invitation to what?"

"Oh, my wedding. Sorry." Even in the dark Jonah could see the guy blush. "Kelly and I are tying the knot next month, over on the Rez. We're doing a whole tribal ceremony and everything. We're hoping you'll come."

Jonah studied the envelope a moment, not bothering to open it. "Are your brothers going to be there?"

"Naw, man." Wayne shoved his hands into his front pockets, nervously shifting from foot to foot. "Finn blew his parole hearing, and nobody's heard from Travis since February."

Jonah tossed the invitation onto the dash and gave Wayne a nod. "I'll talk to Lo about it. Thanks, and congratulations."

"You too," he said, offering his hand to shake. "I mean, on the marriage and stuff. I mean…you know…I know Chloe's happy."

Jonah considered his hand. Wayne hadn't been invited to their wedding. No one had been, officially. Despite knowing his mom would blow a gasket when she found out, the three of them had met in secret at the courthouse where he'd stood as witness for Pryce and Chloe as they exchanged their vows. As much fun as Papa Daniel's and Uncle Cade's wedding had been, none of them had wanted the chaos and attention a big wedding would have entailed. They just wanted to start their life together, and if they'd told anyone, they wouldn't have been able to withstand the pressure to have one.

Once all the legal stuff was done, they sprang the news on his family and Minister Farnes performed a private ceremony for the three of them down by the creek, where it all began. It was the best day of his life.

Of course he still felt guilty from time to time when he saw his mom, but he wasn't worried. She'd forget all about it as soon as Breezy got pregnant. Hopefully he'd get that call any day now. Con and Car were driving everyone crazy since dumping their caffeine habit cold turkey.

He finally shook Wayne's hand. "She is happy. We all are, and I hope you'll be, too."

"We will," Wayne said with a confident nod and withdrew his hand. "Hope to see you there."

Jonah pulled away, tipping his hat at Wayne one last time, thinking he wasn't such a bad guy after all. Maybe one day they might be friends. Stranger things had happened. He'd married his best friend, and the woman neither of them could live without. Anything was possible.

"I'm home!" he shouted a few minutes later as he walked through the front door. He tossed his keys into the basket Chloe had set on the small entryway table for just that purpose and stooped to unlace his work boots. Chloe was every bit as picky as his mom about wearing his greasy boots in the house.

"Lo!"

He picked his way through the stacks of boxes still strewn about the house. Who knew three people could have so much stuff?

"Lo? Are you home?" Her car was in the driveway, and she hadn't texted to say she was going out.

A faint giggle bled through their closed bedroom door. He pushed it open and followed the sound of her voice to the closet where she was pulling clothes from a box as she talked on her phone.

"He'll love it," she said, holding up one of her shirts, the white lace one that made his mouth water every time she wore it.

Jonah snuck quietly up behind her and snagged her around the waist, eliciting a squeal as she squirmed in his arms.

"Oh-m'God! You scared the hell out of me!" She slapped and kicked as he carried her to the bed, Pryce's laughter echoing through the phone.

"What will I love?" he asked, tossing her onto the mattress. He crawled up her outstretched body and took the phone from her hands, clicking the speaker button.

"Don't tell him!" Pryce warned.

With Chloe pinned beneath him, Jonah peeled her shirt over her head and tossed it to the floor. "Fine by me," he said, licking his lips at the sight of her sprawled out beneath him. "I'll just have to torture our wife until she does."

He leaned down and took one of her pebbled nipples into his mouth, loving how she bowed against him, feeding him more with a needy moan he felt all the way to his balls. The only thing better than coming home to Chloe every night were the weekends when Pryce was there to join them.

Pryce had managed to make up the tests he'd missed at the beginning of the semester and landed a part time job at the equine clinic in Billings, where he worked as an overnight technician's assistant on the days he had to attend class in person. Staying the night in Billings saved them gas money and Pryce a lot of unnecessary travel time, but Jonah missed him. He was only a week away from summer break and he couldn't wait.

"Is she naked?" Pryce asked, his voice trembling with the telltale signs of need Jonah'd come to recognize.

"Not yet, but I'm working on it." He slid down her legs, trailing his lips over her heated flesh. He passed the tempting zipper and pressed his open mouth to her pussy, teasing her through her shorts. She bucked beneath him, her hands flying to her button, but he swatted them away.

"Don't tease me, please."

"Oh yeah, tease her," Pryce said. "She deserves it after the picture she sent me at lunch today."

Jonah laughed. "Left you with blue balls, did she?"

Pryce sighed hopelessly. "It's a perpetual condition these days."

Jonah rose up and unzipped her shorts, yanking them and her panties off with one quick jerk. "Then let's take care of that, shall we?" He peeled off his shirt, shucked his jeans and underwear and gripped his shaft. "Tell him what I'm doing, Lo."

Chloe propped up on her elbows, her eyelids heavy as she watched him. "He's stroking his cock, Pryce. I wish you could see it."

"He could if we had Skype sex."

"No!" Pryce shouted into the phone. "I-I'm not in a good place to do that."

Jonah laughed. "Phone sex it is then."

"Is he hard, Chloe? Tell me," Pryce insisted.

"Very," she hummed. "I want to taste him."

"Do it," Pryce ordered. "Suck his cock for me. Let me hear how good he tastes."

Chloe twirled on the bed until she was lying on her stomach in front of Jonah. He stepped to the edge of the mattress and fed his cock into her open mouth, sucking in a breath when her hot, wet tongue fluttered along his shaft. "Damn, Pry! She feels so good."

Chloe hummed around his stiff flesh, the sound vibrating along his cock, ripping a garbled string of curses from him.

"Oh, yeah," Pryce sighed. "I love it when she does that. Fuck her mouth," he ordered with a hushed whisper and Jonah complied, his balls drawing up tight when the tip of his cock met the back of her throat.

Jonah wasn't sure when he lost control of the moment, but he liked it. A lot. Too much. He pulled out, his chest rising and falling with his labored breaths. One more second in that heavenly mouth of hers and he'd be done for.

"My turn," he barked and flipped her onto her back. She yelped when he pulled her to the edge of the mattress and sank to his knees between her thighs. "She's drenched," he told Pryce, nuzzling her slit, taking a long, deep whiff. "You can't imagine how sweet she smells."

"I know exactly how sweet she is," Pryce said on a sigh. "Taste her," he said. "Drive your tongue inside her as deep as you can."

"Mmmm," Chloe hummed urgently. "Pryce, are you here?"

"Shh," Pryce hissed. "Come for him, Chloe. Let me hear you."

"I'm so close already. Jonah, please. Don't stop."

"I'm almost there, too," Pryce said. "Keep talking, Chloe. Tell me how good he feels."

The strained sound of Pryce's voice sent a bolt of need through Jonah. He buried his face in her pussy and drank her sweet release as she shattered in his hands.

"Pryce!"

"That's it, baby. I'm almost there."

His cock hard and throbbing, Jonah hooked her heels over his shoulders and pushed inside her with one long, deep thrust. "Sweet *Jesus*!" It took everything he had to keep from coming. "She's so hot and tight, Pryce, fluttering around me like a damn butterfly."

"Fuck," Pryce mumbled into the phone.

Jonah chuckled at the clunking sound of Pryce dropping his phone, followed by his censored curses. Too far gone to stop, he held himself above her with one arm and reached down with the other to find her puckered star. He gathered her slick release and pressed his finger inside her ass, then quickly added another, drawing out her throaty moan.

"Tell me what it feels like, Lo," Jonah begged, plunging in and out of her. "Tell me how it feels to have Pryce's cock slide inside your ass." He'd dreamed of the day when Pryce finally fucked him. He ached with the need to feel him. They'd talked about it, and Jonah hadn't wanted to push him, but he was nearing his breaking point waiting.

"Burns," Chloe hissed. "Burns so good."

"It sure does," Pryce breathed into the phone, the sound reverberating around the room in stereo.

Jonah glanced over his shoulder to see him standing in the doorway, slack-jawed, his phone still pressed to his ear. Damn if he wasn't a dream come true. Jonah wanted to ask what the hell he was doing there, but his gaze dropped to Pryce's open fly, the rosy tip of his erection peeking out of the top of his boxer briefs.

Jonah licked his lips. With Chloe beneath him, his cock sunk deep into her wet heat, and Pryce standing just feet away from him, he'd never been so conflicted.

"Please tell me you're not planning to stand there and watch."

"Not a chance." Pryce dropped his phone, shedding his clothes as he crossed the room.

"You made it!" Chloe's face lit up with a knowing smile and she beckoned Pryce to them.

"Hey, baby." Pryce gave her a desperate kiss, then turned and pressed his lips to Jonah's, groaning when their tongues met in their familiar dance. "Mmm, surprise," he said with a grin.

"I like your surprises." Jonah snagged Pryce's waist and pulled him further up onto the mattress, guiding him until he could get his mouth around his cock.

"That's so hot," Chloe whimpered beneath him.

Pryce cupped the back of Jonah's head and pulled him closer, forcing Jonah to take him deeper. Jonah willingly complied, loving the new confidence Pryce had found in the last few weeks. Eager for his taste, Jonah sucked him hard, swallowing around the flared head, drawing out a rewarding guttural groan from his other lover as he drove into Chloe beneath him.

"Hold up," Pryce begged.

Jonah hollowed his cheeks as he backed off, diving in for one last taste before Pryce pulled out with a gasp.

"Damn, that was close. So good," Pryce panted as he reached over to the nightstand for a condom and the tube of lube.

Harder than ever, Jonah turned his attention back to Chloe, thrusting inside her a few last times before he made room on the bed for Pryce. "Roll with me?" he asked and she nodded, but before he could, Pryce's hand landed in the middle of his back.

"Not this time."

Jonah froze at the command in Pryce's tone.

Paralyzed with hope, he could do little more than stare at the man he loved as Pryce ran his hand over his back, caressed his side, his ass, squeezing the back of his thigh before he moved behind him. Jonah watched over his shoulder, suspended in time, as Pryce rolled the condom on and coated his cock with lube, giving him a wink as he tossed the bottle onto the mattress.

"Do you still want this?" Pryce asked, trailing his fingers up his thighs to his balls, cupping them and rolling them in his palm.

Jonah swallowed, sweat beading instantly on his brow. "More than you could possibly know."

Pryce grinned as he bent down and kissed the top of Jonah's left cheek, then opened wide and gave his ass a playful bite that made him jerk against Chloe.

Pryce and Chloe laughed and "—oh-mother of—fuck *me*!"

Jonah clamped down against the sudden intrusion, gritting his teeth, the feel of Pryce's fingers inside him making him want to crawl out of his skin. His feet still planted firmly on the floor, his knees threatened to buckle beneath him from the mixture of pleasure and pain.

"What is he doing?" Chloe asked, squirming beneath him to see.

"He's stretching me," Jonah gritted out, doing a fair bit of squirming himself. Holy hell! He didn't know what had come over Pryce, what had changed, and he wasn't about to ask. He just hoped to whatever sex god had taken possession of him that he didn't stop.

The front of Pryce's thighs brushed against the back of Jonah's and he pressed back against him, silently begging for more.

"What were you saying before I so rudely interrupted?" Pryce asked, sliding his free hand up Jonah's spine, tracing his tattoo with the tips of his fingers.

"He was asking what it felt like to have you inside me," Chloe said with a cheeky grin.

"Inside your ass?" Pryce asked, adding another finger, the burning sting stealing Jonah's breath. The pleasure and pain gripped him hard and he jerked against Chloe, pressing further inside her.

"Mmhmm-ah!" Chloe arched beneath him, her pussy clamping around his cock like a vise. Jonah crushed his mouth to hers, unable to contain the rioting chaos of feelings coursing through his body. Was this it? Was Pryce really about to make love to him? Good god he hoped so. If Pryce stopped now, he'd never recover.

Pryce's fingers disappeared and it felt like all the air had been sucked out of the room. Jonah clenched around the void, his body begging for more before he could speak the pleading words. "Pryce, please don't stop. I need this—oh *fuck* yes!"

The soft steel tip of Pryce's cock kissed his pucker and he sucked in a breath. Pryce gripped his hips and pressed into him, the pressure building, the sting intensifying. Every muscle in his body seized.

Chloe cupped the sides of his face and pulled him down to her, pressing their foreheads together. "Breathe," she coaxed. "It's easier if you breathe."

Jonah nodded shakily, pressing his lips together to keep from crying out. He dragged in breath after breath, his chest aching with— "Ffffuuuuck!" he shouted, his knees buckling when Pryce breached his rim, sliding balls deep in one single thrust. Pryce draped himself over Jonah's back, the movement driving him even deeper, and Jonah pressed his forehead into Chloe's shoulder, his arms shaking as his world tilted on its axis.

"Finally," Pryce sighed, his voice a raspy, strained whisper. "I've dreamed about this all week."

Jonah nearly choked on his reply. "Try years," he said, the burn in his ass rolling into an urgent need to move. He pushed back against Pryce, the fullness ripping a throaty moan from both of them.

Chloe rolled her hips beneath him and the onslaught of pleasure pushed him straight to the edge. "Fuck me," he commanded, no longer satisfied with the still bliss of just holding Pryce inside him. "I want it all, Pryce. Don't you dare hold back."

Pryce reared up, his fingers pressing deep into Jonah's flesh at his hips, and pulled out with slow, deliberate determination. Jonah clamped down on the hot friction as he pulled out of Chloe, screwing his eyes closed, waiting for the inward thrust. Pryce didn't disappoint, snapping into him hard, shoving him deep inside Chloe.

"Oh my God!" she cried out beneath him, thrashing her head to the side.

"So tight," Pryce gritted out and slid back, and then inside him again, his thighs and balls slapping against Jonah's.

Jonah's arms shook as the burn in his ass traveled through his muscles. Sweat beaded on Chloe's collarbone and he nearly collapsed when he dipped down to kiss it from her skin.

Pryce shifted his hips and Jonah cried out. "Oh damn! Oh shit!" He clamped down on his bottom lip as the tip of Pryce's cock nicked his gland.

"Hold on." The mattress shifted against the box springs with Pryce's next thrust, sending Jonah crashing down on top of Chloe.

"Oh yeah-that's it-right there!" Jonah held on for dear life, trying his best to hold his weight off Chloe as Pryce pounded into him, but she clawed at his back, pulling him back down on top of her, her head thrown back in a silent cry as she throbbed around his cock.

Pryce bent over his back again, the feel of his teeth sinking into his shoulder sending Jonah spiraling toward his own super-sized orgasm.

"Mmm! Uh! Uh!" His control lost, all he could do was feel as Pryce emptied himself inside him and he lost himself inside Chloe, over and over.

"Christ, I've missed you two," Pryce said a moment later and collapsed on top of them.

Unable to hold his own weight and Pryce's too, Jonah's arms finally buckled beneath him.

"Can't breathe," Chloe laughed as she rode out her own release.

Pryce pulled out but Jonah reached back, holding him against him as he rolled them all to their sides. "I've waited too damn long to let you go yet."

Their legs tangled together, their arms entwined, holding each other close, Jonah closed his eyes and listened to the sounds of their breaths, felt their heartbeats racing to the same frantic rhythm as his own. Surrounded in every way by the two people he loved, he knew their life wouldn't always be this perfect, but in that moment he'd found something he'd once thought he'd lost forever that day in the arena. He'd found himself, and he was finally home.

A True Love Story Never Ends

Thank You

Thank you for reading! If you love the McLendons' stories, please consider leaving a review at the vendor from which you purchased this book. If you would like more fun and sexy stories by D.L. Roan, visit www.dlroan.com.

The McLendon Family Saga Reading Order

The Heart of Falcon Ridge
A McLendon Christmas
Rock Star Cowboys
Rock Star Cowboys: The Honeymoon
The Hardest Goodbyes
Return to Falcon Ridge
Forever Falcon Ridge (2017)

About The Author

USA Today and international bestselling author, D.L. Roan, loves combining fantasy with the real world, giving her readers more than just a romantic story, but an adventure in true love. She writes about life: the good, bad, the silly things, the hard things, and everything in between.

"If I can give someone a break from all the craziness that comes with real life, make them smile, or turn a bad day into a fantastic one, then it's all been worth it." ~ D.L. Roan

She's a native Floridian, a rare breed in a land of snow birds. Scuba diving and hunting for shark's teeth on the beach are two of her favorite things. She loves rainy days, thunderstorms and is an avid dog lover. Yes, size matters. She hopes to one day add a big ol' floppy Great Dane to her family of hounds.

For exclusive details and free stories by D.L., visit her website www.dlroan.com and subscribe to her newsletter.

Made in the USA
Monee, IL
23 March 2021

63576531R00176